M000223499

(ID)ENTITY

TWIN OAKS BRANCH
0000203738349
AUSTIN PUBLIC LIBRARY

ALSO BY PJ MANNEY

(R)evolution

(ID)ENTITY

PJ MANNEY

This is a work of fiction. Names, characters, organizations, places, events, and incidents are either products of the author's imagination or are used fictitiously. Any resemblance to actual persons, living or dead, or actual events is purely coincidental.

Text copyright © 2017 by PJ Manney

All rights reserved.

No part of this book may be reproduced, or stored in a retrieval system, or transmitted in any form or by any means, electronic, mechanical, photocopying, recording, or otherwise, without express written permission of the publisher.

Published by 47North, Seattle

www.apub.com

Amazon, the Amazon logo, and 47North are trademarks of Amazon.com, Inc., or its affiliates.

ISBN-13: 9781503948495
ISBN-10: 1503948498

Cover design by Ray Lundgren

Cover illustration by Adam Martinakis

Printed in the United States of America

To Hannah and Nathaniel:

You are my teachers.

PROLOGUE

I have no idea who I am anymore, thought Dr. Who. But can I know myself? And if I've changed, am I still me?

The gray-haired, heavyset woman hobbled on two canes along the extensive decks. It had been two years, but she had never gotten used to the endless 360-degree vista of ocean and the bitter saltiness that pervaded everything. Sunset, painting the sky with meteorological brushstrokes of puffy pink and green, didn't help. After the world turned upside down, she left a lifetime of beauty and hard work behind in her garden in San Anselmo, California. She missed the creature-soft smell of compost and the velvet of rich soil under her fingers. Even as the slight movement of the floating platform made her queasy, she could see things growing and adapting all around her, like the ocean-sturdy structures of the seastead *Sovereign* that she stood on. Or the salt water–resilient plants she helped tend. Or the sea-adapted animals, so unlike her former gophers, sparrows, and earthworms. Those sea animals included water-loving people.

Dr. Who tried to be one of them, adapting in her way. Regardless, she hummed to herself as a joke "One of These Things (Is Not Like the Others)." Her kids and grandkids always liked that *Sesame Street* song. However, they remained on the mainland and refused to join her. How had she raised such wimps, more afraid of what could lie ahead than the obvious threats back home? She had never felt she belonged anywhere until she had entered the online virtual world in a variety of guises, especially that of Foxy Funkadelia, kicking virtual ass and taking virtual names. If the *Sovereign* still made her feel like a terra firma–loving foreigner after two years, then who was she? Was she a seasteader? An entrepreneur? An economic opportunist? Some might even say a criminal? And what was her name? No one had called her by the name her parents had given her in years.

A lithe young woman in a wetsuit, with wide-set hazel eyes and black hair slick from salt water, loped along the decking toward her and waved. *"Le Médecin!"* Sylvie Thibault loved to call her "doctor" in French as a joke. Years before, another young woman on the run had dubbed her Dr. Who. The Doctor loved it, and with global notoriety, the name had stuck.

"Come, *le Médecin!* See the cobia before it's too dark. So pretty *and* delicious." She pointed to one of several submerged geodesic, metal-screened spheres with flexible walkways leading to hatches at the top. Sylvie scampered up the walkway and threw open the hatch.

"You kiddin', honey?" said Dr. Who. "I'm no goat!"

"I'll let you name them!" said Sylvie.

Following Sylvie along the undulating planking with great caution, Dr. Who said, "Oh, I can eat 'em just fine without baptizin' 'em and payin' for their college!"

Sylvie laughed for a moment, then quieted, studying the fish inside the hatch. She was a marine biologist turned fish farmer. Like many on the *Sovereign*, she had pivoted her intellect and passion away from research and into new industries to help the seastead and the rest of the world survive through new food sources. Sylvie's spherical fish farms had motors, propellers, and GPS that allowed them to deliver themselves to ports around the Pacific, with mature, market-ready fish inside. Some former scientists and technologists on board manufactured algae edibles and biofuels. Others worked on new versions of wave, wind, and solar energy systems. On another part of the *Sovereign* sat nanofabricators, once illegal after 10/26, the greatest terrorist attack in history. Along with 3-D printers, nanofabbers were making steps toward solving food shortages, as well as manufacturing pharmaceuticals, tools, spare parts, and more nanofabricators.

The Doctor had set up her operation here two years ago for the same reasons the others did: to be left alone to do her work in peace, away from global politics, small-mindedness, and government regulations.

"Mmm . . . ," muttered Sylvie, observing the fish, the water illuminated by powerful spotlights. "They are agitated. I do not know from what."

"Sylvie, girl, till they're on my plate with a side of fries, I'm still not interested." Dr. Who peered into the hatch. The fish were all pushed to one side of the sphere, as though trying to escape through the tight metal mesh. "Looks like fish swimmin' to me. What's different?"

"They are trying to school away from something. Maybe in fear?" Sylvie sat at the hatch's edge and put on her diving mask. "Maybe a mesh break? Predator?" She spoke into a waterproof radio. "Agitation in sphere five, Lyle. Look for predator or malfunction for me? I'm going in."

Sylvie's WaterGO, a waterproof version of the ubiquitous handheld communications device, rang a siren and announced, *"Attention, Sovereign. New storm detected west-southwest at fifteen miles per hour. Repeat, heavy storm to make fall in twenty minutes."*

"Non, impossible," said Sylvie. "We are in the horse latitudes, the calmest part of the sea. No storms coming for days." Confused, she looked in the direction of the warning. All she saw were cumulus clouds over a darkening horizon. "Do you see anything?"

"Nope, but I'm gettin' inside anyway, honey. See ya with the fish—cooked!" Dr. Who shivered. It wasn't just from the looming cold, darkness, or storms. Looking at the watery horizon for too long made her feel dizzy.

The *Sovereign* was a big facility to navigate, shaped like an octopus holding large plates at the ends of its tentacles, and she and Sylvie were two out of two hundred who lived aboard her. Its large central hub sat like a high-tech iceberg, fifty feet above and hundreds of feet below the surface of the ocean. Eight connected arms splayed from the central core, and disk-shaped installations at each end housed different industries and living facilities. Like a space station on the high seas, she maintained her location approximately six hundred miles north of Honolulu with GPS and positional motors that responded to tides and weather. She was a model of the newest type of seastead: a single prefabricated unit, midocean, self-sufficient.

Dr. Who entered the elevator shaft that plunged many stories underwater and exited on a floor that hummed with electrical activity. The ocean-current generators powered the biggest computer server system on the seas and one of the biggest in the world.

She poked her head into the control room. Juan Reyes, a twenty-two-year-old Guatemalan, manned an interactive console in a room filled with a dozen screens and racks of servers. He wore mixed reality contact lenses that were common among most technical folks and a good percentage of the wealthier public. They displayed real-time, augmented image overlays to his retinas to help coordinate all the information he was monitoring. With his hands, he moved around the colorful and complex data only he could see. To the Doctor, it looked like Gustavo Dudamel conducting an orchestra. She could see only a fraction of the facility he was supervising.

"Juan, baby, get you anything? 'Cept the right woman?"

"I should be asking you that, *Mamita*."

Even if she didn't fit in, Dr. Who was treated with great respect and fun. She was the seastead's unofficial mama. Age had its benefits.

Juan made sure the IT systems were happy. There was a lot on the line if they fried. With the most active identity, security, and cryptocurrency computers in the world, the *Sovereign*'s systems allowed a billion people to identify themselves without a government imprimatur. When nations collapsed, as some did after the Major Tom revelations, persecuted citizens needed to leave or change their identities. The facility both processed these new identifications and allowed money, goods, and services to be exchanged without national fiat currencies.

Tools that freed people from a system in which governments and corporations were the moderators of all identity and financial verification were grabbed with great enthusiasm after the collapse. The primary tool was the blockchain, a "trustless verification system." While the original blockchain underpinned the first cryptocurrency, called Bitcoin, there were now many blockchains. They were simple databases, shared by millions of computers around the world, through microtransactions of a digital currency. After performing a basic algorithm, the same data was placed in every computer that mined the currency and shared that blockchain. The fact that the data was the same on each computer was how the system verified it was true.

Blockchain technology now verified so much that it was inherent in most transactions: financial, real estate, trade, barter, identity, gambling. Which blockchain you used depended on the transaction and the institution.

However, like anything sold by big business or big government as "trustless" or "bulletproof" or "guaranteed," better to assume it was as full of holes as Bonnie and Clyde's car. Or Bonnie and Clyde, for that matter.

The largest operators of blockchains, and the "miners" of the currencies to run them, were in China. They had turned a cottage industry of high-tech early adopters looking to level global economic playing fields into the biggest verification system in the world. But that didn't mean they were safe. Their blockchains were suspect, and their hardware was, too. Governments discovered Chinese-made computing hardware was linked to Chinese bugging devices. China made the algorithmic chips that operated the world's blockchains. That was reason enough to be suspicious.

There were several uncorrupted blockchains out there, not manipulated by governments and multinational institutions. They were so popular that they created their own currencies. The *Sovereign* created the Shell, symbolic of its ocean environment and a reminder to the world that seashells were one of the oldest and most used currencies in human history.

In fact, there were two sets of servers in this blockchain farm: one online, which participated in confirming the information on the blockchain, and one safely offline as "cold storage." Hackers could infiltrate computers and steal cryptocurrencies, but this system allowed for multiple verifications of a transaction and a place to hide them and any money from hackers. This made people feel safer. As any financier will attest, if people *feel* their money is safe, the truth doesn't matter.

Governments were unhappy with this development. The *Sovereign* was designed to exist as far from legal jurisdictions and their overreactions as possible. The former United States were particularly annoyed. In the wake of the Major Tom revelations, without leadership at the federal level, some states took their gold back from Fort Knox as the basis of a local currency. With a collapsing dollar, new currencies became popular elsewhere, too. Barter systems, sharing economies, municipality dollars—like the multiple currencies in use at the beginning of the American republic, everything old was new again. This strengthened the Shell's popularity around the world.

"Hey, *Mamita*, look at this." Juan pointed at a screen and expanded the image with his fingers. It showed a flood of currency requests, growing larger by the second.

"Follow back to the beginnin', baby." She grabbed her GO to see what news might have motivated a gigantic movement of currencies.

"Yes, Mama . . ." His hand poked, prodded, swiped, and pulled the air several times. "It's . . . everywhere. Do you see any patterns?"

"No. What's the AI say?"

All large cybersystems had their own artificial intelligence programs to find and halt cyber attacks and runs on their "banks." AI pattern recognition was good but not flawless. A combination of human intelligence and AI was still necessary to cover the cognitive bases. Juan ran the patterns through the AI software.

"*Mamita*, nothing yet," said Juan.

Her international infofeed was filled with the usual crap of civilization. Fake news from fake political parties on fake outlets. Another country splitting apart at the seams. Kardashians, like cockroaches, still reproduced and proliferated. But no unusual currency fluctuations.

"Hell's bells!" she said. "A fancy DDoS?" A distributed denial-of-service attack could strike at any time, overwhelming their meshnet-connected servers. They happened everywhere. Every day. Every hour. To every government and corporation on earth. For many years, they were the blunt instrument of hackers large and small, either to punish, extort ransom, or crash a system and take advantage of its failure.

"Yeah. We haven't had an attack in weeks," said Juan.

Her GO was too fiddly to give her the information she needed. "Call Pavla and Chikelu for help. I need my files."

"Careful, *Mamita*! Storm's coming!"

She couldn't move fast enough. It was dark, struggling down walkways hurt the joints in her legs, and the crutch cuffs chafed her arms.

In her cabin, she had a few vestiges of her old life. A state-of-the-art computing system. A bonsai forest under grow lights. A lifetime supply of violent video games and their player platforms. *Grand Theft Treasury III* was paused on one screen. On another, her automated Foxy Funkadelia avatar pole danced, legs spread in a 190-degree, hyperextended standing split, while giving a lecture on anarchocapitalism. Foxy had passed the Turing Test, which early computer scientists imagined would demonstrate a program's ability to exhibit intelligence resembling a human's, but Dr. Who knew Foxy was just a sham of quick wit, salacious moves, and canned responses, designed to distract her viewers with her sexy wiles. Foxy's audience was bright and therefore gullible to slick presentation and jargon, keeping alive the fantasies of those turned on by "smart" people, otherwise known as sapiosexuals. Someone had to do it. But Dr. Who's business wasn't currency. She ran the most successful and lucrative identity-reassignment service in the world, right from the *Sovereign*'s network.

She settled herself with a groan into her chair. It felt good to get off her feet. Averse to surgery, she knew she didn't have long before she would need a robochair or exoskeleton for mobility, but she was determined to put off that indignity as long as possible. Waving her hands toward the images on her screens, she pulled up her identity files.

They were stable. For now.

Dr. Who had earned infamy from her reidentification of a bioengineer and falsely accused terrorist named Peter Bernhardt. She had helped turn him into the avenging cyborg Thomas Paine and later the first uploaded identity, Major Tom. After she was forced to flee her Marin County home in the chaos that followed his revelations about the truth of American power, he promised to send her anywhere. She was clueless about where to go, so he recommended the *Sovereign*. Conscious of her advancing years and legacy, she'd asked him if she could upload her thoughts upon her death, upgrading Foxy into a real sentient digital being in perpetuity—like him. But Major Tom hadn't revealed his uploading technology to anyone but Dr. Ruth Chaikin, who had helped create him, and he wouldn't promise anything.

Identity reassignment was a big business in the aftermath of Major Tom's ascension. When his story hit the world, first came revelation. Then revolution. There were a lot of new customers. Many people needed to get into or out of nations, or just start again where they were. As fast as the world map changed, her business boomed. When each bit of life was codified and immortalized on the nets, and in corporate and government databases, there were many people who wanted a clean slate. These weren't criminals in an ethical sense. Their governments may have branded them as such, but they were pioneers and revolutionaries whom their home countries didn't yet appreciate.

Still uncertain as to what they were dealing with, she pulled up the weather radar. The storm looked small, maybe a waterspout or microsquall. But it was headed directly at them, on an unswerving trajectory, and would land in a minute. The coincidence that an unswerving microstorm was to hit at the same time as a DDoS attack needled her psyche in a way that had saved her life many times over the years, but she didn't have time to dwell on it.

A bright icon flashed, and her system projected an urgent message. *Emergency identity needed and warning. I need the best new identity you have. Cost is not important. And I have a warning to pass on to you.*

When people would pay any amount of money, she was suspicious.

She switched to an audio call and voiced back, "I don't handle real criminals."

The client responded with a delay, "And who is a criminal nowadays? One who follows unjust laws? Or one who breaks them to make society just? And are you one to talk? You should know better than anyone."

The delay could be a TOR router sending the transmission through servers around the world. She grumbled to the empty room. These pretentious youngsters thought they'd invented revolution. Historical memory was too damned short. Frustrated, she inspected the incoming packet and sent a ping to locate the transmission's origin.

It hopped around the world from city to city, with no end. That was bad. And the timing was worse, with the DDoS and a microstorm heading for them. She no longer believed in coincidences. This was a part of the attack. She checked in on the cryptos. Juan and others were holding back the tide, but barely.

"Are ya messin' with our servers?" she asked the new customer.

"Why, heavens. How could you accuse someone like me of something like that? Haven't we just met? Haven't I been civil?"

This was one pompous asshole, she thought. And guilty as hell.

"If you don't pay heed, you will pay regardless."

"Don't ya threaten me, ya noob!" she yelled.

A siren exploded near her room. She leapt in her seat. Over speakers, a voice barked, *"Unidentified intruders. West-southwest. Closing fast. Prepare for defensive measures and evacuation."* She looked at the radar feed again. The weather was moving too fast: about forty miles per hour. She switched to sonar. It looked like an enormous school of fish traveling at faster-than-ship-speed to intercept the *Sovereign.*

"I warned you," the client said and disconnected.

This wasn't a drill. Understanding dawned. Whoever this asshole was, he was trying to distract her. She checked her identity files.

They were there, but she couldn't access them. A growing malware bug was covering them, isolating them, copying them, taking over her system.

She sent an SOS message to two people she thought could help. Then she grabbed her canes and hobbled for the lifepods at the surface. If the *Sovereign* was threatened, she might make an escape inside the evacuation pods along with others.

Dr. Who stumbled over the precarious walkways, legs and crutches threatening collapse in her haste. Other residents of the *Sovereign* flooded toward the pods. Out of the night sky, they saw it: a towering waterspout, moving faster than any they had ever seen.

CRACK! A bolt of lightning shot out of the swirling apex of clouds surrounding the waterspout, hitting the communications tower.

BOOM! The central hub's roof exploded, and the communications tower toppled, crashing through Quadrant Seven.

CRACK! Another bolt of lightning hit one of the seastead's arms, breaking off a walkway juncture from the central hub.

CRACK! Yet another bolt destroyed a solar array. The batteries exploded, raining fire down on several steaders.

Dr. Who stood gape-jawed in amazement. This wasn't natural lightning. It was an electrical or laser weapon inside the freak storm, taking careful aim at the seastead's most vulnerable parts.

BOOM! Boom, *BOOM!* The waterspout tore through three arms of the complex like a tornado, setting them adrift from the core.

As if that were not surreal enough, a giant tuna leapt from the water, slamming a terrified woman off a walkway and into the dark sea below. Other fleeing steaders met with similar giant fish attacks. Two of the evacuation pods were damaged when a half-ton suicidal tuna slammed into each.

Out of the maelstrom, lit by the seastead's floodlights, Dr. Who saw hundreds of small boats, some too small to carry humans, others like Jet Skis for two or three commandos at most. They swarmed like a flock of starlings or a school of anchovies.

All seasteads had defensive weapons, and all personnel were trained to fight pirates. Dozens of armed Sovereigners attempted a counterattack. Ten feet from Dr. Who, a security guard passed, hefting a shoulder missile launcher. He fired at the swarm. It moved as one unit, anticipating his aim. The missile hit the water and exploded, taking a few out, but the swarm still came up fast. Dr. Who grabbed her GO to take a photo to send to anyone who could see it, but she couldn't tell if the message was sent. The DDoS and lightning attacks sent the *Sovereign's* high-altitude meshnet communications system crashing.

"Mamita!" Juan was stranded on the central hub, wearing his life vest. The station's arms were floating away, listing to the sides, burning, and taking on water. The hub seemed impervious to sinking. Juan looked too stunned to fire his sidearm.

"Juan, baby! Swim to the pods!"

He nodded, holstered the weapon, jumped into the water, and swam.

In the distance, Sylvie shot a laser rifle at everything coming toward her. She hit nothing. She caught sight of Dr. Who and cried out, "*Le Médecin!* Jellyfish!" Dr. Who spun and saw huge box jellyfish squirming over the sides of the submerging platforms. The security guard, concentrating on loading his launcher, wasn't paying attention, and a jelly's tentacle stung him on the leg. Within seconds, he grabbed his chest and pitched over the side.

The jelly floated back into the sea, joining hundreds more. Dr. Who turned on her GO's flashlight and studied them. The clear, plastic-like body common to these jellies contained something rectangular and nonorganic near its core. It looked like electronics. In her long and tech-laden life, she had thought she had seen everything, but she'd never seen a weaponized cyborg jellyfish. And she had told Juan to swim.

The waterspout threw off driving rain, making visibility difficult. She hurried to the lifepod station, dodging humans and creatures, but stopped in dismay. All the pods were gone, either ejected, blown up, or sunk with no one aboard. There was one left. She prayed it would work.

Her legs ached, and spasms shot all the way up to her back, but she ignored them, grabbing the handrail and dragging herself along. The last lifepod was ten feet away on the other side of the gangplank.

"*Mamita!*" Juan bobbed in the ocean, waving. He pointed to her pod, indicating that he'd meet her there.

But the jellyfish were headed his way.

She gesticulated wildly. "No, Juan! Get away! The jellies kill!"

He continued swimming toward her. Maybe if she could get to the pod first, she could stop him. She stepped onto the swaying walkway. Her damned legs. So unstable. Her left knee buckled. She stumbled and fell to her knees, yelping in pain. She grabbed at a wire handrail, panting.

There was a clamoring of feet up the sea ladders below her. They were coming. She continued crawling to the last pod. On another arm, Dr. Who saw Sylvie's laser rifle run out of power. As she popped in a new battery, a bullet hit her between the eyes. She was dead before she hit the gantry.

"Sylvie!" cried Dr. Who.

Drenched at the pod entrance, she punched the code to open the doors. Once. Twice. Three times. Nothing. It was dead. She looked out to the sea, where Juan floated motionless, held atop the waves by his life vest, his eyes forever open to the dark sky.

The sound of footsteps came closer. She opened an electrical panel to activate the pod manually. The footsteps went silent right next to her. She looked up. A figure clad in black neoprene, balaclava, and goggles loomed over her. He had no distinguishing markings, as anonymous as Death. When she saw the red laser-sight dot dancing on her copious bosom, she knew it was over.

The pirate pulled the trigger.

An agony erupted in her chest. She slumped backward, grabbing the spot. There was blood on her hand . . . Juan . . . Dizzy . . . Sylvie . . . The sky and water switched places . . . Which was which . . . Where, where was her precious Earth?

The pirate stood over her. He spoke into his headset microphone, "Got her."

Dr. Who closed her eyes as the world went black.

CHAPTER ONE

Floating was no longer peculiar. When Thomas Paine first uploaded his consciousness, it had been, but now, for Major Tom, the disembodied sensation was integral to his digital life. Today, following some ideas regarding black holes, Major Tom swam through an analysis of interstellar quasar transmissions, looking for patterns in black hole accretion disk data. But memory triggers lay in wait in digital waters, like sea mines, ready to detonate with the smallest touch, blasting him back to the past. And he never saw them coming.

As he searched the latest quasar data, he suddenly saw the astronomer's name. Amanda Markovitz . . .

BAM! Memories blew up, spinning, tossing, tumbling. He withdrew in nanoseconds, hiding in his digital home, his Memory Palace. He considered whether going out was worth it anymore. After all this time, being unable to forget felt like a bug in his programming. Not a feature.

Amanda was his ex-wife's first name.

Even with all his computing power, Thomas Paine had caused Amanda agony too great to calculate. Thinking of her brought the flood of pain back. Human emotions, fluid, contradictory, and governed by biological processes, did not translate well into mathematics, for all the attempts of social science and artificial intelligence. Twice

widowed before the birth of her child, by men who had never understood her, abandoned by a world some still blamed her for creating, she
felt betrayed by everyone around her.

He had been betrayed, too, more than anyone could imagine, and
his memories caused as much pain as they had when he'd had a body
to feel it with. He hadn't assumed that when he built the digital system
that housed his thoughts, and he was an idiot not to have anticipated it.

Two years ago, Peter Bernhardt and his vengeful alter ego, Thomas
Paine, had died. He had uploaded his mind into a digital substrate and
become Major Tom, the sole swimmer in this new realm, a human
mind melded with a digital world. In theory, he should have been all
ones and zeros in algorithmic harmony.

Humans could only approximate diving into information with
their physical devices and technologies. But Major Tom didn't pretend
the virtual world was real, like an embodied human. For him, it was as
real as reality got. The vast collection of data that humans had accumu-
lated provided an oceanic playground.

Until he ran into those damned sea mines.

To distract himself from the memories of a wife and child left
behind, he turned on Talking Heads' "Heaven." Relaxed alt-country
riffs, creepy echo, and a methodical tempo conveyed the promise of
a happiest-place-not-on-Earth where nothing happens, comforting
in a self-annihilating way. Then he followed the 24/7 motion-cam
exploits of an undersea expedition at the bottom of the Mariana
Trench, his version of cracking the last beer in the six-pack, watching *The Tonight Show*—now cohosted by a prerecorded, wisecracking,
overweight android—and passing out. Except he couldn't pass out.
He was always on.

His tin can of a net server farm suspended him far above the fray
of humanity. Like those American Revolutionaries before him, the
Puritans, whose tortuous religious view and life experiences taught them
all people were sinners and not to be trusted, he was determined to be

in the world, but not of it. He'd create his own, like a Buddhist hermit in a cave, but with the best net connection in the world, exploring the reality between his ears. Or in his case, processors.

Because the world was nothing but pain and suffering. He had helped make it that way, but without a body, there was nothing he could do about it. And that was the worst curse of all.

Nine months after his deathbed dispatch of his experiences with the Phoenix Club, Major Tom had transmitted a postscript. It was a convenient story to tell the world, pretentious, but he knew what had happened was important, and it needed to be both codified and presented with the necessary gravitas. Hopefully the world would think he was more than he was and grant him his most devout wish: to be left alone.

I am Major Tom, also known as Thomas Paine, formerly known as Peter Bernhardt. I am the first human-born artificial intelligence. Like Diogenes of ancient Greece, I am a cosmopolite, a citizen of the whole world, claiming no land or culture as my own, because there is no one else like me, and my existence means the world will never be the same. As my namesake, Thomas Paine, said in Rights of Man, *"My country is the world, and my religion is to do good." Though I am human no longer, I am still your kin.*

With the help of Dr. Ruth Chaikin, I sent a message as a voice/ text post, before my body's death, to all the net news services, chat rooms, and bulletin boards, billions of them around the world. In it, I told my story and urged my audience to search for the truth themselves and believe they can confront a future that, like all futures, will arrive regardless of whether they like it or not. As mankind moves from the industrial, to the information, to the nano-bio-info-cogno-convergence age, technology will continue to change society and the rules of governance. It always has. And it always will. Unfortunately, the powers that be of every age—whether tribal chiefs, monarchs, religious leaders, dictators, presidents, or CEOs—have tried to stop progress, to keep power for themselves. Their deliberate misunderstanding, resistance, protection of the status quo, and attempts to prevent the inevitable advancement of civilization have resulted in most of the human-caused strife and suffering throughout history.

When the people of the United States considered my words and realized what had been done to them and in their name for so many years, they disbanded the Phoenix Club, threw its members out of governmental, institutional, and corporate positions of power, and prosecuted those they could prove committed crimes. A grassroots campaign took back the country. It spread around the globe. The people of Earth grew up.

I was so proud.

While some of it was accurate, a good deal of it was complete hooey. People didn't grow up. They resented the changes they were forced into. In some places, chaos ensued. It wasn't pretty. He had once told Josiah Brant, "History will continue gratefully without you," and now hoped it would continue gratefully without him. It had. But not for the reason he thought.

There were always unintended consequences.

Major Tom chose to ignore them. His initial report, sent before his bodily death, had mentioned the multiple entities within him: Carter Potsdam, Josiah Brant, Bruce Lobo, Chang Eng, and Anthony Dulles.

But he did not dwell on them in his subsequent correspondence with the world. It was too hard for humans to accept that within his artificial human intelligence, a.k.a. AHI, several partial consciousnesses resided in a big top, with him as the ringmaster, the "Major" in Major Tom. Based on when and how they had died and what brain-computer interface Peter Bernhardt/Thomas Paine had installed at the time, each uploaded entity experienced greater or lesser humanity. Some, like Anthony and Chang, were just pieces of a brain's electrochemical spasms in the moments of their deaths. Others had more substance. Josiah and Bruce shared a more complex interface inside of Major Tom. They all had their purposes, and even partial entities deserved a partial life in a world of their making.

And then there was Carter. He had always been a special case.

Major Tom received Dr. Who's SOS. *Under attack. Need help.*

He focused on the current location of the *Sovereign*, accessing satellites around the planet that his shell companies paid to use. He was connected to thousands of them. They were his eyes, free from the editing of institutions and governments that spun the raw footage for their own purposes. Isolating one feed closest to the seastead, he watched a coordinated attack. These were complete pros, with state-of-the-art, microautonomous swarm ships and a new laser weapon masked in a waterspout, tech too sweet and pricey for anyone but a government or multinational corporation. He assumed SEALs or their equivalent. Perhaps a secret task force? But which governments or corporations?

The view from the atmosphere made the humans below look like a swarm of wasps and startled ants. That's what people were to him now. Insects—masters of shared intelligence, cooperation, and communication. But they were difficult to relate to. He tried, but it grew harder with his computers' timeshares and cycles. He often attempted to slow down the inputs and outputs, to exist in their time frame, but sometimes he just couldn't be bothered. He zoomed in for a closer look. Scanning images a thousand times quicker than a human could, he looked for any sign of Dr. Who, who had helped him so much in his original battle against the Phoenix Club. She had helped create Thomas Paine.

The seastead was destroyed, except for the central hub, which black-clad commandos were pouring over. A limp body with Dr. Who's height, weight, and build was carried by what appeared to be a SEAL team. No teams carried any other bodies. He applied infrared to pick up heat signatures. She was still red. She might be dying, but she wasn't dead yet. Someone must have known they would be observed, because a SEAL threw an infrared-blocking tarp over the Doctor and her bearers, obscuring them from his view. He followed the occasional reddish hand and foot that stuck out from the tarp and watched their progress into a small boat, which sped to a surfaced stealth submarine five nautical miles from the *Sovereign*. It matched a standard US Virginia-class nuclear-powered fast-attack sub that could have been owned by any number of countries or oligarchs. Its silent operation sent no messages he could recognize. Soon, all the mercenaries in the hub came to the surface and returned by their vessels to the submarine. He gathered all the data he could, until it submerged. There wasn't much he could do beyond that, until it resurfaced. He set a search alarm to alert him to any Virginia-class sub sightings.

This wasn't piracy.

Major Tom studied the cycles of history through a transdiscipline called cliodynamics. The word was derived from "Clio," the ancient Greek muse of history, and "dynamics," describing change over time. Created by a group of interdisciplinary scientists, cliodynamics recognized that the data behind human history might resemble that of biological ecosystems, with similar patterns and rhythms that could be modeled mathematically. Instead of predators, it followed oligarchs. Instead of prey, it tracked the poor and dispossessed. Like animal ecosystems, humans reacted predictably to famine, disease, overpopulation, too many predators, and threats from outside the system. In two– to three hundred–year cycles, cultures went through a period of general prosperity, feast, and peace, and then plunged into economic inequality, famine, and war. Every forty to sixty years, cycles of social imbalance and violence could appear and intersect with the larger cycles, causing a convergence of crises and a potential cataclysm for the empire or empires involved. It was a constant, like the metronomic beat of humanity's heart.

When the hard choices at the trough of the cycle were presented to both leaders and followers, it was the make-or-break moment of a civilization. Sometimes humanity chose badly, leading to the Dark Ages or fascism. Sometimes it chose well, like the brief post-WWII period of Pax Americana and global prosperity. It was clear to Major Tom and his fellow analysts that the world was in a special and dangerous time. Metrics indicated that the future of humanity was about to turn upside down again, unless correct decisions were made to protect the most people possible. Unfortunately, all those cycles could instead sync in one global collapse.

The world was fragmenting. Some empires had fallen apart; others were on the move. All the former certainties—money supply, employment, national security, citizenship—were up for grabs. And more change was coming.

Major Tom was afraid. Afraid of what had happened to Dr. Who. Afraid of how delicate civilization was. Afraid of the bigger cycles happening around the world, out of everyone's control. But he wasn't sure what a brain in a tin can could do about it.

CHAPTER TWO

Major Tom received a message from his best friend and intellectual partner, Dr. Ruth Chaikin: *What about SOS from Dr. Who?* The Doctor had sent it to Ruth, too.

He took his time to respond.

Time had a different meaning for Major Tom. The power of a computer or network determined how fast it could complete operations. Computers ran on their own time frames. So for a large and fast system like Major Tom's, a message from a human was laborious. He felt all of humanity was too slow. He could dart from a detailed climate-change analysis to correcting engineering schematics to the latest puppy photo in the pause of a human heartbeat. Communications were deliberate, especially with Ruth, with whom he spent the most time. Responses from his correspondents took what felt like days, weeks, even months. But to the human, his message back could appear immediate.

He often grew frustrated with humans, so he turned to the others inside his own consciousness. After his upload, Dr. Who had made him a gift so he and his fellow uploads wouldn't go crazy. It was the basic layout of the Memory Palace. Based on the ancient Greek and Roman method-of-loci memory technique, it gave a physicalized yet still virtual location for all the entities' memories to inhabit. In the early days, the more complete mentalities, like Tom or Carter Potsdam or Josiah

Brant, hogged the virtual space, choking the energy to the more limited mentalities of Chang Eng, Bruce Lobo, and Anthony Dulles.

To preserve the inhabitants' sanity, Major Tom gave them their own compartmentalized spaces to function in privacy, and he separated personalities that hated one another. They were no threat in isolation and rarely operated, unless he called on them. Except for Carter, their entities were too incomplete for complex thoughts. He might ask them for advice, but they were hobbled creations, fragments of their original brain patterns.

Major Tom's Memory Palace avatar, Tom, walked into the foyer. The image he chose for himself was simple: Peter Bernhardt, before 10/26, when all his troubles began. Shoulder-length chestnut hair, azure-blue eyes, six foot, and broad shouldered, wearing a black T-shirt, jeans, and biker boots. He liked to remind them that the "him" they had destroyed was still somewhere. Before him appeared six large, arched wooden doors ringing a circular vestibule.

He knocked on Anthony Dulles's door. "Dulles? Permission to come aboard?"

Manners were important in relationships that might last for eternity. He felt obligated to behave, listen, and treat his palacemates with respect.

"Ahoy!" yelled Dulles from the other side. Tom entered the galley of a thirty-foot Alberg racer-cruiser sailboat, the *American Dream* ∞. Many decades old, with a fiberglass hull adorned with teak that could have used a good refinishing, the boat was once Dulles's own, given its details from his memory. It was nothing like his superyacht, the *American Dream II*, which had exploded off the California coast with Dulles on board. This smaller craft provided enough space and detail for Dulles's limited mentality to manage. Variable winds, enough chop in the water to keep it interesting, and a blue sky scattered with cumulus clouds that went on forever. This was how Dulles, the old DC and Phoenix Club veteran, chose to define the hereafter.

Tom climbed the wooden ladder out of the galley and into open air. "Beautiful day, Anthony," he said, his voice resonant with the bourbon-and-cigarettes growl that lifesaving intubations had given to Peter Bernhardt. Tom had sampled that voice for vocal reproduction before he died.

"Always is. Pull and cleat that sheet, will you? I'm coming around," said Dulles.

"Sure." Tom did as he was told. The old-fashioned ship's wheel always reminded him of both the eight primary directions of a compass and the Buddhist dharma wheel: eight spokes for the Eightfold Path, the eight necessary behaviors leading to enlightenment. Dulles's karma was to repeat the same soothing sail, regardless of direction, and never get to land. Or enlightenment. No Nirvana for him. Or for any of them.

Tom and Dulles tacked the vessel. Wind rustled the sandy hair of the former spy's thirty-five-year-old self. Tom had seen him in life as a distinguished elder statesman but found it revealing that Dulles chose to live as a young, virile spy in the midst of learning his craft. Tall and handsome, his nimble coordination honed playing lacrosse in prep school and the Ivy League, this was a man once recruited to do whatever his country demanded, legal or not.

"Something troubling you, son?" said Dulles.

"There's a problem. Dr. Who sent an SOS." Tom sat on the windward gunnel and forwarded all the information he had so far received. He wiped his hand along the sun-worn gunnel, gritty with salt, a nice detail from the spy's memory.

Dulles spent a microsecond scanning the data as he laid a course to some meaningless island forever in the distance. "You wonder whether you should rush to save her and see who's behind it? Or not?"

"Yes," said Tom.

"You have reciprocal loyalty, and that's valuable. She did you many good turns, beyond what you paid for years ago. If it were me, I'd examine all the money flowing in and out, to her, her clients, her clients' clients, and so forth. It's amazing how easy it is to see a big picture with money." Dulles had run money-laundering operations for the CIA and the Phoenix Club. That's how he knew the club had horrible plans for the United States, without being directly involved with Josiah, Bruce, or Carter.

He made a small course correction. "Yes. Money tells the truth. People? Never. Problem is, most are too lazy to follow all the leads to the whole picture. But I think you'll do fine."

"Well, Dr. Who's final client seemed to be her undoing. I'll find the rest."

"That was easy," said Dulles. "Now you must weigh the evidence and decide: Is helping her good for you? And is it good for the country? Don't regret this decision later or ask your Maker's forgiveness like I did. It never comes. That's all I'll say."

"There's no United States left," said Tom. "It's all fragmented now. You know that, right?"

Dulles lifted his jaw and stared at the horizon. "I don't believe it."

Tom stood. "Thank you for your advice, Anthony. I hope I did right by you. This isn't exactly hell, is it?"

The spy closed his eyes for a moment, took a deep breath of the pungent sea air, and smiled. "Isn't it?"

Chastened, Tom retreated through the galley and stood in the foyer, considering the other doors. Chang Eng and Bruce Lobo were too limited and would be no help with this question. Josiah Brant still considered Dr. Who an enemy.

He knocked on Carter's door.

Carter was not like the others. His uploaded consciousness was almost as complete as Tom's own. Tom had forgiven his longtime friend and part-time enemy before Carter had died and was absorbed into Tom's brain. He talked to Carter often in the Memory Palace. Charmingly, Carter still called him Pete. But lately, Carter had balked.

Look, Pete, you know I love you like a brother, but I can't be with you all the time. Eternity is fucking long. Please leave me alone unless I send an engraved invitation.

Tom felt it was only fair to do so. Nothing Carter had ever done or said inside the entity had made him doubt his choice, but he needed help. Tom knocked again.

"What?" Carter snapped.

"I need you," said Tom.

"Why didn't you say that years ago?" Carter's voice teased behind the door. "Come in, my dear."

Carter changed his environment regularly. It had been a Saxon castle preparing for a Norman raid. It had been the French court of Louis XIV, with Carter starring as the Sun King. This time, Tom stepped into the front hall of an antebellum plantation. He could see straight through to a back door that would lead to cotton fields. Out the front door, an alley of Southern oaks, heavy with Spanish moss, shimmered in the hazy air. But Tom wasn't perspiring. Apparently, Carter didn't think feeling the discomfort was necessary to embrace the atmosphere.

Inside, the house was a magnificent and meticulous reproduction of the height of the nineteenth-century Southern gentry, with an occasional piece of cutting-edge contemporary art on the wall. Over the fireplace at the moment was a monumental piece Carter would describe as "I can't do that," which meant he thought it worthy of study. This broad category was derived from the famous Gruendemann maxim of the three schools of art: 1) "I can't do that." 2) "I can do that." 3) "My pet chimp Bobo can do that."

Tom looked down the central hall and out the back door into the fields. Black men and women worked picking cotton, singing work songs, and smiling as if to ameliorate the reality of imprisonment and cruelty. Tom felt sick.

Carter paused on the second-floor landing for effect, then descended the curved stairs, a dandified version of a wealthy plantation owner of 1860. His clothing's combination of colors and patterns was more vibrant and avant-garde than the Georgian gentry would have attempted. He chose the version of himself from the age he had died—thirty-seven—as his avatar. Carter had been at the height of his powers and charisma then, and he knew it. At the bottom of the stairs, he opened his arms expansively and asked, "Well? Fabulous or fail?"

"Slaves?" said Tom, pointing out the back door. "Are you kidding me?"

"For Pete's sake, Pete, they're not real. They're atmosphere. I'm having a Scarlett O'Hara moment." He looked down at his outfit. "Maybe Ashley Wilkes, with better taste. And don't roll your eyes. What else do I have to do here?"

Tom got to the point. "Dr. Who's been kidnapped. Possibly killed."

Carter looked surprised as he reviewed the data. "Too bad. She was a good egg. But what do you think we can do, beyond our usual voyeurism? It's not like we have real superpowers. Just some half-assed digital immortality."

Tom must have projected disappointment. Carter shrugged. "My dearest Pete, we're just a sad simulacrum of something long gone. Like my plantation."

"You're right. I don't know what I expected." Tom turned to sit in an intricately carved nineteenth-century Victorian Rococo Revival sofa covered in a rich golden-yellow damask. He looked at it closely. He could have run an image search, but it was easier to ask and might spur Carter to more conversation. "This is familiar."

Carter sat gracefully on a matching sofa opposite Tom. "Made by John Henry Belter. From the White House Lincoln Bedroom. Have to copy the good stuff. Even digital renderings should have standards. Otherwise, we're barbarians."

Tom never thought to do this himself. While always curious, he never brought his interests home. As usual, Carter made him feel inadequate. Even as digital entities, that was still their dynamic.

"You could live anywhere," said Tom. "At any time. Or create a place unique to you. Why this?"

Carter looked around. "History comforts me." He nodded toward the back door. "Even if it seems distasteful. I've stewed in an aristocratic pot all my life. It's who I am."

"You still care about the country? Or what's left of it, after all that's happened?"

Carter looked surprised. "Of course. I know you were born in a manger, but don't you? It's still the greatest social experiment the world's ever known. As former scientists, we should appreciate experiments." He winked.

Tom shifted uncomfortably and bounced. The stiff sofa had old springs, cotton batting, and horsehair internal upholstery. The detail was impressive. "But the experiment is over."

"No, it's not."

"The government and the club . . ."

Carter laughed. "You think you destroyed the country? You saved us from ourselves. Good job there, my dear. We'll be right back where we need to be. Someday." A glass of scotch appeared in his hands.

Tom wondered if a part of Carter's digital mind was not able to grasp reality. He thought of Anthony Dulles on his never-ending sail. "I've done all right by you, haven't I?"

"Who's 'I'? And who's me, for that matter?" teased Carter.

"Come on. Be serious."

Carter smiled benevolently. "Considering our illustrious past? I'd say you did okay. More than I'd have done." He sipped his virtual scotch. "You know what gets me after all this time here? I can remember drinking the best scotch whiskies in the world—some of them with you!—and can replicate that taste memory. But after a while . . . it's boring. You didn't factor in the human craving for novelty when you all built this. Our memories and influences are finite, but even human-like entities need novelty. It's why I change my space so often. Maybe better to be out in the world, for all its sorrows, than an eternity of this."

"We can't be in the world," said Tom. "Look what we did last time. Can you imagine what we might be capable of now?"

"Oh, I can imagine," said Carter.

There was a flicker, the briefest hint of malice on Carter's face. Tom might have missed it if he didn't have perfect recall. It was covetous. Eager. Grasping. Knowing.

Tom wasn't sure why, but he was suddenly afraid.

CHAPTER THREE

Instead of just sending a text or verbal message, Major Tom's avatar appeared in Ruth's computer monitor and answered her back. Face-to-face dialogues were best for humans. It was 0.58 seconds after she had sent her message. "We're monitoring the situation. Nothing to do right now."

"*Sovereign*'s two days away. Under full power. We can see for ourselves," said Ruth.

"These guys are pros. By the time we get there, there'll be nothing left to see. And no communications we can find. We can't chase the sub without endangering you and everyone on board. There's nothing to do right now, except collect data."

For Major Tom, her brief pause of disappointment was a long wait.

"*Keshure,*" was all she said.

But she didn't sound "okay." He viewed her through the cameras on the bridge of their home, the former USS *Zumwalt*.

Ruth managed the Major Tom operating system and program aboard the ship, a decommissioned stealth-guided missile destroyer bought from a disgusted American admiral when he realized his beloved US Navy had fragmented into regional and state forces. Like the Russian admirals and generals after the fall of the Soviet Union, he sold extraneous vehicles and munitions to the highest bidder—within reason, of course. Unlike his Russian counterparts, he refused to sell nukes or chemical weapons. Few could bid higher than Ruth, with their stolen Phoenix Club money. And so minus the guided nuclear missiles, the *Zumwalt* became their home. They automated the navigation systems so Ruth could sail it single-handedly if necessary. With the world fracturing, staying relatively undetectable at sea was a great advantage. Right now, they were located 38.744699 N, 130.303043 W, more than 250 miles off the Northern Californian coast.

It was a strange place for Ruth and Major Tom to call home, maybe the strangest in the history of naval shipbuilding. There were no windows on the bridge, which was two stories tall and completely enclosed. The *Zumwalt* relied on data analysis of its environment to control the complex ship. It was the closest thing to a spaceship on earth, bound only by gravity and the ocean's currents. There were a dozen desks with old-fashioned three-screen wraparound monitors. Another ten desks fit inside half domes, set on their sides, ten feet in diameter. Within the dome's periphery, Ruth could watch a 3-D presentation of 180 degrees of space in any direction, in real time, with depth perception. It was a better visual tool than the mixed reality goggles everyone wore and equal to virtual retina projection affordable only to the rich, a system designed to make the drone pilots feel like they *were* the drone, flying through real space.

But Ruth preferred to have a traditional monitor console all to herself, and to be left alone by the ship's skeleton crew. A *Zumwalt*-class destroyer once needed a minimum of 130 crewmen to run her, but Major Tom and Ruth's improved automation and nonmilitary goals reduced that number to fifteen men and women who provided the hands, feet, and autonomy that Major Tom lacked. They had been recommended by the admiral, and so far, they had proven loyal. Yet Ruth barely knew their names and had never made friends with any of them.

Her head twitched to the side, and she sighed. "I miss the *Pequod.*"

"I miss my body. And my old brain. And all the amazing things it did." Though his memory was perfect and he felt psychological pain, his upload eliminated the more remarkable feats that his previously hacked and jacked human brain could perform. No more clairvoyance. No more manipulation of linear time. No more synesthesia. Thomas Paine's synapses had been copied and recorded, but the nanobots and nanowiring did not replicate themselves in Major Tom. Even after trying and failing to reproduce them after he uploaded, he surmised that a digital copy could not replicate real-life atoms of matter coming into contact with one another and reacting in surprising ways. In the end it didn't matter: his special abilities were gone. It made him wonder if there was an ineffable "magic"—a word scientists abhorred—to having a biological body.

Ruth's muscles twitched in unison in a single convulsion. "I miss a boat. You miss a body. I am not competing. For who has the most loss."

"You know why we had to change ships," said Tom.

"Safety. Always safety. Feh . . ."

Her sadness had slowly permeated the *Zumwalt*, like water passing through a cell membrane, diluting the morale of everyone around her. Here was one of the world's greatest scientists, always battling at the cutting edge of the possible, too depressed even to argue back. Major Tom didn't know how to fix it. Ruth rejected psychotherapy, psychopharmacology, and the usual prescriptions of meditation, exercise, and sunlight.

Humans needed a lot of tending.

"How are our electric reserves?" he asked. "I noticed you stopped working with your hard X-ray nanoprobe beamline. Is there an energy problem?" They had changed the ship's Rolls Royce MT-30 gas engine and generator sets for a tiered-hybrid system capable of utilizing any type of fuel available, as well as ample high-density, flexible solar arrays that unfurled like mats and sails when weather was good and stealth wasn't necessary. Desalinization and food production with grow lights deep below deck allowed Ruth and crew to avoid ports. But it was conceivable they might need more power someday.

"Oder es helft nit oder men darf es nit."

Either it didn't help or it wasn't needed. Tom wasn't sure if she meant the nanoscale microscope or her emotional health.

"And that guy. P-P-Ponnusamy," she continued. "He's bugging us. Again. Why don't you message back?"

"I might have been a scientist, but I don't enjoy being the object of scientific scrutiny. He wants to pick my digital brain apart to make more of me. We can't allow that."

Truth be told, as the world reshaped itself, fewer and fewer scientists had the funds to continue the type of research that might replicate Tom's existence. They were busy trying to survive themselves. Caltech's Dr. Arun Ponnusamy was one of the few still chasing him.

"I'm not your mother," said Ruth. "Don't complain to me."

"You did kinda raise me," said Tom. "Sorry I'm not a better companion." Ruth had raised him, to the extent that a computer-simulated brain could be raised. She tried to make him do what was right, even if he didn't agree or didn't want to. Or found he couldn't. "Ruth, I really am sorry."

She didn't answer.

"I'm sorry I'm so limited," he continued. "And selfish. But I can't fix everything. I don't understand as much as you would want me to. I can't model a perfect equilibrium and have the model work. The world's too complex. My digital brain is still like a human's."

She sniffed. "You are too smart. For that argument."

"I can see and hear more of what's happening in the world and process it faster. But there's no omniscience. I'm not God . . ."

"Danken Gott . . ."

"You said it. I'm no more than I was. I'm less. That superhuman shit's just fodder for bad science-fiction movies. I'm afraid to do anything. I might screw it up all over again."

Ruth's shoulders twitched uncontrollably. She looked like she might cry.

She reached for her old-fashioned keyboard. Her cameras cut out. She'd hit the privacy screen. Their conversation was finished.

He left the question unasked: Was it ethical to do nothing? His emotional programming said no. Major Tom checked the worldwide media. No one had picked up on the *Sovereign* raid. It would have been plainly visible from space by the major countries of the world, but it had been ignored. He checked the currency markets. The Shell was still being traded, but its price was more volatile. Cryptocurrencies were generally cyclical, and he saw the possibility of underlying instability. Vendors of biofuel and fish seemed to expect their deliveries.

No obvious patterns emerged.

Major Tom had one distinct advantage as a digital entity. He could verify and back up his digital "senses." He couldn't "remember" wrong. He had absolutely witnessed the *Sovereign* under attack.

Unless it was an illusion created to lure him into something. It was possible, but he did not think it probable. He studied Dr. Who's message and the footage again, to make sure. All the data looked real. He compared it to footage he lifted off foreign satellites. He could find only one—a South Pacific media satellite—that had captured the entire raid, and it backed up his own data.

He found a headline: "Russian Army Along China's Northern Frontier." The Russian government-controlled media said, "The former Western Empire of homosexual pederasts has fallen to our Russian might! No longer will they humiliate us, steal our money and resources, and torture our brave Russian soul! Having brought our former Western regions back into the fold, we turn our eyes in dismay to the East, to the angry dragon snapping at our Great Bear's ankles. If they cannot be brought to heel, they must be eliminated."

Even with his augmented intellect, there was no rationalizing idiotic propaganda aimed at future cannon fodder.

Another headline: "China Activates Military Facilities in Philippines." The Eastern Empire had created islands across the Pacific for years. When they bumped into another nation's territory, an inevitable soft power struggle ensued. A few missiles lobbed back and forth that never hit their targets, then acquiescence when the aggrieved nation realized there was no one to help them fight back. In the wake of a fascist dictatorship, the Philippines had been taken over as a Chinese protectorate in a bloodless invasion. China had snared Japan and Indonesia into its political sphere of influence. Their ships had been seen near the Hawaiian Islands, with more landfill and construction gear. The Chinese navy had also launched deep-sea military facilities years ago, using the depths of the Pacific trenches to hide a multitude of operations. All this looked potentially relevant, given the *Sovereign*'s location just six hundred miles north of Hawaii.

Major Tom's revelations began a cascade of small and not-so-small revolutions around the world. The American Empire contracted, and the states fragmented into ideological regions. Without clear leaders or a mission, the US military had come home from overseas and hunkered down at American bases. The European continent's cooperative agreements had broken up years ago, victims of the corrosive effects of bureaucracy and warring elites who shared only the language of money and manipulated those beneath them into blaming immigrants for Europe's problems. Russia and China leveraged their investments and resources in Europe, the Middle East, Africa, and Asia to take over the globe in their imperial ambition.

After thousands of years of empires rising and falling, it looked like the world would never learn.

When Major Tom looked at the state of North America, he was confused. He had destroyed the Phoenix Club to stop the political elite from drugging the nation's—and the world's—citizens into conformity and apathy, mindlessly allowing their leaders to do whatever they wanted without resistance. By doing so, he had single-handedly eliminated the overabundance of warring and conspiring politicians and corporate heads who regularly destroy political systems, as had happened in Europe. With fewer players struggling for the top of the Teflon pole of power, the country should have relaxed. That's what cliodynamics predicted, usually. Fewer infighting leaders meant more desirable seats at the eternal game of elite musical chairs, less political polarization, less educational and economic insecurity, and less stress on the entire system. With the Phoenix Club no longer there to tighten the screws of society, the system of American politics should have reset.

Instead, the country was in shambles. He didn't grasp something crucial at the heart of the continent. What was he missing?

The West was fragmented and confused. Without the United States as the world's emperor and policemen, and with Europe in pieces, Russia and China felt emboldened to move into full-blown imperial expansion. Countries that had criticized Pax Americana simply traded one emperor for another. No longer teamed up against the United States, China and Russia feared only each other, and in a scramble for dominance, both looked to pick off what the former United States and Europe had left behind.

Maybe China attacked the seastead, looking for more Pacific real estate, he thought, edging its way toward Hawaii and, eventually, the entire Pacific Rim. But he lacked enough data to make a final analysis.

Regardless, war was coming.

The world was still filled with nuclear weapons. And bioweapons. And technological bear traps. With powerful robotic, surveillance, and energy weapons widespread, he wondered if humanity could survive. Otherwise, he would get painfully lonely, for as long as he had power and working servers. And then, he'd be gone, too.

His daily musical gig in the virtual world was coming up in seconds. Thinking it might be among his last chances to play his music and enjoy the crowds, he kept the appointment. The show must go on, at least for today, he thought. The end of the world could wait. It always did.

CHAPTER FOUR

The Church of Major Tom was created by its users and existed on its own open virtual reality platform, allowing his disciples to access his public thoughts and archives and, from them, build a world. No matter how he had tried to dissuade them, he couldn't stop their adoration. This was in contrast to the coalition of fundamental Abrahamic religionists who thought Major Tom was the devil; or the Americans for a Theocratic World, who thought he was the antichrist; or reactionaries of all political persuasions, who thought he destroyed the world through accelerated change. So he let TCoMT take on a life of its own.

He was surprised how much he liked the virtual reality they created. He would appear in disguise each day at 5:00 a.m. Greenwich Mean Time as a wandering troubadour with a guitar, checking out the scene, eager to perform music the faithful enjoyed. No one knew he was Major Tom. He looked like any other fanboy. The songs were often his favorites, but he took requests, too. His disguise was of a male of Asian descent who looked like Chang Eng. He was no digital artist, and it was simplest to replicate those he knew best. It didn't matter whom he looked like, as long as no one knew he was their supposed messiah.

He materialized at his usual spot, a cobblestone sidewalk corner under a nineteenth-century streetlamp whose puddle of light illuminated him. Behind him loomed a medieval cathedral copied from the design of Chartes in France. The rose window glowed from inside and vibrated gently to the congregants' singing of the primary doxology, Simon & Garfunkel's "Sound of Silence."

He wasn't sure why they had chosen that song, as much as he liked it. It wasn't one he had thought about in his previous life. But it had stuck with the acolytes, one of many hymns adopted by the devout. They created a virtual world in what they assumed was his image, hoping to entice the savior for a messianic return to their ranks.

"You think I'm the narcissist?" Carter once teased Tom. "What do you think this makes you?"

Tom didn't like to admit how much he depended on the devotees' interactions. He received messages, and not only from his fans. Some were images and people he couldn't identify, as if TCoMT had created a hive mind greater than the sum of their individual thoughts. TCoMT was the only place he experienced these visions. He wondered if they were genuine or if someone had figured out who he was and was placing them inside his programming. Either possibility was unsettling.

A month earlier, he had sat strumming his virtual 2001 Manzer Paradiso archtop acoustic guitar on the curb of a cobblestone street. Acolytes appreciated attention to details like the replication of the master's own instrument. That day, he hadn't wanted to play from the official hymnal. Instead, he played Coldplay's "42," singing of Carter, Josiah, Bruce, Anthony, and Chang within their Memory Palace. Remembering everything they did, unable to change the past. They weren't ghosts. But through their memories, they were the undead. A house of ghouls, caught in the machine. As he sang, he had a vision. Dr. Who was conscious and restrained, in tight, gray, utilitarian, windowless quarters, maybe a military ship or submarine. He didn't know if it had happened in the past, present, or future, or instead was a dream. Did he receive a message? Or did the virtual world create something on its own?

He had sent Dr. Who a message on the *Sovereign*: *Just checking in. Are you okay?*

She had been in the midst of teaching a Foxy Funkadelia pole-dancing lesson. "Child, you're gettin' paranoid in your eternal age. If you're here for the splits, stick around. Otherwise, shove off, hon."

The vision had appeared a month before her kidnapping.

He had also foreseen the riots in Washington, DC, the burning of the Capitol and the Phoenix Club, an enraged citizenry scouring the city, looking to attack members of the club. And the final demolition of the Phoenix Club camp outside of Yosemite National Park, where bulldozers knocked down every building and left only the trees behind. These were the rare times he had anything like his former clairvoyance. So something must have transferred in his upload. He just wasn't sure what it meant.

Now, a month later, he sat under the streetlamp and played "42" again, hoping to understand both a prescient vision and the true conundrum regarding Dr. Who. As the music spread, it activated a form of techno-synesthesia. He could hear the sound of silence between the notes. Feel the nothingness he inhabited as he plucked virtual strings. The lyrics of "42" captured the famous artificial intelligence researcher Douglas Hofstadter's work into the torturous nature of memory in *I Am a Strange Loop*. It hinted at the quirkiness of Douglas Adams's numerical meaning of life. And it teased Major Tom's own frustrations at his new identity. Who was he?

The crowd, expecting its bard, had gathered to listen. Coins rattled into his panhandling cup. A woman in all black stood before him. She was tall, delicate, and attenuated to an unrealistic degree. She wore a corseted and studded bodice under a black-leather duster coat. A long black tulle skirt covered black pirate boots. Long, straight blonde hair fell to her waist. Steampunk's requisite Victorian goggles wrapped her top hat. Around her neck, she wore a necklace with an oval pendant about three inches long, painted with the face of a man in the style of a sixteenth-century portrait miniature.

She waited for him to finish the song, then cleared her throat.

"Something you want to hear?" he asked. He strummed, waiting for a response.

She set their conversation to private. "No, Thomas Paine. I have something for you to hear."

His fingers froze on the strings. No one had recognized him before.

"I wanna talk about *Sovereign* seasteaders. And Dr. Who. And a run on the cryptobanks. That hasn't happened yet, but it will soon. Oh! And here's an image file. It's my version of the virtual you. Hope you like it." A freakish, crooked grin split only half her face. Perhaps she hadn't mastered the visual emotion-capture yet.

The image file was of a rectangular fabric banner, white, with gold fringe around its edges. At its center, a man's face designed from the composite images of Peter Bernhardt and Thomas Paine. She had entitled it "Veronika's Veil." It matched the portrait around her neck.

"Who are you?" he asked. "Where are you from?"

The other half of her mouth smiled. "Come on in. Let's talk."

CHAPTER FIVE

Major Tom received the IP addresses of a computer with an old-fashioned mixed reality headset in Santa Barbara, California. That's where she wanted to talk.

After one second, during which he had verified that she wasn't monitoring him in any way that might compromise his security, he asked, "So how do I know you?" In the time it took for her to answer, he learned a good deal about her:

Name(s): Veronika Gascon, born Ronald Gascon. Name change occurred four years ago.

Place of birth and hometown: Santa Barbara, CA

Age: 22

Parents: Anita Gascon (56, webzine editor) and Michael Gascon (57, professor of theoretical physics at UC Santa Barbara)

Siblings: Rachel (26, management analyst) and Robert (24, member of modern dance company)

Records included her homeschool high-school diploma at age twelve, impeccable standardized test scores, and online college classes worth three master's degrees in computer science, fine art, and linguistics.

He found the chosen name of Veronika interesting. "Veronica" was derived from the Latin *vera icon*—true image. As Jesus carried his cross to Calvary, Veronica was the saint who wiped the sweat from his brow and found his face forever imprinted on her cloth. That relic was supposedly in Saint Peter's Basilica and had magical powers. And here she had made her own version of Veronica's Veil with his face on it.

This fan might be a handful.

Major Tom did a cursory search of her home computer. She was the talented virtual world artist who had created much of TCoMT. She made a good deal of money with her digital art and programming services. More than enough to pay for the sizable medical bills that gender reassignment entailed. But was she as clever as she appeared? He also found well-disguised partitions hiding information. And he was sure of a good deal of offsite storage, too. Her system was too clean for a sophisticated digital denizen.

He looked around her room through her monitor and headset webcams. Her TCoMT avatar was an elegant version of the young woman lounging here on a queen-sized bed, dressed all in black: slouchy, shapeless sweater; long cotton skirt; comfy socks. Long, straight blonde hair that could badly use a trim. A narrow, gaunt face and a delicate, almost scarecrow-like build, her knees and elbows sticking out like raw turnips from her branch-like limbs.

Veronika lay on her black-sheeted bed, sheltered by black walls and a white ceiling. Her screensaver rotated a series of images familiar to anyone who had kept up with the news in the last few years. Photos of Peter Bernhardt, the bioengineer and falsely accused terrorist, and his alter ego, Thomas Paine, the mysterious billionaire who had brought down the most powerful and dangerous men in America. The repeating loop ended with the same face from the Veronika's Veil banner: an avatar representing Major Tom. Todd Rundgren's "Born to Synthesize" reverberated through her room. She clearly knew the savior solved problems with music and thought a song about thinking might help.

Since she had invited him into her mixed reality glasses and headphones, he appeared in them for their conversation. "Why an MR headset? You seem state-of-the-art enough for contacts and eardrum sensors. Even the new brainjack's in alpha."

"Earwigs fall out. Like, the last pair I found on my pillow, knotted in my hair." She made a cat gagging sound. "Retinal projection contacts are too limiting so far. More toys than tools. One scratched my cornea. And forget about Essensse's brainjacks. Gotta wait for, like, version 4.0, at least, for wetware on the market now."

Essensse Labs was a small and practical brain-computer-interface firm that competed with Prometheus Industries in the research, development, production, and sale of nano-scaled prostheses for the brain. Their brainjacks were the first marketed attempt at a nontherapeutic brain-computer interface.

"I've hacked these specs to include full haptic coordination and eyetracking," continued Veronika, "voice and blink commands, gyro-recognition, and the full spectrum of language and perceptive input from any sensorium I link."

Her bragging and implicit criticism amused him. "Impressive. Room's very goth," he said.

"Ha. Nope. Very you. Hello, darkness, baby." She pointed to the black wall. "This is my frustratingly banal meat existence." She pointed up. "And that is the purity and light of information. Where we can all, like, be together."

"Dramatic," he said.

"Fuck yeah."

He spied a hunk of half-melted and half-burnt fiberglass in a Plexiglas case on a shelf. He'd seen the ads last year. For $1,499.95, one could fondle a "relic" of Major Tom's past: a piece of Anthony Dulles's *American Dream II* that had exploded off the coast of California, not far from her house, when he was chased by the Phoenix Club. The ad claimed treasure hunters had scoured the bottom of the Pacific for the pieces that proved Major Tom's story, then sold them when the man was hailed as a global hero.

On another shelf, he found a crystal presentation vial, purporting to contain a tiny piece of biological tissue from Thomas Paine's remains. "Your Own Piece of DNA History!" read the label. The flesh would have come from the Sacramento General Hospital morgue, where his body had been taken after his upload. Supposedly, morgue attendants had discovered his identity and taken more tissue samples than necessary. That would have cost her a lot of money.

He knew the boat fragment was fake, but the tissue was real. She was a Major Tom fangirl. He had never met one in real life before.

"Do you put the visions in my head?" he asked.

"What visions? Do they softly creep?" She giggled, braiding her hair.

It was difficult for Major Tom to gauge all her emotional tells with her eyes obscured by the mixed reality glasses. But she seemed quite relaxed. He also didn't want to tip his hand or betray any technical vulnerability. The popular image he portrayed was smarter than he was, and he liked to keep it that way.

"So will you rejoin the world and help us?" she asked.

"Who's 'us'?" he asked.

"Dr. Who," she said. "And the *Sovereign*. And everyone depending on what they do."

"And who are you to them? And they to you?"

Veronika sat up on the bed. "Look, I know what happened. And you do, too."

"What I know is of no use to you. Or me . . ."

"Bullshit," she said. "Only the savior can fix this. You can't live in silence. It's like . . . a cancer. No one in TCoMT knows who or what you really are. They're interpreting false messages."

"That's your pitch? 'The Sound of Silence'?"

"No! I know who has Dr. Who. At least I think I do." She picked at an acne scab on her face.

"And that would be . . . ?"

"This connection isn't secure enough," she said. "Somewhere more private."

"Where's more private?" he asked.

"Please," said Veronika. "I can't tell you yet. But I can soon!"

"We're done here. Good luck on your adventures." He cut off the private communication, and they found themselves back on the cobblestone street in TCoMT.

Her furious avatar tilted her tear-streaked face up at a streetlight and screamed, then turned away to a neon sign on an alley wall. It read, *The words of the prophets are written nowhere and are read by no one.*

He hadn't written that. And he wasn't sure if she had.

The thing he was afraid of had happened.

He knew one thing. He was supposed to come out and fix it. Whatever "it" was. For everyone. And he didn't want to.

There was a part of his personal statement he had never made public. Even though he thought of himself as the creator of the changes in the world, it posed problems:

But the world's people did not see me as their parent. They blamed me. Or worshiped me. Or forgot me. And I, them. I forgave my enemies their will to power and status. But it's hard to forgive yourself. When you have such powerful technologies delivering the riches of the world to your neural-net tips, the troubles of humans grow distant . . . petty . . . inconsequential . . .

He cranked Bowie's "Ashes to Ashes," rising and falling with each twanging digital cubit of sound. In the song, his namesake, the musical Major Tom, still floated in space, adapted to his new life. He wanted to "come down" but didn't know how to break the addiction of his drug: his newly detached self. Bowie also hadn't known how to come down off the drugs he was addicted to, and Major Tom knew that the life he was living was as potent as any drug. It allowed him to hide. Be free. Never engage.

Could he ever "come down"? And where would his home be now?

It was enough to make him pull inside his digital snail shell and lock the entrance. But a thought escaped from a tiny, parceled-off part of him: When did he become such a coward?

This hermetic fear and resistance wasn't him. It had never been him. Something was wrong.

CHAPTER SIX

Major Tom frequently eavesdropped on Ruth to check on her well-being. Ruth knew it. He knew that Ruth knew it, and so on. It was a game that neither enjoyed playing.

Removing her privacy screen, Ruth still sat in her favorite ergonomic chair on the ship's bridge, reading a private message from Veronika Gascon: *I know what happened to Dr. Who and the* Sovereign. *Please help me convince Major Tom that he is the only one who can help them. This will not be isolated. Many more lives are on the line.*

Then Ruth received another message from Miss Gray Hat, the mysterious hacker for whom Ruth held an unrequited geek crush. Ruth had taken Miss Gray Hat's sudden departure from their lives badly. Ruth had given her the moniker *Fräulein Ethische*, meaning Miss Ethical. It was Thomas Paine who had named her Miss Gray Hat, denoting that she was neither a legal white-hat hacker nor an illegal black-hat hacker, but someone in the middle who did the right thing, even if it was criminal. Miss Gray Hat could speak several languages, including Ruth's own Yiddish, and Ruth had always assumed she was a fellow Eastern European Jew.

Miss Gray Hat had also helped when Peter Bernhardt/Thomas Paine had needed her most, by stealing IBM's Blue Gene programming for their own use; protecting him from cyber attacks; setting traps for cyber spies; uncovering and collating data about the Phoenix Club; and along with Dr. Who, spreading disinformation about Thomas Paine to his enemies. She was extremely talented. But Major Tom didn't know if she was even a she. Miss Gray Hat had successfully maintained her anonymity with elaborate encryption, voice anonymization, and contact impersonal enough to reveal almost nothing. After his uploading two years ago, the hacker had departed for computers unknown. Ruth was heartbroken. Major Tom was suspicious. Miss Gray Hat had been such an intense and necessary part of both their lives. Had she taken another gig? Was she upset with them? Was she dead?

Neither had heard from her until now. Was this even her?

Anonymized through the usual feminine voice, the audio message said, "Have you heard from Veronika yet? I know her. Listen to her. She's right. Dr. Who needs our help."

"What do you think, Ruthie?" asked Tom.

Ruth slunk down into her chair and crossed her arms defensively over her chest. "I don't know."

"Well, we know that Miss Gray Hat and Dr. Who worked together for us a couple of years ago. We just don't know how deep the relationship might be. I'm guessing she knows something. Right?"

"I'm allowed? To have an op-p-pinion?" Ruth muttered.

"Always."

"Hmmph . . ." Ruth's shoulders twitched. "That's a first."

"You think I ignore you?" asked Tom.

"Yes," said Ruth. "You withdraw. You leave me alone. You do what you want. With no thought of me. How are you my best friend?"

He was concerned. Ruth had had a crush on Peter Bernhardt as far back as when they were graduate students together in her father's nanotechnology lab at Stanford. "We've been friends and colleagues a long time. And we always will be."

"I want more," she said. "And I don't think you can."

Ruth was never one to dissemble. But she wasn't able to have a traditional relationship, either. Her unique neurological wiring made it painful to touch another human being. Once, she had thought Major Tom would be the ideal partner, because he had no body.

"I'm sorry, Ruthie. You said I was a great mate: 'Toilet seat stays down. Toothpaste stays capped. Never needs a hug.' And I thought we were bound for life with our blood oath." Ruth insisted they perform a blood oath ceremony three years ago, each depositing a drop of their blood onto a single microscope slide and sandwiching them together. Ruth had kept the slide as a sign of their pact to work together forever. He wasn't sure where the slide was anymore.

"Worst d-d-decision I ever made," she said.

With the swipe of a finger, she deleted both Veronika's and Miss Gray Hat's messages, then turned on her privacy screen again.

"Guess that's my answer," said Tom. He was sorry to see Ruth depressed, but he knew she would have to deal with both Veronika and Miss Gray Hat directly. They were making sure of it.

CHAPTER SEVEN

Major Tom and Talia Brooks kept an open AV link between her office at Prometheus Industries and his servers. As CEO, she now ran the firm that he and Carter had created. And she was not pleased to hear from him.

"Why do you need me to do this?" she asked.

His GPS and satellite image of Veronika's robocar showed it parked in the lot, and she was entering the main doors.

"I asked her to come so I could get your opinion. You might pick up something I don't."

"Female intuition is overrated," said Talia.

Tom ignored her sarcasm. "She knows things, and I can't figure out how or why or what. But we owe Dr. Who. How can we help her without more information?"

"Hmm . . ." Talia had a sad, faraway look.

"Sorry. Guess you're in my crap again," said Tom.

"I'm always in it," Talia said. "You just never notice."

Talia had been inextricably linked to Tom for over three years. From the moment Peter Bernhardt's technology came on the scene, she had stalked him, knowing that the Phoenix Club would pounce on its potential. One of the few who understood what the club would do to him, she had struggled to convince Peter that he would be their victim and only succeeded after she saved his life. Talia had helped make him their mutual weapon against shared enemies, overseeing the creation of Thomas Paine in the image of her murdered father. Even though she had feared that his brain technology would change him, she had become his lover. And now, she was a keeper of his flame. Since his and Carter's deaths two years ago, she and her once-past-now-present lover, Dr. Steven Carbone, had run Prometheus Industries. They handled everything Peter Bernhardt had created, but not as he would have wished. But Major Tom had no say anymore, legally or ethically.

"You know I wouldn't ask unless necessary," he continued.

Talia sighed, then focused on the monitor. "It's all about to change again, isn't it?"

Tom didn't answer. He studied the alterations that the last couple of years had rendered in her. She let her hair grow back from a dyed bombshell red to its natural dark brown. She wore less sunblock and pale makeup, so her skin darkened to its natural café au lait hue. The soft curves of her body revealed that she no longer kept it up as her weapon of mass seduction. But she was still gorgeous. Major Tom's digital memory could never forget that, even if he didn't have a body to react to her with hormonal feedback. He might not want to have sex with her, but he knew beauty when he saw it.

"How's the ethics committee going?" he asked. Because of his fear of the technology, Steve had insisted on creating an ethics committee as part of the management structure.

"Doing what it's supposed to: first, do no harm."

Tom made the speaker sigh. "That's the Hippocratic Oath for medicine. Where's the revolutionary or groundbreaking research in that?"

Talia's life over the last decade had been traumatic: the murder of her father, fleeing and fighting the club, and the death of Tom. He hadn't made her life any easier. Fearing the world-changing potential of the various brain-computer interface technologies, Talia and Steve had locked up all research that could lead to another upload event. Instead, they used Prometheus to continue developing technologies and drugs to save lives. The only tech of Peter Bernhardt's that they continued, and that kept the entire enterprise profitable, was nano-medicine. Microbivores, artificial white blood cells designed to destroy any programmed pathogens in their path, eliminated common diseases from viruses and bacteria to precancerous pathogens. Respirocytes were artificial red blood cells that provided drowning, choking, and smoke-inhalation victims the oxygen necessary to survive. They were now car-ried by EMTs and ERs around the world. Thomas Paine had been the first human subject to use them. Nanomedicine made Prometheus Industries a hugely successful biotech business, but it was not as radical as what Tom had once hoped for.

"Still haven't learned, have you?" she asked.

"Guess not."

There was a knock at the door.

"Ready?" said Tom.

Talia shook her head no and yelled, "Come in!"

Veronika Gascon tripped through over the threshold and threw herself into the chair across the desk from Talia. She wore her black shirt, skirt, and boots, but she had the Veronika's Veil portrait in a gold, silver, and enamel oval frame hanging from her neck on a silver chain. A close look revealed that it was a tiny flat digital screen projecting her artwork. Her hands fidgeted. She tugged at her long hair. Major Tom turned on other cameras so he could see the conversation from several angles.

Talia stared at the portrait of Thomas Paine on Veronika's chest, her expression betraying confusion, but it wasn't the time for Tom to explain. She finally looked up into Veronika's eyes and gestured to the monitor that displayed Tom. "He says you know about Dr. Who's kid-napping. Convince me you're not crazy."

"I've been followed. They know I'm here," said Veronika.

Major Tom immediately searched for proof in nearby traffic cameras and available satellite imagery. He found nothing to support her claim. It was possible, but he couldn't prove it.

"Who is 'they'?" asked Talia.

Veronika rolled her eyes. "Whoever attacked the *Sovereign*?"

"That might indicate you're crazy," said Talia. "You're the only person who thinks that happened."

"I'm not. Major Tom knows," said Veronika.

"And how do you know that?" asked Talia.

"Because he didn't say I was wrong."

Talia squeezed her eyes shut in annoyance.

Veronika continued, "I think Major Tom is depressed and can't understand why he needs to help."

"Depressed? How can an artificial human intelligence be depressed?"

"Why not?" asked Veronika. "He has the programming of past emotions."

Talia rocked back in her chair, crossed her arms, and stared deadpan at the young woman. "There's a new job at Prometheus: AHI psychoanalyst. 'Come lay here on my CPU and tell me about your motherboard.'"

"Why don't you admit you know, too?" asked Veronika.

"Because I don't," said Talia.

Even Tom could see the tell in Talia's reaction. He replayed the eye squint and her glance away to be sure. She did know. Talia thought he was depressed, too.

Veronika must have caught it, because her eyes went slightly manic. "You *do* know. So why don't you want to, like, help him? Is it me? Are you jealous of me? That I get to spend time in the church with him? Where he has a body? Is that it?"

He wondered how long Veronika had known Tom was the troubadour. "Veronika, please get back on track."

"No, she's got a problem with me and I wanna know why," said Veronika.

Talia's jaw set, and she sat forward. "Get out."

Veronika shrugged, grabbed her pack, and skipped out of the room with visible relief.

"Why the hell did you provoke her?" said Tom. "We need her information."

"Me provoke her?" said Talia. "I don't want her here again."

"Don't tell me she touched a nerve," said Tom, "when it's Dr. Who's life on the line."

"She's crazy," she said. "If you can't see that—"

"I see she's immature and frustrated because she *does* know things. And I see your resistance, so I have the same questions she does. Why in God's name are you threatened by her? You're probably her hero."

"I don't want to be a hero. Not anymore."

An unidentified videochat got Major Tom's attention. "Wait a moment." He tried to trace the source of the transmission, but even with his extreme speed, it appeared that the location was many places at once. Was that even possible?

He accepted the videochat and immediately saw Dr. Who, tied up and propped on a bunk on some kind of naval vessel. He didn't see a window. She had a hard time focusing her eyes, like they had been recently unbandaged. Or she was drugged. A small red laser light shined off her forehead. The implication was clear.

The scene matched the vision he had had months ago while singing in TCoMT.

"Are you okay?" he asked.

"Don't know . . . Can't think straight . . . They're lettin' me contact ya."

"Why?" he asked.

"So ya know I'm alive, child. Don't know how much longer. Gotta gun pointed at my head, so I can only say so much. Ya have no idea how hard that is with these motherfuckers."

"Careful."

"I'm tryin', hon," said Dr. Who. "Good Lord knows I'm tryin'."

The last location of the transmission was a satellite that supplied data to an abandoned moon base, once financed by a Chinese billionaire developing lunar tourism until the market crashed when the United States and Europe dissolved. But that was impossible. There was no way she could be on the moon. No rockets had launched in months. The construction had never been finished and was exposed to the vacuum of space.

"What will they let you say?" he asked.

"All they say is, 'History is a set of lies agreed upon,'" said the Doctor.

"Napoleon Bonaparte?"

"Glad you knew that, sugar. I didn't." She sighed, shifting uncomfortably. "Don't know much right now, 'cept I don't wanna die. Hard to think . . . Drugs . . ."

Major Tom examined the connection and had the oddest sensation, the feeling of being observed, scanned, and recorded in his entirety. But there was no sense of creation or surge of energy, like when he lay dying during his upload. It felt like a snapshot. He tried to isolate the sensation to analyze later.

Was the observation coming from her captors? Or from somewhere else? It felt too complete to occur over a videochat. But he was concerned about Dr. Who and didn't disconnect the call.

"Anything else you can say?" he asked.

"Yeah." She was breathing heavily now, and her eyes watered. "Pray for me . . ."

The transmission cut off. He repackaged the chat data so it couldn't be traced and sent it to Talia's monitor.

She watched in horror. Tears formed but didn't drop. She mouthed, "I'm sorry."

Tom spoke softly, "Dr. Who needs us. Now."

CHAPTER EIGHT

Major Tom withdrew from Talia to consider the options. He still felt fear, but now the strangest sensation occurred, like a heavy curtain had lifted from him. His usual lack of interest, distraction, and low energy disappeared. Terrified and invigorated, he didn't understand the sudden change in his emotions. He sent energy and engagement data to Ruth and Miss Gray Hat to figure out and, desperate to talk to someone who might understand, hurried to Carter's door. He knocked.

There was no response.

"Carter?"

Silence.

He pounded on the door. "Carter!"

He threw open the door and barged in, triggering an audio file, a live version of David Bowie's "Hallo Spaceboy," performed by Bowie and the Pet Shop Boys. How narcissistically appropriate. In college, they had bonded as friends over Bowie, and Carter had often been compared to him in looks. Carter knew it would dig at him.

The plantation was as it had been when he visited before. Right down to the singing slaves. Tom scanned Carter's digi-scape. Carter wasn't home. But there was no other place he could be.

He compared this scan to his memories of his previous visit. The only difference was on the fireplace mantel. A Victorian calling card of ecru paper sat there, *Carter Potsdam* engraved on it in an elegant cursive. The bottom left corner of the card was bent, which, according to Major Tom's instant research, meant the person was saying goodbye to go on a trip. Tom picked it up and turned it over. In Carter's neatly flowing prep-school script, it read, *Adiós, muchacho.*

If the song was to be believed, the chaos was killing Carter, and he was quite literally saying bye to Major Tom. But was the moon dust a musical reference to "Space Oddity" or connected to the moon-related transmission he had just received?

Rushing out of the plantation and into the Memory Palace's foyer, Tom threw open all the other doors. Anthony Dulles still sailed the *American Dream* ∞ on an endless sea and viewed Tom with alarm as he stormed the deck, scanned the environment, and retreated without a word.

Chang Eng worked in the shed of an idealized 150-year-old Chinese home. It would have been owned by someone successful, before Mao's revolution. Tom could see Chang's mother cooking in the open kitchen, gnarled hands kneading dough for Chang's favorite vegetable-and-egg dumplings. Here, there was no global politics. No anxiety. No want. Just peace and small engineering projects in a shed outfitted only with hand tools, next to a vegetable garden.

"Is Carter here?" Tom asked as he scanned.

The passive expression on Chang's face betrayed the limited mind that had been left after his torture and murder. There was little of his intellectual or emotional essence there.

"No," Chang said.

In the impeccable re-creation of his now-destroyed Malibu beach house, Bruce Lobo paced in tight caged circles, like the predator he had been in life. Beautiful naked women were draped over furniture like silky throw pillows and blankets. He simply growled at Tom's brief presence.

Josiah Brant had once run the United States of America in secret, and in the Memory Palace, he had replicated his gracious Virginia home at the height of its Southern beauty and comfort. Tom burst through his door.

"Where's Carter?" he demanded.

No longer an elderly man, a Josiah of about forty years' age had constructed a tower of wooden blocks on the Aubusson carpet with two young children. The girl, about six years of age, chased a kitten around the room, and when the pet careened too close to the unstable structure, Josiah swatted it away. A small blind boy of eight fumbled with the loose wood pieces. Josiah rose from the floor of a living room overlooking the Potomac.

"Get out," he said. His face might have been forty, but his eyes betrayed a lifetime of disappointment, pain, and betrayal. Tom could see himself and his great negation of Josiah's dreams in that agonized glare.

"Not until you tell me what you know about Carter."

"Such manners!" spat Josiah. "So the benevolent dictator wants to chat?"

Tom tried to find any data that would link Josiah and Carter in a plan. He found nothing. But that didn't mean Josiah was innocent. "Well?"

"Boy, how in tarnation would I know? I'm locked up here for eternity with a little girl and a blind boy."

"Thought you might get parenting right for once," said Tom.

"And I thought you'd finally get smart," said Josiah, reaching for a cold beer in a frosted glass mug on the coffee table.

"Enough Southern charm. You're the only one who might know."

Josiah bowed. "You give this former public servant more credit than I deserve."

Tom didn't believe him. Once the most powerful man on earth, Josiah was going to make Tom suffer for his fate.

"So our boy's left the nest and you're off like a herd 'a turtles, huh?" Josiah smirked.

"I will stop Carter," said Tom. "And that means stopping you, too. Doesn't it?"

Josiah stared unblinkingly, his eyes almost empty of emotion. Almost. "You're not man enough to run with the big dogs anymore. You're dumber than a sack o' hammers. We all are. And if it all goes to hell in a handbasket, it is, as always, your own damned fault."

"But Carter isn't dumb, is he?"

Josiah didn't speak, and continued that unnerving, unblinking stare.

An invitation arrived from Veronika, along with a link and an urgent message: *HELP!*

CHAPTER NINE

M ajor Tom watched through Veronika's MR glasses as her autonomous, electric Fiat 500 sped south down the 101 Freeway from Palo Alto to Santa Barbara in the far lane. It wasn't a fast lane anymore. All vehicles drove the same speed.

Traffic was light and steady. Gridlock no longer existed. Driverless car services and private autonomous vehicles streamed live government traffic data, overruling human decisions. Those who couldn't afford the cars used public robotransportation.

He checked the gauges. Speed: a steady and legal 65 mph. As Veronika's head turned, Tom saw a late-model black Chevy Suburban pulling up alongside on her right, then weaving into her lane. Suburbans were still a ranch house on wheels, the biggest damn roadhogs around.

Her little car's sensors anticipated the possible impact and accelerated slightly, dancing the Fiat onto the left shoulder, half an inch from the concrete barrier dividing southbound from northbound, then back into her lane.

"The fuck, dude! I told you someone's following me," said Veronika.

Major Tom analyzed the Suburban's movements. There was no one in the car. The dodging and weaving would be impossible with the SUV's factory-built autonomous system, unless someone was driving by remote control or had programmed the car to misbehave. The car had no license plate that he could see. No registration he could run.

Had Veronika been followed from Prometheus? Or before like she had claimed?

The SUV didn't accelerate or cut in front of her. It obeyed the same 65 mph limit as all the other cars on the road, except for those directly behind them, which slowed down in programmed anticipation of the swerving autos ahead. It was weird, nerve-racking, and hilarious to watch, like Keystone Kops putt-putting but never reaching the criminals. A high-octane car chase this was not, but lives were still at risk if the Suburban decided to slam the Fiat.

He looked for the Suburban's location on the California DMV traffic flow site. There was no car next to the Fiat. It was all open lane. So there was no ID and no way to hack in and stop the car.

But the Fiat wasn't on the traffic site, either.

"Neither car's on the grid. Give me control of yours," said Tom.

Veronika tried to touch the steering paddles but flinched back like she was afraid. "No!" she said.

"You blacklisted your car. How can I help you?" asked Tom.

"Just tell me what to do."

He watched her awkward movements. "Do you even know how to drive?"

"I passed the test."

"And never fucking drove again. What's with you kids? Okay, I'll talk you through. Get to an exit now. Take Moffett Boulevard, drive through Hangar One, then back to Prometheus."

"Can I do that?" asked Veronika.

"Let's hope," said Tom.

"Autopilot? Reset—"

"No," said Tom. "Autopilot won't speed. Turn it off."

"But—"

"Put your right foot on the accelerator and your hands on the wheel. Then turn it off."

"Oh shit." She did each movement deliberately, like touching a snake for the first time.

"You got this," said Tom. "Now, don't signal. Just put your foot gently but firmly on the break . . . I said gently! Slow . . . get behind the SUV and keep going to the right . . . Fast. Don't give them a chance to brake and hit you."

Shuddering fast-slow-fast-slow, the Fiat slid behind the SUV and passed to the right. The SUV tried to slow to match her speed, but its programming seemed confused by the order to stay in top-speed pursuit. Veronika struggled to keep the Fiat in a single lane.

"Keep merging right. Moffett exit's a half mile away. Get into the exit lane fast and get ready to hit the gas."

"Gas!" said Veronika in half terror, half irony.

"You know what I mean," said Tom.

The Suburban recalibrated and changed lanes to follow. There was an opening ahead of the Fiat with no cars for a quarter mile until the exit.

"Okay, accelerate. Now into the exit lane and go. Top of the ramp, turn hard right . . . Other right!"

As soon as the car's speed exceeded the posted limit, the internal warning system went berserk with beeping, warning lights, and dire buzzing.

"What the hell's that?"

"Nanny car. Calm down." My God, thought Tom, how the hell do these young people have fun with cars anymore? It made him miss his 1968 Corvette Stingray.

The Suburban's program figured out it needed to speed to keep up.

She looked in the rearview mirror. "It's coming. And there's a stop sign . . . ," she said.

"Intersection's clear. Mostly. Punch it."

An autonomous tour bus full of space fans was rumbling to the stop on NASA Parkway and would cross right in front of her.

"No!" She closed her eyes, hit the accelerator, and missed the bus by a foot.

The Suburban was stuck until the bus recalibrated from a near crash, puttering through at a legal fifteen miles an hour.

"Wheel straight. Wheel straight!" said Tom.

"Guard post!" yelled Veronika.

"Ornamental. Keep going. Slight right on Akron, then get to the hangar and make a left on Cummins. Follow it to the north entrance."

Veronika let out a huge breath. "Read the link I sent?"

Tom opened the link: a complete copy of his famous message, detailing his story from the moment of the 10/26 mass murders to the time of his death and uploading of his memories, located in the archives of the *New York Times*.

"I wrote it," said Tom.

"Read it again."

He quickly scanned the document. And it made no sense. He scanned it again, then looked for other copies, on message boards, in e-mails, in the Library of Congress, on media websites. Many were the same as the *New York Times*. And none was his original story.

The message had changed. In this new retelling, Peter Bernhardt admitted to being a terrorist. Everything that happened was rooted in his aggression. His insanity. The Phoenix Club had only defended itself and failed. The weight of the entire world's woes was dumped onto him. He had often blamed himself in his lonelier moments, but here was proof for the uninitiated.

The only copy of his writings that he knew for sure was still completely his own was in TCoMT.

He contacted Miss Gray Hat. *Please, I need your help. As soon as you can, lock down the Memory Palace. All of it. Only I can be let in to the meta structures that remain. Not even Dr. Who. And ask Veronika for help freezing TCoMT's archives into a blockchain.*

He received a checkmark in reply.

Veronika looked in the rearview mirror. The Suburban was gaining fast. "It's coming! Now what?"

"Just get into Hangar One," said Tom. "Don't see on board weapons trained at you, so let's try to shake it."

"Holy shit," she said, craning her head to look up.

In front of her loomed one of the largest freestanding structures on earth, built in 1933 to house airships, including the biggest blimps and zeppelins in the world. Enclosing eight acres of ground space, it stood without a single interior support, held aloft by curved walls 1,133 feet long and 308 feet wide, with a ceiling almost 200 feet tall. It was a marvel of twentieth-century engineering. Even more remarkable, it was built at a time when people still designed with slide rules, pencils and paper, and the belief that anything was possible with enough mathematics. Stripped of its aluminum and insulation shell years earlier in an attempt to eliminate hazardous materials, all that remained were steel ribs and a metal latticework that stretched into the distance. Even without its art moderne exterior, it was magnificent.

Major Tom had searched Moffett Field's servers for access into Hangar One. The building was long ago decommissioned and hardly top secret to begin with. It couldn't still be operated by an ancient, manual Bakelite switch near the door, could it?

The Fiat rolled through the open orange-peel doors. Inside, covered in giant lace shadows, sat the Potsdam Boeing Super 27.

"Pull in more to let in the Suburban," said Tom.

The Fiat crept forward. The Suburban rolled in behind it, then paused. In an open-source NASA Moffett Field training system, Major Tom found an old program to operate the doors remotely. The building rumbled to life. Behind them, the doors shuffled shut. The far doors moved an inch, then another inch. The steel frame shook so much, he wondered whether it was specced to operate both doors at once.

"Isn't that Carter's jet?" asked Veronika, her voice quavering.

"Yeah," said Tom. "Now drive around the hangar."

"Why?"

"Trust me," said Tom.

Veronika sighed and looked at the dash map. "Autopilot, drive around the building perimeter."

"I'm sorry. That's an unknown command." Its bourbon-and-cigarettes voice sounded a bit too much like Thomas Paine's.

"You're kidding me," said Tom. "And no more autopilot. Not until Prometheus."

"Sorry." Veronika bit her lower lip.

The little Fiat crept forward, approaching the Super 27 in the center of the building. The Suburban followed.

"Can you do some donuts around the jet?" asked Tom. "We need time."

Veronika made an uncertain jerky loop under the long wing of the jet, barely missing the Boeing's massive rear tire.

"Keep your eyes on the road," said Tom.

The Suburban followed ten feet behind, like a malevolent stalker creeping after a young woman down a too-quiet street. The cars looped once around. Twice around. Three times. Four, five, six. For Major Tom, it felt like eternity. Finally, with the far doors open almost enough, he said, "Now hit the accelerator. Hard."

"What? It's not open enough."

"Do it!"

The doors rumbled. Another inch, another foot.

She tapped the accelerator, and her car moved forward again.

"Hard!" yelled Tom.

She stomped on the accelerator. Her skull slammed on the headrest.

He double-checked his math. Fiat was 64.1 inches wide. Suburban was 80.5 inches wide. He estimated the distance to the doors, the speed and acceleration of the cars, the width of the gap. The opening was too wide. The doors made a loud grinding sound as they stopped and reversed course, closing too slowly.

"What?" screamed Veronika.

"The Suburban can pass through!" said Tom. "Needs to be smaller."

The doors continued to crank closed.

The Fiat raced on.

The Suburban was right behind.

"Are you punching it?"

"I'm punching it!" By mistake, Veronika slammed on the brake, and the Suburban screeched to a stop just behind it.

"The other pedal!" yelled Tom.

Veronika stomped on the accelerator.

The Fiat flew through the passage with an inch on each side to spare.

With a squeal of tires, the Suburban skidded to the left, avoiding the steel beams by half a foot. It took a few seconds for the program to realize it should go back to the first hangar doors. Even racing to the exit, the doors were almost closed. The Suburban was stuck.

The Fiat continued at top speed from Moffett Field and back to the offices.

"You okay?" Tom asked Veronika.

"Yeah, thanks. Exhausted. Shutting down for a while. See you at Prometheus." Veronika's glasses cut the link to Tom.

Major Tom contacted Ruth. "Head for the mainland. Something big is coming. And I need to be something and somewhere else."

Tom saw Talia in her office and spoke through the monitor. "It's me. I need you to get into the safe room."

"What safe room?" she asked.

"Top right drawer. Reach underneath. Piece of paper stuck under drawer runners. Follow directions and take paper with you."

"Are you kidding?"

"Now! Veronika's coming. She *was* followed." Talia reached under the drawer runner and came up with the piece of paper. She looked at it, surprised, and ran from her office.

Then he messaged Miss Gray Hat: *Destroy the Memory Palace gateway at the server farm, but leave my entity separate in cyberspace.*

R U sure? she responded.

Yes.

It took some time, a lot from his perspective, but she obeyed. The Memory Palace had no more connections, links, or pathways in or out, a digital entity isolated from the rest of reality. He didn't want to extinguish what little they had left of their lives. Their consciousnesses were as valuable and real as his. But he would never let them share their thoughts—or plots—again.

He messaged Veronika. *You were right. Talia is waiting for you. I'll direct you to her when you arrive. We need to work together.*

He was finally terrified. And it felt good to feel more human again.

CHAPTER TEN

As Major Tom waited for the humans to catch up, he thought about the nature of history. Humans lived in a continuum of time that they assumed they understood. But they could never possibly comprehend everything at once, and their interactions with it, so they settled for the simple bedtime story. People assumed history was decided at the moment it happened, immutable from that point on. But of course, it wasn't. The story of a people was written and rewritten by the victors over time, immortalized in the culture, whether by historians like Herodotus or Ibn Khaldun; politicians like Theodore Roosevelt or Winston Churchill; or storytellers like Shakespeare, Tolstoy, or Dumas. Even then, it was revised and revised again. History was not created in a vacuum of desires and experiences. It was colored by personal goals and biases. Humankind couldn't help making stuff up if it tried.

The story of Peter Bernhardt and Thomas Paine was no different—it was the story as he had experienced it, shared as honestly as he could. It was impossible to be completely truthful and accurate, even with his perfect memory, but he had done the best he could to share what he knew.

But this attack on him and his story wasn't an attempt by victors to justify their means to posterity. The lies were created by a single group to bend the world to their will. Again.

At Prometheus Industries, a secret basement room had been designed to keep internal communications as private as possible. There were no air ducts or windows. It could be occupied only for as long as the oxygen lasted, unless you opened the door or took a big pull from a couple of O2 tanks standing in a corner. The door, four walls, floor, and ceiling were insulated with soundproof, baffled acoustic panels. A Faraday cage could be turned on to impede electrical impulses. Inside it was bare bones: white-painted drywall, linoleum floor tiles, a table, a few chairs, some LEDs in the ceiling. An old, large computer monitor hung on the wall, usually unplugged and offline. Today, it was working.

Carter had designed the room after Peter Bernhardt had disappeared, presumed dead, in the explosion of the *American Dream II*. He had thought he might need it someday. It had never been used, until now.

Veronika sat nervously twisting her hair and picking off the split ends.

Talia said, "We're as private as we can be. Let's talk."

All the sound baffling made their voices sound squelched and flat, like a giant sponge swallowed them. The electronics in the monitor were strangely loud.

Veronika wiggled a finger in her ear canal, thinking it might compensate for the strange pressure-filled feeling and lack of sound, then pointed at the monitor. "He's connected online now."

"Yes," replied Tom through the speaker. "But you can't talk to me any other way. I've created a firewalled partition. It's the best I can do. Ruth asked for help from Miss Gray Hat. She promises this'll work."

"Huh," Veronika said, still mangling her hair.

"What are you waiting for?" asked Talia, barely concealing her contempt.

Shifting her jaw around, Veronika tried to equalize her ears. "Whaddaya wanna know?"

Talia gave an incredulous glance at the monitor's camera.

Tom asked patiently, "What do you know about the *Sovereign* and Dr. Who?"

"The seastead was attacked," said Veronika. "They kidnapped Dr. Who and have her on a moving remote location. Probably a submarine. They've taken control of the *Sovereign* servers. I think they're going to sink the Shell. And whatever identity files the Doctor was working on. Maybe someone important is in them?"

"Who is 'they?'" asked Talia.

Veronika gave her another bored look and asked the monitor, "What do you think happened to the Phoenix Club?"

"It was dismantled," said Tom. "Many people went to jail. Others fled overseas. Some are running small regional governments around the country, because their constituents prefer the devil they know. They're popular in some Southern states, with local clubs. It's not what it was."

"That's not the whole story," said Veronika. "You were living in the Memory Palace with the key players. They still exist."

"Not anymore," he said. "Did Dr. Who tell you about the Memory Palace?"

"Yes, dude," said Veronika. "I've done some side stuff for her. You got my big secret. Okay now? And Carter's escaped. You told us that. And you don't think others want the power they had?"

"Organized so soon? Not likely," said Talia.

"You both fought power-hungry psychopaths," said Veronika. "Think they disappear, just 'cause you whack-a-moled a few?"

Talia went pale. "Prove it."

The two women stared each other down.

"MT, pull up the news," said Veronika.

"He's your personal HOME/GO now?" asked Talia.

"Dude. Pretty please," said Veronika. "Look for references to yourself."

News feeds and archives flooded Tom's data-retrieval system. He dived into the information. It was no longer overwhelming, as it had been when he was a living human. He applied a filter for "Peter Bernhardt," "Thomas Paine" minus Founding Father results, "Major Tom" minus music results, and "Phoenix Club." A huge stream of data flowed in from all over the web.

On a singularity weblog that archived his story, on the *New York Times* site, in a chat room that archived a discussion about global oligarchies, the story points were isolated, and the new words replaced the old.

Through the search, the story of Peter Bernhardt changed in real time. Electronic editors crawled all over each mention of him, all over the world, not only in his personal tellings, but in quotes from his message, discussions, memes, quips. He had never thought to check before. He was embarrassed to be considered a superintelligence, because he was a failure at it.

"This is weaponized narrative," said Tom. "And Talia, they're changing your story, too. They've made you a Central American Communist rebel. And Ruth is a psycho scientist who fabricated data for payoffs. Steve broke his Hippocratic Oath and should have his medical license revoked. We're all villains."

"Oh my God." Talia buried her head in her hands. "When were you going to tell us this?"

"Why is the copy in TCoMT the only one unchanged?" Tom asked Veronika.

"I need external access. For just a sec," said Veronika.

Talia looked at Tom's camera.

"I'll do it," said Tom.

Veronika entered TCoMT's site. "It's buried in a blockchain and invisible to outsiders. Did you ask someone to do that?"

"Yes," said Tom. "Miss Gray Hat didn't work with you?"

"I gave her the hashes and keys, but I was driving," said Veronika. "That's okay. She did good. But you have to be a validated church member to read it, and now no one but you, me, Ruth, and Miss Gray Hat can access the original code."

"Are any other copies of his version in other blockchains?" asked Talia. "Those wouldn't be changed either, right? Or they'd generate a completely new private key and we'd know it was changed."

Veronika shrugged. "In theory. No one's tried to break the security of major blockchains . . . yet. But I'm guessing they're trying now."

"How would they do it?" asked Talia.

"A blockchain is based on an algorithm," said Veronika. "What if you had fake blockchains that pretended to be real? Or a fifty-one-percent attack, where a majority of computers generate a different private key for the same transaction. Which confirmation would you trust?"

"It would take enormous computing power to maintain that level of fraud and deceit," said Tom.

"All this shit requires huge numbers of web crawlers, data crunching, and narrow AI, designed just to do this task," said Veronika. "And it would take shit-tons of money. And computer- and man-hours." She thought for a moment, then furiously typed into the antiquated keyboard. "Look. Employment ads and unemployment stats around the world. China, Russia, India, North and South America, Europe. Even Africa. No one can find workers for data verification. They could use corporate AIs trawling for your references, to replace with this data, overseen by humans, for placement accuracy normal AIs can't quite manage yet, because they don't want any mistakes to follow a trail back to them. Also, check the comments sections of any site."

Major Tom avoided comments sections like a computer virus. Cloaked in anonymity, they reflected the worst of humanity. With no consequences, trolls could be as evil as they liked. Every agenda thrived.

She was right. Recent negative comments proliferated. "It's time to unplug this bastard and kill all his helpers." "Thomas Paine has destroyed the world. Time to destroy him." "This is what happens when you let AI run mad. It's the end of humanity."

"Damn," said Tom. "Troll army?"

"For hire, and on a global scale," said Veronika. "Comments appeared too quickly after the changes. All that takes cash. So who has that kind of money these days?"

Talia jumped in. "The Russians had a huge government troll factory for years. But it could be any major government in the world."

"Corruption abhors a vacuum, dude," said Veronika. "Every nation-state and political psychopath has a stake in discrediting Tom and trying to take over during the chaos. If you thought, like, 'Hey, it's my turn to be king,' wouldn't you do the same?"

"Where's the money coming from?" asked Talia.

"Can you see the Phoenix Club accounts?" Veronika asked Tom.

He could, because he had kept information from Mr. Money, the money launderer murdered by the club. The accounts were almost empty. They had originally totaled trillions of dollars. "I thought they were pillaged by the membership for their own benefit."

"Sure," said Veronika, "but after you killed the leadership, who had access?"

Tom paused. "How do you know all this?"

She sat straight up in her chair for the first time, looking almost demented. "Dude, I am a nerd and a geek. I've crushed on you for years. You are my only hobby. I've written fan fiction about you! The only way I can get closer to you is to . . . help you!"

"Why me?" Tom asked.

For the first time, Veronika looked sad. "You don't get it."

"I'm sorry," said Tom. "I don't."

Veronika slouched back into her seat. "You're an example for people like me. People who aren't born into the right body. You're like the ultimate expression of the mutability of humanity through technology and, like, the desire to transcend the physical body."

"Do all transgender people see me as an example?" he asked.

Veronika chewed her hair. "Don't flatter yourself. Only the **über**-geeky ones."

Then she was quiet. No one spoke for a moment.

Talia finally said, "You still haven't said how you know about the *Sovereign* and Dr. Who."

Veronika sighed. "Dark-web chat room. Mercenary recruitment for special marine skills. Former SEALs, naval engineering and laser weapon operating systems. That kinda stuff. Needed really deep tech skills with autonomous vessels. And one superweird ad about working with sea life that got pulled in, like, thirty seconds. I kept tabs on it. And I know folks like Miss Gray Hat. Except I call her the Masked Avenger."

"You live in the dark web?" asked Talia.

Veronika gave her the dead-eyed, hooded gaze of every annoyed young person ever. "You think they post this stuff on the Prometheus bulletin board? The dark web is, like, bigger than the rest of the webs combined and has all the scary shit no one wants to believe exists. And I've read all about you there. My nana would call you a 'piece of work.'"

"Who the hell are you to criticize me?" yelled Talia. "Dr. Who is *my* friend. She saved my life countless times. You're just . . . a child and a poseur. I don't even know why you're here."

"If you haven't noticed, dude, your generation fucked everything up," said Veronika.

"I am *not* your dude," said Talia.

"And I'm not yours. But it's my generation left to sift through your shitstorm and, like, make sense of it again." She looked to Tom's monitor. "So am I, like, the fourth Musketeer or what?"

"So what should we do?" Tom asked Veronika.

"First? Save the stories we can. Store them in safe blockchains around the world, if we can find them. We may have to create them. It's harder to mess with them in our own. Then, who knows?"

"Define a safe blockchain?" he asked.

"Any that aren't related to currency or identity," said Veronika. "If, like, Dr. Who is a canary in the coal mine for the seasteads, those are the targets now. Find a blockchain pitched for something innocuous. Like digital art verification and sales. Or music downloads. Places people go for, like, squishy, feel-good stuff. Not vital, world-crashing stuff."

He did it at once as they continued their talk. Although the high-status copies in institutional libraries were already changed, he found unadulterated copies in places as diverse as a Pakistani madras, a superhero-fan chat room, a South African private school's assignment file, a Peruvian NGO website about political systems, and a news portal for the Mars Team training in Antarctica. There were still many places to tag copies and verify them into blockchains, so even if they were changed, he would have proof that a different version had once existed. He was amazed that he had never thought to do this before.

This was the price of his complacency. Was that part of the digital heaviness, the withdrawal he had felt? Was the depression imposed upon him from outside?

"Figure out our enemies' patterns," Veronika continued. "Then draw them out."

Of course, she was right. It was all about patterns. When the great Cold War KGB cryptoanalyst Yuri Totrov had sought to find undercover CIA operatives in the USSR, he began by looking for anomalous patterns. But the patterns were anything but unusual. They were regular, repeated, and it shocked the Soviet analyst. The CIA blamed Soviet moles for leaking the spies' identities, but it hadn't been anything so subversive. Rather, the CIA was so thoughtless that undercover agents had pretended to be foreign service officers in precisely the same ways, using the same apartments, spending the same unusually large amounts of money, performing the same spycraft, and all exactly different from the behaviors of the real foreign service officers they were impersonating. It only proved that the CIA had been arrogant, lazy, and stupid. But the KGB was no different. Totrov had looked at his own ridiculously bureaucratic country and realized that all civil services suffered the same inadequacies, regardless of political labels. Humans liked their bureaucracies as simple and repetitive as possible, making them easy targets for detection. Most people assumed they were smarter than the dopes next to them, so they rarely bothered to try to outthink them.

Major Tom hoped his enemies were as stupid, but he doubted it.

He concentrated on building a pattern-recognition module like Totrov's, depending on an immutable law of the universe: the low level of human initiative. Based on what he knew so far, the most likely candidates were China and the former United States (f-US).

First, he built simulation maps of both China and the f-US, such as it was, split ideologically and politically between those who wanted nothing to do with the Phoenix Club and demanded to reorganize for themselves and those who wished it was back to running the world.

Certain parts of the country hardly needed an excuse to go it alone. Hawaii's independence movement threw its watery lot in with the seasteaders and ineffectively prayed that China would assume it was too far away for effective occupation, even as the building of Chinese military islands continued. Desperate to repeat its imaginary-independence-for-protection schtick, Alaska played slow and tight with Russia and Canada, hoping for Arctic access and a promise to continue subsidizing its fossil fuels from whatever country would claim it, even though Alaskan salmon—"wild" DNA and nutrients, free from contaminants—was more valuable a commodity. And there weren't many wild salmon left.

Independent regions like the Northeast, Upper Midwest, the West, and the Pacific Coast fractured into states or smaller municipalities. The Northern and Western states began to organize for themselves and forge mutually supportive relationships.

Desiring a strong leader to unite them in a fight back to global domination, the deep South, Texas, Appalachia, the Lower Midwest, and what remained of the center of federal power in Washington, DC, gathered as one sovereign state: the Southern States of America or SSA, or as Major Tom thought of it, the NeoConfederacy. Its leader, Terrence Conrad of Virginia, called himself president of the Southern States of America, lived in the White House, and was treated as such only by those under his firm grip. The rest of the world tried to ignore him.

Conrad was a tall, flawless-looking, narcissistic psychopath on the make, with a needling personality that the weak-willed interpreted as purposeful, a strong, nasally voice sure to cut through a raucous crowd, an aggressive persona demonstrated by a wide stance, and a place in the Southern hierarchy that made him as much of an aristocrat as Carter Potsdam. He had it all: sexy wife, good-looking kids, a plantation corporation that made him buckets of money. His hatred of anyone unlike himself made him a hero to those who wished they were him. His idea of a transportation policy was promising the trains would run on time. And the political kleptocracy around him was no better.

What about Conrad might embolden Carter or the remnants of the club?

China, on the other hand, had suffered from an economic crash after fragmentation and recession dried up its global markets. Top-down governance, tactical use of fear, and a talent for empire building had brought its people back into line after decades of pseudo capitalism. It was a dominant culture ready to take over, and the world knew it.

Then Major Tom mapped the migrations of peoples. In the American past, people had moved to where they felt they had found either others like themselves—culturally or ethnically—or simply where the work had taken them. The Chinese were no different, except that they needed permission to migrate, based on government quotas and plans. So he looked for the patterns and put them in chronological spreadsheets and geographic maps. While he had hidden in his figurative deep sleep, countries had hemorrhaged for and against a new world order. Looking at all this together for the first time revealed surprising results.

China was spreading around the world. America was shuffling people around the continent at a rate as vigorous as the migrations of the late eighteenth and nineteenth centuries. No one stayed put, and that meant unstable systems. And with instability came war.

The Phoenix Club was somehow behind an effort to create or profit from a war. And Major Tom knew which side of the war Carter would take.

Only a few seconds had passed while Major Tom had done his analyses.

"Well, the Southern States of America has big problems . . . ," he said.

"No shit," said Veronika. "Has for, like, four hundred years. Started with the first settlers."

"I mean they lack the means for self-sufficient production," he clarified. "People are trying to leave at an alarming rate. And China lacks markets . . ."

"We all know this," said Veronika.

"But do you realize most of the surviving and nonincarcerated Phoenix Club members are either in the Southern States or in China, right this moment?" pressed Tom.

Veronika grew antsy, plucking errant eyebrow hairs.

"So what's that tell you?" asked Talia.

"If they're working together—" said Tom.

Veronika lurched up. "I hate this room. I can't breathe. I need my stuff. Like from my car."

"Can't until Talia says we break," said Tom. "The door's locked."

Veronika gestured with her hands, executing a computer command. Tom saw it coming but didn't stop it. The door unlocked and popped open.

"Did you think I couldn't figure that out?" asked Veronika.

"Don't be a child," said Tom. "Talia can send someone to get what you need."

"You're not my dad. I'm fine." She loped out the room and slammed the door.

Talia shook her head. "How can we work with her?"

"We have no choice. All I can find so far are trends. She knows more than she's telling us."

"I know." Talia ground her teeth. "I just wish she'd say it and get it over with."

"I'm asking security to stop her from leaving the building," said Tom.

"Fine." Spent, Talia paused for a few seconds. "We'll be hunted again."

"I'm sorry," said Tom. "It was nice while it lasted."

"I need to tell Steve. He'll be so angry."

"I'm sending him a message now to come down. Maybe it's better if I'm not around when you tell him." Tom threw the security footage onto the monitor. The message had arrived too late. Veronika exited a different set of doors than he'd anticipated, and a moment later, security guards ran for her in the lot.

A shrieking sound, something flying low and fast . . .

BOOM!

The building convulsed. Major Tom commandeered all the security cameras at once. A corner of the Prometheus facade exploded, exposing offices and labs as the smoke cleared, like a jagged doll's house, bodies on the floors, two others thrown from the explosion to the pavement outside. A blaze ignited. Fire sprinklers kicked on, showering the dead and the living.

"Steve!" screamed Talia, as she ran from the room, clutching her GO.

Major Tom found Steve Carbone's GO in a room inside the research facility and confirmed the biosignature. The internal security camera wasn't working. Steve's signal was stationary, then moved. He might have been injured, or administering to others. Tom sent a message to Steve's GO: *If you can, join Talia.*

Steve audio messaged back, "Hands full here. Send more first aid supplies."

"No time for triage," said Tom. "Get as many as can be evacuated out with the able-bodied, and then join Talia. There will be another sortie."

"How do you—"

"Trust me. Just do it."

Veronika's car was already gone. He set a program to search for a robo-Fiat 500. So far, none had been found on the streets surrounding Prometheus.

Then the Prometheus security cameras went dead. All of them.

Major Tom switched his vision to a satellite feed, looking for the plane or rocket launcher that had delivered the payload, trying to anticipate the next move.

And then he saw it.

A phalanx of twenty-six unmarked cars and transport trucks rumbled down Sand Hill Road, heading directly for Prometheus. They couldn't have been more ostentatious if they had tried. A truck-carried rocket launcher led the pack, followed by crowd-dispersal laser-heat units. Worse, the sky filled with drones. Large ones with weapons. Small ones with cameras.

GO-clad Sand Hill Road workers and Stanford students recorded the march on the Valley.

Major Tom could only assume that this unknown army wanted staff out of Prometheus and rounded up as quickly as possible so that they could get what they had come for and destroy the rest.

He sent a message as "Prometheus Security" to all employees: *Evacuate immediately—scatter to the west and south. Avoid the driveways and parking lots. Head into Stanford and hide below ground if you can. Do NOT stay in groups. Avoid the drones.*

And an additional message to Talia's and Steve's GOs: *Out through the basement into the tunnels and head west! NOW!*

"Which way is west?" Talia screamed into her GO.

Steve messaged, *Use the GO compass!*

From Major Tom's satellite view, the ants were agitated and moving fast. Thousands of Stanford students, staff, and faculty tried to figure out what had exploded, and where. Sand Hill Road office buildings emptied. Prometheus employees followed orders en masse: jumping fences, hiding, pretending to be with nearby facilities, getting away. There were 1,257 employees and only two hundred drones. Mingling with the Stanford population or running into open buildings might save their lives.

Major Tom had never wanted his body back so much.

CHAPTER ELEVEN

T he audio message said the sender was "Rick Blaine" and included a live AV link. It originated in New Orleans, one of three Southern Exodus ports, along with Miami and Fort Lauderdale/Port Everglades. That voice had the peculiar verbal twang of Louisiana Creole.

"Veronika told me to contact you urgent if *kaka e paye*."

Translation: if the shit hit the fan.

A quick search revealed that the most famous Rick Blaine was the protagonist in the classic movie *Casablanca*. That made sense. These cities might have been in the American South, but they were certainly not *of* the South. New Orleans, Miami, and Fort Lauderdale had become the Casablancas of North America, a byway for refugees who had the wherewithal to flee an increasingly authoritarian regime for the more democratic shores of Northern or Western states, another country, or a seastead. Those fleeing a collection of threats—racial, ethnic, or religious violence; the for-profit prison-industrial complex; or wage slavery—attempted to raise the necessary funds and prepare whatever paperwork was needed. In a world filled with legal, quasi-legal, and illegal demands on governments, bureaucratic mendacity only increased when life and livelihood were on the line.

The GO link went live. A pumping nightclub inside an old industrial warehouse. A twenty-foot, neon-trimmed robot danced to the tightly laced, deep-groove electro-funk of Jonny Sonic's "Seminal." Sweat-slicked bodies, a literal and figurative melting pot, writhed in sync on the dance floor. Both music and lyrics enticed them to get aroused through the irresistible beat and find a suitable sex partner. An array of sexbots for hire lined the walls for those who struck out with humans and still needed to scratch an itch. Some looked almost human, others like giant dolls with unsettlingly close-set eyes, symmetrical features, and Barbie-and-Ken physiques. All were ready to provide erotic fun for the price of a GO swipe through the biometric reader between their robo–shoulder blades, in any currency. Permutations of heights, weights, ages, genders, and ethnicities added to the carnivalesque, something-for-everybody vibe. A handful of prospective clients were grinding against them, getting their android on.

Major Tom watched the GO-cam move from the line of sexbots into an empty sex booth, one among many that hung above the fray off a catwalk. A cappuccino-skinned hand closed a door. Occasional bumps, grinds, and climactic sounds seeped through the walls. The camera turned 180 degrees to face a square head with the same cappuccino-colored skin. Short-cropped black hair, black mustache and goatee. Pale olive eyes with an intense squint.

"Is Veronika okay?" asked Tom.

"Sent me a message a day ago to contact you when I had problems. And I do," said Rick.

"Where is she?"

Rick shook his head. "Don't know."

"Who are you?" asked Tom.

"Identity and currency trader. I work with Foxy. All my accounts are frozen. The Shell is dropping. I can't reach her." Dr. Who traded through Foxy, too. Maybe that's how Veronika knew Dr. Who.

"How do you know Veronika?" asked Tom.

"Occasional hack," said Rick. "Realistic designs for forged papers. She knows what's goin' on. But isn't sharin'. Do ya know?"

"Not much, and I'm a little busy right now," said Tom. "What happens if Foxy's network crashes?"

"Hey, I make *franc* from folks payin' for fun, but if I can't move 'em with new identities, there's gonna be a million refugees stuck between here and Miami with nothin'. No life. No future. Not enough smugglers in the world to move this bunch. And there's rumors Southern military be linin' up at the Exodus Zone borders. Need these folks out now."

"Why?"

"SSA wants poor folks back. Abandoning their country? *Tre térib* for the bosses. The South was never about machines. Cheap, desperate humans with no security net do the work as cheap as robots, so *aristos* and *bureaus* sell 'em God and suck 'em dry." Rick gestured behind him at the dancers. "History, man. Automation my ass. These are still cogs and wheels. And ya know they'll scoop the rest of us up in the nets, 'cause they can. *Vit komm un néklè.*"

As quick as a whip. It was amazing how some phrases still resonated. These emigrants needed new identities and lives as much as anyone.

"Rick," said Tom, "I'll do everything I can to help you get those people out, but I need a favor, too. Right now. I need a sexbot."

While speaking to Rick, Major Tom dove into the vast files of Prometheus Industries: research and development for the Hippo and Cortex 3.0, memos, correspondence, marketing, sales, personnel records. He wanted copies of all of it.

A vindicated paranoid, he also demanded ridiculous levels of redundancy, especially in the aftermath of the destruction of the Phoenix Club. His off-site storage records at Prometheus indicated that eight facilities still held the company's data. At each of them, he observed both satellite imagery and digital traffic. All were under either physical or digital attack.

Except one.

When the redundant systems were developed, he moved one to his own server farm. No one but he knew where it was located. Not even Ruth. It was never recorded as a backup. And the route that delivered the data was circuitous and designed to appear as if it had originated in another location. He checked for that system's files.

They were still there. He copied them to yet another location, in case something happened to him. Somewhere no government or corporation would care about invading, on the other side of the world: the largest data center in New Zealand, on the North Island, near Whangarei, the most geologically sound area in the country. No one disliked Kiwis. Hell, a bunch of wealthy or connected Americans had moved to New Zealand already to run away from the disintegration of the United States. He hoped the information would be safe there.

He followed Talia's progress into the depths of the building. Most people never knew how deep underground a highly technical building such as Prometheus could go. It had to handle a great deal of power, waste, and communications infrastructure, as well as storage and replacement parts. If they needed a helium-neon laser for a state-of-the-art Raman microspectrometer, they couldn't order it for next-day delivery.

"Where am I?" Talia yelled into her GO.

"Under the power plant," said Tom. "Straight for another twenty feet. Then turn right into the next tunnel."

There was the sound of her breathing. Then the sound of flowing water.

"A flood!" she yelled over the sounds.

"Hold your camera up!" She moved it to show water pipes had ruptured. "Can you get through it?" he asked.

"I don't know!"

"Try. And keep your camera up!"

"Shit!" she screamed, sloshing through the water. Her cursor stopped moving on Major Tom's schematic of the building.

"You okay?"

The few seconds it took her to answer felt like several little eternities.

"Yeah . . . yeah, I think so," she said. Steve's GO-map cursor went dead on Talia's GO. "Steve! Is he okay?" In her panic, she stopped moving.

"Yes, he can hear me. Keep going. The GO's probably got water in it. He's moving."

On his satellite, Tom could see another sortie approach. "Talia, turn left. Steve, hold on!"

"But it's too short to stand in!" screamed Talia.

"I know. Trust me."

BOOM!

The structure shook violently. Talia's camera showed that her section of the building held, but Tom didn't know for how much longer.

"Steve?" she yelled.

Steve was still moving. "He's okay!" said Tom. "Turn into the next service duct!"

"You're kidding," said Talia.

"Go!" said Tom. "Steve's following you."

Talia crawled on her belly through the duct, the building rumbling around her, her head and GO above the rising waters. She panted, "Where's Steve . . . ? I have . . . to wait . . . for him."

"I promise you he's behind you. Keep moving. Only ten more feet, then you can stand."

"If you let anything happen to him . . ."

"I'm trying to save you both. Move!" said Tom.

From Major Tom's satellite view, the exterior of the Prometheus building was destroyed. Bloody bodies littered the ground. He ran an estimate of casualties among the Prometheus employees: explosions or weapons killed 5 percent; drones rounded up an additional 10 percent.

"Talia! Turn right, you'll see a—"

"Go up . . . here?" She was climbing the ladder already.

"Yes," said Tom. "Then open the door. Be careful."

She scrambled up the ladder, leapt onto a platform, and flung open the door, still holding her camera up. Steam permeated the air. Loud male voices bounced off the tile walls and reverberated through the facility. She could hear showers running and locker doors slamming. And laughter.

"Just stop playing golf, for the love of God," said an old naked man, holding a towel and gesturing with it at a younger man. "I can't fix you! Square your shoulders, keep your head down, line your feet up to the hole, follow through. This isn't rocket science!"

A towel-clad thirty-something threw his hands in the air. "Dad, I watched the Palmer videos, bought the auto-caddy and the roboswing corrector. What more do you want from me?"

But Dad wasn't listening.

Filthy and dripping, Talia stood in an elegant men's locker room among two dozen naked, betowelled, and half-dressed men, ranging in age from thirty to eighty-five. Conversation quieted. All the men stared at her.

Dad whipped his towel around his waist and marched up to her. "Young lady, how the hell did you get in here?"

"You didn't hear the explosions?" asked Talia.

"Barney," another older man interrupted. "That's the tunnel door."

Barney barked, "I know that, Connie!" He peered at Talia closely. "*You* are not a member of this club. How do you know about the tunnels? And what explosions?"

Younger members could be heard murmuring to one another, "What tunnels?" "What explosions?" "I thought that was a closet!" "There are tunnels?"

The tunnels were a secret Cold War relic in Silicon Valley. The clubhouse had been built in 1962 for the Stanford University elite, as well as aerospace engineers and executives who worked on communications, ICBMs, and NASA projects. They had taken no chances, using the tunnels first as nuclear war bunkers, then to provide cover from the rain between their companies or university and the clubhouse without ever coming to the surface if they felt like it. Most members had forgotten about them. Many decades later, the country club was the playground to the Valley's remaining elite.

Major Tom knew the history because Carter was a member and purposefully maintained the tunnels between Prometheus and the club for his own use, in case he needed an escape route. Peter Bernhardt never knew about them, but Tom knew what Carter knew when he had died.

Talia pointed at a man holding a dry towel. "May I use one?" When he didn't respond, she added with false sweetness, "Please?"

He handed her the towel. She attempted to dry off.

Through the open door behind her, a soaked, dirty, and disheveled Steve stumbled into the locker room. His handsome face had acquired more wrinkles over the last two years, and his fringe of black hair was strewn with flecks of gray. His large and warm brown eyes caught the sight of Talia and went huge, pupils dilating. His beloved was safe. The GO's picture went dark as the camera pressed against Steve's shirt.

The hug lasted a long time.

Tom sent the couple a message.

Talia glanced at her GO and couldn't stifle a manic giggle. She turned to the club members. "I'm supposed to say, 'Carter Potsdam says, "Hi, and thanks for keeping the door unlocked."'"

Barney's jaw went slack, and Connie looked like he'd pass out. The other members were silent. Talia grabbed a bewildered Steve's hand and pulled him with her, grabbing dry towels from the shelves as they went.

The crowd parted reluctantly, making a path for the couple to leave the locker room.

They wandered until they found an empty function room in the clubhouse. The event hall was white-washed and mahogany-beamed, filled with upholstered dining chairs and tables covered in brightly colored linens. The camera caught a quick image of a banner hung from the small dance floor: *AdVentures Capital Family Dinner*. Tom supposed it might be canceled.

Outside the floor-to-ceiling windows, there were men in golf clothes running toward Sand Hill Road. The image dropped quickly to the floor. Talia and Steve collapsed in an exhausted heap. The GO camera focused on the ceiling.

"You can't stay here," said Tom through Talia's GO.

"Give us . . . a goddamned minute . . . for God's sake . . ." panted Steve.

"Talia," said Tom, "I need you in Los Angeles immediately. And Steve, I want you on the *Zumwalt*, to protect you."

"Hell no," said Steve. The camera hadn't moved.

"This is part of a global attack," said Tom. "I need to keep you safe and out of the Valley. This is the first front of a war and we don't know the enemy."

"Are you crazy?" said Steve. "Our people are dead! You're the target. And I don't want Talia standing in front of you!"

Their breathing grew slower and shallower. No one said anything for 42.3 seconds.

"Okay, I need to get to the injured," said Steve. "Where are they?"

"Noninjured are taking them to Stanford Hospital," Tom replied. "Ruth sent word there that they are not to be arrested and to lie to authorities about their identities if necessary. Since we built a new neuroscience wing in her name, I think they'll listen."

"Then I'll go there," said Steve.

"No. You can't. The attackers will find you. We need you and your expertise elsewhere."

Talia let out a sigh. She picked up the GO and looked in the camera. "What time's the flight?"

"As soon as you can get to Moffett Field," said Tom. "I'm operating the airport remotely and found a pilot to fly the old Potsdam jet. Also, some students are dismantling a Suburban in the hangar. With crowbars. They think it's a new kind of engineering project. Ignore it. Amanda won't be pleased we're taking the jet, but hopefully she'll never find out."

"But you don't care what she thinks, or what any of us thinks, do you?" said Steve.

"I care more than you'll ever know," said Tom.

Talia sat up wearily. Steve grabbed her arm, saying, "You can't . . ."

She continued to rise and gently disengaged from his grasp.

"How does he still have control over you?" Steve asked.

"I don't know," she muttered.

"I can't do this anymore," Steve said. "I won't."

"Please, love," said Talia. "I need you more than he does. Help me."

"Not now. I won't let you," said Steve.

"It was never about you letting me, was it?" she asked. "Really?"

"I love you," Steve said.

But Talia was already on her way out the door.

CHAPTER TWELVE

Major Tom's satellite search for Virginia-class submarines sent him new data. A sub matching the kidnappers' vessel had surfaced off the coast of China and sent an encrypted message to a server in Wenzhou. He recorded the location and encryption but needed someone more skilled to break it. He sent it to Miss Gray Hat.

And he kept trying to contact Veronika by any means possible. Via her GO. At TCoMT. Her car had simply vanished. It could only be on purpose. He had no idea whether it was her or his enemy's doing.

The first inkling of their enemy's plan was emerging. A concrete-haired and facial pore–free reporter got to the scene suspiciously fast and was already doing his stand-up, his flak jacket so new, the price tag was still on it.

"The digital entity known as Major Tom, formerly in life a terrorist known as both Peter Bernhardt and Thomas Paine, has destroyed the company he once created: Prometheus Industries." The camera panned around the carnage. "Sources say this is part of a greater plan to destroy what remains of North America for his alleged new ally, the People's Republic of China."

Was someone trying to start a fight with the Eastern Empire?

Miss Gray Hat voice messaged Ruth and Tom. "Received full access to Rick Blaine's identity files for the Prometheus employees' re-identification. Recommend sharing these with Veronika, since she seems to have expertise and knows him. Chinese message decryption will take longer than assumed. Will get back to you."

Tom eventually got a text message from Veronika: *Got files from Miss Gray Hat. Will do what I can. I'm busy. Cryptos are crashing. It's a global 51% attack. Will be in touch.*

"Wait," said Tom. "What the hell? You're okay?"

"Yeah. For now. Let me try to save our money." She went dark.

Our money. Tom had to laugh. She was taking this fourth Musketeer stuff seriously. He decided not to bother her. Their money needed saving. He tracked cryptocurrency fluctuations, and it wasn't only the Shell that was plummeting. There had been global attacks on cryptocurrency server farms. If any entity controlled 51 percent or more of a currency's blockchain mining and computing power, then a single majority controlled both the mining and auditing power of the currency network, as if a banker simultaneously minted a currency, told you how much it was worth, and then repeatedly spent the same money over and over again without showing you an accurate audit. Any currency attached to the attacked blockchain was untrustworthy and potentially worthless in as little time as it took for the news to spread. Which was no time at all.

LooseChange, Bittybits, Foolsgold, Beads, NonStaters, and Rupeedupees were all on the verge of collapse, along with the businesses and regions that used them. The flow of fear and speculation looked like a plague spreading at the speed of digital communication.

Hundreds of millions, if not billions, of people were about to lose their money.

With destructive coordination so meticulously organized, this suggested a global group of attackers who had planned this long in advance, with complete access. This wasn't only a "Phoenix Club," multinational corporation, or government. This was something more.

To pull off a 51 percent attack of most of the important data-carrying blockchains in the world would require vast power. Who had that kind of power? It wasn't the former United States. He was back to either Russia or China. And China kept coming up in his analyses. It was time to find out why.

Tom swamped Veronika's text message systems again: *We need to talk!*

Finally, he received a voice reply. "The hell, dude! Said I'm busy."

She had locked down her cameras to his view, so he couldn't see her, her room, or what she was working on. It was a conversation in the dark.

"Do you want to stop this?" asked Tom.

"Whaddaya think?" snarked Veronika.

"Then we follow the money."

"Har dee har. Didn't know uploaded entities could be so hilarious," said Veronika.

"I need your help for that. Not the currencies themselves," said Tom. "The reason for the theft."

"Who knows?" she said.

"But we do know," said Tom. "We just don't know that we know."

"Dude, no more koans!"

"It may be tied to China and Dr. Who," said Tom.

"Why?"

"The sub surfaced off the coast of China . . . I think they're bringing her ashore."

"Shit . . . ," said Veronika.

"All of this has to be connected. What do we think they will do with her?"

"Like, Dr. Who's the ideal person to use to corner, like, the identity market. They've already destroyed and cornered monetary markets."

"I think it's more than that. If you corner all the markets, you also corner humanity," said Tom.

"Whoa . . . ," said Veronika. "You really think it's the Chinese?"

"There's not enough data to speculate. And they may not be alone," said Tom. "We need more information on the ground. There are too many countries and multinationals threatened. But the Chinese are the biggest players. Makes Russia look like a bunch of whiny Luddite trolls in a cave. This is a substantial weapon for the Chinese."

"They may not see it as a weapon. Every tool is morally neutral," she said. "You have to assume it will be used for both good and evil. Swords *and* plowshares for the win."

"You know you're quoting me back at me, right?"

"Shit," said Veronika.

"But yes, each time a new disruptive technology is created, we fight the same damn fight all over again. So evil doesn't win. And if they're targeting me, they don't want me to stop them."

"Mad props to you, dude," said Veronika. "Who else can say that?"

Miss Gray Hat sent a text message to Tom and Ruth. It was the decrypted message the submarine had sent to the server in Wenzhou: *Doctor is ready. Meet Qi Jiguang.*

All roads led to China.

CHAPTER THIRTEEN

In a back alley in San Pedro, California, near the Port of Los Angeles, a pair of former UC Berkeley robotics students-turned-entrepreneurs and their dedicated employees—both human and robotic—worked out of an anonymous warehouse down by the docks. Its last tenant had been a cheap Chinese electronics importer, but that business had folded with the troubles. Inside the rusty structure, the new tenants fabricated the world's oldest profession.

Rick Blaine had convinced a sexbot manufacturer in California that he wanted VIP treatment for his VIP friends.

Talia had tried to clean up on the forty-five-minute flight aboard Carter's old private jet, but she still looked bedraggled after her escape from Prometheus. Arriving at the entrance, she wore a microcamera transmitter on a pair of AR glasses, so Tom could see and hear what she could, even if the GOs were shut off.

"I don't like this," she said aloud.

"Have we ever trusted anyone, Talia?"

She stopped at the unmarked door and didn't ring the buzzer.

"Is there a problem you see that I don't?" he asked.

She didn't answer, hesitated for a moment more, then rang the bell.

A voice through a speaker said, "Look into the camera to your right."

The small monitor had a camera and a screen with instructions. Talia pressed her hand into the palm scanner and looked into the retinal display, which was more sophisticated and foolproof than an iris scan. Even Thomas Paine had fooled iris scanners with implants. She knew the camera was recording facial biometrics like ears and pores, too.

"Thanks for confirming your data. Come in."

A buzzer sounded, and the door clicked open. She entered, and the door automatically shut behind her. The inside of the warehouse was vast. A sign hung from the rafters in a sexy font made of human sexual positions. It read: *COMPANIBOTS*. She walked through aisles with shelves of wire spools, component parts, and 3-D printers churning out acres of silicone skin in all the colors of the human rainbow. She watched it emerging and couldn't help but touch it: pores, follicles with human-like hair, the mottling and depth of many colors that a dermis and epidermis take from a blood supply and exposure to the elements.

A few aisles down, skinless animatronics were being tested for consistent movement and reliability. The underpinnings of a human-like robot looked anything but organic, with tiny silicon chips; servos; gyros; silicone; and flexible metal "flesh" to pad out a pliable human shape, titanium bones, and wires. Lots and lots of wires.

"Over here!" yelled a youthful, unseen voice. Talia and her camera followed the voice. Near the center of the warehouse, two young men were immersed in mixed reality, their hands moving, and subvocalizing with a throat microphone to live or virtual AIs. They were about thirty years old. One had a prosthetic left arm that he didn't dress with his company's remarkable fake skin. He seemed to revel in its mechanical complexity. He wore a haptic sleeveless shirt under his short-sleeved tee. Tom couldn't see if he had haptic leggings under his jeans. His black dreadlocks flowed out the back of haptic headgear, which looked like a motorcycle helmet. The only thing he was missing was a pair of goggles. Tom assumed he wore MR contacts. The other man had his back to Talia. He wore older goggles, with no tactile input. There was a fat "G" carved in the back of his red buzzcut. Both seemed agitated. The cryptocurrency drop would affect their business, too.

Talia cleared her throat. The redhead turned first and swished his virtual workspace away. She pointed at his head. "'G' for Greg?"

The man in the haptic suit swished his work away, too, and said, "No, I'm Greg." He and his partner shared a concerned look.

"Does that make you Will?" she said to the redhead. "What's the 'G' for?"

He nodded and self-consciously rubbed the back of his scalp. "Green Bay Packers. They don't play much now, but I can't let the world forget they were America's team."

Greg and Will rose and walked quickly across the warehouse floor. Talia tried to keep up.

"Sorry for the rush," said Greg, "but the crash has vendors and distributors in a frenzy. We're trying to hold it together. But Rick Blaine insisted—"

"I appreciate it. Hey, that skin I saw was amazing," said Talia.

"Best in the business," said Greg. "We can't give you a same-day custom model, so you need one off the rack. We're hoping this inventory still heads to Singapore in a week, so there are options. My *usual* pitch is, What's your pleasure? Pick your skeletal characteristics and combinations. Male or female or intersex? Young or old? Tall or short? Thin, muscular, fat? Genitals of all sizes, configurations, and mileage, including models with all possible sex characteristics together or none at all. Skin color in real, plus some fake shades. Same with eyes and hair. We even have some alien and cartoon characters. All legally licensed, of course. They also vary in tech. Some are body-density dolls with bendable joints you carry around. Some are true companions with autonomous movement. They're programmable and learn with each interaction. They can spouse for life, if you wanted a very predictable and controlled relationship."

"Greg calls them the ultimate prosthetic," said Will.

"I want the most advanced, highest level of autonomy, AI, and tech upgrades, with wireless communication and interactivity. It needs to move and talk and think on its own, and we need to talk to it every way we can think of, all the time. Probably male, but otherwise . . ." Talia shrugged.

Greg and Will shared a knowing look. "Even our most expensive models don't have that level of autonomy," Greg said. "You'll need more programing and robotics than most customers are willing to pay for. Some folks modify the hell out of these. I don't care what they do with them in the aftermarket. Once modders invalidate the warranty, it's not my business."

"Then I need your best modders. Only the ones we can trust," she said.

"We know who you are. And we all know Thomas Paine," said Will softly. "Some of us do what we do because of him."

Talia arched an eyebrow at Will. "You make sexbots because of Thomas Paine?"

Will smiled. "No, we redefine what it means to be human."

Talia sighed. "Okay. We'll take the best of everything, including modders."

"Then we have to find a currency to accept," Greg said. "Right now, it's Chinese renminbi or direct transfer to and from a Swiss bank. And we insist on proof-of-transfer before it's out the door."

"Swiss bank is fine," said Talia.

"Look on those five racks at the back. Gotta go make sure the Swiss thing still works," Greg said, then speed-walked away.

The racks were forty-foot wardrobe rods made of strong steel and mounted on large wheels with tires. Each rod had a computer pack with GPS and a motorized system to drive it around the warehouse or out to the shipping dock. The robots hung from a torso harness, with a strap around the neck and a hook that attached to the rod. Most were naked, to be dressed by the new owners. They were covered in a clear protective plastic wrap. The variety was staggering, although Asian-looking robots dominated this particular shipment. And cartoon characters. And young girls and boys.

Talia must have made a physical sign of disgust, because Will said, "It's better they use robots than real children, right?"

Talia and her camera nodded. "Why do they buy from you and not China?"

"We're the best," said Will. "Chinese competitors try to copy us, but they always cheap out. They can't help it. Competition never lasts long 'cause we innovate the shit out of 'em. They're always playing catch-up."

Talia mumbled into a throat mic, "What do you want?"

Seeing all the body possibilities made Tom feel an odd need for familiarity. He said into her earpiece, "Could you stand one that looks like me?"

She laughed. "Which you?"

"It was always your call," Tom said.

She wandered through the racks for a few more minutes. Will followed her. Finally, she stopped cold and gasped.

"This one," said Talia.

The sexbot was a white male, over six feet tall, broad shouldered, and moderately muscular with bright-blue eyes, a square jaw, a cleft chin, and brown hair with chestnut highlights. And an enormous penis.

Will laughed. "In Asia, they call that one Mr. Handsome. Or James Bond. Popular with rich Chinese women."

Talia looked skeptical. "Which Bond do they think it looks like?"

"All of them," said Greg.

To Tom, it looked like Peter Bernhardt, porn star. "You really want to stick it to them."

"You have no idea," Talia said.

"Buy two," Tom said. "You can call them Thing 1 and Thing 2."

"Because one of you was never enough?" asked Talia.

"Because one is staying here," said Tom. "And one is going to China."

CHAPTER FOURTEEN

The *Zumwalt* sailed into the Port of Los Angeles, all pointy
stealth geometry, long and sleek like a needle. LA was still
the busiest container port in the Western Hemisphere, but
a twenty-first-century destroyer was an unusual sight. California and
Washington State had cobbled together a West Coast navy from their
existing bases, but none of them had a similar vessel. When the USS
Zumwalt had been commissioned, the navy ordered thirty-one more
Zumwalt-class ships. Then Congress lowered the budget to three ships.
After that, no more were made.

Instead of docking at the port, which was mobbed with cruise ships
filled with immigrants from former American states and abroad, the
ship pulled up to Island White, one of the THUMS/Astronaut Islands
in San Pedro Bay named after four NASA astronauts who had lost their
lives in the line of duty. A manmade isle surrounding an old oil-pump-
ing operation, decorated in the 1960s, it looked like a Disneyesque
vacation resort full of high-rises, waterfalls, and palm trees so as to blend
in with the Southern California coast's reputation as the playground of
America, while not disturbing the ocean views with ugly derricks and
platforms. The oil had run dry years ago, so it was abandoned. No one
would bother them there.

Talia arrived with the two unactivated sexbots and the young robomodders Greg and Will had recommended: Dev Parashar, Miguel Aznar, and Sasha Orlov. The Companibots boys had some of the best minds in robotics working both on and off the books. The money in the global sexbot trade was that good. Fiscal uncertainty and a general uneasiness about the future might slow down committed relationships, marriage, and childbirth, but it didn't stop folks' desire for a satisfying orgasm. Sex tech always led innovation.

After thorough background checks by Ruth and Miss Gray Hat, Dev, Miguel, and Sasha set up shop in the *Zumwalt*'s empty personnel and engineering rooms. They were only a little younger than Greg and Will and, based on Ruth's research, came from the top robotics programs in North America. They brought with them crates filled with upgrades: new eyes with hi-res sensors and regular, infrared, and ultraviolet filters; extra-sensitive skin and audio receptors; faster motor processors; and the lightest, smallest, most conductive carbon nanowiring produced anywhere. But the most important addition was the new "brain," designed to be dependent on the signal sent from Major Tom's server farm and yet had to be able to act autonomously and with minimal information if the signal was cut.

The two Mr. Handsome/James Bond robots lay on tables in the middle of the room. Dev—tall, thin, with an austere face and eyes that were always squinting—worked on installing the new eyes, a sized plug-and-play model he'd invented to fit any Companibot's product. Miguel—petite with a ready smile, quick movements, and quicker wit—added thick silicone cushioning to the joints, originally specced to be useless for anything beyond a roll in the hay. Sasha—athletic, nervously fiddling with fingers and jiggling legs—toiled through her mixed reality contacts on the communications platform. She had the communications array up, but there was a gap between the dependent and independent thought processes.

"What happens in the time between getting cut from the servers and regaining autonomous control?" Sasha asked Ruth and her coworkers as she shook out her limbs. "And how do we make sure we can get server control back as quickly as possible?"

"I b-begged Miss Gray Hat for help. Says she will. *Danken Gott!*"

"Miss Gray Hat?" asked Sasha. She and her coworkers had worried looks.

"L-l-long story . . . ," muttered Ruth. She sent another message to Miss Gray Hat, requesting her opinion.

Tom was a little jealous watching the young people tinker with his golems. He spoke up from a monitor. "Why did you all decide to work on robots?"

Dev looked up from a robot's empty eye socket. "Isaac Asimov said that one day humans and robots would become so much like one another, a combined culture and species would result. I want to be a part of that."

Miguel chortled at Dev's high-mindedness. "I like the money!"

The room broke out in laughter.

"You can't put the genie back in the bottle," Sasha said. "We will be them someday—and them us. The more I can figure out how to do it right, the better we'll all be."

"Miss Gray Hat has communication for Sasha," Ruth said. "'We can maintain limited computing capability, but much better connected to cloud. Find AI and resynchronization operation. Can lead to inconsistencies, but simultaneous updates can create merge conflicts. Spend some time resolving merge conflicts.'"

Sasha nodded and cracked her knuckles. "Huh. Good idea."

The tinkering took several days. The biggest problem was how to replicate Major Tom's mind in these new substrates. How much would be based on his original download and program, and how much would be independent and autonomous in each robot? What was important to keep, and what could they lose for both storage and efficiency's sake?

Miss Gray Hat lobbied for resolving merge conflicts at each stage. "Major Tom might represent the brains of the operation, but each robot will have experiences and input it needs to comprehend and share immediately. This means their identical programs split and generate their own data. He needs a truth maintenance algorithm to access and sync to every copy of him, so he will always know what each of the robots knows and vice versa. In essence, we're updating their experiences, their model of the world, and their personalities at every step. They'll be working from the same shared information, so every problem is a synchronization problem."

Ruth's lips alternated between pursing fish-kisses and blubbering. "*Nein.* Another problem. He might remember. Too much. It's *meshugenah.* Crazy. He's the worst part of human. And machine. Humans need to forget. Sometimes."

Sasha asked, "So you want to throw out data?"

Ruth's lips stopped twitching. "Only what might cause too much pain . . ."

"No," said Tom, through a console. "We won't know what that is until too late. I need to know and synthesize. I can't forget anything. And I'm not really human. It's simulated pain. We can fix that."

Separate copies in cyberspace would automatically update new information to the original Major Tom. If they were cut off, they could hold their own, at least for a while. It would have to do for now.

Miss Gray Hat called the team. Ruth put her on speaker. "As far as I can tell from the Memory Palace and the data Major Tom sent me regarding his change in energy and personality, he has been under a tempered data attack, with a clock speed slowdown and an input scrambler. It's a computer version of enforced depression, like a human given chemical depressives in their drinking water, making it harder to process information and diminishing the desire to engage with reality. I'm guessing he's had it for about a year. Maybe more."

Ruth twitched and stared at the robots on the worktables but said nothing.

"Miss Gray Hat," Tom said, "would my depression have affected Ruth?"

"Human psychology is not my line of work," the hacker's synth voice replied.

Sasha bounced her legs, cleared her throat, and shot glances at Dev and Miguel.

"Something to say?" asked Tom.

"We read about you guys a couple of years ago, when it all went down," said Sasha. "It's why we're here. And I noticed how close you two are, both in the story you sent and in reality. It's like when one spouse is depressed or addicted and the other gets dragged down in a spiral of depression or addiction. Even though you're the first AHI and human relationship, I have to believe it's possible."

Miguel and Dev nodded to Sasha. The room was quiet for a moment.

"Sorry I dragged you down with me, Ruthie," said Tom.

"M-m-me, too," said Ruth.

"Do we all assume Carter and his group did this?" asked Tom.

The four human heads in the lab nodded. Miss Gray Hat posted a thumbs-up.

"Time to get that fucker," said Tom.

While the technical team sat hunched over mixed reality and haptic computer interfaces, or like Ruth clicked on an old-fashioned mouse and keyboard, Talia sat quietly in a corner of the room, saying nothing. Simply watching. Tom could see the conflict on her face and her withdrawn body language. She had feared him ever since he installed the more complex brain-computer interfaces as Thomas Paine, but she was still here, doing everything in her power to save him.

Steve refused to participate at all. "Your weird fetish for the mechanical makes me sick," he had told them. Now he hid in his and Talia's bunk room, catching up on medical journals.

The team activated one robot at a time. They called the first robot Tom 1. To Major Tom in his server, it felt like an awakening. There had been nothing physically tangible about his world until the moment of activation. Tom 1 didn't understand the conflicting sensations suffusing his processors and couldn't resist trying to resolve the confusion. Major Tom told his body to get up, but all it did was spastically shake so hard that the table jumped and shimmied.

"Haltn!" scolded Ruth. *"Khop nisht di lokshn far di fish!"*

Grabbing the noodles before the fish was like putting the cart before the horse. "Sorry, Ruthie . . ." Major Tom mentally relaxed and cut off his robot's inputs to stop the data flow.

Time still moved frustratingly slowly to him. Interacting realistically with his body and the world around it would require a colossal balancing act of time and space.

"Start again," ordered Ruth. "And pay attention!"

He turned on the data flow again.

"P-p-point your left foot," said Ruth.

He tried, but he couldn't connect the position of the foot with the command in his programing. There was no replicated autonomic brain region that kept the body functioning smoothly without a program or conscious thought behind it. He had to think of each action individually.

"I can't," he said. "Any way to guide me?"

Ruth grabbed the foot and slowly pointed it for him. "Feel that?"

"Yes."

"Now flex it . . . P-point . . . Flex . . . Now left knee . . ." She grabbed his calf and thigh to bend the joint. "B-bend . . . Straighten . . ."

"Ruthie, you're touching me," Tom's avatar said on the monitor.

Ruth froze. Her eyebrows jumped. She dropped the leg and stared at his screen.

"Ruth, how can you touch me?" Tom asked.

Ruth's right shoulder leapt repeatedly to graze her right ear. "I don't know." She thought about it. "You're a machine. Not human."

"Really? Of all people, I would have thought you—"

"D-d-don't want to think about it!" She lurched up, rummaged around the room, found the pile of clothing they had bought for the robot, and pulled a pair of boxer shorts over his leg and up around his waist.

Tom laughed from the monitor. "Why the hell do I need underwear? And shouldn't we activate that? It might end up being my best feature."

"On your t-t-time. Not mine," said Ruth.

Over and over, he'd repeat actions to program and link his physical motor processor to his virtual ones, hoping that sooner than later it would feel natural, unconscious.

"I'm going to regret this," said Ruth. "Open your mouth. Let's get a voice."

Major Tom rerouted his vocal feed from the monitor to the audio speaker in the throat of the robot. After some shockingly loud and dissonant sounds, Ruth ran speech-therapy drills so that his lips and jaws would match the sounds.

"Ready for a sentence?" asked Ruth.

"Yes," said Tom 1.

"Repeat after me: I apologize. To Ruth. For being an ass."

Sasha and Dev tried to keep straight faces, but Miguel burst out laughing.

"'I apologize to Ruth for being an ass.' Does that make you feel better?" Tom 1 tried to smile, but facial expressions hadn't been loaded yet. Instead, his cheeks juddered like Ruth's.

"Nein," said Ruth. She adjusted the isolated muscular motors. "Okay, Genius Boy . . ."

She hadn't called him Genius Boy since he had been alive. The apology must have worked.

"Time for your eyes," said Ruth. "Dev?"

Dev powered up the video connection through his new eye circuitry. Because these worked like cameras, Tom 1 was both extremely near- and farsighted. He could zoom in and out, pan and tilt in a full 180-degree half-spherical plane, and have clarity on any focal plane, even with his fisheye function. He could flip from regular to infrared to ultraviolet filters, allowing heat sensing and night vision. Ruth could see on the monitor what he was seeing through the sensors.

"Bubula," Ruth said to Dev, "nice eyes."

"Enjoy it, Dev," said Tom 1. "I haven't heard her give a compliment in years."

"I am finally working," said Ruth, "with smart people. For the first time. In years."

Sasha, Dev, and Miguel beamed.

Putting it all together would be quite the balancing act. After several hours of running all the body systems through their connective paces, Ruth finally said, "Now, Genius Boy. Get up."

The robot slowly rolled on his side, threw his legs off the table, and stood up to his full height. All eyes were on Tom 1. The techs took notes. Ruth appraised him with a critical eye.

He thought about the move carefully: contract the right mechanical quadricep to lift the right knee, shift the weight forward on the left leg, create the imbalance to relax the right quad, lower the right knee, contact the ground with the right foot, roll forward on the ball of the right foot, propel the next step. And process the visual stimuli, skin stimuli, and vocalizations, all into a seamless whole.

The deliberation was agony, but from his computer's standpoint, time seemed to contract a bit, the simultaneous processing helping to even out the time discrepancies. With all the processes a brain underwent during movement, Major Tom thought, it was hard to believe the first tetrapods ever squirmed out of the oceans and onto dry land 350 million years ago.

But could he manage to operate several copies of himself at once? Right now, two seemed more than enough. More copies would pose all kinds of coordination problems down the line, although theoretically, it should work. Keeping track of all the hims would be possible, but not until he figured out how to keep a single him active and intact.

"He's rocking. Instability in his left hip," said Ruth.

"No more samba, Tom 1," said Miguel as he edited a remote adjustment program. "Correcting . . ."

Tom 1 dressed himself from the clothing pile, considering each move. Talia had provided the bots with Peter Bernhardt–typical black clothing. The clothes registered a contact pressure on the skin from the electronic sensors under the surface. He felt whether he was clothed or not, but the clothing retained the warmth from all the electronics under his skin.

His fingers were still too clumsy for buttons or zippers.

"I'll help," Talia offered. She rose and approached the robot warily. She guided his fingers along the black jeans' zippered fly. It was like teaching a toddler to dress himself.

He tried to smile at her, but she avoided his robotic stare. He couldn't read her face.

Holding his arms out, he turned in a circle. "So? Do I pass the test?"

Ruth grunted. "Not the uncanny valley. The movement, your looks. Still more doll than man."

Traversing the uncanny valley—the creepy discomfort elicited when an image or sculpture was close to human resemblance, but not quite perfect—was the goal of every computer-graphics artist and roboticist in the world.

Sasha stared wide-eyed. "It's amazing, put all together."

Dev grinned. "Yeah, with a personality inside it."

Miguel couldn't stop giggling.

Talia shook her head. And kept shaking it. Major Tom could see in her expression that he looked too much like Peter, doll vibe or not. She was looking at a ghost.

"I need to get into and out of San Francisco as soon as possible," Tom 1 said to the group. He faced the techs. "Can you guys drop me there, then come back here, fire up Tom 2, and pack for shipment? You can tinker some more on me on the way."

"Why?" asked Ruth, her eyelids squinting and twitching hard.

"There's someone I have to see," said Tom 1.

Talia met the robot's stare, looking deep in his glass-and-electronics blue eyes. Then she stormed out of the room.

"She doesn't love you," muttered Ruth.

"No. She loves Steve," said Tom 1.

"Not her!" said Ruth. "The other one."

CHAPTER FIFTEEN

Tom 1 opened his eyes. Sasha, Dev, and Miguel sat next to him in the back seat of a robocab, looking concerned.

"Are you sure you want to do this?" asked Sasha.

"Yeah," said Tom 1. "Thanks for all the help."

Dev took a deep breath. "You know this is the real world, right?"

"The real world has layers even you can't see yet," said Tom 1. He remembered a time when his human brain perceived so much more of reality than a normal brain could.

"Okay, Yoda," said Miguel. "Good luck!"

They dropped him at the corner of Broadway and Broderick in Pacific Heights. He struggled to get his balance as he crawled out of the cab. The three technicians waved, their expressions varying from doubtful to fearful, as the car drove off.

The Potsdam house was still occupied. Tom 1 rang the doorbell. A faint tingle of electrical current ran through the wiring and camera system observing him. When Carter had died and Amanda inherited their estate, she and her then-unborn son, Peter Jr., were set up with enough money to keep themselves barricaded inside forever, along with their housekeeper/chef, Rosinda, and butler/chauffeur, Tony. The couple would care for them for as long as necessary. They were eager to stay. All that money protected Rosinda and Tony from the vagaries of the newly distraught and complex outside world, too.

Tony opened the door. The short, balding butler looked up, aghast, staring at the sexbot's glassy eyes, the silicone skin seams, the rumpled wig, and clothes that didn't quite fit, more proof that Tom 1 had not yet traversed the uncanny valley.

Tom 1 self-consciously patted his hair and shifted his shirt. "Hello, Tony. Please tell Amanda that Peter Bernhardt is here."

Tony flinched. "Yes . . . sss . . . Uhhh . . ."

"I would be happy to wait here, Tony," said Tom 1.

The door slammed. He waited. He tried to use the time productively, contemplating a break-in, running house schematics and the likelihood of success from various entrances. But he preferred not to trigger a police call. He checked the latest on Dr. Who's whereabouts, tracking weather patterns, directing the *Zumwalt* to alter course.

Five minutes passed, during which time the door camera's lens shifted to take in his entire image. Finally, a voice came through a speaker.

"Is this a sick joke?" It was Amanda, her voice ragged.

"No joke, Mandy. It's me. I've come to see you. And little Peter. Sorry if it's not exactly how you expected me."

"I don't know what the hell you are. Go away." Amanda cut the connection.

He stood in place. After another 3.4 minutes, Tony finally opened the door and made a shooing motion with his hands. "Mrs. Potsdam wants you to leave."

Tom 1 took a chance, leaning forward and walking right into Tony. Startled, the butler jumped back to avoid contact. Tom 1 took advantage of the space and shambled quickly, yet awkwardly, into the foyer.

"Mandy? We need to talk!"

"I'm calling the police!" The voice came from upstairs.

Tom 1 headed quickly for the staircase while Tony played a back-and-forth dance, trying to stop the robot but afraid to touch it.

"Please," said Tom 1. "Don't. I just wanted to see you and little Peter. I've never met him. And now, I finally have the opportunity. Please."

He grabbed hold of the banister and took the first few stairs. This staircase was a new topography. He had never been particularly graceful in his flesh-life, but memories of moving through this house with smooth meat-muscle agility taunted him. Acting human was harder than it looked. The idealized patterns in his circuitry were in sad contrast to the actual movements the servos and gears made. They were designed for thrusting and rolling, not the enormous variety of movements that the average human took for granted. He kept climbing, knowing that every gesture would count to Amanda. He had better be the Fred Astaire of robots.

Attempting his first goal, Tom 1 infiltrated the Potsdam computer network. He still had the password from his last visit, when Thomas Paine had tried to seduce Carter and Amanda was pregnant with Peter Jr. She hadn't bothered to change it. He searched through her server and browsers. No messages from Carter. He searched for evidence of any contact. None. But that didn't mean it wasn't there. Carter could have approached her and covered his electronic tracks. He kept looking.

The house was darker than he remembered, as if shrouded in gloom. Was it the difference between his organic eyes and his mechanical ones? He studied the light. The floor-to-ceiling lead-paned windows were grimy with salt and smog, and it was hard to make out San Francisco Bay in the distance. While the atmosphere was dreary, it also made it difficult for outsiders to see inside. It seemed purposeful. The interior was still decorated like it had been when Carter had lived there, all rare antiques, fine art, and comfy sofas. Back then, it had carried the stylish man's stamp. Now, in the gloomy light, and with nothing moved since her husband's death, it felt like a mausoleum.

Amanda stood at the top of the stairs. Her heavy, straight, black hair had grown back, giving her the look of a Native American princess again. But not a young one. The bags under her eyes, some gray hairs, shapeless clothes, and her defeated stance added more than the few years since he had last seen her on an aircraft runway at the Phoenix Club encampment.

Tom 1 paused on the staircase. "Hello, Mandy."

She appraised his figure with disgust. The robot's resemblance to Peter's once-human appearance was too close for comfort. "Are you fucking kidding me?"

"No," said Tom 1.

"So are you Peter again?" she asked. "Or Tom?"

"That depends."

"What do you want?" she said.

"To see you. And Peter. You never responded to my messages," said Tom 1.

"Why should I? You're dead."

A little voice down the hallway behind her yelled, "Mama? Where you?"

Tom 1 carefully stepped up another step. "Please. Let me see him."

Retreating from the staircase, Amanda shuffled down the second-floor hallway. He took this as permission, climbed the last several stairs, and followed.

The hallway was empty, but he found an open door and entered a room across from the master bedroom. It had once been Carter's personal bedroom, used when he wished to sleep apart from Amanda, and it was next door to the room where Thomas Paine had first allowed Carter to kiss him as part of a mutual seduction, a mind game to see who could manipulate whom. So many memories . . . Carter's former bedroom was a nursery with distinctly boy-child decor. The walls and floors were blue. Trains and cars littered the floor. Toys and games filled shelves next to a toddler-sized bed. Absentmindedly gathering up crayons, Amanda sat cross-legged on the floor with a two-year-old boy.

Their son.

The boy had a complexion like his mother's, chestnut hair, and the cleft chin of Peter Bernhardt.

"Thank you, Mandy. This means a lot." He had to keep her talking. "How'd you know it was really me?"

"Whatever's inside, it's annoying and relentless," she said as she put some crayons back in their box. "I remember that. It's what I hated most about you."

Tom 1's processor recognized most of the crayon colors, but some were not differentiated as well as they should be. Were his robotic eyes subtly color-blind, or had crayon colors changed? A toddler's proto-drawings of some sort of vehicle lay scattered on the ground. The same color mistakes were repeated on them. He'd have to ask Dev.

"There's more of me here than you realize," he said. "Does it matter that I was once flesh, but I'm now a machine?"

She closed the crayon box and put it down, looking around for anything to occupy her eyes and hands. "None of you is real. And you'd have no idea if it was."

He couldn't deny that. As real as he seemed to himself, how would he know? "I've thought a lot about you both, and kept track of you, to make sure you were okay. I'm so sorry for what I did. I want you to know I never meant to hurt you."

"Carter," she said. "Play 'Mrs. Major Tom.'"

Tom 1's head swiveled around as fast as it could. "Carter is here?"

Amanda looked at him as if he were insane. "Idiot. I named the HOME after him. It's all you left me."

The speakers played the song by K.I.A., one of the many by singers and songwriters inspired by David Bowie's Major Tom. It was not a subtle message. He waited for her to speak again.

She listened for a minute, then turned to him. "You always thought you could problem-solve through songs. Can you solve this problem?"

"Mrs. Major Tom" was a continuation of the "Space Oddity" story from the plaintive voice of the astronaut's abandoned wife, who was left to rot during Major Tom's disappearance in space. His absence crushed her. Even when he returned, albeit different than before, he was still absent, never hers to begin with. He had always been in it for himself, and that destroyed her. It was not a happy song, and Major Tom was definitely the bad guy.

Tom 1 knelt toward the toddler playing on the floor. The boy pushed a blue wooden engine with a smiling face along a wooden track, to a wooden station, to meet a black engine with a big frown. Back and forth, he rolled the blue engine.

"Hello, Peter," Tom 1 said.

Peter Jr. turned his enormous Bernhardt-blue eyes to his mother, his eyebrows raised in question.

"Toy?" the boy asked her.

"No, love. Not a toy. It's . . ." She tried to finish the thought but couldn't come up with the right words to describe the being in front of her.

"Father?" the robot asked.

Amanda raised her head, bristling. "Peter Bernhardt was his father. He doesn't even know what a father is."

"I am still Peter. In part," he said.

"Can't prove it to me."

"Mandy, I understand your feelings . . ."

"Feelings?" she asked. "You have them?"

". . . but you need to know that the feelings I uploaded are still there. I still love you. And my son. But in a way that might seem confusing."

"What way is that?" Her voice was rough with anger.

Tom 1 thought for a moment. He wasn't sure. He touched Peter's head gently. The painful tentacles of love he had felt on the Phoenix Camp tarmac were still there. They might not make his robot body react in the same ways, but he had always wanted to be a part of his boy's life. This was his chance.

"You selfish . . ." She paused, briefly glanced at little Peter, and mouthed, "Prick."

"You're the first people I wanted to see me. Like this," he said.

"There is no way you can love. Or that I could love you. It's grotesque. Never."

The boy, concerned for his mother, moved to hug her.

"I'm okay, love," said Amanda, kissing his head. "Keep playing."

The child toddled away and rummaged inside his large toy box.

"Regardless, you need to know something else," began Tom 1.

Peter Jr. waddled back with two dolls in his hands. They looked outdated and worn, handed down from much older children, or even their parents. The boy held a Thor action figure and presented Tom 1 with another. It was Iron Man. For a moment, the boy's hands inquisitively touched the robot's, feeling the silicone skin and the padded frame underneath. Tom 1 passed Iron Man between his two hands.

"Thank you, Peter." He reached out to the boy to ruffle the long hair that his mother had been loath to cut, but the little one ducked away and sat back down next to Amanda. Tom 1 wondered if the long hair had reminded her of the child's father, so long ago.

Amanda teared up. "Enough. Just go." Little Peter reacted to his mother's emotions by emulating her. He sniffled softly and crawled into her lap, lacing his fingers through her hair and twirling the strands.

Tom 1 sputtered, "Please. Carter's escaped."

"You locked him up in there," said Amanda. "What did you expect? Can't you leave him alone?"

She knew how the Major Tom entity worked. Tom had never gotten the chance to communicate with her about it, so Carter must have told her. But when? "You know him almost as well as I do. His disappearance isn't benign."

Amanda raised her eyes. "Get out."

"Remember when I told you," said Tom 1, "back on the tarmac, that I'm doing the best thing for everyone? It's still true."

"You have no idea what the 'best thing' is. You've destroyed everything you've touched. Including me."

"But I—"

"Everything wrong in the world is your fault! And why is it *your* choice?" said Amanda.

Peter Jr. whimpered and hugged his mother's neck. She squeezed him back.

Still digging through the Potsdam servers, he found an electronic file called "Doppelgängers/Psychopomps." A doppelgänger was a mythical physical double of a human. A psychopomp was an apparition that led one to the afterlife. In many cultures, it was your physical double, like the Irish fetch. The file's contents made his mechano-body quake for a moment, trying to react several ways at once, locking up his servos. It described ideas about copying humans into different forms and substrates. Carter had proposed all this before he had died.

Was Carter here in the world, too? The Antlers' song "Doppelgänger" seeped into Tom 1's mind. Dreamily and with great languor, it described two images of a person trapped on either side of a mirror. Who would prevail if the twin creature attacked? Who was the fiend, and who was the man? His thoughts accidently played it on Amanda's audio system, a warning for them both of the monsters doppelgängers could become.

Amanda's horrified expression betrayed that she clearly thought *he* was the monster, not Carter.

"Leave Carter alone!" She lunged for his right leg, unbalancing him. As he compensated, his mechanical quadricep and calf flexed shut, and his "muscles" almost crushed her hand behind his knee. She cried out in pain and released him. Little Peter wailed.

Tom 1 uncurled and sprinted from the room.

CHAPTER SIXTEEN

Tom 1 flung open the front door and ran into the street. The déjà vu of losing Amanda and his child, again, was so palpable that it would have physically hurt if he had the biosensors to receive the neurofeedback. He contacted Ruth on a secure line.

"Carter is out here in the data world with me. And he wants a body. Here are copies of what I found on Amanda's servers. Follow them back. Where is he?"

"We're busy!" replied Ruth. "Trying to keep our money! Can't save the world if we're poor!"

"Miss Gray Hat is helping you?"

"No. Veronika is. Moving money to renminbi. And Swiss francs. Like everyone else!"

A feedback warning from his legs reminded him that his knee and ankle joints weren't built for sustained bipedal speed, so he slowed down and walked to Divisadero Street and down into Cow Hollow.

As he walked on, a teenager moving a foot off the ground on a flyboard headed straight for him and shoulder-checked him at full speed. Tom 1 spun. He steadied his gyros, stopped to check whether he was injured, ran a quick diagnostic, and then kept walking.

That bump hadn't been an accident. Tom 1 looked around and actively analyzed his surroundings. This wasn't the San Francisco he remembered: rich, young, arrogant, and bursting with ideas and attitude. It was the middle of the day in September, but kids wandered around. People congregated on stoops or out in the streets with nothing to do and nowhere to go. There were more homeless.

Veronika? Busy? he messaged.

Yeah, she said.

I can't believe what I missed. His gaze scanned the surroundings to show her.

Dude. You're hilarious. Looks like Cow Hollow?

Yeah. His eyes focused on a driverless delivery truck picking up an empty pallet from a lone shopkeeper and unloading a new pallet with shrink-wrapped food containers inside. The grocery manager didn't even direct the forklift. It drove itself. Inside, there were only a few customers and no staff. The entire business looked automated. He refocused on the dry cleaner next door. And the pharmacy. And the fast-food joint. Each run by a single human. Automation took care of the rest.

He had been too busy playing in cyberspace for the last two years. *Did I have anything to do with this?*

Was happening anyway, but you sped things up by getting rid of leaders. When companies only care about efficiency and profits, humans aren't needed. And don't forget our blockchains. Lawyers, financial services, bureaucrats—Poof! Humans go bye-bye. Thank God folks are guaranteed a basic income in California.

Otherwise, said Tom 1, *it'd be another revolution.*

No one told people rebooting their world would be so hard, said Veronika. *But there are a lot of artists and writers now. Silver linings? Anyway, dude, we're busy. Call if you need help. Ciao.*

An old Asian lady held her Pomeranian on a leash while she waved her GO over a reader at an outdoor produce market. The little brown dog lunged for Tom 1's ankles.

"Hey, puppy," said a young woman nearby. "Don't like sexbots?"

Others nearby laughed. A young man came forward and shoved Tom 1 in the arm. "You lost me jobs. I had a good gig going!"

The gathering crowd howled with derisive laughter.

Tom 1 took off at a jog, ignoring the alert from his leg joints. As he turned the corner onto Union Street, a mother walking her two children screamed, "Robot attack!" She grabbed her kids close. A group of men loitering at the corner started toward him, but Tom 1 ran on.

He had never noticed how many people hated robots. He shouldn't have been surprised. They were the symbols of the radical automation that had taken their jobs, changed ways of life, and created a new underclass, the biggest in history.

"Ruth!" he voice messaged. "I've got a target on my back out here!"

"Need a new p-p-plan, Genius Boy," she replied.

An outside message arrived from a burn address.

"Ruth, please deal with it. I can't respond to a video, operate my body, and avoid attacks," he said.

"Should I share?" Ruth asked.

"Yeah, with Veronika, too. I'm trying to stay in one piece."

The message contained a video link with a 3.87-minute movie file. And one sentence: *Did you think she'd give me up for you?*

That stopped him. He scooted into an alley off Union and hunkered down behind a Dumpster so he could focus on the video. A motionless homeless man lay next to him, covered in bubblewrap. He looked to be asleep.

In the vid, a beautiful young woman staggered out of a rave. It was nighttime, and the footage was not clear. She was a tall, curvaceous blonde with cheekbones that could cut a man into bite-sized morsels. Her natural stride and bounce suggested that every last inch was what nature had given her. She was tipsy and tottered in her stilettos as she entered her companion's robocar. As she slid over, her date got in next to her. They snuggled and murmured to each other. Then he stabbed her with a tiny automatic needle. She slumped unconscious in her seat.

The camera cut to an operating room. Quick edits showed her being wheeled into the room and having her head shaved. Cut to a marker-drawn circle on her skull. Cut to her draped for brain surgery. Cut to robotically guided lasers pointed at key sections of the cortex. It could only be a high-tech lobotomy. Neurorigs, resembling Prometheus Industries' Hippo 3.0 and Cortex 3.0, were placed in her brain and overlaid with a new neural microlace in the space between the top of the cortex and the brain's membrane, creating a neural interface that covered the entire brain. A tinny voice faintly directed the medical team, its aristocratic tone devastatingly familiar.

Cut again to the woman in a hospital bed. Maybe a week had passed. A little hair had grown back around the sutures. The woman finished an innocuous conversation with a nurse about what she wanted for lunch, then turned to the camera and said, "Hello, my dears, I'm back!" Then she winked.

She sounded like the woman in the cab, but Tom 1 knew it wasn't her. Not anymore.

Ruth and Veronika watched the message at the same time. There was stunned silence.

Then Veronika screamed, "I know her!"

"From where?" asked Tom.

"Downtown Santa Barbara!" said Veronika. "Met me in a chat room. Friended her at a coffeehouse yesterday and she came on fast."

"Calm down," said Tom.

"Der gehenem iz nit azoi shlecht vi dos kumen tsi im," said Ruth.

"Hell is not so bad as the way to it," repeated Tom.

"Oh my God," said Veronika.

Major Tom scoured the nets for an image of the woman in the video. He found her: Samantha Nugent, a.k.a. Sammi, a biotech sales rep living in San Jose. He called her GO but got only her answering message. Checked her financial records. Her apartment lease was prepaid for a year. Her bills were on auto-pay. When he called her employer, he was told she had quit by e-mail after disappearing two months ago.

"Veronika," Tom said, "let us know as soon as you see or hear from her again."

"Dude, she's coming here."

"Where?" asked Tom.

"My house. Ten minutes!"

While Major Tom set up a satellite feed over Veronika's house, he reran the video for himself. Watching this woman become another victim to his own technology made him consider Amanda's question anew. Why *did* he get to choose?

"Before Carter left the Memory Palace," said Tom, "he planned this, sent a copy of himself without me knowing, found a victim, lobotomized her, and used her body so she'd be completely functional and ready when he left for good. I understand how he did it, in theory. But I didn't think anyone would do it yet."

"Well, that thing is turning up here," said Veronika.

"Carter knows you know me," said Tom. "What do you want to do? I'll help you run, hide, take your family, anything."

"Let's get the mofo," said Veronika.

"Du bist meshuga," said Ruth.

"That means you're crazy," said Tom. "She's not wrong."

"Dude," said Veronika. "This is my turf. Let's figure out what Carter's after. If he wanted me dead, that bitch coulda killed me on the street yesterday. Now nine minutes!"

Thoughts raced. About Carter. About Sammi Nugent. About downloading into robots or humans. About the nature of identity. About the ethics of being human. About the next stage of economics, politics, and society at large.

And ultimately, about why the hell it always involved him.

CHAPTER SEVENTEEN

Tom 1 left the alley off Union and headed up the hill. A young couple in their twenties strode straight for him. Both looked like they hadn't seen a shower in a few weeks. As they passed, the man shoved him with his shoulder, hard. The woman kicked behind his kneecaps so the gyros could not correct the imbalance. He crashed onto the pavement, which sent "pain" signals to his AI brain. He looked down. The skin had torn on the palms of both hands, exposing the inner workings.

Tom 1 was in trouble. This body wasn't designed for hand-to-hand combat. He quickly sent his sensory information to Ruth with an SOS.

The couple dragged him back into the alley, away from the street cameras. They had done this before.

"Help!" he yelled at the sleeping man behind the dumpster.

The man didn't respond. The woman kicked him with her boot. The man didn't move at all.

Her partner sat on Tom 1's chest, and she sat on his knees, making it impossible for him to gain any leverage.

"You run away from your owner?" asked the male.

"No," said Tom 1.

"Ooh, you fancy talker!" squealed the female. She ran her fingers along Tom 1's skin. "Nice hair, too!"

The man studied the robot carefully, opening up clothing, locating the skin seals, looking into his eyes. "Top of the line, plus aftermarket upgrades. This is big!"

A street camera must have sent an alert. A law enforcement drone flew toward them.

"Help!" said Tom 1.

"Don't worry!" said the man to the LED as he shut Tom 1's jaw with his hand. "Sexbot went bonkers. Rebooting it."

The female wagged her finger at Tom 1. "You have to learn to stop turning tricks on the street, or else your privates'll need reprogramming!"

The drone hovered for a few more seconds, taking footage, then flew away. Cops weren't too interested in human-on-robot violence, real or imagined. With the drone out of sight, the female unzipped Tom 1's fly and pulled down his pants. "*Wowee!* Never saw one 'a these out in the wild," she whispered. "You musta cost your sugar momma something!"

"Or daddy . . . ," the male sneered. "Maybe Roberto can move this for us? Not a drone, but big money. He's gotta have a buyer."

"Ruth!" Tom 1 hadn't realized he would vocalize the call. He stopped his vocal transmissions and continued the message. "They're drone thieves!"

"You gotta alarm?" The woman turned to the man. "Told ya it was a sugar momma."

"He learns too fast. Turn him off," said the male. "We need to replace his GPS."

"How much she pay to get you back, puppet?" the female teased.

"You m-m-messed with the wrong sugar m-m-momma!" Ruth yelled through Tom 1's mouth speaker.

"Turn him off!" said the male. "Owner has tracking!"

He got off Tom 1's chest and rolled him over. The woman snaked her hand under a flesh flap near the junction of the neck, spine, and shoulder blades, looking for the off switch. It was enough to allow Tom 1 to free his arms, and he smacked her with all his strength, enough to send her flying six feet away. Her head cracked on the concrete. She looked unconscious, but not dead. He rolled the other way as the male leapt back on top of him. Tom 1 quickly aimed two fingers right into the man's eye sockets. Only one made its target.

The man screamed and grabbed at his bloody left eye. He ran full force at Tom 1, screaming, knocking him back like a battering ram. He hit the ground with a crunch, and the male began to bash his head on the pavement over and over.

First, audio stopped. Then his vision failed with a single fizzle to black. Touch was the last to go. He could feel the beating his mechanical body was taking, but before his touch sensors shut down, he sensed that he was no longer being used as a punching bag. The man must have abandoned his girlfriend and run away to save his eye, leaving Tom 1 in the alley, perhaps to pick up later.

"Ruth, get the robot out of there!" said Major Tom, safe in his server.

"Called robotics team," said Ruth. "With the location. Don't get them hurt! You had to be a big man. Such a *schmuck*!"

"Thanks for the encouragement, Ruthie. But I need a real body. Like Carter's."

There was a long pause before she spoke. "We shipped Tom 2 to Wenzhou."

"I hope it can work there. But I need a real meat body here."

"Bist meshugeh?"

"No. Still not crazy. We're not going to kill anyone. We need to find someone who's the right kind of almost dead."

"Zol Got mir helfen."

"God won't help any of us."

CHAPTER EIGHTEEN

With no body to operate on the ground in San Francisco, Major Tom looked over the figurative shoulders of his team through whatever cameras he could.

"Oh my fucking God," Veronika muttered into her mic. Her hands sculpted the air around her, moving, manipulating, and analyzing file after file of data from her bedroom in Santa Barbara. "All the cryptos. They're just, like, gone."

Ruth shot back from the *Zumwalt*'s bridge, "How gone?"

"Worthless. Some aggressive new stakes in, like, New Zealand and Australian dollars. Put some bets there. Also huge real-estate investment Down Under. And global gold . . . hell, you'd think they just invented the stuff."

Ruth's lips burbled. "Gold . . . If it's from the ground. It must be more real. Fools."

"Hell yeah," agreed Veronika. "All currency is fake. Doesn't matter if it's material or digital. Dudes can't eat gold."

"Is our money safe?" asked Tom.

"We lost some," said Veronika, "but what's left is safe as it can be. For now. Hell, I missed my calling. Shoulda taken my nana's advice and, like, gone into financial markets. Coulda been an oligarch myself!"

"It's not what it's cracked up to be," said Tom. He looked at their new portfolio and agreed with Veronika. For all the world's volatility at the moment, the places Veronika chose were safer: China for its power, Switzerland for its neutrality and banking system, and Australasia for its stable governments and people who ignored the craziness in the Northern Hemisphere if they could. Ruth had been right: they couldn't save the world if they were poor. Too much negative press was lining up against Thomas Paine to create any kind of grassroots support. They would need brute wealth and persuasive leverage on the right people. Most people didn't like the idea that only those with money could play the game. It ruined a "feel-good story" and offended their sense of personal agency, their romantic notions of "the people" saving the world.

In all of human history, quick and powerful change by and for the people had only worked a handful of times, usually with torment, ugliness, death, and a vast communal effort led by a critical mass of highly motivated people, including the wealthy. With Tom's story changed and his name reviled, he couldn't muster that kind of support anymore. People were buying the lies. Nobody would march with him.

Now there was less money than ever, and not only in his accounts. The world had lost trillions of dollars in a few days. Arguably, that value had never really existed but was instead inflated by gamblers using currencies as casino chips. But tell that to the poor people now starving and homeless, their money lost in oligarchic manipulation. Why did this have to happen over and over and over again? Would humanity never learn?

Major Tom received a live link through a TOR router from Veronika's MR glasses, interspersing frames of video with frames of snow with dots. The human eye is slow. Anyone watching would just see her room. But for Major Tom, it contained subliminal messages and links. Veronika had to have created this ahead of time. She was proving to be a remarkable hacker.

On the satellite link, Tom saw a woman approaching Veronika's house. "She's walking up your driveway. Ready?"

A written message in Veronika's frames read, *Thought monsters were outta my league. Let's do this.*

This worried him, too. "What'd she call herself?" asked Tom.

Winter d'Eon. Cool name.

His search for the new name came up empty, but the last name, d'Eon, was that of a famous transgender aristocratic spy in eighteenth-century France. Carter didn't care enough to have created a backstory, but he sure loved to reference French and American history.

Veronika's house was a remodeled two-story tract home along Foothill Boulevard on the outskirts of Santa Barbara. She revealed all the HOME video feeds and ancillary cameras so Major Tom could watch in real time. There were twenty-two cameras inside and out, a more sophisticated rig than a fangirl hacker like Veronika should have had. On one feed, Veronika orchestrated her online life in her bedroom, trying to save crypto-investments. The doorbell rang. On another camera, Veronika's mother, tall, slender, and delicate like her daughter, opened the door. Winter d'Eon, formerly Sammi Nugent of San Jose, stood in the doorframe, dressed like a student. A blue chambray button-down over a rock 'n' roll T-shirt. Jeans. Flip-flops. Her hair was cut pixie short to cover the surgery scar and convey youth with a slight androgyny. She carried a backpack and a brown paper bag.

Her smile was sparkling, white, and lovely. "Hi, I'm Winter. Is Veronika home?"

"Uh . . . one moment. Honey? Your friend Winter's here!"

"Tell her to come up!" yelled Veronika from her room.

"Upstairs, second door on the left. Nice to meet you."

"Nice to meet you, too, Mrs. Gascon. Have a great day."

Winter's smile was warm and comforting. Veronika's mom beamed back. She was accomplished parent bait. She climbed the stairs with a relaxed saunter, in complete control. That worried Tom even more.

The door to Veronika's room opened. Winter strolled in, flopped down on Veronika's bed, and kicked off her flip-flops. Veronika flipped her MR glasses to record.

"How's the farmers' market?" asked Veronika.

"Always yummy. Got some organic grapes and raspberries for us." Winter took in the entire room. "Oh my God, you're a serious Major Tom fan! Me, too!" Then she lounged suggestively on the pillows and offered the brown paper bag to Veronika.

"Really?" Veronika moved to the bed and sat next to Winter.

Winter noticed the Thomas Paine tissue sample on the shelf. "Wow! Now that's something I don't have. Is it real?"

"It's real."

"Shit." Winter crawled off the bed, moved to the shelf, picked up the crystal display, looked at it from all sides, and put it back. "That's impressive. And pricey, I bet. Can't afford that on a grad-slave stipend." She grinned and flopped back onto the bed. "How'd you get it?"

"Long story," said Veronika.

"I'm not going anywhere," said Winter.

"How much do you really know about Major Tom?" asked Veronika.

Winter took a raspberry out of the punnet and held it above Veronika's mouth. "Lots. Studied him for years. He's why I study bioengineering."

Veronika opened wide, and Winter popped in the berry.

"You have good taste," said Veronika as she chewed.

They giggled. Winter offered her another raspberry.

"Yeah," said Winter. "Amazing dude. So innovative and creative. Did you know that he got his start because he played with"—she snapped her fingers, trying to recall a word—"uh, Arduinos? Isn't that crazy?"

The geek-credential competition was on. Tom was incredulous.

"Yeah," said Veronika. "Super old-school dude. Saw one in a museum. But did you know that he's not even from California. He's from someplace in New York."

"Yeah, I know!" Winter looked distracted for a moment. "I'm sorry, you're just so cute," she cooed.

"So are you," said Veronika.

Winter looked toward the desk. The monitor was dark. "Whatcha doing there?"

"Work."

"What kind?" asked Winter.

"It's . . . like . . . hard to explain," said Veronika.

"Do I look dumb?" said Winter. "I'm not. I mean, I could play dumb if that's your thing. But I don't think it is." Her smile was sly.

Veronika laughed. "You're not dumb."

"Then what's wrong?" Winter ran her hand through Veronika's hair.

"Absolutely nothing," said Veronika with a sigh.

"Better not be." She grabbed the berry punnet. With a twinkle in her eyes, she slowly placed a berry between her teeth. Then she leaned in, hovering an inch from Veronika's face. Veronika snatched the berry with her lips. They kissed.

"So . . ." Veronika said with a heavy breath, "you know I'm . . . not finished, right?"

Winter smiled, her eyes tender. "Baby, I'll take you any way you are."

Adjusting her MR unit, which had slipped down her nose, Veronika smiled back with a little sadness.

Winter breathed in her ear as she reached to remove the glasses and said, "It's more fun au natural."

"No." Veronika pulled her head away and winked. "It's more fun with 'em on. Promise. And I just got a hot idea." She gently rolled Winter off her and onto her back.

"I'm so looking forward to this, my dear," Winter said with a sigh.

Kissing Winter's neck, Veronika undid the top few buttons of Winter's chambray shirt and slowly lowered the fabric over her shoulders and down her arms, almost down to her elbows. It had the effect of immobilizing Winter's arms. Winter squirmed, trying to take the shirt off completely, but Veronika whispered in her ear, "I'll do you first. Then you do me."

This is a brilliant and brave young woman, thought Tom.

Raising Winter's shirt over the jeans' waistband, Veronika slowly unzipped the fly, kissing and licking the exposed skin as she went. She pulled Winter's jeans ever so slowly over her hips, pausing with the bunched fabric at the knees, and moved back up to kiss Winter's tiny G-string with puffs of hot breath.

Winter squirmed in delight. "Let me help take them off."

"No, let me," said Veronika. "I have a surprise for you." Languorously sliding her hand between her mattress and box spring, Veronika slowly pulled out a sizable butcher's knife, keeping it out of Winter's line of sight.

But Winter's eyes popped open in anger, and Tom realized that she had infiltrated the cameras in the house. She tried to wriggle away from the weapon, but her clothing bound her.

Scared and no expert with a blade, Veronika flailed, bringing the knife down hard and hitting the mattress. Struggling to pull it out of the foam and fabric, she struck again, hitting Winter's shoulder. Blood spurted.

"Aarrgghh!" Winter roared.

Run! messaged Tom into her glasses.

Veronika thrust one last time, slicing into Winter's thigh, cutting into the quadricep but not severing it. The muscle was too big. The sight of all the blood scared Veronika more than it did Winter, who ignored it, trying to roll into Veronika instead of away from the blade. With a large thud, Winter forced them both onto the bedroom floor, ripping at own her clothes in an attempt to escape. Veronika rolled away, grabbing at the wall for support, but Winter headbutted her in the stomach. Veronika doubled over and hit the wall. Winter struggled with her clothes and her leg wound as Veronika scooped up her backpack, threw the knife in, and staggered out the bedroom door.

Veronika bounded down the stairs, two at a time. "Mom! Get out of here!"

"What, honey? I'm in the bathroom."

"Get out of the house, Mom! Now!"

"Be there in a minute . . ."

She ran for the bathroom door but heard movement upstairs. Terrified, she banged on the door. "Mom! You gotta run away!"

"What?" said Mrs. Gascon. "Almost out."

Veronika screamed, "Save my mom!" to no one in particular, headed for the front door, and dashed outside.

Tom couldn't answer back through the house speakers without giving himself up, but Carter was smart. He'd know from Veronika's entreaty anyway. The outside cameras picked up Veronika, unlocking her car with her handprint, jumping into it. It started. She lowered the window, screaming, "Mom! Please come out!"

Tom's message came up in her MR glasses: *Get away. Now. I will do what I can there.*

"No!" said Veronika. "We have to wait."

"I will help her. She'll survive if you get away. Winter doesn't want her. She wants you."

Veronika thought for a second, then hit a random location. The car pulled out of the driveway and took off to the west.

"Let me into your car's system, so I can get you out of there."

"But . . ."

"Do it!" he yelled.

She did.

He received a link inviting him into her car's automated system. "Got it." He downloaded a driving simulator and loaded the Fiat's robotic software into it.

"Don't touch the steering or brakes!" he said.

She shrunk back, and the car sped off.

"How the hell did you know to stow a knife under your bed?" asked Tom.

"I always have a knife, near me and on me. I'm paranoid. Shit!"

The Fiat barely missed the rear bumper of a large robobus ferrying a high school football team.

"Then learn to use it," said Tom. "And why are you still living at home? You make good money."

"It's safe. My family loves me and wants me to be happy . . ." She started to cry. "Transitioning is hard enough . . . and to have my family help . . ."

Major Tom continued to monitor the cameras at the Gascon house. Winter had dressed and wrapped her wound. She was standing up, her expression betraying concentration.

Downstairs, Mrs. Gascon grabbed her handbag, not understanding the urgency of her daughter's command. As she put her GO into her bag, it exploded, shocking and burning her hand.

Upstairs, Winter heard the scream and smirked.

Bang! A HOME screen exploded in another room.

"Housenet, stop," said Mrs. Gascon.

Bang! *BANG!* The other HOME screens exploded.

"Housenet, *stop!*" she yelled.

The refrigerator's doors flew open, its shelves spewing milk, eggs, meats, cheeses, and bottles of soda and juice. Mrs. Gascon made for the door but slipped on the tile floor and fell, knocking her head hard on the counter. A trickle of blood ran from her hair. The toaster and electric oven continued turning on and off until the fuses shorted. But the alarms were silent, and the sprinklers were off. Stunned and scared, she huddled on the floor.

Winter had hacked into the Net of Things. Up-to-date appliances and smart houses had net connections animating once inanimate objects. Refrigerators put in orders for delivery via robovan or drone. Occupants could turn off lights or ovens, lock doors, or start air conditioners before they returned home, either remotely or on automatic schedules. People had forgotten how to do basic things, and few companies cared how dangerous this might turn out to be if someone or something hacked into the systems. They didn't pay for anything beyond the appearance of security. It was always cheaper to pay off lawsuits than to preempt them.

A small explosion rocked the garage. The solar array and batteries short-circuited. A fire began to smolder, and it would soon spread. Mrs. Gascon sat dumbfounded on the kitchen floor, too confused and in pain to understand.

Major Tom would not let Mrs. Gascon die or let the evidence of Winter's deeds be destroyed, so he sent messages to the local police and fire departments, using the identity of the next-door neighbor, Mr. Alonzo Terranova, who might feasibly have heard the explosion and seen smoke if he had been home.

Winter limped slowly downstairs to inspect her mischief, holding Veronika's DNA relic of Thomas Paine. She stared at Mrs. Gascon, crying and wet in a puddle of milk, eggs, juice, and condiments, her burnt and bloody hand applying pressure to her head wound.

"Please, help me up," asked Mrs. Gascon, who then apparently noticed Winter's injuries. "You're hurt, too! Let's get help!"

A nearby siren sounded. Winter smirked and limped back into the hallway toward the foyer, where she discovered a camera lens discreetly hidden in a wall sconce near the front door. She held up the crystal DNA display and waved it with a smile. "Souvenir!" Then she winked at the camera.

All the cameras went black.

Back in the Fiat, Veronika watched on her GO and wept.

CHAPTER NINETEEN

Your mom's going to be okay," Tom said. "We have to talk."

"Are you crazy? Did you see that?" wailed Veronika.

"I've got fire and police almost there. I know Carter. Your mom's not worth it to him. He's taken off."

"She's probably killing my mom right now!"

"If I could shake you by the shoulders or slap your face, I would. And why did you play Mata Hari up there? Concentrate! How did he find you?"

"Pronouns, dude! *She's* taken off. *She* found me!" Veronika punched at her car's directional control. "I'm going back right now."

"I'm keeping control. We can see your mom on satellite. Look."

Veronika saw a zoomed image of what looked like her mom, staggering out of the burning house toward a fire truck pulling into the driveway. Major Tom zoomed out, and they could both see more fire trucks heading to the house along Foothill Avenue.

"She's okay," soothed Tom. "Now, I'm sorry, but how did Winter find you?"

Veronika's crying abated. She struggled to concentrate. "Someone followed me back from Prometheus?"

"Right, but that was hard. You shut us out from tracking, and I still don't know how you disappeared. If I had a hard time, so would Carter or the club. Can they follow us now?"

(ID)ENTITY

"I don't think so. We're masked as a Toyota Prius in the DMV GPS database."

"Was it always a Prius?"

"No. It randomly chooses a new common make and model every time the engine starts. Unless I disable it. I've got it on a random timed revolution now." She wiped her tears. "At the moment it's a Chevy Malibu that came from the supermarket parking lot."

"What about highway cameras?" Cops didn't bother with live speed traps anymore. With robocars connected to the data grid and obeying the laws automatically, cameras were built into the highways at regular intervals so that old-fashioned cars could be tracked. There were rarely live police on the highways anymore.

"Special optical shield over the entire car exterior. And I've disabled all the built-in identi-chips."

"So the cops can't find us easily if I speed?"

She stifled another sniffle. "Go nuts. We're in a ghost."

The car immediately took off as though possessed, searching for back roads to avoid any police just passing through. It wasn't as fast as Tom had hoped, but what Fiat 500 was?

"How much do we think Carter knows about you?" asked Tom.

"He found my car. He knows what I look like and where I live. But it can't be much more or, like, she would have killed me instantly. It felt like she wanted to get to know me and get, like, information. Or turn me."

"I agree," said Tom. "How much could she get from your room, beyond your obsession?"

"Not much. My setup is too partitioned, and it's activated by biometrics."

"You promise?"

"Yes!" yelled Veronika.

"But she knows your interest in me, with all that crap you've got," said Tom.

"It's not crap . . . ," she said, sniffling quietly.

"And all this is leading us away from Dr. Who. The deeper we go, the further away we get."

"Where's the second robot?" she asked.

"Getting there soon. I hope."

"Is Mom okay?" asked Veronika.

Major Tom zoomed back in. Paramedics took care of Mrs. Gascon while firefighters put out the fire.

"What about your dad? And your brother and sister?"

"At work, probably." Veronika saw they were avoiding the 101 and heading down mountain back roads for the Pacific Coast Highway. "Where are we going?"

"Back to the *Zumwalt*," said Tom.

"But my family . . . ?"

"Messaging them right now." He pretended he was with the Santa Barbara Police Department by sending the message from a real investigating officer's GO.

"You never considered that playing spy would get your family hurt?" he asked.

"I thought I was . . . like . . . smarter than them." She teared up again, curling into her seat.

He didn't want to torture her with all the failures of intellect he'd already lived through, like conspiracies, betrayal, murder, war, and chaos. "Well, now you know. No one—and nothing—is smart enough for every contingency. There's always failure."

"Then why do you do it?" asked Veronika.

"I have no choice. No one else can do what I can. And I started all this."

CHAPTER TWENTY

Reengineered, reprogrammed, and rebuilt—a robot's version of tanned, rested, and ready—Tom 1 swung from a body harness over the Pacific Ocean. He was lowered by winch from an old V-22 Osprey, a long-range tiltrotor aircraft that could take off and land like a helicopter but, with rotors forward, could also fly quickly and far like an airplane. Major Tom and Ruth had liberated the old piece of US military hardware from the same naval admiral who had sold them the *Zumwalt*. On his back was a sizable waterproof backpack full of anything he might need for this journey, including some crucial robotic replacement parts so he could self-repair if necessary.

Below him was a small tanker, painted white with huge red crosses on her sides and stern. Retrofitted into a hospital ship, it plied the Pacific's seasteads and port towns for procedures that were too complicated or expensive for the communities to manage with their own medical support teams. Above the red cross on her stern was her name, *Savior*.

From the upturned faces below him on the ship's deck, Major Tom could see incredulity and concern. He read one man's lips. "What the fuck are we doing with a sexbot? Crew's not that lonely." The speaker was a big, brawny fellow. Curly dark-brown hair. Muscular, but with a beer belly. Full, thick facial hair over olive skin. Smiled a lot. Tom 1 found a single facial recognition hit, deeply buried. It identified him as Franklyn Gottbetter, once of New York. That's all he could find.

Tom 1 lipread the response of a grizzled face next to Gottbetter. "Just catch it in one piece."

From the shaved head to the sea-worn skin to the respectful body language of the other crew to the eyes taking in the scene at once—it all added up to "Captain." Facial recognition and searches of the captain's background came up empty, no matter how far he dug. As Veronika would say, "Dude's a ghost."

So was the ship. Her name was on no ship registry or crew manifest anywhere in the world. The only history was in photos or social media that mentioned the remarkable rescues it had accrued over the last few years. The more unstable the world became, the more work the *Savior*'s team had to accomplish. Major Tom also noticed that no faces or identities were revealed in any links to the ship, which must have maintained a vigorous data-scrubbing team to keep it as anonymous as possible. He could imagine the reasons why. In a world where doctors may not have borders, they could still be targets. He would let Gottbetter know that he found a search hit, so their team could eliminate that as well.

The captain nodded to Gottbetter and walked back to the ship's bridge.

Gottbetter manned the hook that grabbed the drop cable and guided Tom 1 down to the deck. He unlatched the harnesses and got the rig clear, waving to the Osprey crew that they were good to go. They did.

This might be a one-way trip, but Tom 1 hoped not. Despite its balance issues, awkward movements, and limited use, he was nevertheless coming to rely on and even like this ridiculous mechanical body, his mind quickly adapting to its new conditions and parameters.

A handful of crew members stood around, staring at Tom 1. Gottbetter broke the spell. "All right, back to stations. We got folks to take care of!" He turned to Tom 1, looked him up and down. "Okay . . . Sexy-3PO, follow me."

"Are you a doctor?" asked Tom 1.

"Ha! Funny. Do I look like one?" asked Gottbetter.

"I admit you don't act like one."

"I'm the chief officer. And chief cook and bottle washer. And chief cut-up, according to Cap. Short of surgery, I can do most anything on this ship. But I'm a hell of a nurse."

"And what's the captain's name again?" asked Tom 1.

Gottbetter grinned with big white teeth. "That's Captain Anonymous to you, Dreamboat! Can't get me with that one. He pays me."

Inside, the ship looked remarkably like a hospital, down to the lino-leum floors; sound-paneled ceilings; and clever wall-mounted storage and deployment solutions, portable imaging machines, and operating tables. But the ceilings were lower, barely eight feet high, to accommodate as many floors, beds, and operating rooms as possible inside the ship's frame.

They continued up metal stairs and met the captain in a small, spartan conference room off the bridge, painted the same dull white as the rest of the ship and strangely bare. He could see pinholes on the wall that might once have held thumbtacks. And an empty bookcase.

"Captain," said Tom 1, "thank you for taking me to the *Meropis* with you." Meropis was the mythical island invented by Theopompis of Chios as a parody of Plato's Atlantis. According to the ancient Greek writer, life there was bigger, crazier, and more contradictory than the utopian perfection of Atlantis, like an ancient Athenian's idea of Texas.

"The right money talks. Especially now," said Captain.

"When will we get there?" asked Tom 1.

"A day," said Captain. "Give or take."

Major Tom had already calculated their arrival to be in 23.4 hours. Captain was not giving anything away.

"And what exactly will you be doing there?" asked Tom 1.

"We got messages that they were attacked. Pirates. There are survivors, but no more food, medical supplies, or working medical equipment. We're there to pick the survivors up and care for them."

"And when and where exactly did you receive the messages?"

"A week ago," said Captain.

"Captain," said Tom 1, "I understand the necessity of your secrecy, both politically and as medical personnel. But I'm here to play a bigger game, and the more I know, the more I might help you, too. And maybe prevent more of these attacks."

Gottbetter shared a look with his captain. "Cap, he's got a point."

The captain got up and began pacing. He looked out the only small window. Tom 1 could tell he wasn't made for quiet reflection and felt claustrophobic in the small room. "We were still off Lima, Peru, providing care offshore after the food riots. Local hospitals had been looted and burned. No supplies. Doctors in hiding, trying to survive. Complete disaster." The captain's face reflected the tragedy he had witnessed. "Before that, we were providing abortions off the coast of Brazil. Women die there all the time from dangerous pregnancies and self-abortions. With no birth control, they're saddled with sick or dying children. We had a ship full of desperate women. Wish we could have taken them with us."

"Why didn't you?" asked Tom 1.

"Brazil threatened us with kidnapping charges and a declaration of war," said Captain. "Said they'd fire on us if we tried."

"Don't seasteads provide abortions?" asked Tom 1.

"Too far away and still expensive. Women need vessels and fuel money to get there. And most seasteads are profit-centers. Rich women can always get the medical attention they need. Poor women can't."

"And *Meropis* still needs you after all this time?" asked Tom 1. "Aren't you worried there will be no one left?"

"We hope we can help save some survivors," said Captain. "Regardless, they're finished. We're the cleanup crew. And I don't understand how you can help."

"I think I know who's attacking the seasteads. It's a single group. Since the *Sovereign* and others were destroyed and sunk, I need any evidence that remains to confirm it. The *Meropis* is the most likely to give it to me. Only then do we have a hope of stopping more atrocities like these. And making less work for you."

CHAPTER TWENTY-ONE

Precisely 23.4 hours later, the hospital ship made anchor next to the *Meropis*. Until the last few weeks, seasteads numbered in the hundreds around the globe. Some were close to national shores and in cooperation with their local governments. Others, far out at sea, were independent. These were the victims of recent attacks.

Seasteads attracted the same people who, for hundreds of years, had immigrated to the New World: the restless, persecuted, ambitious, subjugated, antisocial, antigovernment, dreamers, builders, and wanderers of every stripe. Seasteads were the new frontier, where pioneers could try out or reboot political systems, economic and business models, and lifestyles. None was big enough to prove that any particular model would work once it was replicated at a large enough scale, but that didn't stop the experimentation.

Unlike the *Sovereign*, which was a self-contained, fully functional, permanent facility and community, *Meropis* was an "archipelago" of attached and semiattached vessels, changeable by design. A central core provided power, desalinated water, IT support, computing power, and first aid, but the rest was essentially building blocks at sea. Participants could motor or sail their vessel in, then join or leave. Ships and barges could link to specially built midocean anchorages. Seasteaders who bought matching modular units could join them to the larger modular community. It was a quirky, do-it-yourself, libertarian's wet dream, the central facilities owned and operated by a core group of investors as a profit-making venture. Who came and went, and what they did while they were there, was completely up to the individual vessels' owners.

As a reasonably successful Pacific seastead, they were busy. Beyond cryptocurrency and blockchain generation, they produced generic and custom pharmaceuticals, away from nations' pharma bureaucracies. Algae farms produced biofuel. Servers for meshnet-based economic markets innovated outside of government regulations. *Meropis* also functioned as a tax haven for companies whose addresses could change with the hoisting of an anchor. If neighbors' disagreements were intractable, aggrieved parties were urged to pick up their toys and find more hospitable waters. *Meropis* represented only one of a few successful archipelago arrangements afloat. None of the ad hoc ventures grew too large for too long, though. Dunbar's Number postulated that the members of any community larger than 100–250 ceased to know one another directly, and so social pressure could not exert enough force to encourage fair dealing. If you couldn't trust someone you didn't know, they probably didn't trust you, either. Good faith was hard to scale. When groups grew too large, governments, "trusted" middlemen, or verification systems like blockchains came in to recreate trust. Those already attracted to such an independent lifestyle were averse to notions of bureaucratic oversight or law enforcement. So there was no authority, for better and for worse.

Unfortunately, despite the connectivity of seemingly endless social media, humans still had neolithic brains. Seasteads worked if the 'steaders cared about their immediate tribe. And the *Meropis* was a tribe, though there wasn't much of it left.

The reconnaissance dinghy from the *Savior* approached the *Meropis*. On board, Tom 1, Gottbetter, Captain, and a triage doctor named Joanne took in the destruction. Only two ships floated at an attached anchor. The first was a 174-foot ketch motor-sailor yacht, with *Independent* painted on its stern. Once a famous luxury craft worth about $100 million, its two masts, booms, all its rigging, and most of the top deck were gone. The other was a large ocean barge retrofitted with prefab buildings atop it, but it now looked like a floating, blackened brick with a drizzling of burnt wreckage.

They motored to the central core, careful to be as quiet as possible. Tom 1 saw no sign of survivors at the surface, and no bodies. He assumed they had been dumped overboard, or taken by the sea or its animals. At the central hub, Gottbetter jumped off the boat to lash the dinghy to an exposed beam of a partially wrecked dock. Captain helped the robot out of the boat and he, Joanne, and Gottbetter grabbed a bunch of duffel and tech bags, including medical kits, Tom 1's backpack, and portable emergency supplies. Tom 1 still didn't have reliable sea legs, although he was learning. They stood around a locked metal door, which they suspected would lead down into the central underwater core of the facility.

Picking up a piece of loose, twisted metal, Captain used it to knock on a sealed metal hatch. The rhythm was —.—.— —.—, the international Morse code for "calling." He did it again. No response. Then a third time. And a fourth.

Joanne, her triage kits loaded on her back, looked worried. "Cap, we could be too late."

They heard scraping of metal on metal from behind the door. The great bolt moved, and the hatch swung open slowly. A shaking, emaciated hand emerged, holding a gun. Tom 1 could see the safety was off, and the trigger finger was too twitchy not to be a threat.

Captain spoke calmly and quickly, "Code name, Deliverance. I'm the captain of the *Savior*. Permission to come aboard and begin patient transport."

The gun trembled in place for a moment, then lowered and disappeared. The door opened wide, and a young man emerged, midtwenties, with long brown hair and a long beard, shirtless and barefoot, wearing only filthy, ripped jeans and a furious visage.

"Took you long enough!" the survivor barked at them.

"We did the best we could," said Captain. "How many of you are there?"

"Down to fourteen. We had three more die after we called you," said the survivor.

"I am truly sorry," Captain said. He nodded to Gottbetter, who stepped aside and contacted the ship to send more medical staff and a larger transport for the patients. The dinghy would hold only six beyond themselves.

The young man saw Tom 1 for the first time. "What the fuck is that?"

Captain deadpanned, "Wish I knew. But he's here to help. What's your name?"

"Tanner Delaney."

"Thank you for your help, Tanner. Can you lead us to them?" asked Captain.

They descended into the bowels of the platform. This seastead design relied on old oil-platform technologies, paired with new sustainable-energy generation from sun and waves. Like many seasteads, it was built like an iceberg: a tiny bit exposed on top, much more space below. The steps were covered in debris. It was dark, so they lit their bodylamps on their hats and vests. Tom 1 couldn't smell, but by all the decomposition of sea life and possible human remains, he assumed it would have reeked. Captain, Joanne, and Gottbetter seemed inured to it, although Gottbetter squinted.

"Elevators are out," said Tanner. "Too dangerous. We have to carry them up. Shut down all unnecessary systems. There's a little power that's reliable since the batteries were damaged. Today's okay, lots of sun and current, but we try to use only what's needed for survival."

Fifty feet below the surface, they reached a reinforced metal door. Tanner knocked in a code. The door unlocked and opened.

Inside it must have smelled even worse. Tom 1 saw Gottbetter involuntarily recoil and wrinkle his nose. Captain remained unaffected and resolute. Joanne rushed in to assess the patients.

There were thirteen men and women locked inside. A thirty-something man in a bloody T-shirt that read *Why* not *me?* was missing his right arm at the bicep, its tourniquet black-red from blood loss. He looked sweaty and gray in pallor. A younger woman had her head wrapped in bloody gauze. Her breath came haltingly, and her eyes looked vacant. Others had a variety of wounds that would prove equally fatal if they didn't get care soon. Six survivors seemed functional, moving about, tending the others. A woman in her forties, who if she hadn't been as filthy as Tanner would have looked like a Silicon Valley executive on a tropical vacation, complete with floral print dress, came forward quickly.

"Are you doctors?" she asked.

Joanne said, "I am. And he's an aide." She pointed to Gottbetter. "And there's several more coming in a few minutes."

"I think she needs help first," she said, pointing to the woman with the head wound.

Tom 1 gently touched Tanner on the shoulder and gestured to him to talk privately. "Do you know who did this?"

"Who the fuck do you think? Pirates!"

Tom 1 walked him slowly away from the patients. "Shhh . . . What did they take?"

"Fuck knows! They tried to kill us all."

"Is there anyone here who's IT?" asked Tom 1.

Tanner tried hard to hold back tears. "Just me. Toni died a week ago. Amir died in the attack."

"While the *Savior* crew evacuates your friends, can you take me to your hub?"

"It's dead. No communications in or out."

"Can it be powered up?" asked Tom 1.

"The core, yes, but to nothing. Transmitter is gone."

Tom 1 was both surprised and excited. "I just need to access your hard drives and servers."

"But—"

"Please. I'm trying to help figure out who did this so we can stop them."

Tanner stared blankly, as if he had finally lost his mind. After all the death and destruction he'd witnessed, he was arguing with a robot. He leaned against the steel wall, as though he might faint.

Tom 1 reached out to steady him. "We can do this. Just take it slow."

Trudging through dark corridors and staircases lit only by Tom 1's bodylamps, Tanner let them into a large compartment with monitors and servers. The server farm was not here. It was in a separate compartment further down, cooled by pipes of icy seawater. Some of these communities could be amazingly low-tech, but as Ruth always said, the older and simpler ways were often best. Too complex a system could fall apart without the means to repair it.

He wondered what that meant for his future.

"I need you to direct power back to the system," said Tom 1. "Can you do that?"

"Yeah, but you won't have power for long," said Tanner. He went to the wall of switches and breakers.

"Don't need it long. We'll all be out of here soon."

Tanner's last bit of willpower finally left him, and he slid down the steel wall into a fetal heap on the floor.

"Are you okay?" asked Tom 1.

"Am I hallucinating?" asked Tanner.

Tom 1 continued to work. "What do you see?"

"A robot operating my trashed system?"

"Not hallucinating," said Tom 1. "There are energy bars in the front zipper of my bag. Please eat."

Tanner had no strength to disobey. Between mouthfuls, he asked, "Why do you have food? You don't eat, do you?"

"No, I don't. But my human friends do."

Major Tom dove into the data on the monitor, searching for patterns, signs, clues. He found plenty of sequestered and malware-ridden files for cryptocurrencies, identity, and the complete history of the seastead. They contained hideous viruses designed to download and send all data to a hidden source. Tom 1 visually cataloged all he could. Unlike the *Sovereign*, this facility didn't have enough cryptocurrency or identity clientele for the "pirates" to keep up the appearance of its continuing to operate.

Among the data, he found sequences, commands, protocols, and malware that could have been the same as what Dr. Who would have dealt with on the *Sovereign*. Security camera footage showed the attack from the *Meropis*'s point of view, with a waterspout, laser lightning, and a microboat swarm, just like the *Sovereign*, except that the attackers hadn't killed all the occupants. The mercenaries had disabled the seastead enough to copy files, infect the hell out of the IT, and ruin satellite communications. Then they left the *Meropis*—and its survivors—to rot in the Pacific. Their mistake was leaving an old-school hobbyist's HAM radio transmitter intact in a seasteader's bedroom. The survivors had used it to send the SOS received by the *Savior*. They should have been discovered for sending a signal, but few paid any attention to HAM radios anymore. Luckily, ships like the *Savior* still maintained fully operational radio rooms for this type of emergency.

Tom 1's eyes recorded what he needed to send back to the team for analysis. But he was looking for something more. He found a verbal conversation recorded moments before the seastead was destroyed. It sounded similar to what Dr. Who had described. And he recognized both voices.

"Tanner," he said, "you took a call before the attack. What do you remember?"

"That guy was a total asshole," Tanner said. "Wanted to do business. But so stuck up and full of himself. I only figured he was trying to distract me when it was too late."

The other voice was Carter's, and Tom 1 had the distinct feeling that he was meant to find it.

But why, with the valuable Dr. Who captured from the *Sovereign*, would they hit all the seasteads? The only threats that seastead culture posed were decentralization, a renewal of nanomanufacturing, lack of regulations, and a belief in the value of individuals over nations. But the movement was still scattered around the globe, on a much smaller scale than nation-states, so what or whom could the seasteads threaten? How were they worth all this coordinated killing and destruction?

Tom 1 sent a message to Captain's GO: *After this, I'll arrange to leave you. Your money is in the account, but I've quadrupled it for additional food and supplies. There will be more midocean seasteads attacked, especially if they're run by Westerners. They may all be hit by now. If there are survivors, they'll need help. I'm sending you the coordinates and contact information. If you need anything else, let me know.*

On it, replied Captain. *And thank you for caring.*

Tom 1 added, *Thank you, Captain. And good luck. We're all going to need it.*

CHAPTER TWENTY-TWO

A crate marked *Companibots* had made its way onto a container ship headed from Los Angeles to the Wenzhou Longwan International Airport, south of Shanghai. In hibernation mode, Tom 2 had been tracked by GPS and monitored until the crate was opened. Standing in nothing more than a covered shed, two import workers—hired by Miss Gray Hat to supervise the crate as it made its way through customs—opened the top with power drills. Under layers of packing material, they found a Mr. Handsome/James Bond model, predressed in a black T-shirt, black jeans, and black boots.

When the light hit his optic receptors, Tom 2 turned on, sat up, surveyed his location, looked at the two longshoremen, and in Mandarin said, *"Nín hǎo."*

Both screamed. One swung his crowbar in shock, but Tom 2 ducked, avoiding a costly accident. Apparently, neither worker expected a life-like android that engaged them right out of the box.

"I am Tom 2, a self-activated robot," he continued in Mandarin. "Thank you for releasing me to meet my masters. I have been programmed to go straight to their offices. I will do that right now, if you would please allow me." He made a little bow of gratitude. The workers just stared.

Climbing awkwardly out of the crate, Tom 2 headed for the door with a little wave. *"Zàijiàn!"* The workers didn't try to stop him.

He exited the airport shed and walked toward town, adjusting his GPS and following the maps. The city of Wenzhou had many skyscrapers, but also a preponderance of older, well-maintained buildings. He loaded up on a local cybercurrency, the *Yāsuìqián*, Mandarin for "lucky money," then logged into the city's network to do a little digging.

Ringed by mountains on three sides and ocean on the fourth, Wenzhou had long enjoyed the advantage of geographical isolation. A small but flourishing agricultural and entrepreneurial center for a thousand years, it was so isolated that even Mao had ignored it during the depths of his revolution. Why bend a secluded region to a political will when it cost so much to get there and enforce authority, and for so little in return? After a millennium of business experience, the culture of Wenzhou thought little of supporting new businesses just to see what might succeed. China had decided decades before that Wenzhou would be a great place for economic experimentation in government-sanctioned capitalism. But the gray and black markets thrived, too, and the residents were a more independent-thinking, risk-taking, and community-minded lot than those in most other Chinese cities.

The isolation even extended to the language: Wenzhouese was its own dialect, nicknamed the "devil language" by Mandarin and Cantonese speakers for its unintelligibility and difficulty to learn. Tom 2 did a quick analysis with the scant translation apps available for the rare dialect.

Thankful for maps, he navigated the streets. Wenzhou was designed by businesspeople for their personal use and concerns. While the big roads made sense, the small streets began and ended arbitrarily in countless dead ends and weird loops.

A female humanoid robot approached him and passed right by. It could have been a sexbot, but it was not as life-like as the American cousins, nor as technically sophisticated as Tom 2's body. Other robots looked like trash cans on wheels, pack-animal couriers, or small scurrying machines that might be collecting ground-level intelligence for the government. No humans shoulder-checked or tripped the androids. Little kids petted the animal-like bots as they passed, then giggled and ran away. Tom 2 spotted three drones in the skies above. He hoped they knew he was here.

Despite all these robots, there was a strange lack of high-tech companies in town, according to his research. The Wenzhouese were heavily involved in real estate, currencies, fashion, and small manufacturing. Their vast international network of business-owning relatives, especially in Europe and North America, meant that a lot of capital, imports, and exports flowed through the city.

At a loss to make up for the drop in manufacturing output after a global recession and geopolitical restructuring, the Chinese government used Wenzhou's networks and independence for more marginal and quasi-illegal activities, pumping capital into fronts for all types of money laundering and counterfeit goods.

All the capital and contracts required a lot of blockchain entries to prove ownership and track the movement of goods. Did the financial blockchain sabotage originate here? Was that why the kidnappers were here, too? And how did Dr. Who fit into their plans?

A uniformed policeman approached, dressed in the traditional summer outfit of the *chengguang* or City Urban Administrative and Law Enforcement Bureau: a light-blue short-sleeved button-down shirt with black patches and silver embroidery, black pants, and black-laced shoes. He was of average height and build for the Southern Chinese, short compared to Tom 2. But his quick, penetrating, and analytical gaze suggested high intelligence, not some cog in the state surveillance machine.

He looked up at Tom 2 and asked in Wenzhouese, "Are you Thomas Paine?"

Tom 2 paused before answering. The *chengguang* were so notorious for arbitrary attacks and beatings that the word became slang for police bullying and terror. Even though he didn't seem like a mere beat cop looking for a fight, Tom 2 would have to answer carefully.

The officer asked again in Mandarin.

Tom 2 took an intuitive leap, which he hadn't done as a robot yet. "Yes. And I'm here to help. And you are?"

"Cai Shuxian. And we hope you can."

CHAPTER TWENTY-THREE

Through Talia's and Veronika's MR glasses, Major Tom monitored them and Ruth as they dodged gurneys, residents, nurses, and family members in the crowded, aging hallways of Los Angeles County+USC Medical Center. The women wore green medical scrubs and forged ID tags with full hospital access around their necks. Even though the practice of medicine was supposed to have become more automated, with robot gurneys, robot nurses, and robot surgeons, the reality on the ground in a huge municipal hospital had not improved much since the twentieth century. Sick and helpless bodies were tended by the healthy. Dead bodies were mourned and removed. The only visible difference was that doctors, nurses, and administrators communicated through electronics.

Ruth opened the door to Room 345, and they quietly entered. She shut the door behind them.

"God, this is creepy," whispered Veronika as she and Ruth approached the bed.

Hugging the walls, Talia would not approach the bed.

"Talia?" asked Ruth. "You okay?"

Talia nodded. "Brings back memories. I haven't been in a hospital room since . . ." She couldn't say the rest.

Ruth nodded. "Since Tom died. Me neither."

The room was darkened by the nursing staff out of habit, but it didn't matter. The young man lying in the bed wouldn't be disturbed by light.

Part of the patient's head was shaved. The rest of his straight black hair, neat but greasy, was combed away from his incisions. His goatee and mustache had overgrown. His skin had the gray pallor of the seriously injured. The only sounds were the beeps and whooshing of the resuscitation machine and monitors.

Ruth waved her forged tag at a sensor and logged into the electronic chart. Major Tom read the chart through Veronika's glasses. He didn't want to leave any more electronic footprints on the original files than he had to, even though Veronika invented a self-destruct program to protect their IDs. All the data would disappear the moment the team walked out the doors.

This was their guy: Rosero, Edwin—male, twenty-one, six one, 195 pounds of pure muscle, only slightly atrophied by his injury and immobility. Worked in a gym. Motorcycle accident, hit and run. Head trauma to neocortex. Persistent vegetative state. Neocortical death.

"He's really a vegetable?" asked Veronika.

Ruth rolled her ticky eyes. "Vegetative state. Not vegetable."

"Sure he can't hear us?" asked Veronika.

"P-p-positive," mumbled Ruth. "Neocortex ECoG is flat. Nobody home. But autonomic system still good. Relatives aren't claiming him. Doctors will pull plug tomorrow. No organ donation. Headed for crematorium and disposal."

Veronika tentatively touched his exposed hand.

"Chilly."

The hand twitched. Veronika yelped and yanked her hand back in shock.

"He knows we're here!" she said.

"No. Involuntary reflex," said Ruth.

"You're sure?" said Veronika.

"Yes! Stop *kvetching*," said Ruth, her mouth twitching in rictus. "He's sp-p-plendid. Talia? Call Steve for the ambulance."

Talia text messaged Steve, *Ready? You're the only one I trust for this.*

He messaged back, *Promise me again I'm not a stooge. That I make my own clinical and ethical decisions. I don't want last time to happen again.*

Promise, she messaged back.

They often forgot that Major Tom monitored their conversations. He didn't like to eavesdrop, but too much was on the line. After Steve's ethical pushback, which had begun three years ago when Tom's brain-computer interfaces were installed, there was no way he'd let Steve stop this now.

After the women prepped Edwin Rosero for transport, the team transferred the young man's body, along with the necessary life-support equipment, into an ambulance. They looked as official as the rest of the hospital staff, and their data checked out, so the LAC+USC medical staff ignored them.

The moment they exited the building, all their data disappeared, just as Veronika had planned.

They loaded the body in the ambulance. Steve arrived and joined them inside. Ruth and Veronika knew that much remained unsaid between Talia and Steve, and they kept their mouths shut.

Talia leaned in, kissed Steve, and took his hand. "It's going to be okay," she said.

He squeezed her hand but avoided her eyes. "You always say that. And it never is."

CHAPTER TWENTY-FOUR

The view of the Wenzhou basin from the Dongtou Islands was impressive. Twisted, bulbous mountains and atolls rose from the sea like the famous eleventh-century Chinese landscape *A Thousand Li of Rivers and Mountains*. Its classic style was no mere artistic affectation. The landscape was torturously vertical and surreal.

Tom 2 and Cai Shuxian stood at a large picture window in an empty dining hall full of round tables and banquet chairs and hung with festive red drapes, lucky banners, and gold-leaf trim. The window afforded a 180-degree view of the mainland and ocean. Cai had escorted him to this abandoned hotel complex in Dasha'ao on the southwest corner of Dongtou Island. Tom 2 wondered why this place was important and scanned every way he could: ultraviolet, infrared, black and white, underwater surveillance, satellite imagery. He zoomed in and out, panning all cameras as far as their mounts would allow. He searched the net for any relationships that might matter. But nothing was obvious.

Major Tom and Miss Gray Hat had run Cai's face through governmental and private security facial-recognition databases, but it would take some time. China was successful at burying their intelligence personnel. People like Cai often had no imprint either on the web or in social media. Thousands of data operators did nothing all day but use search algorithms to scrub the Chinese net of information. Cai and his lot were the ghosts of the information age.

Tom 2 asked Cai, "Why me? Why here? Why now?"

"You are a fascinating technological specimen," said Cai. "A type we haven't yet perfected ourselves."

"So I'm a future template? You plan to keep me?" asked Tom 2.

Cai looked placidly out at the ocean. "No. It is enough to observe your capabilities."

"But that doesn't answer 'why *me*?'" said Tom 2. "Why are you interested in Thomas Paine?"

"In Wenzhou," said Cai, "it's all about *guanxi*: relationships. Our city, national, and international networks are built on *guanxi*, more than any other city in China. Major Tom is now part of those relationships, and we value that."

"Okay, so you won't answer the question," said Tom 2. "A Virginia-class sub surfaced fifty miles off the coast of Wenzhou this morning. Why here?"

Cai sighed. "Yes, we should have assumed you'd see that." He pointed east. "It discharged passengers onto a vessel bringing contraband fish in with a government official's permission to the processing plant. Beijing will turn a blind eye to the activity."

"What's contraband fish?" asked Tom 2.

"Here, whale shark is popular. Wenzhou still finds many uses for it. Lipstick, vitamin supplements, shark leather, shark fin soup."

"Is the boat here yet?"

"We don't think so," said Cai.

"And who exactly is 'we' again?" asked Tom 2. "As much as the uniform fits, you're no *chengguang*."

Cai bowed his head slightly. "It is my fault that I failed to convince you."

"Are you Ministry of State Security?" China's intelligence and security agency was responsible for all domestic, foreign, and counterintelligence gathering, as if the FBI, CIA, DHS, and NSA were a single entity. As such, they were extremely centralized and powerful.

Cai ignored the question. "We're monitoring activity offshore," he said. "Based on its course, the fishing vessel carrying the new passenger is likely to dock here on Dongtou Island first, then proceed to the Port of Wenzhou. Extra passengers, especially one as unusual as Dr. Who, are likely to be noticed at the city port. And a commercial fishing boat docking on Dongtou is unusual. It's a tourist area. Fish is processed on the Wenzhou mainland."

"And 'we' is . . . ?" asked Tom 2 again.

Cai laughed.

Tom 2 needed more information on the islands. He and Major Tom had analyzed a variety of maps from different years and compared them chronologically. There had long been many islands off the coast of Wenzhou, but there were more now than had been there twenty years ago. The manufactured islands were China's first imperial move of the modern era and edged into the territorial waters of Taiwan. After years of "are they or aren't they," China had finally told Taiwan, "You're mine now." Taiwan had little choice. Other island nations followed.

"So this isn't about the annexation of Taiwan, the Philippines, or, say, the entire Western Pacific?"

"Taiwan and the Western Pacific have been ours for centuries."

"Tell the Taiwanese, Japanese, and Filipinos that."

"We do." Cai smiled.

He was right. According to the maps, hundreds of new islands now encroached on Japan's territorial waters. And the Philippines were officially annexed, surrounded by new Chinese islands with landing fields and military bases.

"What do you believe is the significance of the message we intercepted?" asked Tom 2. "'Doctor is ready. Meet Qi Jiguang.' I know who the historical Qi Jiguang is, but . . ." He attempted a shrug.

"The Chinese coast is fourteen thousand five hundred kilometers long," explained Cai. "Over nine thousand miles. That's a great deal of coastline to monitor. The only oceanfront statue of Qi Jiguang is on this island. Since we're looking for submarines and fishing boats, this is the only logical location. And the boat's course is heading straight for it."

"Do you think it's state-sponsored, or gang piracy?" asked Tom 2.

"Possibly both. As in Qi Jiguang's day, many pirates are still supported by the Chinese government," said Cai. "There's much money in it, especially for the sons and daughters of the powerful. One must tread carefully and know when to stop investigating to make any progress. The government wants both law enforcement success and personal protection from it."

"So if we meet them, we don't know if they're independent or paid for by the government."

Cai paused in thought. "Truly, no. And it doesn't matter. Both are correct. And incorrect. Depending on the day, the weather, and the latest headlines."

"Understood," said Tom 2. "Corruption is commonplace here."

Cai bristled for the first time. "Your own banks, and your once ferocious Phoenix Club, hired the same scions of our Politburo for leverage into China's economy. I'd say you have as much corruption as we do."

"I do not represent the former United States. I have nothing to do with the banks or the club," said Tom 2. "I'm here to save Dr. Who."

"We know you believe that. We read your book." Cai grinned. "Or what's left of it."

"Why say 'believe that'?"

"Everything is about money," said Cai. "And therefore, banks. And governments."

"Or cryptocurrency farms in the Chinese hinterlands."

Cai bowed his head.

"And you didn't have anything to do with either her kidnapping or my story's alteration?" Tom 2 continued. "Dr. Who would be valuable to you. As would rewriting history."

"Of course we're not responsible," said Cai. Based on physical tells, he seemed to believe this. "Eliminating the Phoenix Club did China a great service. You are a revolutionary hero to many here. That is why we are helping you now. And if we wanted Dr. Who, we would never have caused so much trouble to acquire her services. She's more valuable to us back with you."

"So what's the next step to find her?"

"We will locate where her ship is and make sure we're there to meet it before they can make landfall," Cai said. "Perhaps someone will let us know."

"And why would they do that?"

"Because, as I implied earlier, Dr. Who is not the reason you're here."

Tom 2 sent all his sensory data to Major Tom's servers, as well as to Ruth, Miss Gray Hat, and Veronika. Veronika had moved onto the *Zumwalt* as an official member of the gang.

"Well?" Tom asked her.

"Oh my God, this dome is, like, the most bitchin' thing ever!" said Veronika. "Like holodeck meets floating in womb space. And, like, so efficient and organic." She had made a nest inside a 3-D dome and had combined her MR glasses with the dome's capabilities. The heightened reality blew her mind.

"Focus. China," said Tom.

"Sorry, dude . . . I'm not sure what to believe yet," said Veronika, simultaneously typing into the air inside her cocoon.

"I think she's coming to the Chinese mainland via islands off Wenzhou," said Tom. "But I don't think it's the Chinese in charge of her delivery."

"Are they selling her? To the Chinese?" asked Ruth.

"No idea," said Tom.

Miss Gray Hat voice messaged the group, "Don't trust them. There's a bigger game. Working on it."

Veronika rolled her eyes. "Of course it's a bigger game. And I think we need to drop Tom 2 right in the middle of it. It's not like they can kill him."

"You want we should lose? All that work?" chastised Ruth. "Those robots. Masterpieces of technology!"

"Ruth," said Major Tom. "They're mechanical representatives, and therefore, expendable."

"It's a w-w-w-waste!" wailed Ruth. "And they can hack them. And find out things. They're not p-p-puppets! They're you!"

Major Tom realized that they were also the only version of him that she could bear to touch. "Then we can't let anyone get them," he said.

CHAPTER TWENTY-FIVE

While awaiting the promised information from Cai, Tom 2 lay on a bed with a shabby bedspread in an abandoned hotel room that needed a new layer of wallpaper and a deep cleaning. Lying supine was the least mechanically stressful position for a sexbot. The dust on the windowsill looked like it was a year thick. A sooty and rain-smeared window faced the ocean, and he looked out every thirty seconds to see if anything had changed. Nothing had, except the position of the sun, the clouds, and the flights of birds.

Meanwhile, Major Tom did some thinking. Why China? Why cryptocurrencies? And why him?

Start with first principles. The most desired state in economics was stability, with growth and reliable markets, which decreased the likelihood of internal insurrection. Add vigorous trade, and it decreases the potential for war between nations. Every attempt at economic innovation throughout history had been an attempt to achieve that desired state. Whether it was indeed the best state was not the point. Only that it was assumed to be, and had been for millennia.

Once upon a time, the big technological change in currencies was paper money. Introduced during China's Song dynasty in the eleventh century, the paper currency had no intrinsic value, but backed by a government and the faith of a community, it was used as a value placeholder in exchange for goods and services. No need to carry heavy gold or silver coins or to barter with a cow or its milk. A banknote was a magical thing. People could accumulate and exchange wealth without having to lug it around. Or hide it in a hole in the ground. Or feed it. People needed only a pocket or purse to hold it. A government could print more when inflation was desirable, or remove it from circulation when not. It made the trade for goods and services easier, more efficient, more likely to spur growth.

Marco Polo brought the idea back to Europe in the thirteenth century. He was so astounded by the notion that he titled a chapter in his travel book "How the Great Kaan Causeth the Bark of Trees, Made into Something Like Paper, to Pass for Money All Over his Country." It took a few centuries for paper money to catch on in the West.

A millennium passed before a new concept for currency was developed, beginning with a digital currency called Bitcoin. As with most technologies, it wasn't the front-end tech—in this case, the currency itself—that became the killer app. Instead, the decidedly unsexy mechanics on the back end made Bitcoin work: the blockchain, which recorded transactions in permanent, sharable, provable, and retrievable digital forms.

But it didn't remain that way for long.

As with so many powerful technologies before it, the creators assumed that an endless revolution in creative, economic, and personal freedom would miraculously continue unabated. With cryptocurrency, money was finally democratic, no longer beholden to powerful, oligarchic, national entities. But technologies never turn out as rosy as they first appear. Eli Whitney thought the cotton gin would free Southern slaves of difficult labors, but it enabled the growth of one of the most successful and brutal slave economies in history, leading to a civil war that took the lives of seventy-five thousand soldiers and left its mark for the next two centuries.

Unintended consequences were hard to predict and prepare for. Major Tom's would-be Buddhist enlightenment clearly hadn't stuck the landing.

Revolutions did result from the births of these technologies, but they weren't all about freedom. The booster's naive faith in rational economic actors; optimism for the future; confidence in their own intelligence; and finally, a lack of understanding about complexity, supersystems, cascading effects, and the unpredictability of human nature fueled a resistance to making such a revolution impenetrable to corruption. Creators of cryptocurrency technologies liked to claim that their systems were theoretically foolproof, because they couldn't imagine anyone going to the incredible trouble of gaming their systems. But they weren't foolproof. Their systems proved only that they were fools.

Their gullible assumptions that the rest of the world possessed the same values and goals was touching. Major Tom was endlessly fascinated by the failure of the supersmart and technologically cloistered to understand how the world worked, again and again and again, regardless of the disastrous examples of history. But perhaps that was for the best. Without their blind trust in the future, technological innovation might not happen at all. Inventors would be too scared to innovate.

He had been one of them, once. As Peter Bernhardt, he had found it impossible to imagine weaponizing his lifesaving technologies. Instead, when the Phoenix Club stole his Alzheimer's cures to use as mind-control on Americans and the world, he had watched as his plowshares were smelt into swords.

But now the eternal battle was swinging back. In short order, blockchain technologies were replicated and privatized by the biggest companies and nations on earth, all in the name of cost reduction and efficiency. Millions of jobs had disappeared. The tools of freedom had become the tools of control. And too-big-to-fail enterprises were all about control.

The Chinese had figured out how to manage the digital, crypto-currency, and blockchain revolutions early on. Control the production of the cheap electronics that run the blockchain, and you control the world. And the Chinese government owned the land, much of it unus-able for anything other than isolated concrete bunkers, powered for free by local hydroelectric plants. And the Chinese loved mining for crypto-currencies. They had a proverb: 轉注/转注—in English, it meant, "A day without mining is like a day without kung pao chicken."

In no time, China had controlled much more than 51 percent of the world's blockchains, which meant enough for a coordinated 51 percent attack. The decentralized processing of cryptocurrencies was, in fact, extremely centralized inside a single nation. That's why seasteads took up the business so aggressively, to combat Chinese control with an alternative to a system too easily gamed by national players with national agendas. The seasteads wanted to put the "trust" back into "trustless" systems.

That explained "why China?" And "why cryptocurrencies?"

The question the world was asking was, Which side will succeed? He wondered what the human cost would be. What was the emotional and practical fallout of another economic crisis, much bigger than the last? How many knocks could civilization endure before collapsing?

Major Tom might help with that.

Cai knocked on the door and walked into the hotel room.

"We found the boat," he said. "And we intercepted a message. They are coming to the Qi Jiguang statue tonight."

CHAPTER TWENTY-SIX

Edwin Rosero's body lay on the *Zumwalt*'s operating table, connected to life support and a gaggle of monitoring machines. While Major Tom and Ruth still had much of the medical equipment they had used for Tom's previous surgeries on the *Pequod*, they added newer robotic machines to complete tasks that would otherwise require a larger medical team. Instead of a pair of superskilled hands, a surgeon was more a robot driver and process overseer, knowing where the robotic hands and tools would go through analysis of hi-res 3-D brain images. The robot would place the instruments in the necessary locations with uncanny accuracy.

Major Tom had paid Dr. José Irizarry to come back. Irizarry had helped with Thomas Paine's transformational surgery, implanting an intravascular nanowire neural-enhancement system into his body and brain. No longer on the run from Cuba's involuntary medical servitude in Venezuela since both countries' collapses, Irizarry was an interventional neuroradiologist in Miami. With Florida poorer than ever and President Conrad's SSA Army on the march south through the state, patients were hard to come by. Irizarry was more than willing to come and try Major Tom's latest crazy idea in exchange for lots of cash in his new Swiss bank account and a new identity in California.

They had moved one of the 3-D domes and desks into a corner of the operating room so both Irizarry and Steve could feel like they, along with the robot, were inside a giant version of Rosero's brain.

Steve looked at the dome with dread. He pulled Talia aside. "I wish the robot could do it all."

"Not so fast," she said, putting her arm around his shoulders. "You thought that image system was amazing yesterday. I saw you playing and practicing in there. Looked like you were enjoying it."

Steve sighed.

"I know," said Talia. "But just like last time, I don't know how to do this without you."

Ruth said to Major Tom, "Yes. Too much déjà vu. All over again."

"*Sí,*" said Dr. Irizarry with a giggle.

Steve smiled. "You still don't know when you make a joke, do you, Ruth?"

Ruth's eyelids fluttered as she tried to squint at Steve.

Talia studied the vials on the table. "I thought you said no more nanobots?" she asked.

"Well," muttered Ruth, "Prometheus's respirocytes and microbivores."

"It's a good idea," said Steve. "So the body heals quickly. And if he gets in trouble later. You can't object, since we sold those bots for the past two years."

Talia rolled her eyes and pointed. "And those?"

"Neural dust," said Ruth. "Much safer than macrosensors and carbon nanowires."

"There are no wires or infection issues that I can see," Steve added. "The dust uses ultrasound for diagnostics and communications, they're smaller than nanobots, and they fit anywhere. Remember, love, 'first do no harm.'" He tried to smile.

Ruth leaned in, in a stage whisper to Talia and Steve. "And he," she said, jerking her head toward the monitor, "can't mess with them. As much. No more psychic *drek*. Like he had last time. With macrosensors. Hopefully. That scared me."

"Me, too," said Talia. "I thought he was insane."

"And you think this isn't?" said Steve.

Ruth pointed at a large syringe. "And inside this. Neural lace. Same as Carter." Neural lace was a flexible mesh of electrical circuitry that could be injected by a syringe between the cortex and the brain membrane. From there it spread to the surface of the brain, making contact, training neural pathways to connect to it, communicate, and learn.

Major Tom spoke from the monitor, "Carter showed us the surgery video for a reason. He wants a human version of me out there with him. Embodiment gives us both agency in the physical world, but it also fulfills some fantasy or obsession he has. I'll take the bait."

"Please don't say you think like Carter now," said Steve. "He's insane."

"Ruth and I are both trying to think like Carter," said Major Tom. "I understand in theory how he did the surgery. I'm betting he hasn't invented anything new. That's never been his talent. We're both taking bits off the shelf and putting them together. So, in theory . . ."

"In theory, this could all go horribly wrong," said Steve.

"Like any surgery," said Tom. "This young man wasn't going to live anyway. If we succeed, it's a miracle. If not, he's no worse off."

Steve sat on a surgeon's stool with his head bowed.

"You know what's at stake, Steve," said Major Tom. "He's tried to destroy all of us. We need to stop him. And I need your help to do it."

Talia approached Steve from behind and wrapped her arms around him. She whispered, "I'm here. Just remember how much I love you." She kissed his ear.

He grabbed her arms around his chest and held them tight. "I only do this for you. You know that, right?"

Major Tom had other things on his mind. He knew Steve would stay and complete the surgery. He knew it would work. Lives depended on it. Winter was proof-of-concept. He played the Flaming Lips' "Brainville" and dreamed of enlarging his space into a human.

CHAPTER TWENTY-SEVEN

After driving through a scenic park, Cai parked the old-model autonomous BMW. He pointed to the Qi Jiguang statue in the distance. "I cannot come with you. I may be recognized, since I do not know who you are meeting. Follow the path and the bridge to the statue. Send me a message when you are finished here, and alone, and I'll come to get you. Good luck."

"Thank you," said Tom 2, getting out of the car.

The robocar pulled away.

The ticket booth for the Qi Jiguang's statue was closed. The Chinese were strict about visitors' hours, and the area was deserted. The sun shone low over the mainland. Shadows lengthened. An owl hooted. Switching his view to infrared, Tom 2 saw more animals. But no humans. He trod carefully past some pagoda-shaped structures. As far as his sensors could tell, they were empty.

A path led down the hillside along a crenellated concrete wall to two heavy concrete posts with attached steel cables. In front of Tom 2 lay a steel cable and plastic-plank, pedestrian suspension bridge, approximately two hundred feet long. The planks looked like large, flat Lego blocks: primary blue, red, and yellow. They led over the rocks and the East China Sea to a tall, rocky outcropping topped with the massive concrete statue of China's great military leader, Qi Jiguang.

Fifty feet tall, Qi Jiguang bravely lunged forward, reaching for his sword in its sheath. The warrior was backed by a loaded cannon, poised to defend the Wenzhou coast from another onslaught of pirates. The Ming dynasty general was legendary. Five hundred years ago, his tactics were relentless and surprisingly modern. He created martial arts that were not pretty, but they were practical and deadly. He trained a nation to grow into a great global power. With his martial skills, China overcame a scourge of piracy from both foreign and domestic enemies. Qi Jiguang fought most of his career from the stronghold of Zhejiang province, including Wenzhou and Dongtou Island. But in an irony not lost on the modern Chinese, Qi Jiguang drew his sword at the island and the mainland, not toward the ocean. The general and his cannon aimed inward, at his fellow Chinese, not out at seafaring, foreign invaders.

Planks of the footbridge jiggled unsteadily under Tom 2's heavy footfalls. Gripping the steel cables with each step, his gyros whirred loudly. He tried in vain to compensate for the complicated physics. If a small child could master this instinctively, why couldn't he?

The bridge swayed slightly, then increased its swing rapidly. His movements were too metronomic and amplified the bridge's mechanical resonance. He stopped after ten steps, trying to imagine jazz syncopation, African cross rhythms, humming a riff, concentrating on matching his movements to the changing beats.

His stiff movements looked like the Tin Man dancing across a bridge to the Emerald City in *The Wiz*. And that was a song with great syncopation. So he danced to "Ease On Down the Road." The concrete Qi Jiguang made a good Wizard in his throne room.

As he skipped, a ping from his automated search on Cai Shuxian rang. After more than twelve hours, even at his servers' fastest processing speed, only one photo had appeared, with tangential links and possible connections. Cai Shuxian's other name was Ye Rongguang. He was indeed from the Ministry of State Security, a high-level operative in the bureau of counterintelligence.

He reached the concrete pylons at the end of the bridge and searched the viewing platforms around the base of the massive statue. More crenellated concrete walls, a play castle by the sea. He wondered if Peter Jr. would enjoy it here.

But it posed a security problem.

He circled the statue, checking over the walls, a precipitous drop, over one hundred feet—and he knew he'd been had. There was no one here. It was a trap.

Strategically, it would be better to head back over the bridge and monitor from a safer location near the park's entrance. But why this place? Why Qi Jiguang?

He studied the statue again. Qi Jiguang was still and silent, ready to attack.

Tom 2 started back over the bridge, dancing to America's syncopated oldie "Tin Man." Maybe there was nothing to gain from the wizard of Qi Jiguang. Like the Tin Man, either he had everything he needed already, or the wizard had given him something of value he didn't know he wanted.

He was fed up with knowing so much but understanding nothing.

Two men approached the bridge. Through his infrared image, they appeared to be Chinese. Tom 2 didn't recognize them. Perhaps these were his contacts. He hurried toward them.

The shorter man broke into a run, pulled a handheld rotary saw from behind him, and slammed it into the first set of steel cables.

With the bridge swaying, Tom 2's gyro core shook. He froze.

The cable handhold on his left side would snap in seconds. He grabbed the one to his right and ran. The friction melted his silicone-skinned hand against the steel cable, then tore his skin away, exposing the metal and joints underneath. It didn't hurt. His sensors only alerted him to stresses or disturbances in his system. There was no pain feedback loop to make him stop.

The railing on his left collapsed.

Rotary Saw concentrated on the steel cable immediately below it.

Tom 2 was only fifty feet away. He took photos of the men and sent them to Ruth and Miss Gray Hat.

With a giant shrug, the bridge fell away beneath his feet. He hung on to the remaining cables with all the strength his awkward body had. The only way out was down, and the two men above him were now intent on finishing the job.

"*Nǐ shì shuí?* Who are you?" Tom 2 shouted.

"*Bùyàojǐn!*"

Mandarin—*It doesn't matter!*—didn't prove whether they were Wenzhou locals or not. Not helpful, Tom 2 thought. He sent SOS and location messages as the men above him worked on the final cable.

He faced a choice. Smash into the face of Qi Jiguang's rock? Or let go at the right time as the cable and planks swung down and jump, trying to time his descent for the least damage possible? He estimated the trajectory and impact zone on the rock face. It was a jagged and uneven surface, sure to split his body in half. He guessed the drop's distance. Gravity would do its worst.

He chose the rock face. In a half second, he put the planks between himself and the face and hit it full force. The planks cushioned his head. But a space between the planks made a wedge. It broke his torso right at the waist. His legs dangled and wiggled, trying to find purchase, but with no leverage to lift his legs, he couldn't push against the rocks with his feet. After useless bicycling, he let his legs dangle. But he still had use of his arms and upper torso. He tried to climb the rope, but he made it only a few feet. More skin ripped from his hands and arms, leaving only metal on metal, and he began to slip slowly down the cable. He gave up and slid as far as he could.

Releasing his grip, he jumped a few feet onto the rocks below. But without the use of his legs, he lay in a crumpled heap at the base of the rock face. And the tide was coming in.

Offshore, he saw a signal light from what looked like a fishing boat. His attackers messaged with a light back. These guys were old-school.

As he tried to figure out if the light was a Chinese equivalent of Morse code, there was a small flare and a *WHOOSH* from the distance. Suddenly, the rocks above him exploded and crashed onto his already broken body. He did an accounting: legs useless, spine broken at waist, arms crushed and dangling. His battery, meshnet, and communications worked. That was something.

He waited for their next move while sending all the data he could back to the team. He knew the rest of his comrades had their hands full with his new meat body, but he needed all the data analysis he could manage to find Dr. Who. If he failed, they'd lose their chance to save her, and he was desperate not to let that happen.

After 20.7 minutes, a dinghy came to rest at the base of the rocks. A man jumped out of the dinghy and came straight for Tom 2.

Time to play dead. Tom 2 made anything that still worked look like it didn't. His only thought: Take me with you.

A deep voice, from the area of the dinghy, yelled in Wenzhou dialect, "Well? Broken or not?"

Tom 2 was shifted, dangled, inspected. He released all his joints and didn't move or focus his eyes. He looked like a life-sized marionette.

In a high-pitched voice, the man holding him answered, "Nothing works." He tried to lift Tom 2. "This thing's heavy! Help me."

"Leave it for the tide," said Deep Voice.

"You're nuts," said High Voice. "One cousin has a doll factory and another does electronics. They could copy this in a week. Think of the money we'll make. Better than whale shark, tuna, even kidnapping!"

"We need to get rid of it before we hand off the *hakgwei*," said Deep Voice. "Don't want trouble."

A quick search of *hakgwei* found it as a derogatory Mandarin term for a dark-skinned foreigner, literally "black ghost."

Cai/Ye was correct. The fishing boat carried Dr. Who. And it sounded like they had her alive.

Tom 2 heard footsteps, then had a sense of being dragged by four arms, even though his tactile sensors were offline.

"Watch out!" said Deep Voice.

They dropped him and leapt for higher ground. Tom 2 heard the wave coming in, then the gurgle of water in his circuits. Qi Jiguang's lesson was clear. Beware of wannabe pirates, regardless of who they worked for. Real pirates would have done a better job.

Then, silence. His audio apparatus had failed. He had failed. He would never find Dr. Who.

Then, nothing.

CHAPTER TWENTY-EIGHT

The body of Edwin Rosero, a.k.a. Tom, awoke to music. Disturbed's angry symphonic cover of "The Sound of Silence" should have been playing from his private server, but instead, songs that he had never heard before invaded his head: the Game's "El Chapo" featuring Skrillex, Kendrick Lamar's "The Blacker the Berry," J. Cole, Future, Pitbull, Lighter Shade of Brown. The overlapping beats made him woozy. A torrent of input flooded this body's undamaged auditory complex, stimulated by his server.

He hadn't expected this brain to do that.

His head and torso were raised, allowing the surgical inflammation to drain. Looking down his body, he saw limbs. He looked down at his right foot and willed it to move. It twitched.

Nausea overwhelmed him. He breathed deeply, trying to relax, hoping he wouldn't retch uncontrollably. But he couldn't reconcile the mental image he had of "Tom" with this body. He had been Peter Bernhardt. Then he had been surgically altered to look like Talia's father, and that body became Thomas Paine. He even identified with the morphed digital image in Veronika's Veil. But this was different. His skin was a bit darker than the cáfe con leche tint that, with melanotan pills, he had maintained as Thomas Paine. At his new height, he didn't fit the bed. His feet dangled off the edge.

A wave of uncontrollable and fluid emotion broke on the sharp edges of his digital intellect. He was alive again. He was human.

But this wasn't him. It couldn't be him. Oh God. What had he done?

A cry escaped his lips, and his eyes filled with tears. He choked on the runoff in his throat. Without thinking, he tried to roll to his right to dry heave off the side of the bed, but the bed's railing was up. He hit his head hard and bounced back onto his pillow. At least he had some control of his body, even if it was involuntary. He cried anew.

Then, remarkably, unbelievably, he felt something he hadn't for a long time: an erection. What. The. Actual. Fuck. He was a weeping, confused, genitally aroused, unholy mess. He hadn't thought about sex since he died, and he couldn't help but wonder if Carter/Winter had gone through the same thing. Or was s/he still that much better at everything?

That's when he noticed Veronika sitting to his left, a mixed reality unit over her eyes, her hands shaping the air. He tried to shift so the sheets wouldn't outline his body so obviously, but he wasn't successful.

Veronika smiled knowingly. "Dude, don't mind me."

He wasn't sure if he was glad or embarrassed that she was here to see him in this condition. He tried speaking, but his lips and tongue felt like they weren't connected.

"Ya . . . here?" he asked.

"Never left your side," she said.

"Wha . . . ya . . . do . . ." His words slurred.

"Hacking government and medical. Gotta dump all of Edwin Rosero's identity, financials, and biometrics on file. He has to, like, disappear from anyplace I can reach."

"Ya . . . know how?"

"Yeah. It's one of the tricks Mama Who taught me."

"Mama. Neva' . . . tol' me . . . how . . . ya know ha."

"How well can you know anyone on the net?" Veronika winked.

"Pre . . . y well." He tried to nod at her air-processing, but the nausea hit hard again. Not moving was the way to go.

"There's always levels you can't get to," said Veronika. "So people give up, and like, work with what they've got. That causes lots of, like, false assumptions. I could have their minds and thoughts splayed out like a dissected cadaver for my study, but we all hold secrets even we can't figure out."

"Tha' why . . . ya . . . follow me? Ya try ta . . . know me?"

"You got me." She grinned.

"Who . . . makin' . . . me now?"

"Who's making your identity?" she asked.

"Ya," he said. It was tiring to talk.

"No one," said Veronika. "No records. No false ID. You'll be a ghost. Rare in the First World. But with, like, something extra."

She reached into her messenger bag and pulled out a plastic baggy. Inside was a miniscule ID tag, more microbullet than circuit board.

"Tag . . . ?" he asked.

"Yeah, and release. Like a mountain lion. But the most connected lion ever. This little baby opens a lot of doors. And you'll leave no trace."

"Ha . . . do . . . ya . . . ?" He stopped, exhausted.

"How do I know? As sure as, well, you can't be completely sure. I am dealing with, like clearances, privacy, deletion codes. I'd say, just kinda, like, I-know-my-shit sure."

Who the fuck was this woman? Tom wondered. "How . . . ?"

"Never ask a woman her age. Or guess her mole friends."

"Or . . . how ya make . . . mo-ney?" asked Tom.

Veronika grinned and kept working.

He was uncomfortable, and it wasn't just the surgery. How did he attract all these women with hidden agendas? The déjà vu was overwhelming. He wanted to disappear back into anesthetic oblivion. How had he done this *again*? Was this the universe's fate for him? To repeat the same cycle of reincarnation into a new face, body, and technology and be used as a pawn until he could figure out the real game plan? Would he ever get off the wheel of *samsara*—the continual reincarnation cycle of birth and death—and stop having to save humanity from itself? And from him? Could he even save himself?

By asking, he knew he wasn't headed for nirvana anytime soon.

Instead, he'd have to undergo physical therapy and mental acrobatics, again, to get this body up and running after its atrophy in the hospital unit—again. The tears came, again.

There was a knock on the door, and a familiar bald head poked in. When Steve saw Tom awake and responsive, he couldn't help but smile. Steve was a great doctor, as attentive and skilled as they came. Tom just wished he were more supportive of the bigger picture.

"Checking in. How do you feel?" Steve asked.

"He . . . lp?" said Tom.

"Sucks to be him," said Veronika. "But he's speaking well. Forgot to tell him he shouldn't bother trying."

Tom tried to stick his tongue out at her, but the room spun and he stopped.

After a quick examination of Tom's vitals, wounds, and neurological responses, Steve pulled up a rolling stool and sat near Tom's head. "You're healing remarkably well," he said. "But you know that. And you know, probably better than I do, how I feel about all this."

Tom simply nodded once. It was all he could manage.

"I want to stay and support Talia," Steve continued. "But you continually challenge me with what it means to be a doctor. I know you're in pain. But I'm in pain, too." He gestured at Tom's bandages around his head. "That's my pain. I didn't go into medicine to do this. I became a doctor to cure people of things that might kill them. So they could see their lives, and kids, and dreams become reality. Do you understand?"

Tom nodded once again.

"I'll be here as long as you recuperate. But then I have to go. And take care of real people. I don't know what that will mean for all of us. I'm sorry."

Tom wasn't up to arguing. Both left unsaid what might happen to Talia if Steve left. She would have to choose between them.

Tom closed his eyes to feign sleep. He didn't have to pretend for long.

CHAPTER TWENTY-NINE

The first words Tom 2 heard were whispered in a deep, motherly, and familiar voice: "Anybody in there? You hooked up yet?"

Tom 2 swiveled a single working eye toward the sound. It was dark, so he turned on the infrared camera. Dr. Who's red-washed face took up the camera's entire frame. She held his head in her hands and was studying his eye socket in a meager shaft of light from the open seam between an ill-fitting door and doorframe.

Confirming first that he was hooked up to his satellite communications, he immediately sent another encrypted SOS to Ruth and Miss Gray Hat so they could get a GPS fix on him. They responded that they got both his earlier messages and were working on a way to free both him and Dr. Who.

His eye swiveled to the maximum of its range. They were in a tight storage closet filled with fishing gear, cleaning supplies, and paperwork. "You fixed me?"

At the sound of Thomas Paine's gruff voice, Dr. Who's eyes filled with tears. She whispered, "Oh, thank the good Lord in heaven. It *is* you!"

"How'd you know I *was* me?"

"I didn't. But ya look so much like Peter Bernhardt. And in a sex-bot? How in the hell didya do that? Didn't know if it was some cruel joke or whether to laugh or cry."

"Miss me?" asked the robot.

"You got no idea." She sniffled. "Thought I'd never hear a friend's voice again."

"Missed you, too, Doc." He wished he had hands and arms so he could pat and console her. "So what kind of mess do we have?"

"Not sure," she whispered. "But I can fake my way 'round a circuit board and did some rewirin'. It was all there. Just jiggled around, salty and wet. Now you got one eye. One ear. Throat speakers weren't damaged, but your jaw's broken and mouth won't move." She pried opened his jaws and looked down his throat. "Pretty cushioned inside." She lifted up a loose arm. It swung on broken hydraulics. "Not much else, sorry to say. Looks like this was a nice piece 'a work."

"That's okay," he said. "We're getting you out of here."

"Hope so, baby." She wiped her runny nose on her sleeve and didn't look hopeful. "We have to stay in here till you figure it out. Only place they don't got cameras or mics, I think."

"How'd I end up with you?"

She pointed beyond the closet door. "I'm in that room. They tried to fix ya, so they rinsed ya with fresh water and stuck ya in a giant bag of rice to dry out. Still in your hair." She picked a few grains out from the strands as she spoke. "Kinda genius, thinkin' ya was just a big waterlogged GO. But they couldn't get ya to work, so they threw ya in here. I crawled into here with ya and cried loud, gave 'em a show, while I worked out what I could do."

"Try to keep me with you," said Tom 2. "All the communications are inside my head, but the CPU and boards are in my chest."

"Torso's hangin' on by a couple of wires near the clavicle to the battery and processors. And don't think I'm runnin' your football outta here under my arm. Can barely walk."

"We'll see." He quickly analyzed the schematics left in files from the Companibots hackers. There were small auxiliary batteries in the head, but how could she access them without tools? And he didn't' know if they were charged or how long they'd last. And could she uncouple the processors from the chest?

While he puzzled out the engineering, he asked, "Any idea why they took you?"

"Sure do." Her eyes were downcast. She said no more.

He waited. Meanwhile, Miss Gray Hat messaged back that they had his coordinates, were analyzing possible destinations based on the ship's travel vectors, and had a suggestion for him to ponder: What if they created a phantom ship?

Now there was an idea.

Dr. Who sighed and finally said, "I'm sorry, honey. They pumped me full 'a drugs. No idea how much I gave away. But I'm just bait, with some bonus pain for the independent financial and identity markets thrown in. Think I was supposed ta work on some blockchain business and mess things up generally, with them threatening ta take my kids, grandkids." She looked like she might cry again.

"That's not bonus pain," said Tom 2. "That's a huge thing they're pulling off. It will change the balance of power in the world. So why are you bait?"

"It's *you* they want. And here ya are," she said.

"They've gone after all the copies of my message they can find. They're demonizing me, changing my history, everything about me. I had to destroy the links to the Memory Palace and hide. What else can they do to me?"

"Not just you, sugar. Ya seen what's left of the US?"

His head tried to snort, but the nasal sounds didn't work.

"You're part of a bigger plan," she continued. "Don't know exactly. But they want to resurrect ya."

"How? Why?" he asked.

"Don't know," said Dr. Who. "That's all I could make of what they let slip."

"Who are 'they'?"

"The voices of some determined and frightened American assholes. Led by some awful lofty and effete voice I'd swear on my mama's bosom was Carter Potsdam. But ya said ya destroyed the Memory Palace, so he'd be gone, too. Who else ya know talks 'bout you like that?"

"He copied himself and escaped. He's even downloaded into a human female named Winter. But it's Carter's AHI pulling the strings."

She looked stunned. "Never thought I'd live long enough to see that."

"I've got a human body, too, back on the *Zumwalt*."

She blew out a puff of air. "Damn, honey, I think you're playin' right into their plan."

He received a single encrypted word from Miss Gray Hat: *Diversion*.

"Okay," said Tom 2. "The gang thinks a phantom ship may work, and they want a diversion. I'm good at that. Turn my head around so I can see what's in the closet." She did, and he saw a mop and some rags. He applied a Chinese translation app to all the container labels: various cleaning supplies, a copious amount of paper saved for government-mandated recycling, and his dispensable parts, anything from the neck down that didn't house the processors and batteries in his chest.

"They may come here soon. Deliver my dinner tray," said Dr. Who.

"Then we work faster. Now open the closet door a centimeter and put my eye to it so I can see what's in there." The room had no windows, and the door was made of steel and had locks on both sides. It looked like they had stripped the room of anything obviously useful and left just a folding metal bed with a bare mattress and an old blanket.

He ran all the items and materials through a search engine, looking for any combination of supplies that might work to free them. Some search results were referenced with the Darwin Awards. They were handed out annually—and posthumously—to those who attempted stupid behaviors that got them removed from the gene pool. Perhaps he and Dr. Who would join their nominees shortly.

His circuits filled with a song: Blur's "Ghost Ship."

Yes. It might work. Or Darwin Awards, here they'd come.

"Okay, now follow my instructions *really* carefully," he said to Dr. Who.

CHAPTER THIRTY

E dwin Rosero was the right choice to become the new Thomas Paine. Physically fit. Powerful, with quick muscle control. All sensory inputs above average. Bright, with high levels of neuroplasticity and white-matter connectivity through the brain's corpus callosum. He could learn quickly, synthesize a lot of information, and remember it, although Major Tom would do that anyway. Only specific parts of the neocortex and medulla were damaged, which the team overrode with the neural net and neural dust connections to Major Tom's servers. But there were still problems.

Ruth, Talia, and Steve sat on the bridge with Tom. Ruth played double duty, monitoring human Tom's biological upgrades and the ghost-ship plan. Earlier, Talia had asked Veronika to help map out the ghost ship with Miss Gray Hat.

"You guys working on Tom," said Veronika. "It's, like, so distracting. And he's spraying testosterone everywhere. Yuck. I'm going to my bunk and work from there."

Steve noted Tom's medical progress. Sitting next to Ruth and Steve, Tom struggled with a mental exercise on the monitor in front of him. The program prompted him to remember a combination of numbers and colors and to coordinate them with body movements: the number 4, yellow, and clenching the fist of his left hand; the number 7, green, and wiggling his right foot. It was like building the synesthesia from scratch.

In his present incarnation, Ruth wanted to make sure that each brain region and the communication network were connected to Major Tom. And Major Tom added music. Peter Bernhardt's original brain processed information musically, as did all the incarnations. Tom listened to songs to embed the new learning along neural and electronic pathways more deeply. First, Major Tom downloaded tunes from his servers to his new brain. But the tones had a distinctly geometric feel. Each sound was flat on the sides, with sharp edges and points where the edges met, like cubes flowing together in a Tetris-like construction of "music."

"Do we have any headphones?" he asked Ruth.

She dug through some drawers and handed him an old pair. Major Tom turned off the direct music input and redirected it into the headphones. David Byrne breathed in and out, singing about men and women, how well they fit together, "Like Humans Do." The sound grew less cubical. But not quite round.

"What are you doing?" asked Ruth, scrutinizing him.

"I'm listening to the difference between sound from my servers and from my ears into this brain, but they're both digital sources. And I'll be in an acoustic world. But I have no acoustic music. Wasn't sure if that might make a difference or not to my brain processing."

"Hmmmph . . . ," said Ruth. She left the bridge.

He went back to his lessons.

She returned five minutes later, holding his 2001 Manzer Paradiso, a magnificent archtop acoustic guitar he believed had disappeared after the Phoenix Club had tried to kill him.

"Where did you find it?" he asked, trying to jump out of his seat, but his body was not ready for such enthusiasm. He groaned.

"Net. Some *schmuck* selling it. No idea what he had."

"Thank you, Ruthie! You really are the best!" He could have hugged her.

Ruth blushed. He didn't remember her ever doing that before.

He reverently took it from her hands. No one had played it in years. With his digitally perfect pitch, he tuned it. Then he strummed. The guitar sounded great, but his muscle coordination left something to be desired.

"Rosero didn't play guitar," said Tom. "No calluses. No muscle memory."

"Still a good neurological test. Play something," said Ruth.

He looked around the bridge, a little embarrassed, although he had no idea why. Peter Bernhardt and Major Tom used to play for crowds. Why not now? And what would he play?

He didn't consciously make the decision. His fingers moved on their own. It was a song he had heard only once, "Glory" by Radical Face. He wondered if Rosero liked it, because it felt comfortable in his mind. As awkward as his fingers felt, tripping over the strings and making the wrong chords, the guitar sang with the clarity and brilliance that the Manzer was famous for, pillowy soft, not sharp like a cube. It reminded him of the differences between live music, old-fashioned vinyl, and digital recordings, but more pronounced.

"Is it a song with words?" asked Ruth.

"Yes," said Tom, strumming.

"Then sing!" she said. "We need more than one set. Of muscular data."

So he sang, of a stolen name, a battle against a wicked world, the pain of having one's head opened, exposing the memories he wished he could forget. Being unable to help everyone who needed it. It wasn't a happy song, but it was appropriate. He thought he'd rename it "Tom's Ballad."

Ruth fluttered her shoulders and looked on with chagrin. "We must give you voice lessons. This one's voice. Not so good. Maybe a neurological malfunction? Or inflammation from intubation?"

Tom looked up from the guitar to catch a glimpse of Talia at her desk. He studied the skin on her neck when she brushed her hair aside. The shape of her breast under a simple white T-shirt. Her small waist, curved to fit the palm of a man's hand. The roundness of her butt. He knew he shouldn't stare, but he couldn't help it.

"Stop ogling Talia!" Steve barked.

Tom hadn't noticed him watching. He stopped playing, glared, started out of his chair, then stopped because he lacked coordination. He'd get his ass kicked. Why was he so angry?

Talia couldn't quite stifle a laugh. "Did he, now? Don't worry, love. He probably can't help it."

Her giggle made his skin rise in goosebumps. Should he fight? Or fuck? Oh, man . . . He sat back down and started playing again.

Ruth studied him. "Teenage hormones. And unfinished prefrontal cortex." She sniffed. "I was wrong. To choose one so young. Given the chance. You'd hump a female rhinoceros."

Steve moved to Talia and quietly said to her, "I think it's time for us to go."

"Not yet," Talia said.

"There's nothing more for me here. Except you," said Steve.

"Please, can we talk about this later?" asked Talia in a whisper.

Tom stopped playing and said loudly, "Can I take a break?"

"Is Dr. Who? Taking a break?" asked Ruth.

"No . . ." sighed Tom. Looking at Talia, her head leaning in to Steve's, he imagined how amused she must have felt by his teenaged attention. What it would be like to have sex with her again. He remembered the last time . . . But was it *him*? Thinking about it was uncomfortable. He subtly readjusted and bent over the guitar again, muttering, "How did I survive this . . . ?"

"What?" said Ruth.

"My teen years," said Tom.

"Ha!" laughed Ruth. "I remember Peter. At this age? It was we. Who had to survive you!"

Tom lay in his too-small hospital bed at night, plugged into sensors that relayed neurological information back to the servers, Ruth, Steve, and Dr. Irizarry. He would need to develop more muscle memory so he didn't fumble or fall at a crucial moment. And emotional control was a problem, so they tracked endocrinological data, too. Maybe they could stabilize the hormonal extremes. He would need more hardware, and possibly some implants that they didn't have on board ship. They would have to find them or make them.

Even surrounded by his closest comrades, he felt distant. Ruth didn't talk to him with the same intimacy. She treated him differently, like a teenager and not an intellectual partner. Talia had Steve. To come between them would be wrong, even though he wanted her physically. He also missed Amanda. And why did he insist on meeting his son for the first time as a robot? He cringed. He wished he could redo it, meet his child for the first time as a red-blooded human. Somewhere inside this body and brain, he felt a fleshly playback of what it meant to touch someone lovingly. The ache was palpable.

He sent a voice message to Veronika. "You up?"

"Yeah."

"Whatcha doing?" he asked.

"Working all day on the Chinese cryptoproblem," said Veronika. "Might be a way to convince the Chinese to play nice."

"Can you come say hi?" he asked.

She paused. "I'm tired. Talk in the morning."

"Okay. Good night." He cut off the messaging. He could guess why she didn't want to see him. Her idol was less than she had thought. That had to be disappointing.

Or maybe he was reading into it. Isn't that what teenagers did? Read into things? And get them wrong?

He tried to roll over, but the sensors poked his skin. The scar tissue near his clavicle was not completely healed, and the pressure near his vagus nerve sent yet another wave of nausea over him. That triggered a new experience, a sensory flashback, of a female hand he didn't know. Stroking his hand. The skin appeared youthful, the nails beautifully decorated with tiny, intricate constellations of stars. The arm was slender, paler than his, with the most delicate dusting of fine hairs. Soft like velvet. And the smell. She smelled of lavender and sunshine and girl. Who was she? A memory of Edwin's long lost love?

Now he'd never sleep.

CHAPTER THIRTY-ONE

The Chinese ship's closet became the tiny workroom for one human and one robotic terrorist. Or revolutionary. Or rebel. Or freedom fighter. Throughout history, the choice of words depended on which side you were on. Tom 2 was sure he'd be called all those names and more.

"Ever hear of Magic Whip?" he asked Dr. Who, referring to the Blur song "Ghost Ship," which had inspired his idea.

"Sandwich spread?" she asked.

"No. A brand of Chinese firecracker. We're going to make our own. But first, you need to cannibalize my non-necessary parts."

It took longer than he had planned for her to follow his directions carefully and detach each salvageable piece. He directed her to key supplies in the closet: paper, cardboard, kerosene, and other fluids.

"Lord in heaven, this stinks," she muttered.

"Open the door more, so you don't pass out," he said. "I'll let you know if I hear anyone." He turned up his auditory sensors.

She worked silently, her hands shaking as she poured the kerosene into the delicate container they had created.

"Someday," said Tom 2, trying to divert her, "someone has to name a combustible device after me, like a Molotov cocktail. It's become my signature."

Dr. Who was panting hard. "How 'bout . . . a 'Paine-ful . . . Tom-ahawk.'"

"That's funny, Doc. Now wrap the green wire around the conduit at the top."

"I'm tryin', honey, I'm tryin'."

He contacted Ruth and Miss Gray Hat. "Where's our ship?"

"We'll overlay as soon as we're finished," voice messaged Miss Gray Hat. "What do you want to call the ghost ship? Only for our reference, so no one's confused which ship is which. By the way, your ship's real name is the *Po Lin*."

"What else do you know about this ship?" asked Tom 2.

"Four on board. Captain, first mate, and two crew. High Voice and Deep Voice are probably the two crew."

"Call our boat *Tai Ching 21*," said Tom 2. "If they discover the name, they'll freak out."

"Why?" asked Ruth.

"Famous abandoned Taiwanese fishing boat," said Tom. "Caught on fire, but no one knows where. They discovered it off Kiribati. Crew had disappeared and no one ever found their lifeboats, preservers, any sign of fatalities, or survivors. They searched the Pacific for weeks. Truly a ghost ship."

"*Tai Ching 21* looks identical and is overlaid onto your location," said Miss Gray Hat. "It's on fire twenty miles off Wenzhou. SOS sent. Pumping image to available surveillance systems. Let's see who we convince."

After 3.8 minutes, Miss Gray Hat contacted Tom 2. "They took the bait. Lots of radio chatter with your coordinates."

After five minutes, fast boats from the China Coast Guard departed from Wenzhou harbor. Major Tom said to the team, "Watch Dongtou Island." After a few more minutes, a modern powerboat departed, not far from the abandoned hotel where Cai/Ye had taken Tom 2.

"Estimated arrival of first rescue boat, sixty seconds, fifty-nine . . . fifty-eight . . . ," voiced Miss Gray Hat.

"You ready, Doc?" asked Tom 2.

"One sec." She bowed her head and said a little prayer. "Ready as the good Lord'll let me be."

She placed Tom 2's head at the open closet door so he could see and hear as much as possible, then crawled quietly out of the closet and screamed at the locked door, "I'm dyin'! Oh lordy, I'm dyin'! Help me! *Help!*"

Feet pounded. Voices yelled in Mandarin. High Voice unlocked the door and threw it open.

"*Nǎlǐ bùduì?*"

Dr. Who didn't know it meant "what's wrong?" but the intent was clear. She ignored it, buying time.

"Speak English!" she yelled, clutching her chest.

"*Nǎlǐ bùduì?*" High Voice repeated, slower and louder.

"Don't speak Chinese stuff! Help me, I'm dyin'!" She clutched his leg with one arm and her chest with the other.

High Voice saw his payday disappearing. He shook her off his leg and ran for help, but he didn't close the door.

Dr. Who crawled into the hall, looking like she'd keel over any second.

Tom 2 heard Dr. Who yell "Ouch!" Then a thud. Then a *BANG!*

Again, thought Tom 2. Again.

This time, the firecracker flew past the door.

Thud . . . *BANG!*

Smoke began to fill the hallways and their room. He could hear the crackle of fire.

Deep Voice, High Voice, and the first mate came running with a defibrillator. They saw the fire, and Deep Voice grabbed a fire extinguisher off the wall and began to spray their end of the hall. The first mate ran back, probably to tell the captain. High Voice dropped the defibrillator and ran into Dr. Who's room.

"What the hell are you doing?" Deep Voice asked High Voice in Wenzhouese.

"Grabbing our other payday!" said High Voice. He gathered up robotic parts from the floor and the closet. He grabbed Tom 2's head last.

"What the hell *are* you doing?" asked Tom 2 in Wenzhouese.

High Voice screamed in an even higher voice and dropped the head.

"There's smoke coming out of ducts on the real ship," said Miss Gray Hat. "Looks good for the rescue team. They're climbing the ladder now."

Tom 2 could hear feet running on the deck above.

Soon the blue-and-black uniforms of the China Coast Guard, led by the first mate and a stunned captain, appeared in the hallway to put out the fires. Then, in the doorway, a familiar face appeared. Cai/Ye, in police uniform, ordered two nonuniformed officers to arrest the captain, first mate, Deep Voice, and High Voice. He regarded Tom 2's head lolling on the floor.

"Are you just going to stand there?" Tom 2 asked. "Or are you going to pick me up?"

Inside the compact dining area of the powerboat, Cai/Ye sat next to Dr. Who. Wrapped in warm blankets, she cradled a cup of strong Chinese tea in her hands. Tom 2's head sat on the table, along with a bag of rice crackers and the teapot. Next to Dr. Who were the remaining parts of Tom 2.

"We want to know if you're Cai Shuxian or Ye Rongguang," said Dr. Who.

Cai/Ye nodded. "You would be interested in the history of my identity, wouldn't you?"

She put her cup down. "Don't be evasive, honey. Makes ya look smarmy."

Cai/Ye grinned. "And you are a quintessential American: direct, clever, and not to be underestimated. You may call me either. I am actively both. Like Peter Bernhardt and Thomas Paine."

"Peter Bernhardt is dead, and technically, so is Thomas Paine," said Tom 2. "There is only Major Tom, manifest in different ways, regardless of what others like to call me."

"I apologize for the misunderstanding," said Cai/Ye. "And please let me also apologize, both for me and my . . . department, for the delay in rescuing you. We would like to help you in any way we can."

"Ha!" said Dr. Who, giving him the stink eye. "Couldn't prove it to me!"

"Your help hasn't been helpful," said Tom 2. "What were you waiting for?"

"We weren't sure about the situation and the players. We are now," said Cai. "From now on, we can work together. This is a long game. And there's a war coming. If you don't win, we all lose."

"You just figured that out?" asked Tom 2.

"Yes. However, we don't know the extent of the potential conflict. And regardless of your AHI capabilities, neither do you. We have run our own AI-generated scenarios that, if they occur, will be devastating to the entire world—including China. It will take generations to recover."

"It's already begun," said Tom 2. A tiny alarm went off in his head. Only he could hear it. "Dr. Who? My battery's dying, and I need to ask you something before I can't."

"Yeah, hon?" she said, still chewing crackers.

"May I call you Mama? Peter Bernhardt never really had one. And I'd be honored if you'd be mine."

Cai gaped at the surprising humanity from the robohead.

Dr. Who swallowed hard, picked up the head, and spoke directly to it. "Oh, baby . . . 'course you can. I'd love to be your mama. That'd make you my boy." Her sad-eyed smile said the rest.

"Battery's almost dead, Mama," he said. "Game over."

"Now you just shut your eyes and let's hope I'll be talkin' to you real soon."

"'Night, Mama."

And she cradled the head in her arms.

CHAPTER THIRTY-TWO

Veronika volunteered to escort Tom's human body to Venice, California, to find Essensse Labs. They advertised hormonal dampers for just the problems Tom was encountering with his teenaged hormones, and he wanted to test-drive the product. Essensse also made the v10 brain-jack system that Veronika wouldn't use yet, but she was still curious to meet them and see the goods. Unfortunately, Essensse suffered collateral damage when Peter Bernhardt and Thomas Paine's message went wide. The public didn't realize that Essensse's products underwent strict and lengthy experimentation, unlike Paine's brain-computer interfaces used prematurely to defeat his enemies.

Essensse wasn't the only one flying under Silicon Beach's tech radar. The entire industry was in shambles. With currencies fluctuating and people distrustful of both technology and money, the economy wound down, and many couldn't afford the new toys that the tech companies had to offer.

Tom wanted to test his body in a real-world setting, so with apprehension, he dove into the freaky maelstrom of a warm-weather Sunday on the Venice Ocean Front Walk, a.k.a. the Boardwalk. Veronika joked that it would be the ultimate test of sensory coordination. And she was right. In a world with little money, the real-life sideshow was free for locals and tourists alike.

Thousands of people darted in all directions on the concrete walkway, stopping short right in front of him, almost running him over on flyboards, stilts, and cycles with any number of wheels. Vendors hawked body modification, costumes, psychic readings, fine art of every type, religious conversion, found-object sculptures, spiritual jewelry, wind chimes, mind-altering substances. Sartorial/cosplay/body-mod eccentrics posed for photos. Musicians played every instrument under the sun. The largest homeless population in North America asked for money no one had. Above their heads flew LEO drones and homemade flying machines that looked like hot-air balloons, bats, or angels, designed by artists that merged tech and aesthetic genius.

Tom looked up. Squatters crowded in bivouacs hanging from the sides of taller buildings. Tent cities lined the roofs. Out past the waterline, near-to-shore seasteads offered housing, 24/7/365 parties, and quasi-legal substances. With no more Feds, California had passed drug decriminalization. And as it had in Portugal and the Netherlands, so far, it was working here.

Tom had to navigate both the gripping feel of sneakers on pavement and the shifting sand. He gauged his body's temperature control. He assessed potential friends and foes around him, including numerous drones: law enforcement drones, kiddie-starter drones, hobby drones, advert-drones. Negotiating the world as a fully functioning human body was more complex than the throngs of people around him gave themselves credit for. How automatic a human could be when he wasn't a big, buff, nineteen-year-old who had just learned to walk.

They passed a panhandler with a ratty cardboard sign. In faded marker, it read: *Fuck Thomas Paine—Give me a dollar.* Tom shook his head.

"Whaddaya think?" asked Veronika, gesturing to the crowd.

"Weird. When I was living in Malibu and fighting the club, I only passed through Venice on my way. But this feels really familiar."

Veronika's lips curled knowingly.

The side of a building at the corner of Windward Avenue and Ocean Park Walk caught his attention. Painted by Rip Cronk, its mural was called *Venus Kinesis*. Modeled after Sandro Botticelli's *The Birth of Venus*, it depicted the longhaired goddess of love, roller-skating along the Boardwalk in a teeny camisole, short-shorts, and leg warmers. She was surrounded by the winds, angels, flying skateboards, gondoliers, chainsaws, dumbbells, artworks, as well as full-length portraits of real locals recorded for posterity. Its sun-soaked Venetian paradise seemed oddly familiar, yet things had changed, time had passed, and a new Venice had transformed under her skates. In the background of the mural, a self-referential and recursive image of the same mural was painted on the same building, with the same Venus skating behind her. Big and little Venus blithely cruised on. In a cartoon thought bubble above Big Venus's head, she concluded, *History is Myth.*

Tom studied the mural. Here was Venus telling him that history wasn't reality. Rather, it was the stories you told, repeated, changed, and came to believe at the heart of a culture, true or not. History copied recursively, like parallel mirrors, or a computer copying data. Like his digital self. Stories were the small version of history. The big version was cyclical, with seismic changes that civilizations rode like monster waves in the Pacific.

"What do you see up there?" he asked Veronika.

"That's the Essensse building," she said.

"What else?" he asked.

She glanced at the wall. "What? Like, Venus on the half-pipe?"

"That's all? You don't see the threat we're facing? You don't see how much the world has changed?" he asked.

"Dude, what do you want me to say? It's cute. Not that clever, and the paint could use some restoration, but cute." She sounded placating. Not like Veronika at all. There was more here, but she wasn't telling.

He let it lie. The physical practice had sharpened his appetite, and he needed to eat. An overpowering craving hit him. "Where can I get a sandwich near here?"

Veronika looked at him strangely. "What kind?"

He smelled food from the eateries around him. His body quivered with longing. "I don't even get where this is coming from . . . I've never had it in my life. It's creamy, supple, mild, and sweet, and tastes like love in your mouth. Like white bread . . . toasted. And grape jelly. And that soft cheese. You know the kind they put on top of beans and rice?"

"You are so weird, dude," she said.

"But what's the cheese?" he insisted.

"You mean *queso fresco*?"

"Yes!"

Checking her GO, she grabbed his hand. "One block. This way."

They walked up Windward, and as they passed a parking lot, Tom noticed another large mural, Jonas Never's *A Touch of Venice*, this one all in blacks, grays, and whites. It was based on an image from Orson Welles's *A Touch of Evil*, shot right on this block of Venice. The painting depicted a Mexican street, lit by party bulbs, with Charlton Heston and Janet Leigh, and a quotation with no source that he could locate: *Like a dream that I remember from an easier time . . .*

Venice was speaking directly to him. All of this felt like a dream. He had been here. He knew those murals. He knew this street. But his body and mind didn't agree about the where or when. He struggled to reconcile his thoughts, but his hunger kept getting in the way.

They arrived at Windward Farms, a couple of blocks off the beach. Veronika ordered a quesadilla with shrimp and mango. Tom ordered his special sandwich at the deli counter. The cook looked at him funny and then glanced at an older man by the register.

"Gross . . . ," muttered Veronika.

"Customer is sometimes right," said owner to the cook.

Veronika paid for the sandwiches, and they wandered outside to one of several picnic tables set up in the parking lot of an abandoned bank. When Tom 2 took the first bite, he felt like had come home. But to where?

With a full mouth and a satisfied grin, he tried to say, "Why do I like this so much?" A gob of sandwich landed on the table.

Veronika laughed. "Because Rosero did. I can't believe you're even asking."

He took another bite before swallowing the first.

At the next table, Tom heard the sounds of the man eating open-mouthed. Moist, breathy inhalations. The salivated crunch of chips. The slurping of a chemical cocktail of sugar, trans fats, and food coloring. Soggy coughs from deep in his lungs. The slip 'n' slide of ill-fitting dentures flapping against his gums. Then a burp erupted, a syncopated rhythm of groans, rumbles, and gasps.

Unperturbed, Veronika seemed to enjoy her quesadilla. But Tom shivered. How could she not hear this? Why was he so disgusted?

Veronika could see his distress. "What's wrong?"

"Being me. Being human."

"Own it, dude," she said.

He tried to block the revulsion by stuffing his own face. "It's so good . . . Can I have another?"

"Don't move or look at it," Veronika said out of the side of her mouth.

A law enforcement drone—LED—hovered near their table. It was painted black and white, with the blue emblem of the LAPD. It appeared to take in the scene with equanimity, then flew away after four seconds.

"If I hack into it here, they'll see me do it," said Veronika. "Assume the worst."

"Then let's get to Essensse," said Tom.

They walked back toward the Boardwalk.

"Eddie?" A shocked voice was directed at Tom. He slowed under a covered portico of large plastered pillars and archways, but he didn't turn toward the voice. Neither did Veronika.

"Yo, Eddie! You're fuckin' alive!" A well-muscled young man in running gear made a dash for Tom, grabbed his shoulder, and spun him around. "Man, I thought I saw a ghost!" He gave Tom a bear hug. Tom felt familiarity and emotion down to his cellular structure. He knew this man was a friend. A very good one. This body felt like "brother." Tom hugged him back, running a facial-recognition search against every image database he could find.

"Hey, man. Yeah. I'm cool. How are you?" said Tom.

"Awesome now!" They released. "Who's this?" He nodded at Veronika. "We heard you were dying, man. What happened?" He gave Veronika the up-down, waiting for an introduction.

"I'm Denise," said Veronika. "His home healthcare provider."

The man looked at Tom quizzically.

"Yeah. Got better. Don't know how. Just woke up. She's helping me . . . figure out if I can live on my own."

It never dawned on Tom to double-check Edwin's previous address. Ruth and Veronika had overseen body procurement, and he had had enough on his plate. He ran a quick search, and there it was: Edwin had lived in nearby East Venice. Tom was furious at himself, but even more angry at Veronika.

She had helped steal the body. She must have known these were Rosero's stomping grounds.

A hit came back on the identity search: Oscar Morales. Employed at the same athletic facility—Gold's Gym—as Edwin.

"That's good," Oscar said. "Does Tina know?" Was Tina the hand and arm Tom saw in his brain flashback on the *Zumwalt*? "Tina will be so stoked, but not about the hot nurse . . ." He jerked his head toward Veronika, winked, then whipped out his GO.

Tom stayed his hand. "Hey, Oscar. Don't. I need to fly low for a while."

"Who you running from?" asked Oscar.

Taking a calculated risk, Tom said, "My accident wasn't an accident."

Oscar nodded. "We figured that."

Tom had no idea who Oscar might have thought guilty. "And it's not who anyone thinks."

"Need help?" asked Oscar.

"Yeah. But I got no GO. Need to rebuild contacts without them knowing," said Tom.

"Done," said Oscar.

Tom took Oscar's GO and dictated a number into it. "Here's how to reach me for now." The number would connect directly to his digital brain.

"Here's mine," Oscar said, sending a message to the number. "We'll get you goin', bro. Whatever you need."

A dark-blue Lexus sedan, old enough to rely solely on fossil fuels, slowed down on Windward. The two occupants, one with a shaved head and one with a goatee, watched Tom and Oscar through dark sunglasses before speeding away.

"Fuck," said Oscar. "Zeros. What are they doing? Get outta here." He slapped Tom on the back and took off at a run.

As they walked away from Oscar, Tom struggled to stay calm. "Why didn't you tell me Edwin's from Venice?"

"Dude, it's no big deal. I wanted to see if you recognized things. Interesting what still remains in, like, the biological brain."

Tom tried to contain his rage, but it was seeping out of his pores, flushing his skin. He could feel the hairs on his arms get prickly with heat. Shoulder muscles twitched, and his hands shook. He dragged her onto Speedway, to hide near some alley dumpsters. "I'm supposed to be on life support. It didn't occur to you I'd be made wandering around here?"

"We're not sticking around! You'll be a ghost again."

He shoved her hard against the steel dumpster. She yelped in pain as her bony shoulder blades took the brunt of the impact.

"What did I just land in?" he yelled.

Veronika was stunned. So was Tom. He hadn't meant to touch her. Or scream. It had simply happened. One brain overrode the other.

"Stop it!" She backed away from him and assumed a defensive crouch. Reaching reflexively into her Doc Martens, she yanked out a switchblade and flipped it open. "Just stop now!"

He wasn't sure how effective her blade technique would be given her inexperience with Winter and the butcher knife. But she had made her point.

Major Tom's and Rosero's brains fought each other. Tom grabbed on to the dumpster for balance. "I'm sorry . . . I'm . . . I don't . . . know what happened. Just snapped. Really. I'm sorry." He hadn't had a violent impulse for two years. Since before he had died. Goddamn this new amygdala, hijacking his brain and pumping fight-or-flight cortisol and adrenaline throughout his teenage body.

As a human, he was unpredictable. Even to himself.

David Bowie sang "Ashes to Ashes," warning him of his new dilemma. Like his namesake, Major Tom had never done anything out of the blue. But once-Edwin-now-Tom had. And probably would again.

Behind Veronika, the old blue Lexus turned the corner onto Speedway and accelerated straight toward them.

Tom leapt at Veronika and grabbed her by both shoulders. She slashed at him and missed, but he spun her so she could see the car barreling toward them. They ran.

He accessed a satellite map, looking for escape routes. Hiding places. But his body ran for the water. Like it knew what to do.

He didn't know why. He was a remote brain, captive to a body. Tom thought it was a stupid idea. He tried to stop his muscles. His body sputtered like a broken puppet operated by a rogue puppet master.

With the Lexus barreling toward them, they rounded the corner back onto Windward and the carnival of the Boardwalk. Tom tripped into a biker and only missed faceplanting when a bystander caught him and brought him to his feet.

"Hey! Slow down, man!"

"Thanks!" said Veronika, grabbing Tom's arm and pulling him away.

The Lexus barreled through barriers, which had a narrow access to allow cops and ambulances onto the Boardwalk and the beach. People leapt out of the way. Pedestrians banged on the car's hood in defiance, slowing it enough to give Tom and Veronika a tiny lead.

There was a police substation on the beach two hundred feet away. But Tom couldn't go to the police, couldn't get caught, and certainly couldn't get killed by whoever these gangsters were.

The two-wheel-drive Lexus would get stranded on the beach. Tom ran to the closest sand.

The Lexus swerved, barely missing a mother and child on two bikes, and skidded to a stop at the sand's edge. Shaved Head jumped out first, sporting a tight T-shirt and serious guns—both his arms and the weapons badly concealed in his pants. He stumbled in the sand but kept coming. His partner, with cheekbones that rivaled a Russian supermodel's, ran behind.

Running was a revelation for Tom. He didn't trip. His arms and legs pumped, and he could feel the shock of adrenaline. The respirocytes did their job, filling his red blood cells with oxygen. This body knew how to run and liked the exertion. A lot. He was surprised at how fast he went. Veronika fell behind, struggling with her long skirt and Docs. He slowed to help, but she screamed, "Go!"

On the sand, a group of police SUVs sat at a distance from a large group of people gathered at the water's edge. Dozens of drums beat, and hundreds of people chanted—the famous Venice Beach Drum Circle. A few stood taller than the others and danced with ecstatic delight on hovering flyboards. A couple of young men in G-strings hung from trapeze suspended underneath large drones, performing a circus act. Robodirigibles floated above, filming the exploits for social media. Drugs, love, good vibes, and bad rainbow clothing reigned. Neohippies clearly enjoyed their tech toys, too, if they could afford them.

Shaved Head and Cheekbones stopped when they saw Tom running directly toward a police car near the crowd. He could read their thoughts like ticker tape. Was Rosero an idiot? An informer? A stooge? What? Their driving stunt had attracted the attention of a phalanx of cops approaching from the giant drum circle on flyboards. Shaved Head and Cheekbones turned and walked slowly back, but they kept looking over their shoulders to watch Tom.

Veronika caught up to Tom. Panting, she said, "How d'ya . . . know? I never . . . told you!"

"Know what?" asked Tom.

"Go to the police!" said Veronika. "Your chip will work with them!"

"What?"

"You're an undercover cop, dude! Any agency you approach. You're one of them."

"Now you tell me?" said Tom.

"Didn't think you'd need it yet," said Veronika. "But now you do. Better I'm not with you. I'm full ghost, so I'm outta here. See you at the ship!"

She peeled off, effortlessly blending in with the neohippies, stoners, junkies, party dudes, Rastafarians, and tourists. She even danced, in her angular scarecrow way. He knew where she was and hoped Shaved Head and Cheekbones would be too occupied with the police to care.

The closer he got to the cop cars, the slower his pursuers walked away. They didn't want to miss whatever was coming. There was someone above them they'd have to report to.

Veronika text messaged him, *Wand ID. That's all they need.*

It would help to know who I am! messaged Tom.

Here's access link for West Los Angeles PD.

He scanned it. Gang and narcotics, previous work in homicide.

Tom slowed down about twenty feet before the first black-and-white. He approached the cops with a respectful and nonthreatening attitude: hands up, eye contact, slow movements.

"Hey," he said.

Two officers—Daryl Robinson, trim with an equally trim mustache, and Raymond Diaz, short and nuggety—intercepted him.

"What can we do for you?" Diaz asked, looking Tom over carefully.

Tom searched the net regarding undercover cops approaching beat cops: how-to videos, academy manuals, bad TV shows. Anything. He found a lot of bad TV, some disgruntled ex-cops spilling some beans, but not a lot he could use. His hands were still in the air, in anticipation of arrest. "Pretend to arrest and wand me," he said to them.

"Now why would we do that?" asked Officer Robinson in a laconic drawl.

"I'm UC. And they're not." According to an ex-police officer's blog, UC meant undercover cop.

A drone hovered over Shaved Head, Cheekbones, and the Lexus.

"Tag 'em?" asked Robinson.

"Yeah," said Tom. He had no idea what "tag 'em" meant, but he assumed the drones and street cameras would tag and ID them for later pursuit if the cops didn't take them in now.

Robinson and Diaz shared a look.

"It's go time," said Diaz. He slammed Tom's head to the hood of the SUV and grabbed both his wrists to handcuff him.

Robinson wanded his body.

Local, state, and federal agencies CNEM-ID tagged their agents in the same place: the upper left arm. CNEM stood for "conductive nanowire embedded mesh," a thin layer of elastomer permanently attached or implanted subcutaneously. It was faster than using biometrics, which they could still use later to confirm ID. The cops' wands—ostensibly used to check for hidden weapons and illegal substances—also contained a CNEM-ID reader that could distinguish LEO tags from others. The drug trade had taken to chipping mules with CNEM/GPS so they could be accounted for at all times. So had gangs. Cops needed to tell the difference between criminal tagging and agency tagging while making sure no one else could.

When the wand hit Tom's arm, the secret data popped up on Robinson's LEO-GO: *Detective Saul Alonzo. Age 22, Long Beach Police Department, Gang and Narcotics Division.* Tom had no idea if his pursuers had anything to do with drugs or gangs, but it gave him a good cover story.

BZZZT!

His brain buzzed. And blinked out. A shock cascaded down his trunk and spread to his extremities. From an outsider's perspective, it might have lasted only a second, but from his digital perspective, it felt both like a brief cut in the system and a potentially huge loss of data. His entire body spasmed. He seized stiff for 1.3 seconds of full body catatonia. Then he collapsed.

"Shit!" said Robinson.

Both cops dropped to assess Tom. Robinson checked his pulse. Diaz checked his mouth, to make sure he hadn't swallowed his tongue.

"Put . . . me in . . . car," Tom sputtered.

Diaz hustled him into the back seat, got in front himself, and began inputting information into the dash computer. Robinson stood in front of the door. He spoke into his live collarcam, requesting an ambulance.

"No!" moaned Tom.

"You're having a seizure!" said Robinson.

"It'll pass . . . Always does. No hospital. They'll find me."

"Cavalry rides again?" joked Diaz.

"Trust me. It's okay. Happens once a month. Since I was a kid. Probably outta shape. All that running . . ."

The cops laughed. Robinson said, "And they let you pass the physical with that?"

"I'm that good," said Tom.

The cops laughed harder.

Tom sent a diagnostic analysis to Ruth and Miss Gray Hat. Maybe they could see what the problem was. From his body's perspective, it felt like a wiring issue.

"What d'ya need?" asked Diaz.

"Ride to Long Beach. Belmont Pier, near Queen Mary. Gotta make a drop." A small craft from Island White would be at the pier to pick him up.

The partners looked at each other again, now incredulous. It was over an hour away in traffic. "We're no robocar service," said Robinson.

"Call it in," said Tom.

Robinson looked to his partner. "That's commitment, man. He's a fuckin' animal . . ."

"Thanks. Mind if I rest back here?" asked Tom.

"Fine by me," said Diaz. He sent the request, which was accepted, then programmed the dashboard. The SUV rolled away toward the pavement.

As they drove past the Lexus, Shaved Head and Cheekbones gave the cruiser the glare of death.

Tom slumped into the worn back seat, which smelled like flop sweat, urine, and blood. The facial-recognition search for Shaved Head and Cheekbones finally came up: Reggie "Coops" Cooper and Jerry Santiago. Both had been accused, but never convicted, of a variety of crimes, including crypto-laundering and tainted synthopioid production for a cartel based in Arizona. There were connections in Nevada to bankers and a state senator.

ZZZAP!

His body spasmed, but the two cops didn't notice. Jaw clamped shut and vocal cords frozen, Tom struggled to breathe. He tried to send an SOS message to Ruth, but while he had external access, Major Tom's server access suddenly went only one way. He couldn't transmit.

Frozen in the back seat, he was helpless.

And that's when the video arrived.

The video message was sent only to Tom. The sender was anonymous. He looked for a time stamp. It was live.

He recognized the location immediately: the Potsdam house in Pacific Heights, San Francisco. The fish-eye lens captured a wide shot of the kitchen. Amanda faced away, standing at the sink, cleaning dishes. Peter Jr. hummed happily in a playpen in the corner of the expansive room.

"Mama?" said Peter Jr.

"Yes, love?" said Amanda.

"Juice?" said Peter, jumping up.

"Juice what, love?"

"Pease? Juice, pease?" He jumped faster.

Amanda walked to the fridge and took out a container of apple juice. As she put it on the counter and reached for a cabinet, Tom watched the back of a young woman—statuesque with short, choppy blonde hair—enter the kitchen with a slight limp.

In the reflection of the shiny appliances, Amanda saw the intruder creeping up behind her. She screamed and spun. "Who are you?"

Winter held her hands up. "I'm here to give you a message. From Carter."

Amanda shook. "But . . . how . . ."

Extending her right hand, Winter slowly brought it to Amanda's face, settled a palm gently on her cheek.

"Will you let me tell you what he wants you to know?" asked Winter.

"Y-yes," said Amanda.

Leaning in, Winter whispered something unintelligible, her lips hidden behind Amanda's hair. By the message's length, Tom guessed it was about ninety words long. Amanda's eyes went wide. Winter nodded. Then she kissed Amanda.

In high-definition video, Tom could see Amanda's carotid artery pound in terror. Or was it excitement?

Winter reached her left hand into her back pocket, and a tiny syringe appeared, attached to the ring on her finger. She caressed Amanda's neck, then clasped it firmly.

There was no struggle. Amanda's eyes widened in terror, then slumped, and in seconds she was out. Winter gently lowered her to the floor.

"Mama! Mama!"

Winter subvocalized, and two armed lackeys appeared with a large black canvas bag.

"Where you, Mama?" asked Peter Jr.

The video followed Winter into the corner of the breakfast area where Peter played. She looked around at the Legos. The trains. The drawings.

"Where Mama?" the boy asked again.

"I'll take you to her." Winter reached down and hefted the toddler up in her arms, placing one hand around his tiny neck. She stared into those uncomprehending Bernhardt-blue eyes. Tiny hands explored Winter's face. With an unreadable expression, she stared for 7.9 seconds at the boy's innocent face, then sighed. She looked straight at the camera. "Goddamn you," she said. And she ran out the door with the boy.

CHAPTER THIRTY-THREE

Tom couldn't fathom what he had witnessed. Unexpectedly, the damper on his outside messaging lifted, and his body stopped seizing. He could move of his own volition. Panicked, he sent Miss Gray Hat the video and the data about his server attack.

"This isn't easy to decrypt," she said.

"Just do it!"

In the meantime, he searched. He hacked into the server at the Potsdam house and looked through all the security cameras. The house was eerily empty and quiet. He checked San Francisco city cams and couldn't find Winter and her goons. Nothing from satellite cameras or drones. They seemed to have materialized in the house, then disappeared.

Panic flooded his body with adrenaline, more intensely than it had at the beach. Why was he covered in fresh sweat? His heart wanted to explode in fear. Contemplating harm to Amanda and his child was more than his body could manage. Seeing Winter threaten Peter Jr., imagining the toddler's murder . . . the feelings were devastatingly different from when Tom 1 had visited them.

If this was parenthood, then damn biology.

Miss Gray Hat interrupted his reverie. "I found an inbox. We can send them a message back."

"Damn right," responded Tom.

Robinson looked at Tom in the rearview mirror. "Where do you want us to drop you?"

Tom tried to speak, but it took a few tries, and he sounded hoarse. "Supermarket at Ocean and Termino, thanks."

He sent a message to the mysterious inbox. *How could you have managed this all by yourself? You never could before. You always needed me.*

In ten seconds, a video reply appeared. The footage was taken in a dark room. It didn't look like the Potsdam house. Winter's smile was coy. Seductive. Kissing the top of the little boy's head, she said, "You've always underestimated me, my dear. And yourself. Together, we're really something."

And then it cut out.

Fresh sweat broke out over Tom's body.

The SUV pulled into the supermarket lot. With great effort, Tom pulled himself upright and waited for Robinson to open the door.

"Funny place for a drop," said Robinson.

"I need food," Tom said.

"Adios, amigo," said Diaz, and he held out his fist.

Tom's body didn't respond quickly, as though he didn't know what an extended fist meant. Then he bumped it.

Diaz looked at him with squinty eyes. Robinson missed the exchange. "Okay," Diaz finally said. "We're outta here." He tapped Robinson, and the two got into the police cruiser.

Groggy, Tom stumbled down 39th Place toward Belmont Veterans Memorial Pier, where a launch craft for Island White and the *Zumwalt* would be waiting. He wanted Ruth and Miss Gray Hat to run diagnostics as soon as possible. How did Winter get inside his system, and why did she let him go? Did she plant a virus or malware? Was she a cat to his mouse?

He trudged toward the end of the pier, where at water level, a small dock was housed next to a bait-and-snack shack. The sun was setting over the HMS *Queen Mary*. Even distracted, he was impressed by how the beauty of refracted light touched his biology in ways it couldn't when he was a digital entity reading a landscape from a streetcam. It was magic hour, where the air glowed golden and the clouds splashed in streaks of orange and purple, but the lights along the pier had yet to turn on and ruin the show. Attracted to sunlight at a cellular level, he could enjoy the real world again.

A young woman stood among the fishermen packing up their gear to head home with the day's catch. He could see only the back of her, leaning on the rails, seemingly admiring the sunset. Her choppy blonde hair made him freeze midstride. She turned, her face bemused.

"Hello there, my dear," said Winter.

All the mental and physical jangling back in the SUV had knocked Tom off his game. How could Winter be here if she had been in a dark room with his son? And how did she know where he was? He looked around, confused.

She seemed to read the thoughts broadcast on his face. "My dear, you're stupider in each incarnation. I recoded the time on the video. It happened yesterday. Not now." She shook her head sadly and pointed toward Island White and the *Zumwalt*, a mile and a half away, west-southwest. "Should have stuck with the *Pequod*. Much classier vessel. This hideous hunk of steel is about as stealth as my hot bod. By the way, you haven't complimented me on how marvelous I look."

Tom tried to tamp down the rage rising inside him. He could feel his blood vessels dilating, his heart racing, again. But he had to stay calm. Keep this creature talking. He recorded a live feed and transmitted it to the team, his eyes like cameras, though the images would be distorted through neural-transference disturbance.

Winter sauntered down the pier, and Tom had no choice but to follow. "I knew the moment that boy's body was missing, it'd be the one you'd chose," she said over her shoulder.

"Why?"

"Oh, sweetheart . . . It's so"—she gestured at his body and squished up her face, prettily—"plebeian. Does anyone take you seriously?"

"As usual, you're a fucking peacock."

Winter sniffed. "I'm special. And I always will be."

"At least I didn't kidnap and kill mine."

Winter looked surprised. "I'm not dead! And neither are you. This girl's having a hell of a more interesting life than she would have!"

"Can you hear her screaming inside? Do you enjoy it?"

Winter's face fell, her charming affect wiped away. "Took care of that. No more dual processing system. Just mine."

"You bastard. Can't even let her go when you're done with her."

"Why would I let her go? I'm quite partial to this body." She seductively slithered closer. "I like who I am. If you haven't noticed, I'm pretty fucking fabulous!"

Tom noticed. His visual cortex, gonadal steroids, and penis noticed.

Winter saw it and giggled. "Oh, Pete. How cute. Youth becomes you. You know, in some ways, it's quite freeing, especially since I ripped out anything that might get in the way. Like a uterus. Nasty things." She stroked his cheek slowly, like she had with Amanda.

He breathed in, and her scent overwhelmed him. She smelled of sex and oblivion, cloaked in the smooth silk of possibility. He took a quick step back out of her reach and said through gritted teeth, "I thought you wanted children."

"I have a child, last I checked." Her eyes glittered. "He's so much sweeter than I thought he'd be. Those blue eyes . . ." She sighed. "Missed them. That little honey's going to be a ladykiller someday. Unlike his daddy."

Winter kicked at his groin, but Tom saw it coming and dodged. Instantaneously, she spun again and landed a kick square to his head. Tom staggered back, a trickle of blood running from his ear. He responded with a blistering one-two combo assault on Winter's solar plexus.

Clearly they had both downloaded martial-arts techniques. They could both speed-compute punches and kicks. She knew Tae Kwon Do, a graceful, elegant martial art, surprisingly deadly. It suited Carter's dual personality well. Major Tom had downloaded Brazilian jiujitsu, but it didn't feel right, so he let Edwin's body lead, funny moves like running in place before a punch. It wasn't pretty, but Rosero knew Krav Maga. Quickly accessing suggestions from the web, Tom kicked, sweeping Winter off her feet. He dodged and weaved, grabbed legs and arms, and landed some satisfying punches of his own.

People on the pier moved in closer. Some whipped out cameras. Winter rushed Tom, pushing him closer to the gathering GOs recording a young Latino male beating up a pretty white woman.

Was Carter purposely staging this narrative? And what was the story?

Winter reached down her cleavage and pulled a knife from a sheath. The crowd cheered, thinking they were in on a joke. Unarmed, Tom didn't know what else Winter might have stowed. Time to get to the ship.

"Where's the launch?" he voice messaged Ruth.

"Entrance ramp. Four hundred feet on left. Docks in ten seconds," said Ruth.

"Bring it in, keep running, but don't fully dock!"

In the distance, the sound of sirens erupted. He turned and ran down the concrete pier. Winter chased after him, losing some ground because her legs were shorter, but it was clear she had trained for her new persona. He guessed microbivores and respirocytes, too, like him.

Tom reran the last few minutes of his memory. Winter had only breathed when she spoke and after thirty seconds of running. Just like him. Perhaps she also took enough steroids to build muscle. Perhaps they were both designed for this.

He pumped his arms and legs as fast as they'd go. Second fight-and-flight in a day. And it still felt good. What kind of life had Rosero lived, that this was his body's preferred state?

Careening down the long ramp to the boat dock, Winter was only twenty feet behind.

He approached the slip, where the launch idled a few feet from the dockside . . .

BZZZT!

The tremors shot through his head, cascaded down his torso and extremities. Full seizure. He fell hard onto the concrete dock, bruising his hips, shoulders, and head.

Winter ambled up to his body, flipped him onto his back, and straddled his hips, grinding into his pelvis. Then she put her hands around his throat and squeezed.

"You took respirocytes, too, so this might take a while," she said. "But hey, it's a nice evening for a strangulation. And between the lack of air, your youth, and—well, if I say so myself—me, you should pop up underneath me like a turkey timer." She winked. "Or I could hurry up and crush your windpipe, or break your neck and dump you over the side. You'd be completely helpless. Shall I? I'd love to see what happens. You know, out of scientific curiosity."

Her head suspended over his, Tom could do nothing but watch her. He had some oxygen left, but he wasn't sure how much. She leaned over slowly, tightened her grip, and licked his face with a long, languorous brush of her tongue. "I want you to know what humiliation feels like. Because from where I'm sitting, it tastes *so* good." She rose. "You'll get up when I let you. Bye-bye, sweetie." She winked again, blew him an air kiss, and sauntered away, hips swaying insolently.

The young launch pilot, Calvin, killed the engine and docked the launch. "Sorry, sir . . . I'm supposed to stay put, sir, but I don't know what to do." He knelt down, made sure Tom wasn't swallowing his tongue, then laid his hand on Tom's chest to comfort him.

When Winter was back on the pier and well out of reach, Tom's body stopped seizing. He lay there, trying to comprehend the bizarre encounter.

Calvin asked, "What can I do, sir?"

"Get . . . us back," said Tom, his voice sounding as crushed as his neck felt.

Calvin helped him up, and Tom limped into the launch and collapsed on a seat. Calvin took the helm and motored for the *Zumwalt*.

As Tom sat watching the final rays of the setting sun, one thought ringing through his head, on a loop, over and over and over, cycling in nanoseconds, millions of times: How had Winter hacked him, and why had she let him go?

CHAPTER THIRTY-FOUR

L ike Stanford University in Palo Alto to the north, Pasadena was wealthy, a sheltered community enveloping the precious minds at the California Institute of Technology—known around the world as Caltech. Wrapped in a bubble of protection, privilege, clean treelined streets, and gracious architecture, it allowed these minds to think big thoughts with minimal distractions. But unlike Palo Alto's obsession with the next big thing out of Stanford, few Pasadenans thought much about the incredible work being done right under their noses at Caltech. It was too way out in the stratosphere to capture the public's attention.

Caltech was unique. Its tiny size belied its incredible influence in science and technology. Attracting the world's best and brightest to train in technical fields and applied sciences, it was famous for running, training, and supporting NASA's Jet Propulsion Laboratory in its mission to explore beyond our Earth, managing six of the world's most important astronomical observatories and performing some of the most elaborate and successful college pranks of all time.

But there hadn't been a lot of pranks lately.

The day after his fight with Winter, Tom sat a block from campus at the 1960s-themed diner, Pie 'n Burger. While he waited to meet the only man who might be able to prevent Winter's next attack, he ate a cheeseburger with grilled onions and the diner's famous homemade

Thousand Island dressing, with a side of fries. He hoped the man would come voluntarily.

Around him construction workers ate an early lunch, and a handful of students studied textbooks with titles like *Engineering Mechanics/ Dynamics, Vol. II* and *Fundamentals of Aerospace*. Neuroscience had proved that information gleaned from paper texts was remembered with greater accuracy than from digital texts, and printed books had made a comeback. The students took any advantage they could get. The pressure on these young men and women was no longer to make huge scientific strides, or create a successful technology, or get into the top graduate school program. They now had to save the world. Hunched over tables and counters, oblivious to distractions around them, they felt that pressure distinctly.

Tom dug into his burger, a perfect combination: the softness of the bun, the crispness of fresh iceberg lettuce and pickles, the sweetness of the dressing, the tanginess of the grilled onions, the gooeyness of melted cheese, meaty warmth, a bounty of textures and flavors wrapped in a little parchment-paper envelope to prevent all that contradictory goodness from falling apart. He stared covetously into the Plexiglas cabinet with pies of twenty-six varieties, eyeing a piece of peanut-butter pie. Neither Peter, nor Tom, had eaten peanut-butter pie, but he assumed Rosero had loved it, because he felt the desire all the way down in his toes. He had never craved what in his last life he would have considered junk food. It was a revelation! He suddenly understood so much more about the why of American eating habits. Sugar plus bad fat plus too much salt equaled *awesome*. He'd be dead well before the food got him anyway.

Next to his captain's stool at the counter, he held an open seat with a copy of Dr. Arun Ponnusamy's textbook, *Artificial Human-like Intelligence: Next Steps to AHI*. The waitresses frowned at his saving a seat, but it was still early for the lunch crowd, which usually lined up out on the sidewalk, even during these troubled times.

The door opened precisely at 11:00 a.m. It was Ponnusamy. A fit thirty-two-year-old of Southern Indian descent, he wore an Ohio State T-shirt, crisp jeans, and new running shoes and had a collection of prayer beads and blessing bracelets wrapped around his left wrist. A professorial messenger bag was strapped diagonally across his torso. He stood for a moment, his eyes adjusting from the bright sun in the dark diner.

Tom nodded to him. Ponnusamy sauntered over.

"Subtle," said Ponnusamy. "Sure you're not a comp-sci or neuro-groupie? Or a desperate Caltech prospective?"

Tom removed the book and gestured for him to sit. "Nope." He pointed at Ponnusamy's shirt. "I don't remember Ohio State from your CV."

"My religion is the Buckeyes."

Tom snorted.

"The message," Ponnusamy continued, "said that I was meeting someone to see Ruth Chaikin and the Thomas Paine AHI." He looked around tentatively, as if feeling that this meeting was for naught.

Winter was right. Tom felt chronically underestimated in this new body. "Yep. That's me."

"You know them?"

"As I said. That's me."

It still wasn't registering. "I'm kinda busy . . . midterms . . ." He fiddled nervously with his bracelets. A waitress came to take his order. "Thanks, Denise, not yet." She nodded, flicked a glance at Tom, and left.

"I'm part of the Thomas Paine AHI," said Tom.

Ponnusamy rose from the stool and swung his bag around his back. "And that's my cue . . ."

"'Integration of a biological neural network into an AI is by no means theoretical. The example of Peter Bernhardt/Thomas Paine, while doubted by those scientists whose egos he bruised by accomplishing it first, is to my mind clearly existent and demands to be studied in depth. The key technologies that record memories became the bedrock of an AHI consciousness in Peter Bernhardt's Hippo and Cortex 3.0, endovascular nanowire implants, combined later with the nano-sized macrosensors, which have been replicated in animal studies as both an output of neural stimuli and an input for digital information. But what hasn't been revealed is the "magical upload" process, which supplanted the previous . . .'" Tom sighed. "Do I need to go on?"

Ponnusamy stood still. "Anyone with half a brain could have memorized a paragraph in a paper."

"'That paper hasn't been published. Yet. It was your letter of introduction to Ruth Chaikin. But it turns out I have more than half a brain. Probably two, maybe more. If you include the net, the size of one's 'brain' is hard to quantify. And I wouldn't have to memorize it, although I really can't help it. I could have been reading it off the e-mail. And by the way, your message manner annoys the hell out of both Ruth and me. You're a persistent ass."

Ponnusamy sat back down, and his eyes narrowed. "Why are we meeting here?"

"Your campus has too many cameras. In the old days, NASA, DARPA, NIH, NSF, GE, GM, IBM, and who knows who else watched on the other end. In our new world, who's watching now? You still have money coming in. You sure where it's from? And every student I see has a self-designed drone and posts everything, all the time, to social media."

"And there are no cameras here?" asked Arun.

"Other than the diner's GOs, no. I checked. Apparently, your new grantors don't care about cramming students. An error on their part." He looking longingly at the pie case again.

"If I pissed you off, why are you contacting me?"

"We need your help. My AHI is under attack, and we're not sure how they did it. Or what they may do next."

"Flattering. But you still haven't proved to me that you have anything to do with Thomas Paine or AHI."

Tom shook his head. "Accept the chat in three . . . two . . . one . . ." He pointed at Ponnusamy's pocket with his GO inside.

The GO buzzed. Arun grabbed it from the pocket and looked at the screen, accepting an anonymous live screenchat.

Ruth was waving from her favorite ergonomic chair on the *Zumwalt*'s bridge. "Dr. P-P-Ponnusamy? I p-presume? I'm Dr. Ruth. Chaikin." Ruth had become quite famous two years ago and possessed a face, voice, and mannerisms that were hard to forget. "You don't believe? That young man? He is part of our AHI. He p-p-placed our call. His brain is a download. Of Major Tom. And we need your help."

Next to her, a monitor displayed a Thomas Paine avatar on it. "We greatly appreciate any assistance you can give, and we'll give you complete access to our AHI. We would like to host you on our ship if you would go with Tom. After he finishes his burger, of course. He never stops eating."

"But how do I know this is real?" asked Arun.

The Thomas Paine avatar looked at Ruth and said, "See? I told you. Again, in three . . . two . . . one . . ."

Every GO in the room vibrated or rang at once. Patrons and employees checked the unlisted number or answered a caller that hung up.

Arun waved Denise over, barely looking up from his GO screen. "The usual, Denise. Thanks."

"Veggie burger, strawberry pie, iced tea . . . ," Denise said.

"To go," said Tom. "And peanut-butter pie, please. Make that two. All to go. We're in a rush." He was grateful there would be no kidnapping. He took another huge bite of his burger. God, it was good.

One of Tom's conditions was that Arun not be allowed to return home or pack a bag. Talia picked the two men up in a 1995 BMW 325i, gas-powered, built before black boxes or GPS came with cars. They headed to the *Zumwalt*.

"Why are we going to New Orleans?" asked Arun.

"I made a promise to a man named Rick Blaine," said Tom. "For access to information and the robots I've used, I promised to help him with the refugees in New Orleans and South Florida."

Arun looked at him like he was crazy. "Won't that take you away from dealing with Carter Potsdam?"

"No," said Talia. "Carter's part of the refugee crisis. He may have helped create it."

"How?" asked Arun. "I thought this was a battle of AHIs."

Tom laid his head back against the seat. "I wish it were that simple. I'm not sure how yet, but he's connected to whatever the hell is happening in the Southern States of America. The Phoenix Club isn't dead."

"And we have to help the refugees," said Talia. "It's the most important thing we'll ever do. These boys can play their brain games later."

For a moment, the only sound was Arun's fingers twiddling his bracelets.

Tom sighed. "Talia's my moral authority. You heard her. We're doing both."

CHAPTER THIRTY-FIVE

The *Zumwalt* cleared the Panama Canal with difficulty. The Panamanian government had lost control over the canal. Long-unpaid lock workers extorted large amounts of the *Zumwalt's* consumables in exchange for passage. Ruth was concerned that this would happen at each stop, and they needed massive quantities of food and supplies for their next mission. At thirty knots, they had only two days left at sea until reaching New Orleans.

Talia and Steve worked at a conference table on the bridge, planning the logistics of saving hundreds, then thousands, of homeless humans from the clutches of the SSA.

Major Tom's primary goal was to find and stop Carter. Below deck in the surgical theater, he lay on an examination table, his body covered in so many sensors, wires, and contraptions that he looked like a fly caught in a massive spider's web. They could have gone wireless, but as Ruth often said, the old ways were best. Based on discussion with Arun Ponnusamy over the past four days at sea, Ruth ran diagnostics on the AHI information systems. Veronika manned the console, linking the data streams to get a bigger visual picture of the vast system.

Arun asked Tom, Ruth, and Veronika a million questions, poked and prodded physical and electronic systems, and paced. "You're screwed," said Arun, twiddling his prayer bracelets. You're melding biological and digital systems. Works well in small doses. The world's filled with medical cyborgs. And your hypotheses are valid, but you're doing it over huge, complex, and interconnected body systems, all at once, with no testing. You're the only lab rat. How can we be sure if it's working? Or harming you?"

"There are two lab rats," said Tom.

"Yeah," said Arun, "but I can't analyze Winter."

Ruth pursed her lips, and her left arm quaked. "You understand less. Than I assumed."

"Come on, Ruth," said Arun. "I explore AHI concepts and apply them to deep learning and intuitive systems. I don't deal directly with flesh and blood, but I'm not an idiot. Some of my best friends build brain-computer interfaces." He smiled with faux condescension.

Ruth's head twitched, her lips burbling in disdain. She turned to look at the EEG.

Arun pulled a chair up to the examination table and, for the first time, gently laid his hand on Tom's arm. "You realize all these electronics will probably shorten your biological life, right? If someone doesn't murder you, you'll certainly die from something you did to yourself."

"Like cancer? Or a stroke?"

"Yeah. Could be anything interfering with this body's normal operation. Electronics and cells didn't evolve together. You must know this."

Tom sighed. "Of course I do. I've minimized the impact and keep medical help nearby. But one doctor, well, he likes the money and does what I tell him. The other probably wouldn't mind if I shuffled off the mortal coil. Or slunk back to my server. Or just disappeared. I can't dwell on personal consequences. Or I couldn't do this."

"The second one wants you dead?"

"Well, out of the way. I'm ruining his life."

"Great docs to have in your corner," Arun sneered.

Tom wanted to itch where a sensor was glued, but he resisted. "There are trade-offs in life. I make bigger ones than most, and trust me, it's not as fun as it looks."

"Well, it's still more fun than dying," said Arun, "because you get a second chance. And a third. The rest of us don't. How long can you prevent the inevitable?"

"What? Dying for good?" asked Tom. "Or others trying this?"

Arun nodded, impressed that Tom understood the ethical implications. "Both."

"Same answer. As long as it takes so that I don't hurt anyone ever again."

Arun sat back in his chair and crossed his arms over his chest. "I'm betting you won't make it that long."

"Thanks for the support." Tom closed his eyes to shut him out.

But Arun didn't stop. "No. I mean you know how to do this, and Carter Potsdam does, too. How can you be sure he won't share the tech with everyone? Or I won't, for that matter? A Nobel Prize looks mighty nice on the mantel." He winked.

"They're overrated . . . ," muttered Ruth.

Tom shook his head. "You won't want to share this if you spend enough time with me. And Carter? He's not big on sharing. This is the most powerful technology ever created, and he's enough of a narcissist and strategist to keep all the power for himself. For now." Tom said nothing more for a few seconds, running statistical modeling scenarios for how long Carter might keep the secret. None of them made him feel better. "Can we please focus on getting Carter out of my head?"

Arun asked, "Can someone show me where you keep the data that came from outside his servers since he left his digital home?"

"There is nothing. I went over this," said Ruth.

Veronika said, "But we never checked, like, before he left the Memory Palace."

Tom was surprised. "Are you sure?"

"Let's go as far back as the program goes," said Arun. "To before you were uploaded. There must be bugs, or malware, in there. Can we contact this Miss Gray Hat and compare systems?"

231

Veronika said, "I've got it up already."

Tom mentally dove into the programming himself. The code looked good to him.

Arun turned to Veronika. "If I was going to put a body override into a virtual AHI, it could be really hard to find and eradicate because the goal function can be distributed all over the intelligence."

Veronika studied the data in her glasses. Tom looked from the outside on the table, and Major Tom from inside his server.

"Wow," said Veronika.

"What?" asked Tom.

"You don't see this?" she asked.

"See what?" he asked again.

"Both of you, throw what you see onto a big screen," Arun said, "so we can compare them." Veronika split a HOME screen and displayed her programming on the left, Tom's on the right.

Arun considered both. He turned to Tom on the table. "You, my strange friend, are leading a double life. You think that's you, because that's what you see," he said, pointing to the right. "But that's you, too," he added, pointing to the left. "I'm not sure you've ever been in control of you, since the Memory Palace began. If we don't fix it, they've got you. For good."

Arun's declaration took Tom aback. "Wait, you're saying I'm not me? And someone or thing created a version of me that I think is me?"

"Bingo," said Arun.

Tom studied the programs, but this was out of his league. "Help?"

Veronika and Arun shared a look of concern. She pointed to a line of code on the HOME screen. "This, like, right here, replicates you in another location."

"Can we fix it?" asked Tom.

Veronika studied the screens and chewed her hair. "Maybe."

Arun regarded the team with incredulity. "Look, I know you like your little scrappy band of rebels—and hey, thanks for the secret handshake—but we need more help. I'm guessing your opponents have ten times the help you do."

Tom sighed. "Try a thousand times, maybe hundreds of thousands if you include all the AIs and data processors changing the story of my life around the world."

"Well, don't you think—" said Arun.

"Shhh," said Veronika. She was typing.

Arun stood over her shoulder, watching as her fingers moved feverishly in the air on her virtual keyboard. After a couple of minutes, he said, "You're the most interesting coder I've seen. Maybe ever."

"Huh?" she muttered.

His eyes never left the screen. "You're making higher-order leaps that I didn't have to explain, with incredible intuition for someone so young. But you've also got a rigorous, analytical mind. You usually see one *or* the other."

Tom watched the code blossom across the screen, wondering if Veronika's ability was intuition or if she knew more than she was letting on? She was too good to have been hidden for years in role-playing alternate realities like TCoMT, or even cryptocurrency and identity coding. She could have been a programming superstar anywhere she wanted and made a fortune by now.

"That's 'cause I got, like, a secret weapon."

Arun looked bemused. "And what's that?"

"If I hadn't started out as a computer-obsessed kid in a male body, then transitioned, I couldn't do this."

Arun looked at Tom questioningly. Tom nodded. Then Arun nodded. "That's . . . so cool. Never occurred to me it would affect cognitive processes like that. But it has to."

"Hell yeah, dude. Big blasts of, like, adolescent testosterone, then estrogen meds? I grew up with a typical male-brained, intensely logical, analytical approach. Then the hormones made me have, like, intuition,

I guess. My brain does both equally. And you learn you need both, too. You see the world from both sides now."

Tom snorted at Veronika's reference: Joni Mitchell's classic "Both Sides, Now." The song began to play through the speakers.

Shaking his head, Arun said to Tom, "Yeah, we know your tricks. Pipe down." Then he turned to Veronika. "Any interest in Caltech after you save the world? You could teach."

"Ha! Nah, dude. This is the best buzz ever."

The song burrowed into Tom's mind, wiggling around. "Not playing around," he said. "Think about the last three stanzas. About how experience changes us, and friends not liking that change. About being abandoned. And how it's all revealed to be an illusion. There's something there. Isn't that what we're dealing with here? I experienced it back when I had the original implants. And I still am."

Arun's face grew pinched. "Not on your wavelength, sorry."

Tom caught a smile flicker across Veronika's face. And then it was gone. Was she in agreement? Or had she planted the thought purposefully? The song flooded his system with memories of shame, abandonment, and illusion. Of installing the first Hippo and Cortex 2.0 in secret from Carter and Amanda. Of Amanda's miscarriage. Of demonstrating the new systems and failing at the Phoenix Club encampment. Of his supposed colleagues—Carter, Josiah, Bruce, Chang—all betraying him, trying to kill him. Of Steve fighting him on installing the 3.0. Of Talia hating what he had become. Of dying and living again in completely new forms.

An alarm on the console sounded. The cyberhacking detector had found an intruder.

"Shit!" screamed Veronika.

Both men looked at the HOME screen.

"There!" yelled Veronika. "Hacker inside." They all watched the Major Tom code change in real time. The AI was trying to combat it but was not winning. "No way! Not now!" She commanded the AI to take care of lower-order attacks and jumped back into the code.

"Disconnect from the network!" said Ruth.

"No!" said Arun. "We need to see how he's getting in. If we can see the changes, we can try to find the access. And we'd have to turn off all of Major Tom. Complete shutdown. Tom might die."

"Miss Gray Hat built trip wires into this system," said Veronika. "This ass is tripping them."

Ruth sent a voice message to Miss Gray Hat: "Need your help now! MT is under attack!"

The battle was on. Watching Veronika and this mysterious cracker working against each other was like watching them lob grenades, except each throw happened in a few seconds with letters, numbers, symbols— and a lot of deleting—across the huge screen. Some of the code was familiar to Tom. With help from Ruth and Miss Gray Hat, he had writ- ten a little of it himself before he uploaded. But some of it was new, written by Dr. Who, Miss Gray Hat, Veronika, and Ruth.

Arun snapped at Tom, "Stay down! Don't move." He quickly tied Tom down on the examination table with the restraint straps. "They're after your spinothalamic pathway."

Tom watched the code on screen. It was not the same route into his systems that they had used in Venice and Long Beach. Arun was right, and he had no time to . . .

"*Aaaaahhh!*" he screamed.

If a pain signal were a loudspeaker in his brain, this signal was so loud that it ran through all the major biological systems in his body, broadcasting in agonizing bursts to his muscles, skin, head, torso, arms, legs, internal organs. There was no intensity scale to describe it. It was pure pain. He prayed it didn't cause a heart attack. In this body, there were no nanosensors in his bloodstream that he could order to cut his pain receptors. How could Major Tom have been so stupid? He writhed in agony on the table, the restraints preventing him from ripping off the sensors, crashing to the floor, and injuring himself.

Steve came running in.

Frightened at Tom's distress, Veronika couldn't concentrate. She started singing "The Sound of Silence," off-key, to block him out and focus on freeing him from the hack.

Steve yelled, "What the hell are you doing to him?"

"Not me. Hacker!" screamed Veronika. She continued singing the Simon & Garfunkel classic. Only Tom understood. It was like her Lord's Prayer. Tom would have laughed, if he could stop screaming.

Steve ran for a crash cart and prepared a syringe of Nalbuphine, a synthopioid to ease the pain.

"No!" said Tom through clenched teeth. "Not . . . yet!"

Ruth stood close, without touching Tom's body, shaking as much as he was. "P-p-p-please! L-l-let Steve help! Miss G-G-Gray Hat doesn't answer!"

"Opiates . . . might interfere . . . with feedback! She needs . . . to see . . . feedback!"

Ruth knew he was right, but she couldn't take his agony. She ran to the corner of the lab and crouched down, twitching and shivering like a frightened terrier.

Veronika stopped singing. "Fuck! I know this guy!"

"How?" asked Arun.

"Like, his rhythm. And readability index. And his obsession for, like, hidden stupid lady-part words. It's unusual. Get on that terminal!"

Arun ran to another monitor and logged in.

"He's American," Veronika said. "Used to do business, and then, like, he asked me out. Fucker. In Grand Rapids. Try this link." She sent it to Arun. "And this code. And here's the local power grid accesses. Go after it. Just long enough for me to finish. Let's shut that fucker down."

"But how do you know . . . ?" asked Arun.

"What about hospitals and—" said Steve.

"On generator backup. Do it!"

"You're sure?" said Arun.

"If not, we'll know quick!" said Veronika.

Arun did as ordered. It was terrifyingly easy. In less than a minute, Grand Rapids, Michigan, had no power. "Damn. I've never broken the law before."

"Welcome to the shit show, dude," said Veronika. "Look. He's gone. Hired a fucking amateur. Even I had my own solar and battery array."

Her hands danced in the air in front of her. "Just need . . . ten more minutes, then we, like, lock, load, and bury this screed where no one can find it."

Arun sat back, stunned. "I really hope we don't hurt anyone in Grand Rapids."

Veronika looked smug. "Santa Barbara had blackouts all the time, till the state went full solar. We survived."

Tom's eyes flashed open. He gulped a lungful of air, struggling against the restraints. Steve bent over him and listened to his heart, took blood pressure and pulse, checked his eyes and reflexes. Tom lay there exhausted. "When we get that little shit back up," he said, "I want to exploit his system. Figure out who he's working for. And then hurt him. Badly. Leave him as an example not to fuck with us."

Ruth, Arun, and Steve traded uncomfortable looks.

"You know who's behind this," said Veronika softly as she typed. "This one's taking orders. Like, a little fish looking for coin. Throw him back. We'll dismantle his system later and look for others. Then we'll see how to strengthen the cyberhack system. Relax." She took a deep breath, trying to unwind herself.

"Did you see what I just went through?" yelled Tom.

"Yeah, dude, I did. And I know he, or someone like him, set fire to my house and hurt my mom. But he's small fry. And he's done. Next stop for him was fast food, but that's manned by robots now."

She was right. Tom took another deep breath and tried to clear his thinking. Why was he behaving so vindictively? So illogically? Oh yeah, he was human. No one could think purely logically and without bias, no matter how intelligent. Either one lacked knowledge, and therefore thought they knew more than they did. Or they possessed knowledge, and assumed they knew more than they did. Put another way: no matter how much anyone knew, they were usually wrong.

Regardless, with everyone assuming their way was the best way, there would be trouble ahead. He knew the team's plan to save refugees had sieve-like holes. And one question pulsed through his mind like a heartbeat after every attack: Why was he still alive? Why was he still alive? Why was he still alive? His only answer so far: Carter was waiting for a showdown. Winter versus Tom, round 2. For all his knowledge and predictive analysis, he wasn't sure who would win.

CHAPTER THIRTY-SIX

Two days after the cyberneural attack, Tom's human body still recovered below deck. The *Zumwalt* entered the mouth of the Mississippi River as stealthily as a six-hundred-foot naval destroyer could. He didn't want anyone to see him yet, for fear his human identity might become too well known, too soon. But he could watch the first step of their operation almost as well as if he was there.

Only the barest sliver of moon shone on the ship's security cameras, and if one noticed the big, dark mass at all, it was from a hole of blackness surrounded by the shimmer of reflecting water, or by its blotting out lights from the opposite shore.

He heard gunfire, miles away. Conrad's army hadn't arrived yet, but violence was already breaking out. Rick was helping them with identities to get the refugees out of both New Orleans and Port Everglades and in new lives elsewhere, untraceable by the SSA. Tom just wished it went faster. Every moment Carter had before they arrived in Florida would make him stronger.

Talia and Ruth exited a huge hangar door on the stern deck to meet a small craft, its lights out, approaching from the riverside. There was no breeze to move the humid air, and the tinny sound of the putt-putt engine sounded in the dampness. The small boat came along side. A lithe man quickly climbed the *Zumwalt*'s side ladder to the deck.

"Bonjou!" whispered Rick Blaine as he came on deck. "Welcome to the craziest port town in the country."

Talia shook his hand. "So good to finally meet you. Hope we can help."

"Glad Tom kept his promise. How many beds for my people?" Rick asked. He extended his hand to Ruth.

Ruth backed away and twitched. "Only a few hundred. No more available."

"What's your problem, lady?" Rick asked. "The SSA is sending Conrad's army. Now."

Major Tom checked a satellite camera feed of the Southern States of America. A large military presence was massing in Biloxi, Gulfport, and Picayune, Mississippi, and along state borders further west, ready to cross into Louisiana.

"We can't get a big enough ship into the ports here for you," said Talia. "The draught's too shallow and the docks are too small. Big ships can go to South Florida. We're trying to round up more small ships for you."

"Batars!" fumed Rick.

Talia touched his arm. "We're doing the best we can. We can move twenty thousand in two ships from Port Everglades in Fort Lauderdale, so I need your top picks for this ship to help us there. And you."

"I can't leave," said Rick.

"Conrad's army is coming," said Talia. "You said it yourself. We need you for identity assignments."

"Veronika can do it." Rick gestured toward the dark of the riverbank. "If I go, who helps my people get to your future ships? This is my city. *Se kreyol mo yè.* Can't call me Creole if I don't have a parish 'a friends and a hidey hole."

"We must move fast," said Ruth. "In the gulf before sunrise."

"I can register new identities as they load," said Rick. "Veronika can do back-end detail work. Exact number you can take tonight?"

"Three hundred," said Talia. "That's bodies in every place we can manage. This ship is huge, but it's not designed for people. And we've only got enough food to get to New York. Ideally, we want to get them to Canada. We know they're accepting Southern refugees."

"Come on, *mes amis*! Give me some wiggle room! Can't we put 'em on the deck?" Rick waved his arms at the enormous and empty platform. "Tent city? Something?"

"We must remain. As stealth as possible," said Ruth. "This ship is important. And we are p-p-prey if found."

Rick muttered quiet curses in Louisiana Creole. He plopped down cross-legged and feverishly text messaged on his GO, which Major Tom and Miss Gray Hat had hacked back at the nightclub in New Orleans. He was contacting the three hundred people he had chosen for the first wave to pave the way for more folks who would follow. Talia and Ruth left him to it.

Soon, a flotilla of small boats headed for the stealth behemoth. Pontoon party boats, inflatable dinghies, small skiffs, and sportsfishing charters came with human cargo from shore. It was a clever mix of refugees: some leaders, some followers, some with great skills, some with no definable skills—yet—but all begging for opportunity. As with most refugees, the largest demographic was under the age of eighteen. Families with children felt they had the most to lose and were the most eager to flee. They were also those most likely to settle quickly in a new home, assimilate, and establish a community for others to follow.

Talia saw the hope in their faces and understood. "Rick, you're a wise and compassionate man. For all your hustle."

"*Mèsi.*" When she looked confused, he said, "Thanks."

The silent, orderly boat parade approached the *Zumwalt*, dropped off passengers, and went back to pick up more. On a boat, a baby cried. Its mother bounced the infant to quiet him. On another, a child whimpered, apparently afraid of the looming dark ship. It did look like

241

something out of a nightmare, with a dark, hulking shape that didn't look like anything a child would recognize.

As the migrants climbed aboard, Rick and Talia re-registered each subcutaneous CNEM-ID tag with Rick's reader, assigning them new identities so that no government, real or imagined, could order them back. Then they headed below deck, to be directed by Ruth to their crowded, barebones accommodations.

As Rick watched the last few disappear into the hangar doors, he grabbed Talia's arm. "You promise they'll be safe? These folks. They're more than clients. They're human beings. We're all human beings . . ." The pale city lights bounced off the clouds and reflected in his watery eyes. "They deserve to be free. Find happiness . . ." His throat caught.

Talia took his hand. "I hope we do right by you and your community, Rick. We'll keep in touch."

Within three hours, the full complement of three hundred was aboard, and Rick was off to secure the next shipload.

It was time to say goodbye to someone too valuable to keep on board.

Arun Ponnusamy paced the tiny bunkroom where Tom rested in bed. "Come on, you still need me! What if Carter hijacks you again?"

Tom smiled sadly. "I'm sure he will, but maybe not in a way that you can help with."

"But I'm learning, too. I've got incredible new ideas for—"

"That's why you need to go," said Tom. "I need someone to continue what we did. Get back and work. You have no idea how grateful I am that you helped us."

"But what am I going to do now?" asked Arun. "I can't share this information. I can't even tell anyone where I went."

"But you can build from it. And you're right. This body won't last for long. I'm hoping a better AHI will. It needs to evolve to survive.

And I need you alive for that. You can be a warrior on another front."
Tom studied Arun. "What do you know about smart-body prosthetics?
Like autonomous exoskeletons."

"A little," said Arun. "Why?"

"I have a side job. You can give an active life back to the most
incredible woman in the world. And I promise you'll love her as much
as I do."

Within minutes, Arun was ferried to a boat that would take him
to Playa Bagdad, Mexico, where a car would take him to Matamoros
to board a private jet that would fly him to Burbank, California, and
back to Caltech.

The *Zumwalt* set sail for Port Everglades.

CHAPTER THIRTY-SEVEN

The next day, Talia crawled inside a 3-D dome on the *Zumwalt* bridge and monitored a camerafeed near the ship's bow. It was dawn on Florida's southeast coast, and the landscape looked peaceful from a distance: beaches, luxury hotels, cruise ships, palm trees waving in the gentle breeze. But when she zoomed in, she could see people. Hundreds of thousands, all desperate to leave. During her childhood and young adulthood, when she had been Marisol Gonzales, this had been her home. Then her father was mistakenly murdered by the Phoenix Club when a member fulfilling his initiation orders had intended to kill her instead. She had been on the run and living under a fake identity ever since.

Talia changed her feed to HOME media, scanning news, social, any content with the hashtag #SouthFlorida. Local media was a flood of images and catchphrases. The poor flocking to the ports were compared to pigs in dirt, monkeys in trees, rats fleeing a ship, terrorists with bombs, thieving bums, foreign immigrants. Anyone whose skin was darker than whatever constituted "white" to other whites was accused of being lazy or evil. She flipped through quickly. Her eyes watered.

Tom sat in a console next to her. "You okay?"

She was silent for 6.3 seconds, her eyes never leaving the screen. "Never thought I'd have a reason to come back. Too many memories of a shitty life. You know, even though I was forced to run, I couldn't wait to escape. These were my people, and yet, it wasn't my place."

"Is that how you convinced Steve to stay on board? Because you knew he'd be needed back where you both came from?"

"He's a sucker for real people in need. And *his* people?" She tried to smile at the irony, but it didn't reach her eyes. The tragedy ahead of them was stunning. "Neither of us could imagine not trying to help. How can any country in this century do this to its own? No less ours?"

"You think our country is special," said Tom. "It's not. Except for pockets like New Orleans and South Florida, the South didn't treat all their citizens like citizens. And it's not our country. Not anymore."

"But it is." She waved at the millions determined to leave at whatever price they could manage. "They tried to live within its rules, and they're punished for it. The state claims allegiance and demands obedience. But it gives nothing but pain in return. There's no social contract. How could this have happened?" She stared glassy-eyed at the screen.

Tom knew it was a rhetorical question. She'd been fighting the culprits for years, and one cause of this humanitarian disaster was his fight with Carter. Tom believed it would have happened eventually anyway, but probably not so soon.

Although no one wanted to believe it, civilization's veneer was paper-thin. The smallest change could burn it away and reveal the chaos underneath.

"You focus on the refugees," said Tom. "I'm going to focus on Carter and the club."

Talia nodded. The console beeped. She pressed the receiver button.

"CAS *Theodore Roosevelt* calling *Zumwalt* . . ."

CAS meant a California ship. This was the former USS *Theodore Roosevelt*, an old Nimitz-class nuclear-powered supercarrier, designed for naval aircraft and personnel. There were newer and larger carriers, but none could accommodate as many people nor remain at sea for six months without visiting a port. With its nuclear engine still intact and another ten years of fuel, the ship had plenty of good years left in her.

Talia jumped on the com and struggled to sound upbeat. "*Zumwalt* here. Hello, Rough Rider, so good to hear back. How far away are you? And remember, talk to me like I'm an idiot."

The communications officer laughed. "Eleven hundred nautical miles. Arriving tomorrow, oh-nine-hundred hours."

"Thank God," she said. "I don't know how much longer they'll hold out."

"Captain Curtis says to say, 'Anything for Talia . . .' I'm not allowed to comment."

"Tell Geoff I'm more grateful than he'll ever know. How many does he think you'll take?"

"We can manage seven thousand back to San Diego. They'll sleep in rotation on tables, in the halls, and maybe on deck, depending on weather, but we'll go for it."

"Governor Woods will still let them in?" she asked.

"Yes, ma'am. Far as we know, California is ready for them. But don't worry. We're not called the Big Stick for nothing."

Talia and Tom could hear laughing on the other end of the call. California maintained its home ports' naval fleet under the condition that the fleet had some autonomy for humanitarian missions. No smart governor was going to disturb that agreement. And Governor Woods had already publicly stated that California would accept SSA refugees.

"But ma'am," Rough Rider continued, "we do anticipate an issue entering Port Everglades. I understand you know this area well?"

"Yes. What's the problem?" asked Talia.

"Satellite and drone images show that the army of the South has infiltrated South Florida and taken it over. No battles. Just rolled right in and stopped outside large encampments, like Port Everglades. New Orleans is next. At the mouth of Port Everglades, there's a naval surface warfare base, as well as a coast guard base. The naval base was mostly for requisitions, but the coast guard could be a problem. Dover Air Force Base is sending us reconnaissance. There's unusual weapons movements near the port, but also near the northern borders of the SSA. Also, you gave us info about Winter d'Eon. We shared it with Dover. They've spotted someone in Fort Lauderdale matching her biometrics. They're nervous as hell."

Tom nodded to Talia.

"Please send whatever information they're willing to share," said Talia. "Could the SSA hurt your ship?"

"Ma'am," said Rough Rider, "if fired upon, I believe we would hurt them more than they could hurt us, but you know what they say about assumptions."

"Any word on the *Ocean Harmony*?" asked Talia. The *Ocean Harmony* was the biggest cruise ship in the world. Its regular capacity was six thousand passengers and twenty-four hundred crew. In a wartime scenario, it could be commandeered and converted to carry at least ten thousand troops. Maybe more. Talia was hoping to board at least twelve thousand, including crew, for the trip back to San Diego.

"Captain Curtis said he's working on Captain Alessandro right now. One moment, ma'am," said Rough Rider. They muted transmission for six seconds, then came back. "Captain says Alessandro'd have to go AWOL with a two-billion-dollar ship, find a thousand crew, and set sail against his company's and President Conrad's orders. It's mighty unlikely. But it's sitting in Port Everglades waiting to be boarded if Alessandro says yes."

Tom sent Talia a private message: *Tell them I will help with that.*

Talia repeated the message.

"Don't know how that would work, ma'am," said Rough Rider, "but we'll be there to help, too, if they do."

"Thanks, Rough Rider. Give Geoff and your crew my best."

"He says 'right back at ya,' ma'am. Rough Rider out."

She sat back and turned to Tom. Her forced smile dropped. "So how do you think we can convince a cruise-ship line, the president of the SSA, and the captain and crew of the biggest ship in the world to do what we want?"

Tom leaned forward and took her hand. "By telling them it's not happening."

CHAPTER THIRTY-EIGHT

Tom had studied Fort Lauderdale and Port Everglades in 3-D via satellite views and a multitude of security cameras he had hacked into. With countless superimposed snapshots, a multi-layered image coalesced. Like a cubist painting exposing all the subject's sides at once, it revealed the simultaneity of time. His experience was no longer linear. As time stretched, space compacted, allowing events that had occurred over the days to play out all at once. Suns rose with a variety of intensities and hues, shown bright and cloudy at their height, and set, revealing a tight patchwork fabric of moons, stars, clouds, and darkness. People occupied many locations at once, some passing through, others frequent visitors.

Cameras on the *Zumwalt* focused on different parts of the city. The monitors and domes showed the team the new Fort Lauderdale as they approached. Storefronts were closed and boarded up along city blocks. *For Lease* signs hung on almost every commercial space. Streets were dirty, and sidewalks were covered in trash.

The big, white high-rise hotels were empty of vacationers. Temperatures averaged one hundred degrees, with unbearable humidity. Squatters occupied most rooms. The police would clear them out, only for more to figure out a way over, under, and around the fences and barbed wire. Beaches had disappeared under the rising sea. Blue-green algae blooms choked the entire Florida shoreline, clinging to the first-floor walls of once luxurious buildings. Soon, ocean currents would destroy the foundations and even the squatters would have to evacuate.

A tent city of over one hundred thousand people huddled around Terminal 18 at Port Everglades, home of the deepest cruise-ship berths in the world. Refugees were forbidden by the state governor from sheltering inside the Fort Lauderdale Convention Center, so they made do wherever they could. Tens of thousands of refugee tents looked like colored candies on asphalt-gray trays. Parking structures were repurposed as open-air apartment buildings, with tents set up close but haphazardly, as befitted an emergent, unorganized process. They filled parking lots, streets, grassy areas between storage tanks—anywhere that might remain unmolested, even for a short while. They stopped at the fences that ran along Eisenhower Boulevard and Southeast Nineteenth Avenue. The docks themselves were barricaded, with gates manned by a small battalion of local law enforcement officers armed with leftover military gear for which they had little training. Sound cannons and laser-heat arrays intimidated refugees and kept them in place while making the LEOs feel secure.

Lined up along the docks, the enormous hulks of oversized cruise ships blotted out the skies, casting great shadows on those standing closest to them. Each was a self-contained town on water. But those floating hamlets were empty of people. Terminals 16 to 22, where the largest cruise ships docked, once transported their passengers through the Caribbean and the Gulf of Mexico. Passengers had lived fun-filled days and enjoyed sparkling nights, warm beaches, an endless supply of food and alcohol, live entertainment, and mixed reality centers where they could pretend they were someone or somewhere else. With humanity, the grass was always greener.

After the Major Tom revelations, when the troubles started, the cruise ships had come back to their home ports to shelter at dock, manned by skeleton crews awaiting a more buoyant economy. But that had taken longer than most companies had anticipated. The skeleton crews now knew that any day, their meager pay would stop completely. As they stood on the decks, eyeing the crowds nervously, Tom could read their expressions and body language: tense faces, crossed arms. They were as full of fear as the refugees.

The biggest ship of all, the *Ocean Harmony*, lay alongside Terminal 18 like a giant horizontal high-rise, covered by balconies and a festive paint job. Talia planned to load over twelve thousand onto the ship, with first choice to former passenger-ship employees and navy and marine veterans who knew how to run such a behemoth. It was a small percentage of the refugees, but Talia hoped to provide an example that others could follow. The refugees would need more than one reliable lifeline out of the social disaster that President Conrad and his followers were creating.

The CAS *Theodore Roosevelt* steamed along the Stranahan River, into Port Everglades's Lake Mabel. It slowed outside the breakwater, awaiting permission to dock. The *Zumwalt* followed closely behind.

Captain Curtis called via a rarely used encrypted frequency. He didn't hide concern. "I never let anyone order my ship who isn't my commander. You sure this will work?"

"No," admitted Tom. "But we won't get in otherwise."

"Last time I was here was for fleet week," Curtis mumbled. "A lifetime ago."

Captain Curtis's communications officer called into the harbormaster using an old-fashioned radio receiver. "This is the CAS *Theodore Roosevelt*, accompanied by the CAS *Zumwalt*. Rough Rider calling for docking and repair privileges for both."

"Far from home, Rough Rider," said the harbormaster. "Don't usually take naval vessels."

"Understood. We're returning from humanitarian mission in Haiti. Dominican drone hit communications relay. Only radio working—and barely. Would like to get home sooner than later, but with full communications capability. *Zumwalt* offered help, but they need it, too. Hoping either local yard or Orlando might sell spare parts."

"Why not Norfolk?" asked the harbormaster. "And what about your spares?"

"Ran out," said Rough Rider.

"Please send yours and *Zumwalt*'s logs, Rough Rider."

"Done. Also sending permissions code from Captain Garvey of the *Zumwalt*. Should help with processing."

"A moment to check with Southern Naval Command. Hold steady, Rough Rider and *Zumwalt*."

"Will do."

With Dr. Who and Veronika's help, Major Tom had created a fake itinerary, along with ship's logs and damage log for both ships. He knew they would be scrutinized.

They waited for 5.63 minutes.

"Welcome, Rough Rider and *Zumwalt*. Terminal 22 for *TR*, 25 for *Zumwalt*. Sending instructions and permissions for both captains."

"Thanks. Rough Rider out."

Because they had to appear to have communications problems, crew on both ships sent confirmation messages via signal lamp in Morse code.

"I guess Veronika's ID chips and programming do work magic," Talia said.

Ruth pursed her lips like a kissing fish. Her eyes blinked rapidly. "Less her chips. And more our data."

Back on the encrypted frequency, Tom contacted Captain Curtis. "Can we limp more? We don't look disabled enough."

Captain Curtis paused in thought. "Yeah, that was too easy."

"We're on guard," said Tom. "And we've got a lot more convincing to do."

On the bridge of the *Zumwalt*, Ruth paced and twitched. She hadn't sat in hours, the movement hypnotic. Ruth had proved a remarkably accurate bellwether, and they all had learned to pay attention.

"What's wrong?" Talia asked Ruth.

"They allow us in?" said Ruth. "I know. We sent false data. But I agree with Curtis. T-t-t-t-too easy."

Tom had to agree. But they had committed to his plan, and now they would see it through.

Guided by tugboats, the two ships slowly made their way to Terminals 22 and 25 as the harbormaster had assigned them. Tom, Veronika, and Talia in side-by-side domes on the *Zumwalt* bridge.

"It's time," said Tom. "Ready?"

Veronika nodded and typed commands. First, she completed her hack into the Southern Naval Command's port cameras. She replaced their views with computer-enhanced versions of her own. Major Tom did the same with the Miami law enforcement cameras distributed in a five-mile radius from their ship. From the police and the military's point of view, the CAS *Theodore Roosevelt* and the *Zumwalt* were doing exactly as they had promised: lowering their gangplanks and preparing a handful of people from each ship to disembark for parts.

In fact, their gangplanks did lower in time with the manufactured images. The longer and more closely their fake images replicated reality, the longer they had to pull off this stunt.

Talia received an encrypted call from Captain Philippe Allesandro of the *Ocean Harmony*. Without asking his permission, she shared the audio transmission with the *Roosevelt* and the *Zumwalt*.

"Is this Ms. Brooks?" asked the captain.

"Yes, Captain Allesandro. Thank you for calling back."

"Hard to ignore you when you're next door."

"We're here," said Talia. "Are you on board the *Harmony*?"

"Arrived yesterday. The company wants her away from this situation, in a safer port that can handle her size. We're trying to determine exactly where that might be."

"Can you help us?" asked Talia.

"You realize the bind I'm in?" asked Allesandro.

"Yes, we do."

There was a long pause from the captain. Finally, he said, "This makes me sick as anyone. Can you guarantee it'll work?"

Talia closed her eyes and lied. "As much as is possible. We'll fill the *Harmony* first and get you on your way. And we have right on our side."

"Don't lecture me on ethics!" barked Allesandro. "I'm responsible for all the people aboard the biggest ship in the world. Your . . . heroics," he spat, "are meaningless to me."

He hung up.

Talia looked crushed. "Keep an eye on what he does," Tom said softly, "not what he says."

Within five minutes, crew members had removed the upper and lower barriers to the gangway and opened the doors of the *Ocean Harmony*. Two officers stood at the bottom of the gangway and gave a subtle thumbs-up signal.

"Captain Curtis," Tom voice messaged, "please post your personnel to vet sailors. It's your call who gets assigned to which ship."

"On their way," said Curtis.

Meanwhile, Tom signaled to the crew members loitering at the barricades, indicating that they should open some gates and tell the refugees to walk, not run, in a line toward the *Ocean Harmony*. Other crew members were to occupy the nearby LEOs with false communications proving they had permission to take on refugees for transport. That would keep some occupied for a while.

"Can I let him know?" asked Talia.

"Sure," said Tom.

Talia called Steve. "Hey, baby, set up the medical station aboard the *Harmony*. I'm sure we'll have a lot of folks who haven't seen a doctor in too long."

"On my way," he replied.

"He'll be happy to work finally," she said to Tom.

Miss Gray Hat's facial-recognition program was loaded with every identity known to them, friend or foe. A pop-up diverted Veronika's attention from the slow stream of refugees. "Tom," she said. "Look."

Through a nearby law enforcement camera, Tom watched an aged, open-topped convertible Jeep Wrangler, probably hijacked from some poor refugee family, slowly making its way to the edge of the crowd. The contented face of the driver made Tom shiver: Winter. A body-sized canvas bag filled the back seat. She parked the car, climbed in the back, and hefted the bag upright. Opening the zipper at the top, she revealed a head with chestnut hair, pale skin, and a dimpled chin.

Ruth gasped. "He has our robot?"

Winter shimmied the bag off, found the power button at the robot's neck, and turned it on. The head animated. Eyes blinked and looked to Winter for approval. A smile broke out on the silicone face.

"Don't you look dashing, my dear," Winter said as she helped the robot stand. She adjusted its collar and clothing. She shifted the waistband, exposing the familiar shape of a gun under the shirt near the right hip. And another on the left hip. At least two concealed weapons.

"Well, of course I do," said Tom 3.

The voice was Carter's.

They watched, transfixed. "Shit! They made a Tom 3," said Veronika.

"And they're playing to the camera," said Tom. "They know we're watching."

"Kein ayin hara!" said Ruth. Then she spit three times.

The most rational person in the room was warding off the evil eye.

Tom studied the images in extreme close-up. Winter had a Mr. Handsome/James Bond sexbot. The Chinese had kept the pieces of Tom 2 for themselves, but it was possible that Carter had arranged to use those salvaged pieces in this robot. Tom looked more carefully. The robot was freshly skinned, but he had a sick feeling that at one time, some part of this robot had been him, which meant that even though they had erased as much as possible and cut contact from the mangled bot, Carter might know how the robot had been used.

If so, then the Chinese were playing both ends against the middle. Typical.

"Talia," said Tom. "Make sure all the Companibots staff and hackers are okay. All of them."

Talia nodded and turned to her console.

Back on the ground, Winter winked at Tom 3. "Tom's going to love you. Just like I do." Then she rubbed herself up against the robot's supersized genitalia, which were always in a state of tumescence.

The robot winked back. "Of course he will. I'm you!"

"She has a *schtick!*" said Ruth, in horror.

Winter stopped her erotic play. "Change the voice back."

"Okay," said the robot, now in the gravelly baritone of Thomas Paine.

Winter sighed and slapped the robot's ass. "Okay, enough jerking off!" She pointed her right index finger and jerked her thumb like an imaginary gun, directly at Tom 3's face. Then she winked, jumped into the Jeep, threw it into gear, and drove away without a goodbye.

Tom was stunned by Carter's bizarre Frankenstein creature: part Peter, part Tom, part Carter, part Winter, part robot, part unholy amalgamation of who knew what else. Winter's crass behavior had Carter's mind spewed all over it. Indeed, Thomas Paine had once seduced Carter, to manipulate him. This was simply payback.

"He might have a direct line into us," said Tom.

"But I remote wiped Tom 2's memory and cut off the relays just after his batteries ran out," insisted Veronika. "He's empty hardware."

"You're assuming Carter and his team are less capable than we are," said Tom. "You're wrong." He felt sick to his stomach.

"Now we have to destroy two of them," she said.

He didn't argue. They watched as the robot moved among the tents, making its way slowly toward the pier. "Not from here," said Tom.

"They're in the crowd. We might hurt someone. Maybe we can isolate them—"

"Tom," interrupted Talia. "None of the Companibot people are responding."

He felt sicker.

"*Schmucks!*" yelled Ruth. "How dare they mess with my kids! Our work!" She stopped pacing, grimly manned another console, and barked, "Don't *futz*! *Di shversteh arbet iz arumtsugain laidik!*"

"The hardest work is to go idle," Tom repeated. But no one realized how hard the work would be.

CHAPTER THIRTY-NINE

The false story told to the harbormaster, and anyone watching their cameras, was about seven mechanics exiting both ships and making their way casually toward the harbormaster's office to arrange for repair and parts. In reality, crew members walked to the barricades and struck up casual conversations with both refugees and law enforcement officers. After convincing the LEOs, they opened gates and let through refugees.

If Talia had finally taught Major Tom anything, it was that it's one thing to believe something through evidence, but it's another entirely to experience it. He had been trained as a scientist to think otherwise, but the human brain will always believe its experience, no matter how faulty our memories or how misleading our awareness.

Experience trumps all. He didn't need nanowire- and bot-induced prescience to know that things could go wrong. He had patterns from both his digital and meat lives to base his decisions on, and this body was proving surprisingly competent at staying alive. He would keep listening to Rosero's gut.

Tom stood. "I'm getting ready," he said. "Message when you need me."

"Ready for what?" asked Ruth.

"Anything. Everything," he said. "It's coming." Then he left.

It was time to protect this body so he could protect others. Inside the *Zumwalt*'s armory, Tom put on a 3.0 flak jacket and helmet, designed to stop not only bullets, but also low-grade laser weapons, with a nanoparticle-layered mirrored surface that deflected most of the laser's light. He grabbed a laser rifle and handguns with extra-large magazines. He strapped on a couple of assault knives at both shins, under his pants. Sometimes the old ways were adequate.

He exited onto the large aft deck and looked out at the port. Refugees had already crossed the barriers and begun loading onto the *Harmony*. Some were sent on to the *Roosevelt*. Those aboard the *Zumwalt* made room for more, and Talia motioned for them to come her way.

From a multitude of hacked cameras, Tom observed one hundred thousand people lining up on the docks and spilling over into the streets, parking lots, holding areas, and port service buildings. The crew divided them into singles, couples, families, and most importantly those with proof of either naval or passenger-ship experience. The word had gone out that oceangoing expertise was needed, and they came by the thousands to apply, whether they had it or not. Those who could prove it moved to a special line between the two boats, and they were the first to embark. Then families with children, then couples, then singles.

The air tingled with tension, hope, and despair. So many needed so much, which could be given to only so few. Viewed from afar, swarming people had used to remind Tom of ants, but no longer. With blood in his veins, as red as theirs, he could imagine that they each had a need to be rescued, a story to tell, and a life worth living. He estimated the number that had passed the barrier would soon exceed the twenty thousand berths on the ships, and he sent a message to halt the flow of people and send the rest back.

He felt a tightness in his chest. He hadn't felt a stressed and broken heart since before he had died. He took several deep and long breaths. What good would he be if his emotions derailed him?

Ruth made her way to the gangway of the *Zumwalt* and wrinkled her nose in disgust at the raw-sewage odor of the algae bloom. A crew member holding a body wand and examining each new passenger looked worried.

"Dr. Chaikin," he said, waving the wand over a young woman's bicep, "the readers are finding some people with embedded CNEM-ID tags with global satellite locators. I put those we found over there to wait." The young woman exchanged a frightened look with a man who looked like her brother.

Once used to track animal migratory patterns via the now abandoned International Space Station, the technology had been placed in new satellites, and corporations began attaching them to what looked like standard human CNEM-ID tags. Many in the SSA insisted that their employees have these implants, claiming safety and security concerns. Ruth knew each of these global location tags could be followed anywhere, betraying the *Zumwalt*'s location. Those the crew had separated were standing in a patch of shade created by the ship. They were unhappy. And scared.

"*Nein! Zumwalt* c-c-c-can't take them," said Ruth. "They must go. To another ship!"

Those waiting to board did not take kindly to this news. The young woman's older brother, a muscular and imposing man, loomed large over Ruth. "Whaddaya mean we can't get on? I was a navy seaman. I can make this thing go!"

"Does he have the same tag?" Ruth asked the crewman.

The crewman waved the wand over the brother's body. "No, ma'am."

"You can come," said Ruth. "She cannot."

"I'm not leavin' her for these monsters!" insisted the brother.

"This is a stealth ship. They may find us. B-b-b-because of her!" said Ruth. "Or we do surgery. Right here!"

"I don't care if they find a needle in a goddamn haystack," the brother said. "I'm not leavin' her behind!"

There was a sound, soft as wind at first. It grew louder, like a marauding swarm of a million insects, heard before they could be seen. The argument stopped. Everyone froze.

Then the flying drones came into view.

The brother whipped around. "No . . . ," he said, softly at first. Then, "No!" He grabbed his sister. "We gotta go!"

The humid air stirred with the buzz of tens of thousands of tiny propellers, the largest drone-weapon array ever assembled. They were converging on Port Everglades. Refugees scattered, but no one knew where to go.

Ruth fought a swell of bodies on the gangway, desperate not to touch them. But they were impossible to avoid. Each brush against a person brought a full-body convulsion and a scream of disgust. Tom heard her screams and came running.

"*Nein! Nein!* I c-c-c-can't do this!" she yelled as he reached her on the deck. The crowd heaved and shoved, and he caught her as she fell into him. Ruth shrieked with terror, like a panicked horse, staring at the railing as if thinking of jumping over.

"Shhhh . . . shhhh . . ." He stroked her head as he held her close, cradling her, protecting her from the crowd.

She wept and convulsed against him, her brain short-circuiting with each touch.

His own body couldn't avoid the roiling fear. It felt like cavitating molecules that vibrated so fast, his more rational self was unable to function. He twitched in unison with Ruth, feeling that this body had dealt with terror before. Part of him welcomed it.

He grabbed the closest person who didn't look panicked, a sturdy middle-aged woman. "Who are you?" he demanded.

"Uh . . . former petty officer first class Rebecca Brown."

"Please take Dr. Chaikin to the bridge. Hand her over to Talia Brooks and figure out how to help organize the military already on board."

"N-n-n-no!" insisted Ruth. "You n-n-need me!"

Tom shoved her to Rebecca. "She'll fight you, but stay with her and keep her safe. She's the most important person on board."

"N-n-n-no! You are!" cried Ruth.

"Uh . . . yessir!" The woman grabbed Ruth, and they struggled through the crowd to the doors that led inside.

Tom needed to find Winter and Tom 3. And destroy them.

Through a hacked port camera, Tom saw the ripple of commotion start from the back of the crowd. He heard screams. The drones shepherded the refugees into a tighter group. Tom assumed the plan was to slaughter them. Running down the gangway onto the dock, he switched to a broader satellite view. The crowd surged like reeds in a strong wind. Those still outside the perimeter fence ran away from the port, but in the confined space of the docks, surrounded by fences of unbreakable graphene-coated steel, the rest were penned in.

Plastic, ceramic, metal, and carbon-fiber locusts descended from the sky. The early prototypes had actually been called LOCUST: low-cost unmanned aerial vehicle swarming technology. Tom located a staging point where they were being ejected from tube-like launchers positioned at the top of the Broward Convention Center, north of the docks.

He voice messaged Captain Curtis: "Take out the launchers on the BCC."

"Impossible," said Curtis. "You're asking us to fire on an independent, sovereign state that has not fired on our vessel yet. That's war. We will do our best to reposition and take as many away as fast as possible."

Curtis was right. As soon as people boarded the ships, they seemed safe. No weapons were directed at either the ships or their passengers.

More drones were released. These were small surveillance drones, designed to pursue visual targets. From the back of a large truck to the west of the port, they came at first in dozens, then hundreds, then thousands. Each had a little tendril that hung from the bottom. Touching it triggered an electric shock. Like little flying Tasers, they swarmed the crowd, shocking it into submission.

The mob's panic surged.

Larger drones had weaponry suspended from their bases. Lasers used to blind and burn. Older models with guns and bullets, others with small sound and heat cannons for incapacitating targets. The buzzing of so many machines grew deafening. People dropped to the ground, holding their ears.

These were the first to be trampled.

BOOM!

An explosion rocked the northwest corner of the refugee camp. Tom directed a camera to search the perimeter and found a smoldering wreck. It was Winter's Jeep. But there was no body near it who looked anything like her.

She must still be out there, and she had probably set off the explosion herself.

It was an effective herding device, forcing those fleeing to the north back toward the drones.

Tom watched in horror.

A mother ran, her small boy in her arms. The boy wriggled and cried out in pain. A drone's laser caught the mother in the back of the head. She collapsed to the ground. A shirtless man next to them grabbed the child from her arms and kept running. She tried to rise, the back of her head an open, burnt wound exposing flesh, bone, and brain. She was swept under a wave of terrified refugees and did not rise again.

A young man tried to rally with his friends, throwing rocks, bottles, anything they could gather. Some had constructed makeshift nets and lassos. Nearby drones hovered out of reach, anticipating their aim. The drones' AI employed terrifyingly accurate evasive measures. The protestors successfully downed a few, and the falling drones' propellers still cut and crushed those fleeing underneath.

A large spider-like drone with a machine gun mounted on its undercarriage flew in and hovered, suspiciously still. Spooked, the crowd tried to flee, when . . .

B-B-B-B-B-B-B-B-B-B-B!

The drone peppered the crowd's edge with bullets. Throwing himself in front of his wife, a husband shielded her from the rounds, but the ammunition ripped through his flesh and hers, embedding in people behind them. They fell like dominos where they stood, the man's limp body still shielding his dying wife.

Those who were penned in were slaughtered. Those who weren't might still die. Tom wondered if killing the refugees had been the plan all along, and his rescue attempt had been the cover for atrocities.

Talia manned the bridge on the *Zumwalt*, fielding communications. Captain Alessandro, from the *Ocean Harmony*, filled one of her screens. Captain Curtis, from the *Roosevelt*, filled another.

"Ms. Brooks," said Captain Alessandro, "we are setting sail immediately! I don't care who is or isn't on board. I will not jeopardize this ship and my crew. We are defenseless!"

"The *Harmony* is between Rough Rider and the battle zone," said Curtis. "He's got to get out so we can defend ourselves if we need to. We're all too vulnerable in here."

"Go!" said Talia. "Both of you. I know we can't help you, but I can't leave without Tom."

"This is a disaster! Crazy fools!" said Alessandro. And he cut off.

"Even with all your digital trickery," Curtis said, "they knew we were coming, and what we planned. This was a trap."

She had turned off the monitor closest to her, with its camera feed from right in the middle of the port. Black, brown, white—it didn't matter. They died. The carnage was unbearable. Their only crimes were poverty and the desire for a better life. "I'm so sorry, Geoff," said Talia, holding her head in her hands. "We were trying to do the right thing."

"Now we have to do a different right thing. Get Tom back and get out of here. I'm moving into position outside the port to defend your and Alessandro's withdrawal. Get moving."

Talia teared up, unable to process this disaster she had helped to create. "Thanks, Geoff."

"Rough Rider out."

Talia voice messaged Tom. "You saw all that?"

"Yes," said Tom.

"So get back here," she insisted. She slumped in her chair and swung a camera to follow Tom's progress through the port.

He was running and jumping over bodies. "I can't. I have to stop Winter and Tom 3."

Talia could barely hear him over the screaming on the dock. "They're bait. You know this. Get outta there!"

"They're more than bait," said Tom. "Do what Curtis says." He ducked from drone fire, turned, and blasted the drone with a laser gun. "Get everyone out!"

"We can't leave you behind."

"If I die," he said, dodging another, "you can make a new one."

Talia ordered the ship to prepare to set sail. "I can't!" she cried, throwing her headset.

CHAPTER FORTY

Veronika sat in a corner of the *Zumwalt*'s bridge, having never left her mixed reality command nest. Tom imagined her plugged into so much data, she couldn't untangle her mind. Disaster is a powerful novelty, latching on to a brain with a fresh hell each minute, refusing to let go.

"Tom, I can't find the system running these drones," said Veronika. "It's not Southern Naval Command or Conrad's army. And I can't get into Winter's head to deal with Carter. This is crazy!"

"I can't help you," said Tom.

"Carter's infiltrated, like, everything else. Think he got into the Church of Major Tom? Maybe he's working from there?"

Tom was running visual-data-recognition programs, avoiding drones, and trying to keep out of the mob's way. "Good idea. Figure it out. Just link me to your feed so I know what's up."

Dressed in her steampunk regalia, Veronika entered TCoMT. She placed herself at the doors of the cathedral, the center of the world she had helped create. She sent an emergency text and voice message to all congregants: "Major Tom and his team are under attack IRL Port Everglades. We need your help."

The congregants stopped, processed her message, then continued on their business.

"No! Really! We need your help!" insisted Veronika.

On the cobblestone walk in front of the cathedral, a tiny fairy asked, "Where is he that he asks us to help? Shouldn't the savior show himself?"

"Tom? I need you here," said Veronika. She got no answer.

"Don't use the savior's name in vain," chastised another, dressed as a munchkin.

A priest in a Bernhardt-azure-blue cassock exited the cathedral doors and descended the front steps toward Veronika. "You're creating a disruptive presence, miss. Please behave, or the moderators will have to suspend your account."

"I *am* the chief moderator!" she said.

"Well, you're not a good one," clucked the priest.

"Have you seen what's happening, like, out in the real world? There's an attack in Port Everglades. Major Tom is trying to save refugees. Why aren't you helping?"

"I haven't heard or seen anything of the sort," said the priest.

Veronika contacted another moderator named Fitzy and showed him what was unfolding both inside TCoMT and at Port Everglades.

"Holy shit!" Fitzy replied. "Is this for real?"

"Yes!" said Veronika. "Help me convince them."

In TCoMT, a crowd gathered outside the cathedral, brought by the sound of the argument. Veronika said, to no one in particular, "That's because you're all obsessed in here. Tom's right, being a deity sucks."

A beautiful, statuesque woman emerged from the gathering crowd, her long blonde hair flowing to the ground. Dressed all in white like a Greek goddess, she stood next to Veronika's goth princess.

"She lies," said the goddess to the crowd. Her voice was beautiful, modulated to persuade. "She's trying to divert us from the truth."

Major Tom scrutinized the avatar. There was something familiar. It wasn't a design element. What was it? Veronika displayed the avatar's membership information for Tom and Fitzy. It had joined and created itself soon after TCoMT had been created, but it hadn't been used until today. Real identity and payment information had been scrubbed.

The goddess turned to the gathering crowd with authority and grace. "My dears, we've been duped. This is one giant con. Major Tom isn't a god. He's a devil. And he certainly doesn't care about you. He'll destroy us all!"

It could be only one person.

"No. Not here you won't," Veronika threatened the goddess.

"Oh, you poor sweet things," said the goddess. "Such a waste." She studied the crowd for a moment. Then she opened her mouth and began to sing an a cappella version of the Tea Party's "Empty Glass." Written thirty-five years after the musical astronaut's first appearance in "Space Oddity," David Bowie's Major Tom is revealed to have abandoned Earth. Now humanity must wait for another "star man," another "diamond dog" to avoid losing their souls.

The ever-growing crowd was mesmerized. The goddess stopped midstanza and pointed to the horizon in horror. "No! Your Major Tom knows I sing the truth! Look what he's doing to us!"

The crowd turned in unison to see its world disappear.

It started at the edges. Space folded in on itself. The landscape curled up and rolled inward toward the cathedral, slowly at first, then gaining in speed, deleting entire neighborhoods, businesses, and characters in its inexorable advance. In their place was nothingness.

Back on the *Zumwalt*, Veronika struggled to stop TCoMT's crash, desperate to save the world she and others had created, even if they didn't know enough to save themselves.

"Lock it up!" she voice messaged Fitzy.

"I'm trying!"

But there was no saving anything. Her link to Fitzy through TCoMT disappeared. Her avatar was gone. Her world was gone. She ripped off her mixed reality glasses, covered her eyes, and cried. This hit harder than the devastation in the port below.

Tom sent a message: *I'm so sorry.* She didn't see it until later.

CHAPTER FORTY-ONE

On the southwestern corner of the port, outside the gates, a late-model Mini Cooper drove against the flow of people. Tom zoomed in. A transport company sign lit the front window. It should have been looking for a fare. There was no driver, and no passengers. It didn't stop to pick anyone up. It looked too small to be threatening, and refugees made way for it to pass. Some tried to commandeer it, but the doors were locked, the windows would not break, and the car kept moving.

Tom looked back in the direction it had come from. More empty cars headed their way, and no one could get into them. This was bad. He'd seen what one car had done today.

Running toward the first car, he tried to scream above the din of weapons and terrified humans. "Get away from the car!" Few heard him. They were too consumed with trying to escape.

He reached the gate leading out to the street. It was locked. A biometric reader topped a steel post to his left. He ran to it, looking for anything he could hack . . . And the gate opened. The ID reader had accessed his chip. Veronika's little gizmo was coming in handy.

The Mini Cooper puttered on just thirty feet away. He screamed, "Away from the car! Get out of here now!" He grabbed a middle-aged man and shoved him in the opposite direction.

"Hey!" the man yelled. "Don't—"

BOOM!

The Mini Cooper exploded. The fireball was larger than the Jeep, incinerating those near it. Tom dived to the ground, covering the man, then leapt up and ran to help anyone he could.

BOOM! BOOM! BOOM!

The cars behind the first exploded in quick succession.

His visual recognition pinged. It had found Tom 3 heading toward the ships. Both guns were out, and he was shooting at refugees indiscriminately. His aim wasn't great, but it didn't matter. People saw a Peter Bernhardt–look-alike sexbot shooting into a crowd. Headline news.

The car bombs were meant to lead Tom away. He grabbed the nearest able-bodied person, a woman with a baby in a pack on her chest. "Please, help organize anyone who can be carried away to safety."

"Why can't you?" she asked.

"I have to catch the ones doing this."

Tom 3 marched in the direction of the *Ocean Harmony*. Firing with both hands, he mowed down anyone in front of him. Tom kept out of Tom 3's range, wondering how he could stop the robot.

It wasn't like harming a human. A single shot to the head or the center of the chest would not take him down. The shot could miss all the crucial mechanisms and electronics. Tom ran an analysis of his own robots' schematics, searching for vulnerabilities.

But Carter would assume Tom would look for weaknesses. Could Tom 3 have been altered so an obvious attempt to stop the robot would hurt others?

He voice messaged Ruth: "If you were going to sabotage Tom 3, so anyone trying to harm him would be hurt, where would you do it?"

"Most important part? Central processing unit. And memory chips. In the chest. Two inches above human heart."

He wouldn't aim at the chest. Tom ran.

Three hundred feet from the cruise ship, Tom 3 stopped, turned, and faced Tom, raising his submachine guns.

ZZZZZP! Tom shot at the robot's hands, destroying them and damaging the guns. He raised his sights to the elbows.

ZZZZZP! Elbows burnt and crispy. Forearms fell to the ground.

ZZZZZP! Off came the right foot. Then the left. Tom 3 stumbled and toppled over.

Next, Tom destroyed the knees, separating the lower and upper legs. Tom 3 had only thighs and upper arms. The robot tried to rise but didn't have the programming and engineering to do it without full limbs. He wriggled around on the asphalt like an injured beetle on its back.

Tom approached carefully, fearing an auto-destruct, and reached for Tom 3's neck. The robot turned its head and tried to bite him. Tom leapt back. "Man, you're a nasty piece of work."

"You would know," said the robot.

Tom kicked it in the head, hard, and shot the power switch. The machine went silent and still. He took a deep breath and started to back away. One down.

Tom 3 waited for 3.5 seconds. With a whir, the robot turned on again, righting itself with one upper arm. It turned its head jerkily at Tom. "Surprise!"

Tom knew—he *knew*—he should come up with a better idea, but he couldn't control his hands. They shook. Sweat poured into his eyes. He had had enough. He scooped up Tom 3's submachine gun and aimed at the neck.

B-B-B-B-B-B-B-B-B-B!

Until the robot's head had been shot clean off. Then he went after the rest of the body, avoiding just the chest.

B-B-B-B-B-B-B-B-B-B!

Tom 3 was reduced to a heap of metal, fake skin, and rags. Like the mangled remains of a twin that he had once inhabited and that knew what he was feeling.

The disembodied head buzzed, then clicked. It's one working eye winked.

Tom ran.

BOOM!

He staggered from the blast. It killed at least a dozen people and injured dozens more.

Tom 3 was not just a bomb. He was an IED, a shrapnel machine. Recorded by all the cameras—security, drones, GOs, news services—so the world would see that Thomas Paine's robot was a part of the terrible story. The new plotline written by Carter: Tom 3 was part of Major Tom. The robot killed everyone in its path. The footage was edited to make it appear that Tom, when he had come upon the robot, had flipped a switch on it, turning it into a bomb, and run away.

Carter was shooting a movie, and government media would call it news.

CHAPTER FORTY-TWO

The *Ocean Harmony*'s hospital comprised a handful of small rooms on Deck Two at the ship's lower entrance, near the tender platforms. To keep people moving up into the ship and avoid an unmanageable crowd at the doors, Steve set up his triage unit on Deck Fifteen, outside, in a sports complex with plenty of light, room, and fresh air. After triaging with the help of some medics borrowed from the *Zumwalt* and the *Roosevelt*, Steve sent the serious cases back down to the hospital.

Tom messaged, *Sure you don't want to set up in the ballroom?*

"Air-conditioning isn't on yet. We're fine," said Steve. "I can keep an eye on things here. And no drones." He waved to another medic and pointed to a man having sudden difficulty breathing. "Hey, Chaiprasit! Red tag! Stat!"

Dr. Steve Carbone was in his element.

A satellite cam showed the outer decks of the *Ocean Harmony* filled with refugees. Suddenly, passengers on board staggered as the ship lurched from the dock without the help of tugboats. Steve regained his balance and looked over the side. The gangways were still coming up, even with refugees waiting to board.

He voice messaged Talia through his MR glasses. "We're leaving now?"

"Yes. I'll explain later," she said.

He jogged over to a new patient, a teenage girl. Her leg had a gangrenous wound, probably a week old. Someone had attempted to dress it using ripped clothing, but without proper first aid supplies, she was showing signs of sepsis. She had no identification papers and no one with her to tell him who she was. He took her fingers and pressed them to his GO to record her prints, then linked his glasses to record and spoke quickly, sending her triage information down to the hospital deck where the pharmacy would prepare IV antibiotics and a nurse would set a time for surgery. By the looks of it, he had gotten to her in time to save her life, but she'd lose most of her leg.

Suddenly a blinding white light blasted everything.

Sound was sucked away. So was sight.

The *Ocean Harmony*'s screens went dark.

"Steve!" screamed Talia from the *Zumwalt* bridge. She had been inside a dome with his MR feed on her screen. It felt like she was there with him. She leapt from her seat and ran for the gangway.

Major Tom zoomed the satellite cam out. The rear wall of the *Harmony*'s bridge was gone, but the room was not destroyed. He could see Captain Allesandro and other officers collapsed inside. For Tom, it was sickeningly familiar. He quickly analyzed the images he collected. Light covered only the central part of the ship. Apparently there were limits to the size of the target that Josiah Brant's favorite satellite laser weapon could cover. But who had control of the weapon now? The Phoenix Club? The SSA? Another country?

As the light faded, Tom saw that the midvessel was completely gone, vaporized in place. Seawater below boiled from the intensity of the laser's heat. The fore and aft of the vessel hovered in place, then slowly collapsed toward each other like falling giant redwoods, their hulls rising. From ten and twenty stories above, bodies flew from the decks and exposed rooms onto the dock or into the sea.

Tom bolted toward the ship.

The fore and aft of the *Ocean Harmony* took on water and sank. Tom watched helplessly as Steve tried to save himself and the young woman he held. He grabbed her, one arm around her torso as they slid to a stop at a fence surrounding the tennis court. He tried to reorient them as the deck turtled over. Then the aft section lurched to starboard, pitching Steve and the young girl off the fence and down into a sliver of black water between the dock and the sinking ship.

Talia watched it all on her GO as she ran across the gangway to the pier. "Tom, you have to save him!"

The ends of the ship continued their torturous, groaning submersion, until only a part of the fore and aft hulls peeked out of the water. Running to the edge of the dock, Tom saw a few flailing survivors but mostly dead bodies, either burnt from proximity to the laser or crushed from the fall. He unstrapped his flak jacket and helmet, blew out all the air in his lungs, and took a deep breath, facilitating the respirocytes that would allow him not to breathe for several minutes. He dived into the murky algae-clogged water. The wrecked ship's shadows made it impossible to see underneath the muck. He bumped into arms and legs, some flailing, some still, too late to save.

Steve had pocketed his GO. Tom pinged the signal before water could destroy it. It was still there. He kicked hard, swimming down toward it.

He bumped into the body before seeing it. It drifted limp and unresponsive. Tom knew how badly injured Steve was the moment he touched him, but he grabbed him and kicked hard again for what he hoped was the surface. Battling tangled bodies in the dark, he finally emerged, the goop at the surface stuck to his face, dragging Steve's body up after him.

On the dock, two refugees—a middle-aged man in a mechanic's shirt with the name Balthazar embroidered in red on a badge, and a scrawny, malnourished teenager with his chest covered in tats and wearing only shorts that hung off his bony hips—dove in to help Tom carry Steve up the ladder and onto the ground.

Tom pulled out a gun and handed it to the teen. "If anyone tries to hurt us, use this."

The teen's eyes went wide.

"Help me," Tom said to Balthazar. They placed Steve on the ground, where Tom saw for the first time the head, neck, and torso injuries Steve had sustained. But there was no blood. Tom checked for a pulse. There was none. He cleared the gunk from Steve's face, laid him on his side, and tried to open his airway. Water poured from Steve's mouth. They performed CPR, the mechanic doing compressions and Tom breathing. He exhaled, filling the drowned lungs with enough unused oxygen to give Steve a chance.

Talia rounded the corner, skidded to a stop, and gasped. She stood helpless as the men continued CPR. First for a minute. Then two. After four minutes and no response, Tom stopped the artificial respiration, held out his hand to stop the mechanic, and turned to Talia.

"Steve!" She dropped to her knees, weeping.

"Let me save him," said Tom. The mechanic and the teen looked at each other, confused.

"How?" wailed Talia. She hugged Steve's body.

"Injection of preoxygenated respirocytes, then get him cold to preserve what's left. Every second counts." He sent an urgent message to the medics on board the two remaining ships, asking if they had respirocytes in their stocks and whether they could get them to him. Respirocytes had been invented to bring oxygen to drowning and fire victims. Tom had invented them. Steve had made them available to EMTs and ERs around the world. And they were not available to them now.

Talia cried, "No. *No!*" and rocked back and forth.

"I can upload him!"

Tom had assured Arun that he would never offer this to anyone, and he wasn't sure it would be successful. But this was Steve. To whom he owed so much. Steve might not have thought so highly of Tom, but Tom owed him. And he owed Talia even more. He would do everything in his power to keep Steve alive, even if he had to make it up as they went. Major Tom began to map out plans for the preservation of Steve's brain.

"Never," she said.

"What?" Tom said. "You realize what I'm offering?"

"No!" Talia screamed. "Get away from him!"

"I'm saving his life!" said Tom.

"No! You're not!"

"Talia, please," Tom begged.

At that moment, he knew he had lost not only Steve, but Talia, too.

Horrified, he laid his hand on Steve's head for the last time. Talia yanked the body back, but Tom's hand stayed, and she allowed him a moment of his own grief. Emotions he struggled to contain clawed their way to the surface. Tears formed. His chin twitched. Then he gave up the little control he had left and wept.

Why did Steve, the real hero at Port Everglades, have to die?

Why couldn't Tom have been smarter and not walked them right into a set-up?

Why couldn't he anticipate all these disasters?

But it wasn't just his fault. It was Carter's, too.

And Carter would fucking pay.

He looked around him and through the cameras. The *Ocean Harmony* had sunk. Thousands had been murdered. His friend was dead. Another blamed him for it. The time for sadness had passed. He felt an overwhelming urge to kill, but it didn't come from Major Tom's servers. This body's cells shook with a bloodlust he could barely contain.

He put on his flak jacket, helmet, and weapons, then turned to his two helpers and knelt. "Talia. You have to leave now, or you'll die here, too."

"I want to die," she cried.

"And I can't let that happen." He reached under her arms and lifted her from the ground.

"No!" she wailed.

Tom handed her into Balthazar's arms and gave the teen another handgun from his holster. "Keep the guns. Get her back to that ship." He pointed to the *Zumwalt*. "And get on board with her. I hope I see you there. And good luck."

Then one thought overtook Tom's mind: Find Winter and Carter. And make them pay.

Tom sent an order to the *Zumwalt*: *Get out of here as soon as Talia and the guys board.*

"Are you nuts?" asked Veronika from her dome nest.

"No," said Tom. "No more deaths. No more. Follow the *Roosevelt* out."

"And how the hell are you getting back?" she asked.

"I'll figure it out," he said.

After 2.3 long minutes, the image alarm pinged. A camera had captured Winter in bizarre repose, leaning against a fence with her arms crossed over her chest, a laser gun in her right hand. Her long, curvaceous legs crossed, and a smile rose on her face as she watched the end of the world unfold.

She was only a quarter mile away. So like he had done all day, he ran.

She deigned to notice him at a hundred paces, even though she would have tracked him the entire time, even as he had searched for her. Tom stopped twenty feet from her.

"Fancy seeing you here," said Winter with a coquettish simper. Then casually held the gun at the head of a terrified girl.

279

"How could you do this?" he asked.

Winter smirked. "Because I love you." She winked and kissed the air.

Tom felt a level of rage he hadn't known he or Rosero possessed. He focused all the attention he had spread among cameras, ships, people, data sets, and media toward a single purpose.

Kill the bitch.

As he lifted his weapon, Winter lifted the girl like a human shield. The girl screamed, kicked, and tried to wriggle away. Winter put the laser gun to her temple. "Settle down or you're dead," she ordered. The girl froze.

Tom did not lower his gun.

"Would you really?" Winter asked him. "For the satisfaction? You know it's meaningless."

"Talia thinks you're bait," said Tom.

"But you're smarter than that. And smart guys always turn me on." She whispered into the girl's ear, "Do they turn you on, too?"

"What a fucking psychopath," said Tom.

Winter grinned, baring her teeth. "And you made all this. So what does that make you?"

"Why all this?" asked Tom.

Winter turned serious. "It's necessary. You'll figure it out. Well, maybe not. Your latest incarnation is especially stupid."

Tom's hands shook. He tried to aim at the part of Winter's head that was exposed behind the girl, but while he had decent aim and a laser scope, he could still miss.

Veronika text messaged from the *Zumwalt*: *I can help.*

Do it, messaged Tom.

"Come on, my dear," said Winter. "Get the balls and shoot us both. Don't the ends justify the means? What did Talia call you once? Dudley Do-Right? Didn't like that, did you, sweetie?"

"Ask her for place names! Make her say them!" said Veronika.

Tom took a step closer to Winter. "You're right. You were always right. I'm the idiot. I'm the monster. So now what? Fight? Where? In the real world? Virtually?"

"See? Was that so hard?" Then Winter blinked. And blinked again.

"How? *Mano a mano?* Rock 'em sock 'em sexbots? Just pick a place. Palo Alto? San Francisco? Malibu? Venice? DC? The old Phoenix Camp? Hell, I'll go to Antarctica."

Winter started to answer, but then shook her head, as though to shake mental cobwebs free. She looked accusingly at Tom. "Who's in my head?"

Back at Caltech, Arun found a path remotely tracing Winter's program far enough back to find the digital version of a backup vault. Carter was a narcissist and kept his backups offline in multiple places for posterity. If they could access one and find a single merge conflict with the other backups, they could insert that conflict and wreak havoc. The conflict would be a word, image, or behavior, anything that didn't replicate properly.

Arun had found it. He noticed that Winter never verbalized anything related to place names. On the Long Beach Pier she had twitched while attempting to say Island White. There had to be a merge-conflict glitch in Winter/Carter's thoughts of place names. And Arun had let Veronika know only minutes before.

"Where?" said Tom, moving closer. "Just say it! What's your problem? Are you an idiot? Just say it . . ."

"D-d-d-d-d-d-d-d . . . ," Winter sputtered. Spasming like Ruth, her hands sprung wide, dropping the laser gun. She released the girl, who took a moment to realize she was free. Then she bolted. Winter fell over like a shuddering toy.

Tom held the gun in front of him and walked slowly toward her.

Twitching on the ground, Winter said, "P-p-poor Ruthie. Now I g-g-get it." She looked without fear down the barrel of Tom's gun. "You know every t-time I die, you lose a little m-m-more of yourself. This'll hurt you m-m-more than it will me, m-m-my dear. *Adiós, m-mucha-cho.*" Then she tried to wink, but her eyelid only fluttered.

Tom pulled the trigger, drilling his laser into her frontal lobe. Her eyes remained open, her mouth stuck in a smile. Then he shifted his aim to her heart, driving a stake of light through her like she was a vampire. Perhaps she was one. Maybe he was, too.

But Winter, and Carter, were wrong. It didn't hurt him. Revenge felt satisfying, even tasted good.

But he knew that if he paused to enjoy it, he would be jeopardizing his own life. Turning away from Winter's body, he looked out toward the harbor, linking back to the cameras, taking in the enormous devastation, and planning the next move. The asphalt was a wet, dark reddish gray. The sounds of the terrified had lessened. Those who could escape had scattered. Those who couldn't were strewn all over the port, injured, dying, or wandering. The drones had accomplished their goal: there were no more "refugees" on the ground at Port Everglades. Only "enemy combatants" and "victims," as the SSA had wanted all along.

The sounds of the aftermath haunted Tom. First, there was quiet. The drones had left. Human moans colluded in a low, gentle hum. A few GOs rang. Then a few more. Soon, a ceaseless medley of ringtones, sound effects, song snippets, and comedy punch lines. The noise was as terrifying as weapons discharge and the cries of agony, the sound of thousands of family and friends trying to find out if their loved ones were okay.

A GO rang two feet from Tom. Its owner looked the same age as Rosero, his limbs tucked around him in a protective fetal posture, still. He was covered in blood. The face was familiar. Not to Major Tom, but to Rosero. Tom reached for the man's pocket, removed the phone, and brought it to his ear.

"Hello?"

"Oh my God you're okay thank our lord you're okay please tell me you're okay are you okay?"

"I . . . I'm . . . I'm sorry, I'm so sorry," stuttered Tom.

There was silence on the line. Then a shrieking, the name Aaron, over and over. He placed the GO gently near the young man's ear.

Staggering away, Tom tried to focus both his mind and body. While the digital brain functioned, the human brain had frozen. Major Tom took control, turning Rosero's head to take in the scene. At the nearest dock, the *Ocean Harmony* lay in two sunken chunks. Out beyond the breakwater, the CAS *Theodore Roosevelt* sat in the open ocean, its big missiles and guns ready to fire if fired upon.

The strategists of the SSA were not foolish. They had killed the refugees to assert dominance over a territory that remained a thorn in their side. Knowing that any military commander worth his or her salt would never start a shooting war unless fired upon, they didn't threaten the CAS *Theodore Roosevelt*. The SSA had no intention of starting a war with anyone who would fire back.

Defying Tom's orders, the *Zumwalt* hadn't moved. It sat at Terminal 25, engines running, ready to go. Any drone not recognized by the LEOs as their own had been shot down. Citizens had once had the legal right to film violence that transpired in public, but those rights had been abolished in the SSA. As of last year, drones had no rights, nor did their human operators.

A new wave of drones arrived to explore the carnage. Official state news outlets sent flying robots in lieu of costly mortal journalists. As they had after 10/26, the world tuned in to the horror. The revolution would not only be televised—it would be carefully staged and edited.

CHAPTER FORTY-THREE

Tom regained some integration between his brains and his body during his dash to the ship. Dodging the living and the dead, he leapt onto the gangplank. As soon as his feet hit the steel walkway, it began to raise. He ran down its length and onto the ship as it headed toward the breakwater to join the *Roosevelt*.

He had killed the two entities he set out to, though it was feeling more and more like that was a part of the plan. He tried to save others, but by the end, he was the only target left at the port. Carter allowed the *Zumwalt* to escape. He could have destroyed Tom and the ship at any time. But he hadn't.

Tom was no longer needed in their Port Everglades narrative. The club was building a larger narrative with him as the villain. Carter's new version of Thomas Paine's story went out on all media: Major Tom had control of the terrifying orbital laser that had killed refugees and destroyed the *Ocean Harmony*. He had used the orbiting laser to murder the 10/26 terrorists and his compatriot Bruce Lobo. He had killed innocent people. But his story had changed so many times that people couldn't remember how many versions there were or which was correct. In their confusion, only one thing was clear: Thomas Paine was the enemy.

Tom lurched through the ship, passing passengers he was unable to forget. Most were from New Orleans, fewer from Port Everglades.

Their faces and wounded bodies taunted him. If he had seen them even once, terrified or injured or on the run, he couldn't forget them, their experiences repeating, repeating, repeating.

His mind fragmented in furious anguish. Was he standing in a cramped hallway on the *Zumwalt*? Was he back on the dock, killing Winter? Trying to save Steve? Confronting Talia's face, its expression confirming that he would never have her heart or trust again? He didn't know. Maybe if he tried to compartmentalize the day, lock it up tight in a private digital vault, he would feel grounded. But even as he tried to keep the gates shut on his memories, his body couldn't forget what it had experienced. Or the number of people who had died, all because he had thought he could help.

He felt faint. He grabbed a hallway doorknob to steady himself, but his hands shook no matter how tightly he grasped.

Coldplay's "42" started up in his head. He could hear it in qua-drophonic sound: stereo from both his servers and Rosero's brain. The dead would be in his head forever. Because he was dead, too. He leaned his forehead against the door and gently bumped it against the metal. Stop it. Stop it. Stop it . . .

A young girl shoved up against him. She looked frighteningly like the patient Steve had tried to save before he died. "Hey. Are you that guy?"

He looked at the girl, wide-eyed, shell-shocked. "What?"

"That guy. Who killed people?"

Muscles spasmed through his body. He felt like Ruth on amphet-amines. He jerked back from the girl and staggered down the hall for the bridge.

Ruth, Talia, and Veronika sat motionless in their bridge chairs. Each wore her own expression of devastation and loss. Talia wouldn't look at him. It was unbearable.

Rising out of her chair, Ruth marched up to him. Her right hand rose and shook violently. She looked like she wanted to slap him in the face, but instead, she spun around, picked up a navigation manual, and whacked him across the face with it.

"*Geh in drerd arein!*" she yelled. *Go to hell.*

He had a better idea. The countless dead in his head told him what he had to do. He sat carefully in an empty console seat and, closing his eyes, searched his own programming to find the files and the commands.

An alarm pinged on Veronika's monitors. The Major Tom program displayed on her screen was changing, but Tom had authorized it. She turned to him and asked, "What are you doing to Major Tom?"

"What? D-d-doing what?" asked Ruth.

Studying the commands, Veronika said, "I think he's trying to access his memory files."

Ruth's eyes widened. She screamed, "*Nein!* You will not d-d-do this!"

Talia whispered, "He's erasing his memories?"

"Stop him!" Ruth ordered Veronika.

Veronika jumped into the routine, typing fast. "I know it hurts," she said to Tom, "but you don't understand what you're doing!"

"Don't make me remember this. I won't. I . . . can't!"

"You will!" Ruth yelled back. "You will never f-f-forget it. I will make sure of that! I have copies. When it disappears? I will add it back. You have no right to f-f-forget!"

"Please!" Tom begged. "Sever the server connections and cut the power. Let me go dark."

Ruth crossed her arms in refusal. "And kill your human body, too? Have you no compassion? For the boy?"

Lack of compassion was not his problem. He had too much of it. Rosero's body was pumping his digital system full of anger, rage, terror, grief, and regret. He could feel Steve's body pitching off the ship's deck, hitting the sides of the boat on the way down, breaking his head and neck, and dropping into the sea. That lukewarm, dark, disgusting water had stopped his breath and his heart and his mind. Forever. Tom could hear the instantaneous pain, the emptiness of all those vaporized when the *Harmony* was laser-pulsed. Each refugee gunned down by drones.

He had had enough. It was more than anyone could sustain.

Ruth stood her ground. *"Ale tsores vos ikh hob oyf mayn hartsn, zoln oysgeyn tsu zayn kop."*

Tom chose not to translate out loud. *All problems I have in my heart, should go to his head.*

"Nein," she continued. "You will see what you d-d-do. You will not run away. You must care! Or you are just another Carter." Then glanced sorrowfully at Talia, then back at him. *"Mit a krechts batsolt men nit a choiv."*

You cannot pay a debt with a sigh. Tom owed Steve and Talia more than could be measured. And he had given them nothing but the dubious honor of joining him in a crusade they agreed with but had lost their stomach for years ago. The only payment he could give, they refused. They were bound to one another, but he was still a monster to them.

No, he was a monster only to Talia. He would be forced to remember that. Only Talia now.

The bridge was suffocating. So was his body. So was life. "I have to go. You can't make me stay," he said.

"Oh, for you?" scoffed Ruth. "T-t-t-time is meaningless. But for me? For T-T-T-Talia? You have consigned her. To hell."

Talia hadn't moved. Her eyes looked dead, her voice without affect. "No. Let him go. Rest. We all need rest." She got up deliberately, as though she had only just remembered that she was capable of standing, and wandered off the bridge toward her bunk on the ship. Tom hoped she would sleep. And sleep and sleep. For his part, he never wanted to wake up.

Ruth turned to Veronika. "Keep an eye. On him. Don't let him do. Something stupid." She turned on him. "Go away, too, *pakhdn!*"

She had called him a coward. And like a coward, he fled. But his body didn't know where to go. In desperation, he staggered back through the throng of refugees to his own bunk. But his mind needed to hide, too.

Now that TCoMT was gone, there was only one other place he could go. He messaged Veronika, asking her to send her avatar to join him at a certain location in cyberspace that he had never shared with anyone. And to bring an avatar for him.

CHAPTER FORTY-FOUR

In her trademark black steampunk ensemble, Veronika's avatar
appeared at the appointed location. With her, she had a Major
Tom body of her own design: an amalgamated head and body
constructed of Peter Bernhardt, Thomas Paine, the sexbots, and Rosero,
dressed in the black T-shirt, jeans, and boots long favored by Peter.

Tom inhabited the avatar like an old set of clothes, grateful to adapt
to Veronika's human reaction time. Exhausted and miserable, he wanted
to think as little as possible. But he grudgingly animated the avatar and
tried to show some appreciation. It was difficult. "Thanks. You just had
this? All ready to go?"

"Ummm . . . *yeah*. Do you even, like, know me?"

"I'm starting to. I'm another Veronika's Veil?" He matched a new
portrait miniature around her neck.

"The Catholics said it had the power to raise the dead. We'll see."
She looked around the anonymous white foyer. "Where are we?"

"It's a hidden backup. I copied it, just in case."

Her avatar looked surprised. "There's a hidden backup of the entire
Memory Palace?"

"This isn't the Memory Palace. If my housemates ever got out of
hand, I could jettison or destroy it, and come here. Which we did. That
was Dr. Who's advice when she built both. Smart lady."

He pointed at the simple white-paneled door. "I've never shown this to anyone." His hand touched the paneling, as though to check if it still existed. "I need to hide for a while. But I'm afraid to be alone. I might try something again."

"I won't let you self-destruct. Promise."

"Please, don't tell anyone about this."

"Dude," she said. "I'm your friend. I would never hurt you."

He paused, silent for a few seconds. "Okay. Here goes."

He opened the door, and they stepped into a wonderland.

As a lapsed Catholic, Peter Bernhardt had always held a grudging respect for the Jesuits. They were the religious order that had never forsaken intellectualism, observing and recording reality while still engaged in their evangelical mission. No matter how discordant the concepts, many Jesuits were capable of holding the often contradictory pursuits of knowledge and faith separate and equal. Dr. Who had helped Major Tom design the ultimate Jesuit sanctuary for himself: a recreation of the Admont Abbey Library in Austria. A baroque delight for the mind and the senses, it was the largest monastic library in the world. Over its ivory and gold-curlicued walls and bookcases, its seven baby-blue and pink-domed ceilings depicted the journey of human understanding in paintings by the Baroque master Bartolomeo Altomonte. Beginning with thought and speech, they progressed through the sciences and arts, finally culminating in divine revelation in the central cupola. Major Tom's idea of the divine did not correspond to that of the Jesuits occupying this splendid space, but he appreciated the effort to reconcile different kinds of knowledge with a most imperfect human understanding.

Veronika's avatar gasped in wonder. "I can't even . . . Dude, this is so . . ."

"Weird? Wonderful?"

"Yeah! And, like, fabulously elitist. Why would you ever leave?"

He tried to see it through her fresh eyes. "I never spent much time here. Now I might stay."

A song played. He hadn't programmed it. Bouncy and peppy. Women's voices. Veronika bopped and grooved around the open space, dancing in her quirky, long-limbed way. Even as an elegant avatar, her uniqueness was apparent.

A quick audio search brought the revelation: The Veronicas' "Revolution." "Seriously?"

"Hey, listen and maybe you'll learn something about the optimism of women." She danced up to a bookshelf and pulled out a couple of volumes of sixteenth-century natural history. She opened one. It was in Latin.

"Do you keep any of your own files here?" she asked.

"No. This was intended as pure escapism. That would defeat the purpose."

"You should think about it." She put the book back and stopped short. Next to the shelves was a gruesome yet exquisite statue: Josef Stammel's *Death*. One of a series of The Four Last Things that included *Hell*, *Heaven*, and *Resurrection*, it stood adjacent to the central bookshelves. A winged skeleton wielded a drained hourglass in one hand and a dagger in the other as it dived down upon a helpless old monk, ready to stab the mortal and send him on his eternal way.

She studied the statue. The music faded out. "What's it like to die?" she asked.

"I'm not sure I ever did." Tom touched the old man's hand, which held a walking stick. In his mind, it had as much mass and immutability as the real thing. So how real is anything? If he could replicate reality here and convince himself it was enough, could he stay forever?

Veronika watched his avatar, his mind lost in thought. She snapped her fingers in his face. "Hey, dude! Stay present!"

"Sorry! I mean, my body did die technically, but . . . You can't compare my experience to others. I think most just . . . end."

"Unless you can upload." She caressed the cheek of a putto, a chubby baby angel, holding a soap bubble at the old man's feet. Forever on the brink of dissolution, the bubble's impermanence haunted him. He struggled to stay engaged. "In my experience, if done right, death is an illusion preceded by love. If you're lucky. Just like life."

Veronika took off her top hat and draped goggles, levitated heavenward, and placed it on top of Death's head. It made the skeleton look jaunty. Satisfied, she floated back down. "So Carter never knew this place existed?"

"No. At least, I hope not."

"Why?" asked Veronika.

"I needed something he can't influence. I don't understand how or why we're linked. But we are. Until one or the other of us is destroyed. Maybe both. And now I need a place to hide. I just wish I could forget." He sat on the marble parquet floor, at Death's feet, and rocked back and forth. "But you won't let me forget, will you?"

Veronika ignored his question, sat next to him, and said with great irony, "I think he'd love this place."

Tom found it difficult to talk. "Probably . . . He'd say, 'Pete, you finally acquired some taste.' Fucking asshole."

She could see he was close to tears. "Why did you stop, like, helping people when you uploaded?"

"What do you mean?" he asked.

"Well, like, you were some weird ghost flitting around the web. You never interacted beyond singing in TCoMT. Never touched down. Until I contacted you."

Tom wondered how she knew. How far had she followed him online? As a fan, or a stalker, or something else? With all that had happened, he had set aside his concerns about her honesty, her agenda, her identity. As with Talia in his past life, he was deeply involved with someone he didn't really know. Was he that desperate for companionship? Or to be understood?

"You mean, until now," he said.

"Yeah."

"I'm a scientist and an engineer," said Tom. "I study, then fix things. I wanted to make machines to save people's memories, their sense of self. Like my pop. And I did. But so much happened. So many people died. Some of them were innocent, like my pop. And the people of 10/26. Others were horrible and deserved it. And some . . . got caught up in things they didn't understand." He rocked more. "I want to get out of this alive, whatever that means. With everyone I care about. But Steve's gone. And so many others. And I can't fix anything. Or anyone." He gave up controlling his emotions and wept, but he wasn't sure if, as a digital creature, he would feel an emotional release or not.

Veronika reached over and wiped away his tears. "Not true. You're a hero."

Her touch reminded him of Talia's, when she had wiped his tears in a hospital bed once. When Steve had saved his life. "You have an inflated view of me," he said.

"I don't think so," she said.

"But you do. See, there's a sickness at the heart of the world. It shapes all of us. We're wet clay, until the world tests us, molds us, burns us to its purpose. Into . . . its avatars, I guess. In the fire, good men become petty and weak. Bad men commit heroic acts. All of us are batted from one threat to another, trying to find moments of happiness, before the next blow strikes our hearts and we're forced to act. We're all sick and trying to survive."

Veronika reached out and held his hand. "Dude. That was righteous."

"Not righteous. Even the enlightened suffer, until the day they die."

"Or don't, in your case." She let go of his hand.

"Or don't. As a scientist, I couldn't believe in reincarnation, but I'm living proof," Tom said. "Except I remember past lives and how I fucked up each time, and I still can't seem to get it right. Welcome to my special ring of hell."

"It's not such a bad place." She sidled next to him, laid her head on his shoulder, and took both his hands in hers.

Grateful for a friend, he kissed the top of her head.

After a quiet minute, she pulled up her bustled skirt and straddled him, her long legs wrapping around his waist. Then she wrapped her arms around his back.

He was stunned. "What . . . are you doing?"

"Shhh," she whispered in his ear. "I think you need this." She squeezed him harder, kissed one cheek and then the other. Then his mouth.

He had never felt so vulnerable and grateful at the same time.

He could feel the soft pressure of her lips and tongue contrast with the harder pressure of her pelvis on his jeans and genitals. His avatar—which Veronika had constructed with a surprising level of detail and anatomical accuracy—was connected to both a fully simulated body in a server and a physical flesh-body back in his bunk. She could make him feel what she did, but she could only experience this moment through her MR glasses, without the feedback of muscular pressure or the sensation of touch. She was a voyeur in her own fantasy.

He wrapped his arms around her and hugged her back. "I wish you could feel this."

She caught her breath, then smiled dreamily. "I can."

"How?"

"Trust me," she said. And she hugged him back.

He ran his hands around her body. Over her delicate shoulders. Down her long, lean back, where he could feel each vertebra like piano keys. Up the front to cup her breasts and kiss the lace of her Victorian blouse. Her head lolled back in delight, and he kissed her long, arched neck. With an instant shift of pixels, his clothes disappeared. She was beautiful, naked and astride him, kissing him, her tongue exploring the soft contours inside his mouth. She worked her way to his right ear, licking it in constricting spirals. He moaned. She nibbled his collarbone.

Somewhere, in a bunk on the *Zumwalt*, his nineteen-year-old body's testosterone production went into high gear. The sudden rush of androgens made him woozy.

He couldn't believe she wanted him, in spite of who he was and what he had done.

"I can be anyone you want," she breathed into his ear between kisses. Her figure morphed into different bodies, an athlete wearing only cleats, a dancer in a tulle tutu, an equestrian in boots with a riding crop. "Who do you want me to be?"

"Stop," he choked out. "You. I want you to be you."

No one had ever said that to her before. Except Winter. And the bitch hadn't meant it. Veronika moaned, switched back to her own avatar, and ground him harder, running her fingernails through his hair, nibbling his nipples. He sped up his run time so he could program a soft mattress. It appeared in 5.3 seconds. It looked like a stale piece of sliced bread and felt like sandpaper.

She stopped moving and arched an eyebrow. "Not your talent, dude." She kissed his forehead, then made the bed disappear. "We don't need it."

"But the floor is cold," he said, shifting his ass uncomfortably on the marble.

"Oh, poor baby," she teased.

The books and bookcases around him seemed to sink. Below them, the floor slipped away as they rose above the parqueted stone. Soon, their heads were even with the angel of death in Veronika's top hat.

"Newton's third law," he said. "Zero-g sex won't work . . ."

Veronika put her index finger against his lips and pouted seductively. "Programmer makes the rules. And you're, like, way too literal. Shut. Up." She kissed him hard to make it so.

They floated out to the middle of the central cupola, now equidistant from *Death*, *Hell*, *Heaven*, and *Resurrection*. Above them, in the fresco of *Divine Revelation*, robed religious archetypes floated in a blue-and-pink sky. The central figure, Divine Wisdom, was a woman. The men, including Moses and the four great Latin fathers, Saints Gregory, Ambrose, Augustine, and Jerome, listened to her.

Maybe he should start listening to Veronika.

Veronika flipped herself around like a circus acrobat, her head hovering over his erect cock, and her ass floating near his face. Slowly . . . so slowly . . . she lowered her lips around his shaft, then plunged his cock deep into her mouth. His body jerked in shock. She began a languorous rhythm.

He figured turnabout was fair play, so he grabbed her ass and maneuvered her clitoris to his mouth. He licked gently . . . Her ass vibrated with desire.

They spun delicately through the air, which supported them like the feathers of the angels' wings depicted around them. A distant part of him knew she was still the ultimate fangirl, having the ultimate fantasy. He didn't care.

She stopped, released his cock, and turned her head around. "Still cold?"

He spun her around, face-to-face. "Don't tease!" he roared, then grabbed her ass, threw her legs around him, and drove his cock inside her.

She screamed. It echoed off the wedding-cake walls. She rode him vigorously in the air, meeting each thrust of his with her own, making sure he knew that he was not the boss here, even in his most secret place.

They thrust faster and faster, deeper and deeper, until he lost track of where he ended and she began. She fused their avatars, creating one sexual being, a beast with two backs, part biology and part fantasy, their bodies locked in thrusts that seemed never-ending.

They climaxed in unison, screaming. The statues trembled.

After the echo died away, they floated limp in the air, then drifted down like angel feathers to the cold, marble floor. Their bodies separated. They became individual beings once again.

"That . . . ," he gasped. "That was unreal."

"You're welcome," she said, nuzzling her head into his neck.

While he enjoyed their acrobatics and physiological release, there was no forgetting. No oblivion as he had had in his past life with Talia. He still felt like shit. And he didn't forget the questions he had about Veronika when they entered the Admont Library.

Veronika saw his expression change. She caressed his face. "Dude, what's wrong?"

"What do you want?" Tom asked.

"I think that's obvious."

"No. Not sex. Not some fangirl fantasy. What is it you really want?"

She shifted off him. Staring at the floor, tracing the parquet with a finger, she said, "I want to be like you. You know, like, an upload with a body. All the bells and whistles."

Years ago, he had offered Talia the same brain-computer interfaces he had implanted in Thomas Paine, the chance to be like him, to share their minds and feelings. She had been horrified. He had at first assumed that she thought the intimacy would be too much for her, the stakes too high if something happened to either of them. Only later had Talia admitted that even though she loved him, she was frightened of what he was. But here was a woman who wasn't scared. He should have been thrilled to have found someone who would join him forever, in whatever form they took. And yet her eagerness concerned him.

"I'm not a real boy," he said. "I've still got strings."

"I know what you are," she said.

"That's why you're here? With me? You want me to give you that?"

"I mean, look at this place! We could live here. We don't need TCoMT. And this is who I want to be. I could make this—"

"We're not the same," he said. "Back on the *Zumwalt*, you mentioned the Joni Mitchell song 'Both Sides Now.' I told you that it related to me, and you said nothing. But you had a reaction. Why say it?"

Her face fell. She had played her cards too early. "I get all of this. I get change. And abandonment and isolation. Better than you know. This is me, too. I wanted you to know I understood. I'm like you."

"No," he said. "You're not. I'm using tech to upload and download and manipulate what living means, because I'm so far gone, I can't care what happens. I'm not a me. I'm the biggest lab rat in the world. You're using technology to become the real you. There's a difference."

"But I could help so much more! And, like, I just want to be with you . . . *uhhh!*" She slammed her hand on the floor in frustration. The library shook.

"I'm sorry," he said. "I can't give you that."

She slipped farther away and hugged her knees into her chest. "So you go back to real life."

"Not necessarily," he said. "I could turn my back on everything and live here forever."

She looked confused. "But, you said to me in the car you had no choice. There was no one else like you."

He turned away from her. "But there is. Carter."

She shook her head. "You're not the same. And only you can stop him."

"Once again, you have greater faith in me than I do. Carter's been more than a step ahead since I met him back in college."

Ruth interrupted with a text message for them both: *Wake up. And look at this. Now.*

CHAPTER FORTY-FIVE

He opened his eyes in real space to find Veronika wrapped around him. They were in his tiny ship bunk. Their clothes were still on. She wore a haptic bodysuit under her T-shirt and long cotton skirt, the same body-sensation unit that the Companibots owner had worn. Their bodies still shivered from the physical expression of their digital experience. His crotch was wet and cold. She still looked upset.

Ruth's news was another video from an anonymous and encrypted source. Amanda stood at an antique wooden conference table. Her hair was cut in a sleek, attractive bob and dyed the same shiny black that it had been before her pregnancies and the troubles. Her copper-toned features were enhanced with tasteful makeup. Her once bushy eyebrows were plucked into graceful arches. She was dressed in a chic, form-fitting suit and projected a vision of feminine power and authority that he had never seen in her before.

It appeared that a meeting had just broken up. He noted the hastily abandoned glasses of water and cups of coffee, the heavily upholstered chairs around her, the antiques, the classical molding around the ceiling, and a single-paneled door leading into the room. There were no windows.

She stared with confidence into a camera. "Hi, Pete. I think you need to see this." She gestured to a large HOME screen behind her.

News clips ran. Major Tom, a.k.a. Thomas Paine, had committed an act of war on the sovereign Southern States of America, killing tens of thousands of the homeless waiting at Port Everglades for help from President Conrad. Tom had whipped the homeless into a rebellious fervor, then slaughtered them. Conrad was denouncing Tom as a terrorist, and he and his comrades as dangerous coconspirators. A consortium of nations was banding together to eliminate Major Tom, and the SSA would crack down on anyone caught helping the fugitives. Martial law would be instituted.

Amanda's smile contained a touch of pity. "Pete, you can see, can't you, that there's no way out? Carter's way is the only way. I don't want to see you or him hurt anymore. I can't stand it. Come help us, instead. We can be the Three Musketeers again. Please, Pete. Come back."

As freshmen at Stanford, Amanda and Carter had both called the three of them The Three Musketeers. Back then, they had indeed stood all for one and one for all, even if Amanda and Peter had paired off and married. But this didn't seem like Amanda. She wasn't as soft in her movements, nor as angry or pricking to his ego. Amanda knew how to get under his skin in an indirect way—like when she had wanted to get pregnant, or when she had miscarried, or when he had visited her as a robot—and she was not doing it now. Her most potent weapon was going unused. Carter had rarely seen their fights. They reserved that behavior for each other in private. Tom saw no evidence in her mannerisms indicating how much both men's actions had devastated her. She would have used that, too.

"Turn it off," Tom said to Ruth. Amanda disappeared from their screens.

Veronika saw his expression and froze. "What's wrong?"

"That's Carter," said Tom.

The *Zumwalt* continued north in the open ocean, avoiding the territorial waters of the SSA. They were monitored by the occasional submarine, and Tom was sure that high-atmosphere surveillance UAV and satellite cameras followed them, but otherwise it appeared that they were left alone.

On a loading dock, Tom pulled a black T-shirt over Tom 1's head and helped him into the sleeves. Tom 1 looked back at him with the blankness that off-the-shelf sexbots exhibited until engaged. To protect the server farm, Tom 1 was disconnected from Major Tom. The robot no longer shared a single mental entity, so Tom could not know what Tom 1 was thinking. Or vice versa. To allow Tom 1 to act autonomously, the team deleted as much information as they could and packed him with as much computing power as possible. There wasn't a lot of "Major Tomness" left.

Tom wondered if the robot could still be considered sentient, or whether it was another Foxy Funkadelia, a deceptive Turing Test. And yet he had the oddest sensation they were connected by blood, as if he were sending his brother off to war.

"You know what to do?" asked Tom.

"I ask for Conrad," said Tom 1, engaged and animated. "I look for Amanda. I look for anyone else I might recognize from the memories you left me. I get you information. Then employ my initiative for mayhem. Is that correct?"

"That's right," Tom said. "Now go get 'em." It was a suicide mission. But Tom still felt connected, as if he had just handed the robot the weapon to kill them both. He was nauseous. Perhaps he had adapted to his distributed, multisubstrate personality too well? He had taken for granted that the robots would always be there for him, monitoring the world, expendable on his behalf, a part of him. With Tom 2 destroyed and Tom 1 cut off, there was now only his human body and the server farm. He was losing himself, one by one. Recognizing his own fear of abandonment, Tom pushed the feeling back.

"Bye, Tom 1," said Tom.

The robot's eyes tracked to stare into Tom's. He smiled the same, sad smile as Tom.

"Bye, Tom," said Tom 1.

CHAPTER FORTY-SIX

The large wooden crate arrived at the delivery bay of the Hay-Adams Hotel in Washington, DC, only a few blocks from the White House. Tom 1 lay cushioned within. When it sounded like the area was clear, he turned on the lighted drill in his hand and opened the box from the inside.

Cameras tracked Tom 1 as he walked toward the White House.

The location was not familiar to Tom 1. Tom remembered the *allée* of trees leading to the White House through Lafayette Park, where Carter had convinced Peter to meet with Josiah Brant and join the Phoenix Club. But those and other memories had been wiped from Tom 1. Memories are complex, webs created of innumerable strings. Cut one and others are affected. Tom 1 ran mathematical calculations and language tests, but despite his best attempts at concentration, he was no better than a human with cognitive deficits. He could speak coherently and process others' sentences and ideas. He could do basic logic and make conceptual connections. He had desires and some memories. But he wasn't going to solve complex problems or have eureka moments. Having once known the whole World Wide Web, he was now confined to a small room, adequate for his present purposes, but not what he was used to. Tom wondered how he felt.

Tom 1 approached the sentry post at the gate on Pennsylvania Avenue with his hands up. Armed security detained him, and the

Zumwalt lost visual contact as he shuffled into the White House with six armed SSA marshals escorting him.

Unseen by the marshals was a tiny fly, barely larger than a mosquito, which flew unobtrusively from Tom 1's hair and landed on the collar of an agent behind him. It was a MAV, a micro-air vehicle, which used both wings and six legs for transportation and carried a tiny camera that could record and transmit.

Once inside the White House, the MAV activated its camera and began transmitting. Tom 1 was led to an examination room in the basement. Major Tom directed the MAV away from any sensors, toward a hallway wall nearby, where it landed, waiting.

Six hours later, a web-search alarm rang on all shipboard consoles. Tom, Veronika, Ruth, and Talia gathered to watch a live all-media broadcast from the White House. Tom 1 had not resurfaced.

A press conference for favored media was in full swing in the briefing room. The press secretary made contradictory statements: "The robot surrendered itself." "We found and captured the robot." "A robotic weapon of mass destruction." "The robot has no ability to hurt the president." A gray-bearded engineer took the podium and explained the odd appearance of a robot identical to the one discovered killing refugees at Port Everglades and that Thomas Paine had then detonated as a bomb. Behind and next to the press secretary stood a mixed group: computer and robotics engineers in casual clothing to one side, bureaucrats and security in bland, ill-fitting navy suits, blue shirts, and striped ties on the other. In case it all went sideways, the administration could spread blame among these representatives, and thus blame no one. It was a DC specialty.

"We've examined the robot thoroughly," said Graybeard. "It's a bizarre, jerry-rigged contraption, but harmless. Completely harmless."

No media outlet wanted to pay for reporters to do location work if they didn't have to, especially now that the White House was in a different country than either New York or Los Angeles, so reporters literally phoned it in, their faces projected on large GOs atop remote-controlled robots. The White House could turn them off at will if they asked questions the press secretary didn't like.

A robot flashed its red light, indicating that its reporter had a question. The name of the news organization was displayed at the top of its GO screen. Graybeard pointed to the robot. "Yes, *Atlanta Journal*?"

"Is it true it's a sexbot?" the reporter asked. The attendees laughed, including other reporters.

"Yes, it is," said Graybeard good-naturedly. "But we can't be sure its sexual equipment has ever been used for its intended purpose. Unless *that's* been weaponized. Watch out, ladies!" He laughed loudly, giving permission to the rest to laugh along. One young engineer looked uncomfortable. Tom sensed the discomfort wasn't about sex jokes. Graybeard shot a glance at him and continued, "This thing can't do squat."

When Tom had been Peter Bernhardt, he had witnessed this dynamic often: a youngster discovered something that the project lead hadn't found, or wouldn't acknowledge, and the hierarchy shot the young one down. Consensus was only safe in the room, not in the field. Consensus always led to mistakes. Sometimes fatal ones.

It was sadly human error to ignore a lone voice of warning. And the young engineer was right. Tom 1 was, in fact, a nasty little Rube Goldberg machine of destruction.

The press secretary explained that capturing this robot was the first step in President Conrad's prime objective: to find and try Thomas Paine and his compatriots as enemies of the state. The sentence would be death. Cash awards would be given to anyone with correct information leading to their capture. The threat to the nation would be eliminated.

Tom 1 was led into the Oval Office. The reactivated MAV had settled back into his wig, then alighted on the curved wall to transmit the scene to Tom and the team back on the *Zumwalt*. Behind the *Resolute* desk—built from the timbers of the British arctic-exploration ship HMS *Resolute* and given by Queen Victoria to President Rutherford B. Hayes—sat the president of the Southern States.

Terrence Conrad lounged back in his desk chair. His flawless postsurgical face—almost as robotic as Tom 1's—creepily skirted the uncanny valley. He wore a grimace. Eight Secret Service agents, two at each exit, stood at attention, with laser and mini-electromagnetic-pulse-disruption weapons.

Tom 1 stood still in front of the desk.

As he watched through the MAV's camera, Tom felt an unnerving sense of déjà vu. The office was exactly as he had seen in visual reenactments and the news. Few realized that the windows had been replaced with antisurveillance tech, including sound scrambling and opacity technology. Surrounded by the dark-brown sheen of the glass, the room felt like it was cast in perpetual night. Tom referenced the visual archives of the world's most famous oval room, laying images from different times on top of one another. The colors and decor had changed with each administration. Franklin Delano Roosevelt's administration had rebuilt the room to help the crippled president access the White House's private residence more easily, but its essence had remained throughout the decades. Conrad's decorators had implemented a bilious pastiche of red, white, and blue. A flag stood in front of each blackened window: the Stars and Stripes to the left, the presidential flag in the center, the Confederate flag to the right.

Back on the bridge, Veronika gasped. "You don't think he'll blow himself up now?"

"N-n-n-no," said Ruth, who turned to Tom. "He knows better, right?"

"We'll see," said Tom.

Talia watched without saying a word, her arms crossed, her lips pursed, her face taut. Tom thought, Please, Tom 1, don't kill the president. Not yet. He has something to say. And we need to hear it.

They watched breathlessly as Conrad rocked back in his chair, breathing through his sensuous lips in a display of obvious dissatisfaction. "You're the infamous Thomas Paine? A sexbot?"

"I come in all kinds of packages," said Tom 1.

The president gently scratched his coiffed head. "Didn't think your type was good for much other than a little—" He vocalized a sound like squeaky springs and pumped his fist horizontally in the air.

"Are you prejudiced against robots," asked Tom 1, "or can we discuss terms?"

"Terms?" said the president with a smirk. "I got you here. We'll dismantle you, figure out how you work, and find the enemies behind you."

"You already dismantled me," said Tom 1.

Conrad's eyes narrowed. "We determined you weren't a threat. Now we'll take you apart like some kid's Christmas present."

How Tom hated that bromide: dismantle-and-understand, as though his complexity could be reduced to some chips, wires, and gyros. Even as an engineer, he had known he was more than the sum of his parts. Dismantle-and-understand sounded stupid when the far smarter Josiah Brant had said it in the club bunker before he died, and it sounded imbecilic out of this wannabe strongman's mouth.

"You've got nothing," continued Conrad. "I'm dictating terms. This was all part of my plan to capture you."

"Ask him why, damn it," Tom muttered to himself on the bridge. "This bastard loves to hear himself talk."

Tom 1 said, "What was your plan?"

Conrad straightened his spine, widened his large blue eyes, and took a deep breath. "We had a surplus of unhappy people. They are dangerous for a new government and have to be dealt with. The first people who leave in a crisis are the biggest troublemakers. They hate it here. They can't become part of the fabric of life. They leave, or die trying. The next wave is doubtful. They might be convinced to stay and behave. Or not. Any wave after that is waiting to see what happened to the first two. They see success, they'll keep fleeing, like a leaky drain. But we made sure you killed them. Now they'll stay where it's safer. With us." He pointed a finger at Tom 1. "We'll take care of them, because you will always fail."

Score a point for Conrad. Tom had led the victims into Conrad's trap. The president was the devil they knew, Thomas Paine now the devil they didn't. In times of perceived trouble, people elected strongmen, autocrats, and bullies. Subconsciously, they wanted to be led, even into an abyss.

"Automation is expensive," continued Conrad, "and only necessary when the cost of labor goes up. We're not raising labor costs. Don't need to. Never needed to, as long as we kept a strong hand on the workers. And eventually? We'll clone the ones that work best. Strongest. Efficient. Obedient. Everybody's happy."

Tom 1 winked. "I bet 'Dixie' is your favorite song."

On the bridge, Tom laughed out loud. He hadn't thought the robot could make jokes anymore. He hoped that meant that Tom 1 was capable of making nuanced decisions as well.

"Playing the smartass won't save you," sneered Conrad.

"I'm not smart. I've got few brains left," said Tom 1.

"We wouldn't have accomplished our goals without you. You think we need to be as smart as you all to stop you. Not true. Too smart gets you nothing in this life. Too smart gets you stuck at some college with a bunch of other too-smart idiots who don't understand how the world works."

"And how's that?" asked Tom 1.

"Well, for starters, every place is different. Those San Fran and New York values . . . lifestyles"—he made air quotes—"they don't mean much here."

"Values? Like freedom?" asked Tom 1.

Conrad laughed. "Freedom? The only folks deserving of the word have to earn it. Or inherit it. Prove you're good stock, a productive citizen, decent, clean, hardworking, and then you've earned the right to freedom. Some in our country aren't much more than talking animals. They don't need"—air quotes again—"*freedom*. They wouldn't know what to do with it."

"Earn . . . or inherit it?" repeated Tom 1. He looked confused.

"Well, sure. How the world's always worked. You think people change, just because we got new toys?" Conrad gestured at Tom 1. "Bottom line: We had a labor issue and chose to use the manufacturing assets we had, instead of uptooling with fancy technologies that need replacing every two years and that we'd have to buy from other nations, or worse. We're stopping the outflow. We'll build a wall around the entire South. Including New Orleans and Florida. We're doing what's best for everybody. You'll see." He smiled broadly, his white teeth gleaming.

"A wall . . . ?"

"Not a real wall. A military wall. Air, land, and sea. No one in or out without our say-so. Lock us up tight as a bug in a rug. Safe and predictable. Our citizens love it. Everybody's happy."

Tom 1's head cocked to one side. "How did the Phoenix Club pick you?"

His ego pricked, the president stood up, his wrinkle-free face reddening under his makeup. Leaning his hands on the desk, he said, "I'm the president of the Southern States of America. And you're not, so watch your mouth, dipstick. I got here because I'm the best. The best." He pounded the table for emphasis. The cheek under his right eye twitched.

More likely, the club had reckoned that Conrad was both the most photogenic and the most expendable, should it all go to hell. His ascension had the stink of Josiah Brant all over it: make a figurehead and let him fall if it fails, just as he had tried to do with Thomas Paine. But Josiah's mind had been locked up in the Memory Palace since his death, and destroyed after Carter's escape. Could Carter have learned Josiah's lessons so well? Or was Josiah copied along with him?

"So it was the Phoenix Club," said Tom 1.

"The Phoenix Club built this nation! We wouldn't have accomplished all the good we did without it! And you act like no one likes me. There are millions who love me—millions!—who would do anything I ask. You? I can live without your love. You're done. You're not even human."

"One last question, sir," said Tom 1, "and then you can dictate terms."

"Damn right I'm dictating terms, you creepy puppet," muttered Conrad.

"Why are the seasteads gone?" asked Tom 1.

"Really? That's all you got? Simple. You're either an ally. Or an enemy. The near-shore economic zones? Fine. They can stay. They know they're just a small military exercise away from annihilation. But the deep-sea freaks? You can't negotiate with those fools. They're anarchists! They don't follow anybody. They're a threat to the global order. They have too much power over things they can't handle. Money, identity—that's important stuff! So we said goodbye! Everyone agreed, and chipped in with weapons, vessels, anything we needed to protect our nations."

"Everyone?"

"The club, Russia, China . . ." He stood taller. "All the important players. We're protecting the planet."

"China and Russia? Aren't they North America's adversaries?"

"They know what they're about and will do anything in their power to accomplish it. We have a lot to learn from them."

"So it wasn't about Dr. Who?" asked Tom 1.

"Dr. Who? Who's he?" Conrad seemed genuinely puzzled. The club leaders still siloed information as "need to know." Dr. Who was above this man's pay grade.

"Doesn't matter," continued Conrad. "We got what we wanted. Safety and global compliance. Sold the data to the highest bidders for a good profit. The American way. Now everybody knows who's boss." He assumed a wider stance.

"But the seasteads were a small threat in the scheme of things," said Tom 1.

"Kill it in the cradle," said Conrad. "Anarchists undermine our way of life."

"What if they could have helped you?" asked Tom 1.

"A bunch of water-loving, flag-burning anarchists? No way."

Tom 1 let a moment of silence hang. "And your terms?"

"You and your comrades committed seditious conspiracy, an act of war, and crimes against humanity," said Conrad. "Surrender, and I have prisons waiting for the humans. A bed and three squares for a while. We'll bleed you all dry for information, then finish you off. Better than you deserve. Don't surrender, and you'll be hunted down and killed like the animals you are. You're terrorists now. The world is searching for you, and we will find you. Can't make it simpler than that."

"I'm just spare parts," said Tom 1. "I'm not going anywhere."

Conrad rolled his eyes. "Not you, dummy. The humans."

"How do you plan on letting them know? I've got no communications back to my people. I'm just a mini-recording of a partial personality. I'm cut off from my source."

Conrad snickered. The eight Secret Service agents snickered with him. "We know about your MAV. I'm talking to Thomas Paine right now, aren't I?" He waved around the room. "Hey, Tommy Boy! How do you want to die?"

Tom 1 stood still, said nothing.

Watching the robot carefully, Tom said, "They've got to be filming this, too, for propaganda later. Don't do it."

The robot's body rocked, his eyes twitching.

On the bridge, Veronika said, "Oh my God, he's got contrary commands." The others watched, breathless.

Tom was amazed. "He's still so human."

"What a weird little bot you are." Conrad snickered, mocking Tom 1's odd movements. The Secret Service officers laughed.

The team watched as Tom 1 reprioritized his commands. The robot stopped his bizarre movement. "Now that we know your terms, we will all see what the future holds, won't we?"

"No. You won't," Conrad said. "You're finished." His hand made a slicing move across his neck, and Tom and the team watched as Tom 1 was dragged away by the agents for a final disassembly. As the MAV tried to fly away, a pair of giant hands grabbed it, and the image on the bridge went to static.

CHAPTER FORTY-SEVEN

The team on the *Zumwalt* bridge rewatched the surveillance video, searching for any new information. Even with the robotic face's limited expressions and affect, Tom knew what Tom 1 had been feeling. He felt it, too. No longer linked as a single mind, Tom 1 was an identical twin behind a silicone mask. Tom said a silent and final farewell to him, grateful that the machine had retained enough of Major Tom's wisdom not to self-destruct and take President Conrad with him.

"Am I, like, the only one mesmerized by Conrad?" asked Veronika.

Tom was as fascinated as Veronika. Conrad was a type that humans regularly propelled up the razor-wire social ladder, even though their leadership would be society's undoing. The tragedy was that autocrats gained power from the fear they generated and exploited. Humans were vulnerable to fear. The cycles of history never ceased to taunt those forced to see them. Would humanity ever learn? Or would it have to evolve?

"Dr. Who was a sideshow, meant to distract us," said Tom. "They knew we couldn't abandon her. But the Chinese and Russians? They're no sideshow. What if the SSA brings them in to a real conflict? And against who? It can't just be about me. The Northeast? The West? California? Who's the enemy?"

If the SSA were to declare war on Thomas Paine, and bring two empires into it, would the SSA become a patsy of the club and its global partners? Autocratic leaders loved pretending to hang out together while screwing one another behind their backs. They had the same goals: carve up the global pie, control their populations, run sufficiently successful economies to enrich themselves, and stay on top. He could see why autocrats would be "friends." Psychopaths tended to congregate. They didn't see their mutual behavior as abhorrent. Just smart.

"Right now, I'm more worried about Carter and Amanda," said Veronika. "And their bigger plan. They're working directly for the club, and, like, now rising empires? Doesn't make sense."

"And I'm worried. How they get. In your head," said Ruth. "You are vulnerable."

Talia sat forward, engaged for the first time since they had gathered to watch Tom 1's finale. "Tom, if you were Carter, where would you send her?"

"I'm not sure," he said. "We need eyes on the ground."

"What kind of eyes?" said Ruth. "I will message Miss Gray Hat for help."

"What do Carter and the club use?" asked Tom. "Same as us. Drones, satellites, surveillance cameras, old CCTV? Commandeer people's GOs and HOMEs? Surveillance MAVs. We need anything with a camera."

"Too much data," said Ruth, twitching her shoulders in discomfort. "Too hard to cull through."

Talia said nothing. She turned her chair away, her silence a censure.

"On it!" said Veronika, swiveling back to her monitors. "We're not looking for, like, a thousand different things. We're looking for one face and body we already have a lot of data for."

"Where is Miss Gray Hat? Why haven't we heard from her?" asked Ruth.

"Do we need her?" asked Veronika. "I can handle this."

Tom leaned forward. "She's got this. Let's focus on—"

Ruth shook her head so hard that her curly hair jiggled like tiny springs. "We need higher-level data analysis. Veronika has skills. But Miss Gray Hat is better."

Veronika spun in her chair. "Excuse me? Have you seen, like, what I've done since you met me?"

"Yes," said Ruth. "And we still need help."

"What the fuck, dude!" said Veronika. "Talk about ungrateful."

"Veronika, stop it," said Tom.

"Why so d-d-defensive?" barked Ruth, now twitching. "Can't you learn from those b-b-better?"

Veronika removed her MR glasses and looked at Ruth with her own two eyes. "Sure. If there were any."

"Such arrogance!" Ruth threw her arms around her torso in disgust.

"Ruthie, Veronika, please," said Tom. "Calm down."

Both women ignored him. But Talia didn't. She was watching Tom with a growing expression of horror.

Veronika rolled to Ruth's monitor and began typing. "Miss Gray Hat is a mirage."

"Get off my system!" said Ruth.

"You won't believe me unless I show you." Veronika pointed to Ruth's screen, which displayed a text message to Miss Gray Hat: *Help us!* She rolled back to her own monitor, put on her glasses, and typed a few commands. A scrolling script appeared on Veronika's monitor.

Ruth stopped twitching and sat motionless. Then her entire body sprung into shuddering. "You l-l-l-lied to us! How c-c-c-could you?" she wailed. She swung to Tom. "D-d-did you know?"

"No," he lied.

"Oh! So clever!" said Ruth to Veronika. "Messages! From both! At the same time!"

Miss Gray Hat was no longer an enigma. Ruth's greatest intellectual crush was flesh and blood, wearing a baggy black skirt, a Ziggy Stardust

T-shirt, and high-top sneakers. The proof was there all along: a quick, slight smile when Ruth would compliment Miss Gray Hat. Veronika hiding when maintaining both personas simultaneously was too difficult. And they had been too busy trying to save themselves and the world to see the truth.

"I protected you!" roared Veronika. "If you had known I was Miss Gray Hat, someone else could have found out. How could you have trusted me if you knew I was some girl living with her parents in Santa Barbara?"

"*Nein,*" barked Ruth. "*A linger darf hoben a guten zechron!*"

"I . . . I don't understand," sputtered Veronika.

Ruth lunged at her keyboard and cut the link to Veronika's—and Miss Gray Hat's—messages. "N-n-no longer the great linguist? N-n-no hiding behind a computer. With translation! 'A liar must have a good memory.' And you have n-n-none!"

"But you can't seriously—" said Veronika.

"*A ligner hert zikh zeineh ligen azoi lang ein biz er glaibt zikh alain.*" Ruth's body shook so hard, she would have fallen to pieces if she had been a robot.

"'A liar tells his story so often that he gets to believe it himself,'" said Tom.

"I just wanted to be with you," said Veronika, softer now. "All of you. You're my heroes."

Talia faced Veronika. "Where's the server farm?"

Panicked, Veronika looked at Tom. "Dude. No."

Tom sighed, then nodded. "They have more invested in all this than you do. They deserve to know."

"It's, it's . . . like, 45.846605 S, 170.474149 E."

"And where is that?" asked Talia.

"Dunedin, New Zealand," Veronika blurted.

Ruth and Talia looked surprised, but not Tom.

"Safest place I could find," said Veronika. "Nicest, most resilient, reliable people. Speak English. Least likely to join a war. No nukes. Ass end of the world. And not, like, the most active area on the Ring of Fire. I took an old server farm used for movie special effects and built it there. Students from the University of Otago do the maintenance. They think it's an AHI simulation project."

Ruth was incredulous. "You? How?"

"I made, like, a shit-ton of money. Kept a little for me . . . like, to do what I needed to become who I always was, help my family out. But the rest . . . I put into building the place where Major Tom would be safe. Dr. Who knew this. Ask her! She knows I'm telling the truth!"

Ruth turned to Tom. "True?"

"As far as I can tell," he said.

Talia was stunned. "Dr. Who knew? Why didn't she—"

"Because she knew Ruth would appreciate my talents. Accept my help as an anonymous hacker. But she didn't trust your reactions. And you sure never trusted me or Tom!"

"Enough," said Tom.

Veronika ignored him. "You didn't even, like, want him to evolve! And he'll evolve more than this. What are you going to do then?"

Talia considered this. She did a terrible job hiding her fear.

For the next few hours, only Veronika and Tom worked. Talia had retreated to her bunk. Ruth sat cross-armed, her eyes twitching, staring them down. It couldn't last.

"Found something. Street cam," said Veronika. She put it up on a screen. A figure that looked like the made-over Amanda got out of a car, her door opened by a chauffeur. She entered the side door of an elaborate neoclassical building that was under reconstruction. But the scaffolding didn't hide a building Tom knew well.

"How long ago?" he asked.

"Looks like . . . an hour?" said Veronika. "1733 16th Street, DC."

Ruth's eyebrows shot up. "But that's the Phoenix C-C-Club!"

During the riots that had followed the Major Tom revelations, the Phoenix Club's DC headquarters had been attacked by mobs. But in the two years since, either the Southern States of America or the club, or both, had decided to renovate. An SSA flag flew from the roof's flagpole.

Tom zoomed in. There was something in the back seat that Amanda had vacated. It looked like a child in a safety seat. Little legs kicked.

"Is that—" asked Veronika.

"Yes," said Tom.

Veronika fast-forwarded the footage, stopped it, and pointed to Amanda getting back in the car and leaving.

"They want us to follow her," said Tom. "So let's do it."

Veronika looked unsure. "Okay? But we'll always be behind her. She could lead us into an ambush."

Ruth asked, "Can we use an algorithm? To guess where she's going in advance? And beat her there?"

"Can you think like Carter?" asked Tom in return.

"N-n-no. But you can," said Ruth.

"Exactly." Major Tom dove into his memories of Carter, a creature of habit and comforts, obsessed with his personal history and its ties to his former nation. Major Tom had held hints all along. He tried to think of all the places Amanda might go. "Veronika, tag the following places: the Phoenix Club, the Hay-Adams Hotel . . ." The Hay-Adams was north of the White House, near the Phoenix Club. Peter, Amanda, and Carter had stayed there before Peter Bernhardt's first initiation. Tom sent Tom 1 there for his final mission. "Also Reed House. It's Carter's family home on the Main Line outside of Philadelphia." Amanda could go there, but he doubted it. Only Carter's mother was still alive, but pickled as she was from gin and benzodiazepines, Carter would not want to create a scene. "What other properties does the family own? Or maybe once owned. Or we visited together?"

He dug through family trees and title records going back centuries. And as soon as he found it, he knew immediately that it was what Carter would choose. "I need a helicopter to Dover, Delaware."

Delaware was a special case among the former United States. It was tiny—only ninety-six miles long and between nine and thirty miles wide, the second smallest state, after Rhode Island. Like many coastal states, it had lost some seafront: originally thirty-five miles at its widest, the rising waters overtook the low-lying beaches of Rehoboth and Bethany. It was technically north of the Mason-Dixon line, which jogged south near the Atlantic Ocean to trace Delaware's border. It had stayed in the Union during the Civil War, even as a slave state. It was also the only slave state where no Confederate armies or militias had assembled. Later it had created special laws of incorporation that made it a tax haven so cheap and legally advantageous that half the large corporations of the formerly fifty states incorporated as Delaware businesses, including most of the banks. Riding the fence of history was a locally cultivated cultural trait that the Potsdams had inherited.

Most pertinent of all, one of Carter's most prominent ancestors, John Dickinson, had owned a plantation in Dover. Known as the "penman of the revolution," Dickinson was famous for writing documents urging Britain to change its ways and spurring the colonies to independence. "Letter from a Farmer in Pennsylvania" and "Petition to the King" had beseeched the Crown to treat the colonies with respect. And yet, with a Quaker's faith in pacifism, Dickinson had prayed it wouldn't come to a fight. Holding out hope for diplomacy, he had refused to sign the *Declaration of Independence*, believing it would incite violence. Instead, he had helped write the *Articles of Confederation*. Then when war was imminent, and contrary to his Quaker upbringing, he had fought in the revolutionary army. A complex man of deep Quaker feelings, he had been the wealthiest and largest slaveholder in the Delaware colony. Dickinson's plantation alone had once spanned thirteen thousand acres. During the revolution, Dickinson freed his slaves, the only Founding Father to do so during the war. He remained a devoted abolitionist for the rest of his life.

Twelve acres around John Dickinson House remained, owned by the state of Delaware. There had been no money to maintain it since the troubles and little interest in anything as "unproductive" as a historical museum. Once again, when a people most needed to know their past, they rejected it as superfluous. Closed up and fenced off, it awaited future generations to appreciate its importance.

But there was a catch. Dover was both the state capital and home to Dover Air Force Base, one of the largest in North America. Dickinson House was less than a mile from Dover's landing strip. While it was not yet under the control of the SSA, Dover AFB was on constant alert.

That's where I'd go, thought Major Tom.

Tom outlined his destination, what it would involve to get him there, and why he was doing this. He wanted no misunderstandings.

"You can't be serious!" said Ruth. "Alone? With that *Lominer gaylen?*"

Colloquially, it meant clumsy fool, but literally it meant a golem, the undead monster created by a fictional Lominer rabbi.

"I thought I was the golem," said Tom with a grimace. "Out to kick ass for our little tribe."

Ruth blew air through her lips. Her shoulder twitched.

"Are you nuts?" said Veronika. "No way I'm letting you go alone. We're your Musketeers. All for one, and like, all that crap, right?"

While Ruth and Veronika objected, Talia took an encrypted call from Captain Curtis on the *Roosevelt*. Her not sharing the call concerned Tom. She had made it clear she didn't trust him, so he couldn't trust her. He listened in.

Curtis's tone was gruff, his anger close to the surface. "Here's your last favor: I contacted Dover's commander, Colonel Bryce Keating, directly. We all know what really happened at Port Everglades. I swore on my men and my ship you won't hurt them. I'm probably a fool, but—"

"You're no fool, Geoff. We were outstrategized, outmaneuvered, and outnumbered. I'm sorry I involved you."

Curtis ignored her. "Dover won't interfere. There's no love between them and the SSA, with DC so close. And they don't have short memories, either. Just don't make any sudden moves. They're nervous enough as is. Rough Rider out."

Tom felt guilty. Talia was still in his camp.

Pacing back and forth between consoles, Ruth muttered, "I don't like it."

"What, Ruthie?" asked Tom.

"You alone with them. You are not strong enough. To fend them off."

Tom looked down at his youthful physique. "You think I'm weak?"

"Not your body," said Ruth, waggling her hands toward him. "Your mind. They know your buttons to press. They installed them."

CHAPTER FORTY-EIGHT

It wasn't yet dawn. Viewed from the V-22 Osprey, the twelve acres of John Dickinson's plantation appeared dark and abandoned. The main house, outer buildings, gardens, and trees occupied the south end of the property. A large contemporary barn and parking lot occupied the middle of the land and functioned as a visitor's center. The north half was an empty, overgrown field. There were no cars in the lot, nor anywhere nearby. No movement. No lights. Through an infrared scanner, they saw only rodents, a large owl looking for a final meal, and nesting turkey vultures.

Talia sat at the rear of the transport, avoiding eye contact with Tom. She had come reluctantly. She wasn't armed, but neither was Ruth.

Veronika was armed with who-knew-what in her backpack, but she wasn't proficient with weapons. This worried Tom more than the unarmed women.

"Whatever you do," he said to Veronika, "don't try to protect me. Just protect yourself, Ruth, and Talia."

"Why?"

"Because this is a test. And I'm not sure if I'm supposed to pass or fail."

Two red spots flared on the infrared display. Then a brightness suffused the image, originating from two windows and a chimney. Someone had lit a fire in the fireplace.

Amanda was there. Maybe Peter Jr., too.

The pilot and Tom had a tense conversation with air traffic control at Dover AFB, but once the copter was on the ground in the north field, Dover's tower seemed placated. For now.

The four trudged through the knee-high grasses and weeds toward the house. The helicopter would have tipped off anyone inside, but Tom knew that Amanda and Carter were waiting for them anyway.

Dickinson House did not feature the antebellum columns and *Gone with the Wind* grandeur of Carter's construction in the Memory Palace. Built 121 years before the fictional Scarlett O'Hara swished down a curved staircase into a civil war, Dickinson House was a Northern-style, eighteenth-century federal redbrick house with two small additions. Its trim and shutters were painted a faded yellow, the door a peeling green. Old wooden sheds ringed the house.

The team crept up six back stairs and opened the back door. Inside was a foyer with a staircase and a few doors to adjoining rooms.

Next to the staircase, Veronika cried, "Oh!" and leapt back.

It was a mannequin of a black male slave or servant in eighteenth-century garb, posed to look like he was welcoming visitors.

"Shut. Up," snarled Talia.

They proceeded toward the drawing room, where two figures' shadows danced with flames. One was another mannequin: John Dickinson posed in his wig, dress coat, and breeches, standing to the side of his portrait above the fireplace mantel. The other was Amanda, tidying the kindling. She wore black slacks and a slim black top. She didn't appear to be armed. For a moment, Tom was taken by her beauty. Then he remembered who and what she was.

"You're smarter than I thought," said Amanda.

"Maybe I know you," said Tom.

"Maybe." Staring up at the portrait of Dickinson, Amanda said, "You know Harriet Tubman came here, right? There's no official record of it, but Dover was part of the Underground Railroad, and she wanted to honor Dickinson's memory as a Founding Father and a slaveholder who freed his slaves. He tried to abolish slavery in his new state and in the US Constitution. Didn't work. At least he tried."

"Why the history lesson?" asked Tom.

"Because, my dear, even remarkable people do the strangest things. The purity we expect of our heroes is ridiculous. Here was a revolutionary who would not agree to revolt. A pacifist who led an army. A slaveowner who fought for abolition. Sometimes, you can exhibit contrary behaviors and still, eventually, do the right thing. We are large. We contain multitudes. We do terrible things and call it justice."

"Don't flatter yourself. Whitman didn't mean all this."

"Oh, Pete," said Amanda. "You underestimate us both. History is identity. And sometimes both are more complex than we would like."

"And like all narcissistic psychopaths, you have a God complex. Am I Lucifer in your grand vision? Or Job?"

"We don't know yet." Amanda turned toward the door they had come through. "Peter? Where are you, sweetie?"

"Mama! Here!" The toddler's little feet pattered against the wooden floor as he entered the room, holding a piece of paper and a crayon. "Look!" He handed her a picture. It was a house, a couple of swirly lines, and an attempt at a square.

"That's lovely, Peter! Good job!" said Amanda. She scooped him up and kissed his forehead.

"It's time," said Amanda. She walked out of the living room with the boy on her hip. The team looked at one another in surprise, then followed her out the front door and into the yard. Dawn's light was just appearing around the edges of the landscape, and the fire through the windows cast a tenuous light.

Nearby was a well, three feet high, three feet wide, with a two-foot mouth. The protective grating had been clipped open with wire cutters, leaving sharp, metal spikes around the edge of the hole.

Stopping next to it, Amanda lifted the child over the mouth. Her torso made a visible twitch, as though her mind had one thought and her body another. A single tear ran down from her right eye. The left eye remained clear and focused.

The group froze, stunned at the torn figure before them.

Tom knew that both Carter and Amanda were inside her body, and he struggled with speech. "I . . . thought you loved him?"

"Amanda loves him," said Amanda. "You can see her pain. But he's coming between you and me. It's so much simpler if he's not a part of the equation."

Ruth mimed spitting three times. *"A messa mashee af deer."* But how horrible the death she cursed Amanda with might be was anyone's guess.

Tom took a small step toward Amanda. "I know what it's like. To have part of someone inside you."

A teardrop fell off the right side of Amanda's chin. "No, you don't. Not like this."

"Carter's tried a hostage before," said Tom, slowly removing the laser pistol from his holster. "He knows how it ends."

Amanda lifted the boy higher. "Do I? Do you? You're armed. I'm not."

Little Peter giggled, kicking his legs and waving his arms. "Up, Mama! Up!"

"Shoot!" said Veronika.

"Nein!" said Ruth. "She'll drop the boy."

Tom reholstered his weapon, held his hands up, and took a deep breath. Slowly he approached Amanda, stopping with a foot between them. Her body shook harder and harder, her hold on Peter even more precarious. Tom extended his hands and placed them on her cheeks. And then he kissed her.

Salty tears flowed from both her eyes, reaching their mouths.

He could feel the blow to Veronika without looking. He ignored it.

Edwin Rosero had never touched Amanda before, but her skin felt familiar. And yet not. Her smell was almost primal, reaching to a place he didn't know existed. The taste of her mouth was a favorite flavor he had forgotten he craved. He could feel a tiny bit of her mind inside her, hanging on by threads, by instinct. The touch of her skin unleashed an onslaught of memories. His servers began running as fast as they had ever computed before. The entire life history of Amanda and Peter Bernhardt and Thomas Paine played both in fast-forward and in an overlapping mosaic of image, sound, taste, smell, touch, and movement.

Amanda and Carter were right. Their histories were their identities, and both changed when he least expected it. Her arms shook. The boy dropped by an inch. Then another.

Tom hoped she, too, was feeling their previous lives. Back at the PAC dinner when Josiah Brant had introduced Thomas Paine to the Phoenix Club for the first time, Amanda had held his hand and recognized her former husband at once, in spite of all his physical changes. But the moment he stepped away from this kiss, the spell would be broken for both of them. He needed to appeal to both her and Carter. Desperate, he held on.

Without breaking the kiss, he guided her arms away from the well. Then, with a quick movement, he grabbed the child.

"Don't let her go!" he yelled to the team.

The women surrounded Amanda, who still appeared stunned.

For the first time, a human Tom held little Peter Jr. in his arms. The boy wiggled, uncomfortable with this man's body. The flooding sensation of oxytocin-induced love and security was so dizzying, Tom's knees folded. He sat down, hugging the boy closer. With more-than-human eyes sensing more-than-visual information, he could better understand the child's similarities to Amanda and Peter Bernhardt. The boy's vulnerability—big eyes; large head; soft skin; downy hair; and a small, unmuscular body—targeted all the instinctive nurturing impulses

Rosero and Tom had. Rosero's body didn't need to share actual DNA with the child. Knowing that this was his kin, in need of his protection, was enough. Tom's hormonal floodgates opened, and he didn't know whether to laugh, or cry, or cheer.

He would protect this child forever.

Peter Jr., whose copper color was so close to his mother's, had a smudge of dirt on his face. Licking his thumb to wipe it away, Tom saw that the child was otherwise clean and his clothing fresh. He looked hydrated and well fed. Whether as Winter or Amanda, Carter had taken his parental responsibility seriously. The boy was cared for. Or maybe all the incarnations of Tom and Carter felt the same urge to nurture the boy that Tom did? He hoped that given time with his son, he might come to understand. Someday.

Amanda said, "Charming, isn't he?"

Ruth was right. Between Amanda and Carter, they knew each button to push. It felt like the greatest organist in the world was pulling all his stops.

Tom kissed the boy's head and handed him to Talia, who took him, looking surprised.

"Why did you do this?" Ruth asked Amanda.

"Don't understand yet, Ruthie?" Amanda asked.

Ruth crossed her twitching arms. "N-n-no. I do not."

Amanda said, "You will."

"Show me what you did to her," said Tom.

"What could you mean, my dear?" said Amanda.

"Carter, show us what you did to Amanda," he said.

"Sure you can handle it?" teased Amanda.

"You had to kill her to do it. Show us!" demanded Tom.

"I'm not dead yet!" yelled Amanda in Tom's face. "And you know it!" Her body jerked and shimmied, its personalities wrestling for control.

"Amanda, if you can hear me," said Tom, "Carter's in control of your brain and your body. There's not enough of you left to survive alone. I don't care what he told you. He's a sick liar."

"No, you're lying now," said Amanda. Carter was back in the saddle. Tom doubted he'd let go of the reins again.

Carter sent them a link. Ruth and Talia stood transfixed on their GOs, Veronika on her MR glasses, and Tom on the images inside of his head. The recorded video showed Winter, standing next to a hospital bed in a small, nondescript, windowless bedroom with institutional furnishings. Propped against pillows lay Amanda, her hands tied to her sides. An IV drip needle was inserted in the vein of one forearm. A bag hung on a stand near the head of the bed. Winter opened the IV drip and sat on the edge of the bed.

"Please. Let me see Peter," begged Amanda.

"Don't make this harder for you," said Winter. "Or for me."

"Why do you hate me so much?"

Winter closed her eyes and shook her head. "My dear, I don't hate you. I've never hated you." She opened her eyes again. "I love you."

"Then why are you doing this?" Amanda yelled. "To me? To us?"

"You know why." Tears formed in Amanda's eyes. Winter placed her fingers on Amanda's hand and stroked it. "Because it has to happen to change him. This is so much bigger than you or me. Or him. Or anyone. You know that."

Amanda's tears fell in earnest. "I don't want to die."

"You won't." Winter squeezed her hand. "I promise. We'll be together in a way you can't even imagine." She stood and kissed Amanda's forehead, then watched as Amanda's eyes grew cloudy. Her eyelids sagged. Her mouth drooped.

She struggled to speak. "Don't . . . leave . . . me." Her eyes shut, and her breathing slowed.

"I never will." Winter's eyes watered for a few seconds, but she wiped them, and the moment passed. She rose and approached the camera. "And I won't. And you could never promise her that." Then she smiled and closed her eyes.

A surgical crash team burst into the room, unlocked the bed's casters, and wheeled it away. When the door closed behind them, Winter's eyes popped open. *"Adiós, muchacho."* She winked, and the image cut to black.

Tom stood on his feet by the well, but in his mind, he was curled in a fetal position. He struggled to speak. "This . . . reincarnation . . . into others . . . has to stop!"

"It will never stop," said Amanda. "Not as long as we can find a justification."

"Did you copy anyone else? Josiah? Bruce?" How many Carters were there?

"God, you're pedantic." Amanda shrugged. "It doesn't matter if I tell. You know already. Only Josiah's any good. The rest are damaged toys, but they'll have a use someday." Her eyes narrowed angrily. "It was cruel of you to keep us conscious like that. No freedom, no autonomy. No lives. You, the great liberator!" She snickered. "At least I turned them off. For now."

Amanda made a feint to run. Tom threw himself at her, and they fell hard to the ground. He didn't care if a piece of his ex-wife was inside this monster. The creature was mostly Carter and all evil. He rolled on top of her and grabbed her shoulders, slamming them and her head on the ground. Amanda went limp below him, but the beating continued.

"Why?" Tom cried. "Why am I always asking you why?"

Amanda grimaced as her head rag-dolled back and forth. "You watched that . . . and you still don't . . . get it? You still . . . don't know . . . shit . . . I knew this would . . . get under your skin . . . sweetie. Bad."

Tom dropped her as though his hands had burned. He sat back on his heels. "You're torturing me?"

"No, my dear. You're torturing yourself. I'm just information," she said. "Amanda's DNA. Carter's brain patterns. We can copy it. Move it. Change it. This is all about your reaction to us. To events. You could have walked away. But you didn't. So much for your pseudo nonattachment."

Tom held his head in his hands. In each incarnation, he was starting from scratch. It felt like the molecules, hormones, and neurotransmitters in his brain were shifting in real time. "You're changing me . . ."

Blood from a gash on Amanda's head throbbed out under her black hair. "We already did. You think you're the same person who graduated Stanford with us? Who created Biogineers and Prometheus Industries? Who battled the Phoenix Club? Here I thought you were the Buddhist who couldn't step into the same river twice."

Her contempt felt more like Amanda's just then. But did it matter anymore? Tom knew they were both right. In Buddhism, as in neuroscience, there was no constant self. And here, lying on the ground next to him, was the most tangible proof imaginable. Amanda, Carter, both and yet neither—and far less attached to themselves than he was.

"My family's been saving America for four centuries," Amanda said. "You're not going to stop me now."

"Whose America?" demanded Tom. "If Amanda can hear me in there, it certainly isn't her family's America. All those Native American, Latino, African American, and poor white immigrant ancestors were too busy surviving your people's vision. Spare me your noble lineage."

"But it *is* your America. It's everyone's. We will reunite this country. Or die trying."

"The American experiment is over. We've driven over the cliff. Look around you. We're not even a country anymore. It's time to start something new again!"

"My dear," said Amanda, shaking her head, "humans don't understand analyses. Or history. They understand pain. And we've made sure
you plunged them into agony. They understand a common enemy. And
that's *you*. It's the only way humans have ever united. So they'll join
together to fight you with all they've got, to keep that little bit of their
old life, even if it kills them. And we'll lead that fight. Against Thomas
Paine and everything you represent."

"What the hell do I represent?" asked Tom.

Amanda smiled. "Doesn't matter."

"So 'History is a set of lies agreed upon.' It's propaganda."

"Bonaparte was a smart guy," said Amanda. "But Winston
Churchill's better: 'History will be kind to me for I intend to write it.'
He understood that his story could change if he willed it so. If only he
had a blockchain, too, right?" She laughed.

"But history is the opposite of a blockchain," said Tom. "Victors get
to tell their stories. People get erased. Vilified. Beatified. Made martyrs.
Villains. None of it is real."

"And . . . ?" said Amanda.

"And what?" said Tom.

Amanda sighed. "Blockchains aren't real, either. We proved it.
With enough firepower and a large enough digital attack, they can
be manipulated, just like history. The poor, sweet saps who invented
them thought they couldn't be corrupted. They were all idealists, and
idealists make cool stuff, but they never accept how the world works
because it affronts their personal beliefs. Just like *you*. Bless your little
cotton socks."

"So no one will remember what really happened?" said Tom.

Amanda's bloody smile filled her face. "And *now* you get it!"

"But blockchains don't matter, either," said Tom. "Even if we record
things, humans have short memories. Shorter-term goals. They don't
look back. Real history's too complex. We forget our mistakes and
repeat them. Every time."

Amanda nodded in approval. "And *that* was the purpose of the Phoenix Club. To prevent our nation's amnesia. To save us from ourselves. But we're all human. We had the same fears and greed and desires as anyone. Ironically, it was men like Josiah that understood it best, although we can argue whether his solution was any good. And you, my dear, had to kill him."

"But he wanted to brainwash the world!" said Tom.

"For everyone's *good*," said Amanda. "They'd be happy, rather than miserable and on the verge of self-destruction. And as I said back then, you and I could have undone Josiah's plan."

"But why you? Why me?" asked Tom.

"When will you stop asking this? You refuse to accept your experiences. As much as I made you, my dear, you made me. We're a matched set. Scotch and soda. Sticks and stones. Matter and antimatter. And you know what happens when *they* come together." Amanda winked. "As much as the world needs people like you, it needs me, too."

"Manipulators? Autocrats?"

"We move things forward. We don't care who we hurt to get it done. But greatness is the result. No one gives a shit about the process in the long run. Want to remake the world? Call me whatever you want, sweetie. Just call me." She blew him a kiss.

"Even if that means it's a world we don't want to live in?" asked Tom.

"That's your opinion. But sure."

"And you can't do it without me."

"But now I have Peter Bernhardt, the earliest digital version of your upload, with memories from Carter, Amanda, and anyone else we could find. We've tweaked and adjusted it to resemble Peter's mind as much as possible. *He* was a man with a vision. He is the version of you we've always wanted." Amanda gestured toward Ruth and Talia. "And who *they've* always wanted. We loved you. Or at least that version of you."

Tom turned to Talia. "Once you called me 'Naive. Sweet. Infuriating.' Is that who you want back?"

"Yes," said Talia, tears in her eyes. "I knew what to do with that man."

"Ruth?" asked Tom.

Her face wore a puzzled expression. "I do not know. Who you are. Anymore."

Amanda sighed and rose to a kneel. "Are we done arguing?" The others stood around her in a circle. She looked up at their grim faces.

The circle drew in tighter.

"We may understand," said Veronika. "But you can't leave."

"No! Mama? Here, Mama?" Peter Jr. looked uncomprehending at his bloody mother, big teardrops in his eyes. Reaching out to Amanda, he tried to wiggle out of Talia's arms.

Talia held him tight. She took a step back from the circle.

Tom looked away over the marshes and farmland to the east. It was morning. The sun rose, painting the sky with screaming swaths of flamingo, lemon, and orchid. Azure-blue sky peeked through, the color of Peter Jr.'s eyes. And once, in a lifetime before, Tom's own. Light rays stretched through the clouds, like fingers of the infinite, taunting him with endless possibilities. Of discoveries yet to be made. Of lives he could have saved. Lives he could have lived. Lives he could be living right now . . .

Veronika broke his reverie. "Dude, I know what this looks like. But she has to go, at least in this form. Carter *is* torturing you."

"Like you know Tom's w-w-w-weaknesses," muttered Ruth.

Veronika ignored her. "Who wants to do it?"

Talia took another step back and pointed at the pretty colors in the sky, trying to distract Peter Jr.

Ruth stepped back, too, waving her shaky hands. "N-n-n-no . . . *Nein.*"

Amanda looked up at Ruth. "That's my Ruthie. That's why I did all this. To prevent more bloodshed." She jerked her head toward Tom.

"He will never get that. Think of all the people he killed. Or let die. He caused many deaths, didn't he, Ruth? Untold pain and suffering. And you helped, against your beliefs. How can you continue to help him?"

Ruth looked at Tom. Her intellectual partner and best friend inhabited the body of a young man she had helped to create. She had made so much possible. Her shoulders ticked. Her face contorted in spasms. Her eyes watered. And then she turned away.

Veronika turned to Talia. "Well?"

"This isn't my fight," Talia said. "Not anymore." She bounced Peter Jr. in a gentle rhythm.

"Of course it is!" said Veronika. "You dragged Peter Bernhardt into it! You helped make him what he became to satisfy yourself!"

"No. We finished the Phoenix Club. It's over."

"How can you say that?" said Veronika.

"This isn't about the club," said Talia. "This is between the two of them. And we're all pawns." She looked into Peter Jr.'s guileless eyes, then back to Tom. "And I hate what he's become. It has to stop."

Tom reached down and ran his fingers through Amanda's bloody hair. They recognized the thick, smooth texture, the oval shape of her skull. He thought of a song: David Bowie's "Killing a Little Time." Carter would have appreciated that.

Tom pulled Amanda's head back and stared in his ex-wife's eyes. On her knees and with her defiant expression, he could think only of a Native American woman resisting the pioneer invaders for the last time. Carter, ever the performer, was milking it for all it was worth.

Abraded by Bowie's discordant melody, he was falling, choking, fading away. "Why can't you let me go? Let her go?"

"You don't listen," said Amanda. "You need to figure out why for yourself."

Tom released her hair and staggered a few steps away. "I can't. You knew it. I can't do it."

Bowie crowed in pain. The band played arrhythmically, out of time, like a broken heartbeat, as if the song itself were unhappy with his refusal to kill.

Veronika moved to Tom and whispered, "Dude, Amanda died a while ago."

"No," said Tom. "You saw it. There's a little bit left."

"She's Carter's puppet," said Veronika. "Like, a hostage forever. Do you think that's what she wants?"

Amanda watched their exchange, bright-eyed, as though she knew something they didn't.

"So much for merciful," Veronika said. "Heroes suck. They're never what you want them to be." She stepped away, dug around in her backpack, and pulled out the same butcher's knife she'd used on Winter in Santa Barbara.

Amanda giggled. "No, my dear. Heroes all contain the same parts. The good, the bad, and the ugly. You just don't like looking at slimy things under the rocks. But I do." She sneered at Veronika. "I remember wanting your mother to die. I thought it might be fun to see her burn alive. See?" She gestured to Tom and then at herself. "We know what that's like. But I didn't kill her. Stupid bitch wasn't worth the effort. I saved her life. So was I a hero? Or a villain?"

Shaking, Veronika held the blade high above her head. "You crazy-ass motherfucker!"

Laying a calming touch on her arm, Tom gently removed the knife from her hand. Holding it by the grip, he stared at it for a moment. Bowie raged, roared, falling, choking, bleeding. Tom whipped around and thrust the blade under Amanda's sternum and up to her heart, lifting her body off the ground.

"Monster," he said, an inch from Amanda's face. "You will never know me." He wiggled the knife, then yanked it out and threw it on the ground. His hand dripped bright red. Amanda collapsed into the dirt. The song finished abruptly.

Talia hadn't covered the toddler's face in time. Peter Jr. wailed.

Looking into Tom's eyes, Amanda gasped for breath, her lips trembling. "Pete . . . we . . . love you . . ." Was that Carter or Amanda? Was it true or a lie? Did it matter?

She died with her eyes open and a smile on her face.

Tom had been manipulated. Killing Amanda had been the game all along, and he couldn't stop it. For a moment, he wondered what the two personalities had experienced inside Amanda's dying body. Had she wanted to die? Had it felt like Carter's first time dying in the basement of the Phoenix Club's bunker? Or more like the second, when Tom had killed Winter? Was Carter getting good at this? Was he taking Amanda with him? And if Tom's present body died, would death be the same for him?

"You . . . You are the monster!" cried Ruth, stepping away from him. "P-P-Peter would never. Have made that choice!"

"Of course Peter did!" said Veronika. "Carter's a manipulative shit, and he's trying to destroy us all! Can't you see that?"

Talia spun on Veronika. "No. You think you're in control, but you're a pawn in their game, like the rest of us."

Still in a murderous musical daze, Tom turned to Talia. "You never trusted me. Never . . ."

"Who's next?" asked Talia. "Me? Ruth? Will you kill us all?" Talia handed Peter Jr. to Veronika with a sneer. "Take him. I've got no father to offer this child. You and Tom deserve each other."

"Port Everglades was *your* idea!" insisted Veronika. She regretted it the moment she saw Talia's expression of grief.

Talia stiffened, marched up to Tom, and leaned in close to his face. "I will *never* forgive you. Not for Steve. Not for me. Not for Amanda. Not for Peter. Not for anyone."

"Years ago, you said you were my guardian angel," Tom said.

"And now I hope you rot in hell," Talia spat. "Come on, Ruth."

Ruth reached into her worn khakis and removed a small specimen bag. Her hands shook as she opened it. Wrapped in a piece of cotton wool were two glass slides, sandwiching two droplets of blood. Since she and Peter Bernhardt had memorialized their intellectual and business partnership in a lab at Stanford University, this memento had come to represent everything they had done together and meant to each other. She threw it to the ground and tried to crush it under her ratty sneakers, but her shoes and the dirt were too soft to damage it.

"*Katsevte,*" she said. She spit at Tom's feet, then spun on Veronika. "*Un a shtik fleish mit tsvei oygn.*"

Tom was a butcher. And Veronika was a piece of meat with two eyes.

With one last dead-eyed glance back at Tom, Talia led a sobbing Ruth away. The last words Tom heard were, "They are d-d-d-dead to me!"

He knelt in the dirt and picked up the glass slides. The blood droplets had turned black with age. His gut knotted. These women had loved him, each in her own way. They had saved and even created his body multiple times. And now they hated him. He pocketed the slides.

CHAPTER FORTY-NINE

Talia and Ruth headed for the Osprey. Where would they go? What would they do? The two women who knew more about Tom than anyone else, in some ways more even than Carter, were now his enemies. They knew his physical, mental, and technological strengths and weaknesses. They had all the information about his plans. Ruth controlled the hash keys and codes to his existence as an AHI. Talia had once controlled whatever was left of Prometheus, and he assumed Carter had access to it all. They were sure to take advantage of it.

They would fall right into Carter's plan. They would join Carter, and whatever version of Peter Bernhardt he claimed to possess. Now that they had left, Carter would make sure they found the man they loved.

Tom sent a message to the Osprey pilot: *Take Talia and Ruth anywhere they want to go, within your fuel constraints, except the* Zumwalt. *They are never to step foot on board again. Then come back for us.* He turned to Veronika. "Let's get out of here. I'll need you to help me lock Talia and Ruth out of the Major Tom and *Zumwalt* systems."

She looked shocked.

"Please," he continued. "I think they've left to find their Peter Bernhardt. They'd work for Carter in order to do that."

"I can only do, like, so much from here," said Veronika.

Tom headed away from the well and Amanda's body. Veronika followed, trying to carry the boy, but she couldn't get a grip on him. Peter Jr. seemed to sense the insecurity of her grasp, and he sucked in larger gasps of air with each scream. As his distress grew, so did Veronika's, a classic feedback loop of adult-child anxiety.

Tom wiped his bloody hand on his clothes. But as he grabbed the child, red smears still covered the little blue T-shirt and jeans. Tom put the boy down and held his hand, hoping they both might relax. He searched expert opinions as they walked, but there was no information about "How to Calm a Child Who Just Watched You Kill Its Mother."

Still crying, Peter Jr. let go of Tom's hand and grabbed Veronika's leg. "Is it just us?" she asked, struggling to pick the boy up again.

"Maybe," said Tom. "I contacted Dr. Who. Told her the whole story. We'll see who convinces her."

It was Tom, Veronika, and little Peter against the world. Overwhelmed, he screamed at the sky. "Carter, you bastard!"

"You don't have to yell," said a familiar voice in his head. "You're clear as a bell, my dear."

Not what Tom wanted to hear. He grabbed his hair, yanked at it in chunks, and shook like a madman. Little Peter whimpered.

"What's wrong?" said Veronika, clearly frightened. "You're scaring the kid."

"Carter's in my head!" Tom yelled. "Leave me alone!"

"Hey, Peter, let's just sit for a sec. Okay?" She dug around in her backpack, pulled out a GO, keyed it to an interactive cartoon site, and handed it to the boy. "Go nuts, lil guy." Still scared, the child half-heartedly pressed buttons and soon lost himself in the screen. Veronika sat on the ground next to him, pulling on her MR glasses. "He's not in your server," she said to Tom. "He's just messing with you on some communications network. I'll cut him off. Need a minute."

An image arose in Tom's mind: Carter, waving a white flag covered in tiny gold fleur-de-lis. *Vive le Roi-Soleil!* he said with a grin.

Long live the Sun King. He brandished the flag of French monarchy, used for four hundred years until it was supplanted by the revolutionary republic's *tricolore*. The fleur-de-lis's three petals represented the three social classes under the control of kings: workers, clergy, and warriors.

They would all be warriors soon.

"Get him out!" Tom begged Veronika.

"Of course you know, this means war," said Carter. "Or as your dear Veronika likes to say, 'Corruption abhors a vacuum.' Or simply, there always needs to be a leader. Most aren't capable of the task. So when you find one who can do the job, you hitch your wagon. Or your star. I've got one named Peter Bernhardt."

"We will stop you," said Tom.

"You can't, my dear. This is part of larger historical processes. We've both been playing roles for a long time. We have to see this out. To the end."

"Why are you dragging the whole world into this?" asked Tom. "Can't you and I just fight it out, once and for all?"

"Why do you always assume this is all about us? It isn't. It's about the nation. It needs to rise again, like it always has, every few generations. Like a phoenix."

"Empires don't always rise again. Rome ended. And the Holy Romans. Victoria's British Empire ended. Byzantium, Babylonia, the Cholas and Ottomans and caliphates. They all end."

"But they don't," Carter said. "You know better. They just layer over each other. The Roman Empire crumbled, reorganized, and became the Holy Roman Empire." Carter displayed a map of Europe, evolving, morphing, and remaking itself again and again through the centuries. "Then the Thirty Years War, then a bunch of pseudo revolutions and unifications, then a stupid attempt at a mythical Third Reich. Then the European Union. Then the dissolution we see now. They're creating, dissolving, and recreating the same empires through time. We've had two empire-reshuffling wars already: the American Revolution and the Civil War. Revolutions, civil wars, they're all the same. They burn away the fat and flab of civilization, and we start again. It's time for number three."

"And with them came death and destruction," Tom said. "You're dragging billions into chaos, maybe extinction—an event horizon, a point of no return—all for a vision no one wants but you."

"War is hell," Carter said, "but sometimes it's the only way. This isn't an event horizon. It's a phoenix horizon. Doomed to reincarnate forever. You're the Buddhist-flavored upload. Should be familiar." Carter transformed into a Civil War general, but he wasn't wearing blue or gray. His uniform was bloodred. He suddenly appeared on both little Peter's GO and in Tom's processor. "So long, my dear. Until we meet again, on the field of battle." He saluted, winked, and disappeared.

Tom knew he wasn't kidding. There would be dark days ahead.

"There. He's gone," said Veronika.

Collapsing in the dirt, Tom said, "No, he's not."

A video link arrived, marked *URGENT*. Tom shared it with Veronika.

Dr. Who appeared. "Watch this," she said. "Then let's talk."

Back in a warehouse in what Tom assumed was Los Angeles County, Arun adjusted a pair of MR glasses to record the event.

"Uh, coming in clear?" he asked. "Or is it too dark?"

"Looks good, Arun," a young voice responded.

"Okay," said Arun, "so I know Major Tom and the gang are probably busy, and I hope you get to see this, but this is what we've been up to since I left. Fingers crossed!"

In front of Arun was a large mass, covered in a white, plastic sheet. In the distance, four students—three young men and one young woman—guided a stretcher with a patient on it.

The patient was Dr. Who.

She pointed to the mass. "That's it?" she asked Arun.

"Yes, ma'am," he said. "We got explicit instructions from you-know-who that you be as protected, comfortable, and independent as possible. Otherwise, what did he say? You'd whip my ass." He laughed. "Take a look."

She reached over and yanked off the plastic, uncovering a convertible wheelchair/exoskeleton. She didn't say anything at first. It looked like a clever machine, but Tom could see the doubt in her eyes. The machine's multipositionable tank treads could climb and descend stairs and hills. Its hoverboard technology would allow it to rise above the ground about six inches for a smoother ride on uneven terrain. Below the seat, locking leg and hip braces made of superlight carbon nanofibers could hold her body and raise her upright while providing her legs, hips, and back the stability and strength she had lost. The exoskeleton's lower half could also detach, its micromotors allowing her to walk. It even had autopilot.

She frowned. "Guess all things come to an end."

"And a beginning," said Arun. "We've got some private medical help lined up in a secure facility near Caltech. They'll check you out, and then I've got orders to make sure you get to wherever you need to go."

"Hon," said Dr. Who with a sigh, "if only I knew."

"Doc, you're a legend. If you want to stay with us at Caltech, I can guarantee hundreds of young acolytes to take care of you. Not everyone can say they know the real Foxy Funkadelia."

The four students traded shocked looks, then grinned.

"See?" said Arun. "You got 'em hooked already."

"Okay, okay, ya wore me down," said Dr. Who. "Let's take this rig on the road and see how she handles."

"She?" asked Arun.

Dr. Who's vast bosom jiggled with laughter for the first time in weeks. "Hell yeah, son. Ya think somethin' that stands ya up, sits ya down, and wipes your ass is male?"

The image cut to a live feed. Dr. Who sat in her exochair and wheeled around a tiny yard. It looked to Tom like California. A coast live oak grew in the corner. Manzanitas edged the yard. Someone respected the native foliage. Dr. Who was hiding her geolocation. He guessed she was with family, but then again, maybe not. She certainly looked much happier among the dirt and greenery than she ever had on the water.

"Arun so wanted ya to see that," she said. "He misses ya all somethin' fierce."

"I miss him," said Tom.

"Bet ya do," she said. "Honey, you're in a heap 'a manure right now."

"I know, Mama. And you should call me from inside."

Dr. Who nodded. "You're right. But I missed my hands in dirt. Best healer there is. Hey, check this out." The chair rose on a cushion of air, pivoted, and landed without a jostle. "Even my baby Talia left ya?"

"Yeah. And I understand if you do, too. You have much longer loyalty to her than to me."

"To quote a wise man, 'I'm too old for this shit.'"

"Mama, I don't know how I would have done it differently."

"Why would ya?" asked the Doctor. "From my perspective, you saved my ass, child. An' I can see my family again. That's not nothin'. I know ya don't think like your old biological self anymore. Relyin' on logic, ya coulda just focused on Carter's bigger game. Most AIs woulda focused on the top-down goal. But ya didn't. You 'n' Talia tried to help all kinds 'a people. Most woulda died anyway, child. And who knew an AHI could feel so sorry for itself?" She laughed, and her copious bosom heaved with mirth.

It made Major Tom a little happier to see her laugh again. "How so?"

"We're havin' this conversation, right? There's still some Peter Bernhardt left in ya. And don't ya dare let 'em convince ya otherwise."

"Mama, why do the people I love hate me?" he asked.

"Oh, child," she said with a sigh. "Bein' out on the ocean taught me this: there's no one right way to do anythin'. And too much 'a anythin' turns into disaster. Ya showed 'em there's no right answers, but nobody wants ta hear *that*! The people who love ya the most will hate ya the most, just for showin' 'em they ain't got faith in ya. Think 'a what ya meant to those four people. They loved ya. You showed 'em the great paradox at the center of existence, and they lost their worldview. Nobody gets awards for that."

"So what do I do now?" he asked.

"We figure out their goals, their strengths, and their weaknesses. And then we fight."

"We?"

"Honey, I may be old, but I'm ornery, too. Foxy was fun, but this here's a better thrill than any virtual world. And ya got my girl, Veronika. She's a hoot 'n' a half, but no one's got your back like her. And Cai/Ye is my new pen pal. Never lets me forget he's around, within state security and diplomatic parameters, of course. Anyway, he says he's there when we need him. We'll see. And let's get Arun back on board. His kids did a great job with this hunk 'a junk." She banged on the armrest of her exochair. "I know he ain't done fiddlin' in that brain 'a yours, and I got some crazy ideas. Might just work."

"Oh . . . oh, Mama . . ." He wanted to cry, but they'd be happy tears. For the first time, he felt hope. With Dr. Who, Veronika, Arun, his son, and perhaps even the Chinese government with him, he wasn't alone after all.

Veronika sent them yet another Veronika's Veil, the morphed face of Tom comprised of tiny portraits of all the people who had supported Peter Bernhardt and Thomas Paine, or who had been helped by him: his new family, his pop, Ruth's father, the employees who worked at Biogineers and Prometheus, the mercenaries he had employed over the years to help him run every kind of vehicle and vessel, the survivors of the *Meropis* and the crew of the *Savior*, the refugees who escaped on the CAS *Theodore Roosevelt* and the *Zumwalt*. There were thousands of them. Together they made up the face of her composite, a new banner for them all to march behind.

They weren't what most would call a family. And not an army, either. But they were his. And maybe through their eyes, he might finally figure out who he was, and why he was here, attempting the impossible.

When he died the first time, it had felt like all the love in his life had gathered together and showed him the way. He had lost so much. He had proved that the road to hell was paved with good intentions and their unintended consequences. But he couldn't stop now, just because he'd alienated his best friends. There were bigger priorities, and he hoped he could help them all see that someday. It might take a war, but he hoped they could forgive him.

EPILOGUE

Tom, Veronika, Dr. Who, and Arun watched in real time as the story of Major Tom changed yet again in blockchain servers around the world.

He wasn't just a terrorist.

He wasn't just a destabilizing force for the entire world.

He was the juggernaut, the ceremonial wagon that pulled the Hindu Lord Vishnu from his temple and crushed the devout, in their desire to be near him, under its wheels. He was a rogue technology, relentless, thoughtless, cruel, bent on destroying anything in his path. He was the ultimate enemy.

But Peter Bernhardt's story had changed, too. He was a good person, with a brilliant mind, until he had experimented on himself with brain prostheses, nanowire implants, and nanomedicine. Peter was a victim of his own hubris, a symbol of the dangers of technology without ethics. He was a victim who wanted to be a hero, until the thing he had become undid him. Perhaps, the new story suggested, Peter Bernhardt could be used to protect the world from his monstrous creation.

News stories proliferated. "To make America whole again, we must fight the forces of dissolution and disruption." "The only way to stop Thomas Paine and Major Tom from destroying that which we hold dear is a battle for the Union of America!" Port Everglades was cast as the new Fort Sumter. President Conrad was the new Lincoln. Tom was the new Jefferson Davis, instigating anarchy and divisive disasters in his wake.

It wasn't literature, but it worked as propaganda in a world turned upside down.

For the first time, Major Tom, as a human being, a digital being, and a member of his new little tribe, committed to a purpose that gave him an identity. He would lead his band, save as many people as possible, and put an end to the suffering promised in Carter's vision of the future.

Civil War 3.0 commenced.

ABOUT THE MUSIC

As with *(R)evolution*, Major Tom solves problems and cognates musically, even in his new nonorganic substrates and adopted bodies. Like him, my daughter experiences her life through a continual soundtrack and builds her mental world with music as its foundation. She is my model. And I think that's supercool.

(ID)entity was inspired by the work of David Bowie and his creation Major Tom. After Bowie wrote "Space Oddity," in 1969, the character of Major Tom took on a life of his own, not only throughout Bowie's later music and videos, but in music and artwork created by many others. I've touched on a handful of references in *(ID)entity*. Don't worry, Bowie fans, there will be more in the next book, *(CON)science*.

Since my creative process is cyclical, moving between music and writing, there are many more songs that inspired the book than made the final cut. I mentioned fewer songs in *(ID)entity* because it just felt right.

While you can enjoy *(ID)entity* without listening to the playlist that follows, doing so adds a layer of Tom's thought process within his hacked 'n' jacked brain. There are some Easter eggs within the lyrics, too, so I hope you take as much pleasure puzzling them out while listening to this playlist as I did in making it.

(ID)ENTITY PLAYLIST
(in order of appearance)

"One of These Things (Is Not Like the Others)," Joe Raposo, Jon Stone, and Bruce Hart/Sesame Street

"Heaven," Talking Heads

"Space Oddity," David Bowie

"Sound of Silence," Simon & Garfunkel, *The Paul Simon Anthology* live solo version

"42," Coldplay

"Born to Synthesize," Todd Rundgren

"Ashes to Ashes," David Bowie

"Seminal," Jonny Sonic

"Hallo Spaceboy," David Bowie, with the Pet Shop Boys (1996)

"Mrs. Major Tom," K.I.A.

"Doppelgänger," The Antlers

"Brainville," The Flaming Lips

"Ease on Down the Road," Charlie Smalls/The Wiz

"Tin Man," America

"Sound of Silence," Simon & Garfunkel, covered by Disturbed

"El Chapo," The Game featuring Skrillex

"The Blacker the Berry," Kendrick Lamar

"Ghost Ship," Blur

"Like Humans Do," David Byrne
"Glory," Radical Face
"Both Sides Now," Joni Mitchell
"Killing a Little Time," David Bowie

ACKNOWLEDGMENTS

As in all things in life, my mistakes are my own.

So many people deserve thanks. I have wonderful friends and acquaintances with expertise on many subjects who are willing to suffer through my newbie questions about things they've thought through and pursued with rigor for many years. Thank you to: Itamar Arel, James Clement, Nikola Danaylov, J. Dax Hansen, Randolph Hencken, Orna Isakson, Alex Kawas, Richard Loosemore, Oscar Morales, Joe Quirk, Christopher Rasch, Sophie Robert, Edwin Rosero, Russell Rukin, Peter Turchin, Reichart von Wolfschield. And the biggest thank-you possible to Monica Anderson. I couldn't have done this without you.

For this series, I relied on the writings and work of Theodore W. Berger, James D'Angelo, Robert Freitas, Benjamin Goertzel, James Hughes, David Levy, Rodolfo Llinas, Ralph Merkel, Steve Omohundro, Bruce Schneier, and Wendell Wallach.

I'd like to praise these books as great primers on their subjects: *Seasteading: How Floating Nations Will Restore the Environment, Enrich the Poor, Cure the Sick and Liberate Humanity from Politicians*, by Joe Quirk with Patri Friedman; *Robot Ethics: The Ethical and Social Implications of Robotics*, edited by Patrick Lin, Keith Abney, and George A. Bekey; *American Nations: A History of the Eleven Rival Regional Cultures of North America*, by Colin Woodard; *The Nine Nations of North America*, by Joel Garreau; and most especially, *War and Peace and War*, by Peter Turchin, researcher in the remarkable discipline of cliodynamics. These are important works that more people should read to understand where we've been and where we're going.

Thanks to my great lawyers, Neal Tabachnick and David Hochman at Wolf, Rifkin, Shapiro, Schulman & Rabkin. I know you have my back.

To those who lent your names: let's see, one of you was resurrected, one creates AI, one is a great friend, one is a brain surgeon, and one ran away to sea. And my two college housemate physicians are still smushed into one. My work here is done.

To my dearest friends who always have my emotional and creative back: Karen Austin, Belinda Todd, and Jonathan Westover. Go *mishpucha*!

My incredible team at 47North/Amazon Publishing really is the best in the business. Jason Kirk, you are the most wonderful editor a writer could hope for, even beyond all our weird connections and coincidences. I am one lucky author. Thank you to copyeditor Josh Overbey and proofreader Jill Schoenhaut for making sure this dyslexic and grammatically challenged author writes in English. Kristin King, and formerly Britt Rogers and Sarah Shaw, of the Authors Relations department, you always know how to take tender loving care of our 47North tribe. Laura Costantino, thank you for marketing this book so well. And Kimberly Cowser, PR gal extraordinaire, you are a joy to work with. To Adam Martinakis, the remarkably talented artist behind my beautiful and evocative book covers: I am so grateful we get to work together. Your work is magnificent! And thank you to Ray Lundgren for your excellent design skills in putting all the visuals together.

Thank you to Richard Manney, my science-fiction-fan father, who fed me a constant diet of SF classics. And my mother, Gloria Manney, who doesn't know Yoda from Yogi Bear, you are my eternal representative of the *vox populi*.

As always, my work is a family affair, and this series wouldn't exist without them as teachers, helpmates, and motivators. Nathaniel, thank you for the endless discussions on plot, characters, cryptocurrencies, cliodynamics, the blockchain, history, economics, and politics. And thanks for lending your hair and the Green Bay Packers. Hannah, I could never have written *two* characters in this series without your life as my inspiration. Your story and character instincts are so good, you're my go-to brainstorming gal. And to my husband, Eric, you are my partner in all things. Thank you for your tireless editing, action ideas, flights of fancy, backrubs, and endless support. I'm the luckiest person on earth. I lurve and luff you all.

Los Angeles, California,
2017

ABOUT THE AUTHOR

Photo © 2014 Kevin Warn

PJ Manney writes the same way she lives—with an abiding passion for exploring new, exhilarating, and utterly unique experiences. A devotedly positive futurist, she was chairperson of the board of directors of Humanity+, an international nonprofit organization that advocates the ethical use of technology to expand human capabilities. Manney has also been active in communications, public relations, and film production. To date, she has written numerous scripts for television pilots and has also worked on shows such as *Hercules: The Legendary Journeys* and *Xena: Warrior Princess*. She has lived as far afield as New York and New Zealand and loves delving into the cultural landscape of wherever she finds herself. Whenever she's not working on her novels, she continues to expound on her perspective of a technology-driven posthumanity while encouraging hopeful visions of the future. She lives with her husband of twenty-eight years and their two children.